ps·4

No Longer
a Gentleman

**Center Point
Large Print**

Also by Mary Jo Putney and available from
Center Point Large Print:

The Lost Lords Series
Loving a Lost Lord
Never Less Than a Lady
Nowhere Near Respectable

**This Large Print Book carries the
Seal of Approval of N.A.V.H.**

No Longer a Gentleman

❧{ THE LOST LORDS }❧

MARY JO PUTNEY

CENTER POINT LARGE PRINT
THORNDIKE, MAINE

This Center Point Large Print edition
is published in the year 2012 by arrangement with
Kensington Publishing Corp.

The text of this Large Print edition is unabridged.
In other aspects, this book may vary
from the original edition.
Printed in the United States of America
on permanent paper.
Set in 16-point Times New Roman type.

ISBN: 978-1-61173-405-8

Library of Congress Cataloging-in-Publication Data

Putney, Mary Jo.
No longer a gentleman / Mary Jo Putney. — Large print ed.
p. cm. — (Center Point large print edition)
ISBN 978-1-61173-405-8 (lib. bdg. : alk. paper)
1. Women spies—Great Britain—Fiction. 2. Large type books. I. Title.
PS3566.U83N6 2012
813'.54—dc23
                                                    2012005406

To the Mayhem Consultant for his
patience and good nature.
It isn't always easy to live with a writer!

ACKNOWLEDGMENTS

To the Creative Cauldron. How many stories have we knocked out of the ballpark together? *A lot!*

And to all the great people at Kensington, who take such good care of my books.

Chapter 1

Time to dance with the devil again. Cassie wielded Kirkland House's dragon's head knocker, wondering what mission awaited her this time.

The door opened. Recognizing her, the butler bowed her inside. "His lordship is in his study, Miss Fox."

"No need to show me the way." Cassie headed to the rear of the house, thinking that it was about time Kirkland sent her back to France. For years, she had moved secretly between England and France, spying and acting as a courier at Kirkland's direction. The work was dangerous and grimly satisfying.

Outwardly a frivolous gentleman of leisure, in private Kirkland was a master of intelligence gathering and analysis. He'd kept her in London longer than usual this time as part of a team working desperately to uncover a plot against the royal family. They had succeeded, a wedding and Christmas had been celebrated, and now Cassie was restless. Working to undermine Napoleon's regime gave her life purpose.

She knocked at the door of the study and entered at his call. Kirkland sat behind his desk, as well tailored as always. He rose courteously as she entered.

With his dark hair, broad shoulders, and classic features, the man could never be less than handsome, but today his face was etched with strain despite his smile. "You're looking more anonymous than usual, Cassie. How do you manage to be so forgettable?"

"Talent and practice, since anonymity is so useful for a spy," she retorted as she chose a chair opposite him. "But you, sir, look like death in the afternoon. If you don't take better care of yourself, you'll be down with another attack of fever and we'll find out if you're indispensable or not."

"No one is indispensable," he said as he resumed his seat. "Rob Carmichael could do my job if necessary."

"He could, but he wouldn't want to. Rob much prefers being out on the streets cracking heads." Rob had said as much to Cassie—they were close friends, and occasionally more than friends.

"And he is so very good at it," Kirkland agreed. "But I'm not about to fall off the perch anytime soon." He began toying with his quill pen.

"It isn't like you to fidget," Cassie said. "Have you found a more than usually perilous mission for me?"

His mouth quirked humorlessly. "Sending agents into France is always dangerous. My qualms increase when the mission is more personal than of vital interest to Britain."

"Your friend Wyndham," she said immediately. "Bury your qualms. As heir to the Earl of Costain, he'd be worth a few risks even if he weren't your friend."

"I should have known you'd guess." He set the quill neatly in its stand. "How many times have you followed possible leads about Wyndham?"

"Two or three, with a singular lack of success." And Cassie was not the only agent to look for proof that the long-vanished Wyndham was either alive or dead. Kirkland would never give up until there was evidence of one or the other.

"I haven't wanted to admit it, but I've feared that he was killed when the Peace of Amiens ended and all Englishmen were interned so they couldn't return to England." Kirkland sighed. "Wyndham wouldn't have gone tamely. He might well have been killed resisting arrest. He hasn't been heard from since May 1803, when the war resumed."

"Since he isn't in Verdun with the rest of the detainees and no other trace of him has turned up, that's the most likely explanation," Cassie agreed. "But this is the first time I've heard you admit the possibility."

"Wyndham was always so full of life," Kirkland said musingly. "It didn't seem possible that he could be killed senselessly. I know better, of course. But it felt as if saying the words out loud would make them true."

It was a surprising admission coming from Kirkland, whose brain was legendarily sharp and objective. "Tell me about Wyndham," she said. "Not his rank and wealth, but what he was like as a person."

Kirkland's expression eased. "He was a golden-haired charmer who could beguile the scales off a snake. Mischievous, but no malice in him. Lord Costain sent him to the Westerfield Academy in the hope that Lady Agnes would be able to handle Wyndham without succumbing to his charm."

"Did it work?" Cassie asked. She had met the formidable headmistress and thought she could handle anyone.

"Reasonably well. Lady Agnes was fond of him. Everyone was. But she wouldn't let him get away with outrageous behavior."

"You must have a new lead or you wouldn't be talking to me now."

Kirkland began fidgeting with his quill again. "Remember the French spy we uncovered when investigating the plot against the royal family?"

"Paul Clement." Cassie knew the man slightly because of her ties to the French émigré community. "Has he provided information about Wyndham?"

"Clement had heard rumors that just as the truce ended, a young English nobleman ran afoul of a government official named Claude Durand," Kirkland replied. "I know the name, but little more. Have you heard of him?"

Cassie nodded. "He's from a minor branch of a French noble family. When the revolution came, he turned radical and denounced his cousin, the count, and watched while the man was guillotined. As a reward, Durand acquired the family castle and a good bit of the wealth. Now he's a high official in the Ministry of Police. He has a reputation for brutality and unswerving loyalty to Bonaparte, so he'd be a dangerous man to cross."

"Wyndham might not have survived angering a man like that. But Clement had heard that Durand locked up the English lord in his own private dungeon. If that was Wyndham, there's a chance he might be alive."

Cassie didn't need to point out that it was a slim chance. "You wish me to investigate Clement's information?"

"Yes, but don't take any risks." Kirkland regarded her sternly. "I worry about you. You don't fear death enough."

She shrugged. "I don't seek it. Animal instinct keeps me from doing anything foolish. It shouldn't be hard to locate Durand's castle and learn from the locals if he has a blond English prisoner."

Kirkland nodded. "Dungeons aren't designed for long-term survival, but with luck, you'll be able to learn if Wyndham is—or was—imprisoned there."

"Did he have the strength to survive years of captivity?" she asked. "Not just physical strength, but mental. Dungeons can drive men mad, especially if they're kept in solitary confinement."

"I never knew what kind of internal resources Wyndham had. Everything came so easily to him—sports, studies, friendships, admiring females. He was never challenged. He might have unexpected resilience. Or, he might have broken under the first real pressure he'd ever faced." After a long pause, Kirkland said quietly, "I don't think he would have endured imprisonment well. It might have been better if he was killed quickly."

"Truth can be difficult, but better to know what happened and accept the loss than be gnawed by uncertainty forever," Cassie pointed out. "There can't be many English lords who offended powerful officials and were locked in private prisons. If he is or was at Castle Durand, it shouldn't be difficult to learn his fate."

"Hard to believe we may have an answer soon," Kirkland mused. "If he's actually there and alive, see what must be done to get him out."

"I'll leave by the end of the week." Cassie rose, thinking of the preparations she must make. She felt compelled to add, "Even if by some miracle he's alive and you can bring him home, he will have changed greatly after all these years."

Kirkland sighed wearily. "Haven't we all?"

Chapter 2

"Time to wake, my beautiful golden boy," the husky temptress voice murmured. "My husband will return soon."

Grey Sommers opened his eyes and smiled lazily at his bedmate. If spying was always this enjoyable, he'd make it a career, rather than something he merely dabbled in. " 'Boy,' Camille? I thought I'd proved otherwise."

She laughed and shook back a tangle of dark hair. "Indeed you did. I must call you my beautiful golden man. Alas, it is time for you to go."

Grey might have done so if her stroking hand hadn't become teasing, driving common sense from his head. So far, he'd acquired little information from the luscious Madame Camille Durand, but he had increased his knowledge of the amatory arts.

Her husband was a high official in the Ministry of Police, and Grey had hoped the man might have spoken of secret matters to his wife. In particular, had Durand discussed the Truce of Amiens ending and war resuming again? But Camille had no interest in politics. Her talents lay elsewhere, and he was more than willing to sample them again.

Once more indulging lust led to drowsing off. He awoke when the door slammed open and a furious man stormed in, a pistol in his hand and two armed guards behind him. Camille shrieked and sat up in bed. "Durand!"

Grey slid off the four-poster on the side opposite her husband, thinking sickly that this was like a theatre farce. But that pistol was all too real.

"Don't kill him!" Camille begged, her dark hair falling over her breasts. "He is an English milord, and shooting him will cause trouble!"

"An English lord? This must be the foolish Lord Wyndham. I have read the police reports on your movements since your arrival in France. You aren't much of a spy, boy." Durand's thin lips twisted nastily as he cocked the hammer of the pistol. "It no longer matters what the English think."

Grey straightened to his full height as he recognized that there was not a single damned thing he could do to save his life. His friends would laugh if they knew he met his end naked in the bedchamber of another man's wife.

No. They wouldn't laugh.

An eerie calm settled over him. He wondered if all men felt this way when death was inevitable. Lucky that he had a younger brother to inherit the earldom. "I have wronged you, Citoyen Durand." He was proud of the steadiness of his voice. "No one will deny that you have just cause to shoot me."

Something in Durand's dark eyes shifted from murderous rage to cold cruelty. "Oh, no," he said in a soft voice. "Killing you would be far too merciful."

Chapter 3

London, 1813

Cassie returned to the private boardinghouse that Kirkland maintained for his agents near Covent Garden. She stayed at 11 Exeter Street whenever she was in London, and it was the nearest thing she had to a home.

Packing didn't take long because whenever she returned from France, she had her clothing laundered and folded away in her clothes press to await the next mission. It was winter, so she selected her warmest garments and half boots. All were well constructed but drab because her goal was to pass unnoticed.

She was finishing her selections when a knock sounded on the door and a female voice called, "Tea service, ma'am!"

Recognizing the voice, Cassie opened the door to Lady Kiri Mackenzie, who was balancing a tray with a teapot, cups, and a plate of cakes. Lady Kiri was tall, beautiful, well born, rich, and confident to the bone. Amazing that they had become friends.

"How did you know I was here?" Cassie asked. "I thought you and our newly knighted Sir Damian were still honeymooning in Wiltshire."

"Mackenzie and I returned to town yesterday. Since I was near Covent Garden, I thought I'd take a chance and see if you were here." Kiri set the tray on a table. "Mrs. Powell said you were, so behold! I arrive bearing tea."

Cassie poured a splash of tea and decided it needed more steeping. "I'm glad you returned in time for a visit. I'll be leaving by the end of the week."

Kiri's face became still. "France?"

"It's where I am useful."

"Do be careful," Kiri said worriedly. "Having had a brief encounter with spying gave me a sense of how dangerous it can be."

Cassie tested the tea again and decided it was ready. "That was an unusual circumstance," she said as she poured. "Most of what I do is quite mundane."

Kiri didn't look convinced. "How long are you likely to be gone?"

"I'm not sure. A couple of months, perhaps more." Cassie stirred sugar into her cup and settled back in her chair. "Remember that I am half French, so I'm not going to a foreign country. You're half Hindu, so surely you understand that."

Kiri considered. "I take your point. But India can be dangerous even though I'm half Indian. The same is true of France. Rather more so since we're at war."

Cassie selected a cake. "This is my work. My calling, really." The cake was filled with nuts and currants and very tasty.

"From what I can see, you're very good at spying." Kiri chose a spice cake. Mrs. Powell's kitchen could always be relied on for good food. "Does Rob Carmichael mind you going away for so long?"

Cassie's brows arched in surprise. "I beg your pardon?"

Kiri flushed. "I'm sorry. Was I not supposed to know about your . . . your relationship?"

Kiri must have seen Rob and Cassie together. Not surprising since the women had lived under the same roof for several weeks. "Our relationship is that we are friends," Cassie said astringently.

"And I should mind my own business," Kiri said, her voice rueful. "But he's a fine fellow. I . . . I thought there was something more than friendship between you."

Cassie felt a sharp pang of . . . envy, she supposed, that Kiri could believe in love. Not that her friend hadn't had problems to overcome. Her father had died before she was born, and since she had been raised in India with mixed blood, she had faced prejudice when her family came to England.

But Kiri had a loving mother and stepfather, not to mention wealth, position, and beauty to protect against an often cruel world. Cassie had been born with some of those advantages but had lost them early, along with her faith in happy endings.

Newly wed and madly in love with a man worthy of her, Kiri lacked the experience to recognize the many ways men and women might connect. A desperate need for warmth could draw people together even without love.

Not wanting to try to explain that, Cassie said merely, "Friendship is one of life's great blessings. It doesn't need to be more."

"I stand corrected." Kiri made a face. "I appreciate how patiently you've educated me on worldly matters."

"You learned quickly." Cassie chuckled. "Kirkland said he'd hire you as an agent in an instant if you weren't unfortunately aristocratic." She paused. "He probably has put you to work listening to what is said at Damian's since so many high officials and foreign diplomats choose to do their gambling there."

"The possibility might have been touched on," Kiri said with a twinkle in her eye. After demolishing another cake, she opened her reticule. "While in the country, I spent some time playing with a scent you might find useful." Kiri pulled a small vial from her reticule and handed it over. "I call it Antiqua."

"Useful?" Cassie accepted the vial with enthusiasm. Kiri came from a long line of Hindu women who were perfumers, and she created marvelous scents. "I thought perfumes were for allure and frivolity."

"Take a sniff and see what you think," her friend said mysteriously.

Cassie obediently unstoppered the vial, closed her eyes, and sniffed. Then again. "It smells . . . a little musty, in a clean sort of way, if that makes sense. Earthy and . . . very still? Tired? Not exactly unpleasant, but nothing like your floral and spice perfumes."

"If you caught this scent in passing, what would you think of?"

"An old woman," Cassie said instantly.

"Perfect!" Kiri said gleefully. "Scent is powerful. Dab on a bit of Antiqua when you wish to be unnoticed or underestimated. People will think of you as old and feeble without knowing why."

"That's brilliant!" Cassie sniffed again. "I detect a hint of lavender, but I don't recognize anything else."

"I included oils I don't use often, and when I do, they're usually disguised by pleasanter fragrances," Kiri explained.

"When I'm in France, I often travel around in a pony cart as a peddler of ladies' sundries. Ribbons and lace and the like. I make myself look plain and dull and forgettable, and this will add to the effect. Thank you, Kiri." Cassie stoppered the vial. "Would you have time to make more before I leave?"

Kiri pulled out two more vials. "Once I thought the scent worked, I made a larger batch." She chuckled. "I put some of this on and crept up on Mackenzie and he didn't recognize me until I caught his attention by doing something highly improper."

Cassie laughed. "If you could creep up on Mackenzie unobserved, this scent should make me invisible."

Kiri pursed her lips. "If you're going to be traveling as a peddler, I have a remedy that might be a good item for you to carry."

"Perfumes that aren't quite up to your standards but are still lovely? That would be wonderful," Cassie said.

"I hadn't thought of that," Kiri said, "but it's a good idea. I have a number that aren't quite what I wanted, but pleasant and too full of expensive ingredients to throw out. You're welcome to them. But what I had in mind was thieves' oil."

"What on earth is that, and why would any honest country housewife want any?"

Kiri grinned. "I found it when researching ancient European scents. The story goes that during the Black Death, some thieves were caught robbing the dying and dead. In return for their lives, they offered the formula that allowed them to commit their crimes without catching the disease. There are different recipes, but they're usually based on an herb vinegar infused with other herbs like lemon and clove and rosemary. Herbal vinegars are traditional remedies, so that's a good start."

"Fascinating," Cassie said. "Does it work?"

"I have no idea. Perhaps it might prevent someone from coming down with more usual ailments like coughs and colds. Since I'm usually healthy, I don't know if the thieves' oil is making a difference. The version I settled on is pungent but not unpleasant, and it smells like it ought to do some good. Perfect for a peddler who won't be around if it doesn't work."

"I'd love to have some," Cassie said. "I'll use it myself. Traveling through the French countryside with a pony cart in the dead of winter is a recipe for catching colds. I'll let you know if the thieves' oil keeps me healthy."

"I'll send some tomorrow, along with my surplus perfumes." Kiri foraged in her bag again and produced an exquisite bottle of scarlet glass with a delicately twisted stopper. "One last thing. For when you return to England and can be yourself again."

Warily Cassie opened the bottle and placed a drop on her wrist. One sniff and she became still as stone. The fragrance was an exquisite layering of lilac and roses, frankincense and moonlight, vanished sunshine and lost dreams. And underneath, the shadows of darkest night. It caught at her heart with painful intensity.

"Now that I know you better, I decided to create a personal perfume," Kiri explained. "What do you think?"

"It's superb." Cassie reinserted the stopper with rather more force than necessary. "But I'm not sure when I'll have occasion to wear anything like this."

"You hate it," her friend said sadly. "I thought you might."

Cassie gazed at the lovely little bottle resting on her palm. "I don't hate it. I . . . just don't want to wear this much truth."

"Perhaps someday you will."

"Perhaps." But Cassie doubted that.

Chapter 4

Castle Durand, Summer 1803

Once he realized Durand didn't want him dead, Grey fought at every opportunity. Resistance didn't get him killed, though he acquired numerous bruises and lacerations.

If he'd known what lay ahead, he might have tried harder to get killed.

Durand's men were well trained and brutally

efficient. As soon as Grey was captured, one of the guards appropriated his finely tailored garments, gave him coarse peasant clothing and shoes, and ordered him to put them on.

After Grey dressed, he was shackled, gagged, blindfolded, and tossed into a smelly cart. Foul straw was thrown over him. He struggled frantically for breath as the cart began rumbling over the cobbled Parisian streets. When he fell into agonized unconsciousness, he was sure he would never wake again.

But he did. When he recovered his senses, he learned that he could breathe if he didn't move too much or allow panic to flood his mind.

As cobblestones became roads and then rutted rural lanes, he thought he would go mad from terror and anguish. Grey had always loved sunshine and bright lights and good company. Now he could not see, could not speak, could not even howl with despair.

He lost track of how long he rattled around the cart. Several days, but it was devilish hard to tell how much time passed when he was in constant darkness.

Morning and evening, he was fed and watered and allowed to relieve himself. His body was so stiff from its bindings that he could barely walk. Chilling spring rain sometimes fell, but his damnable good health spared him from lung fever.

At last the nightmare ended. The cart clattered

into a stone courtyard, the ropes securing his ankles were unshackled, and he was marched into a building.

Being blindfolded sharpened his senses. He recognized that the building was large and old and mostly stone. A castle, perhaps. He stumbled down narrow stairs with uneven stone treads that supported that theory.

The guards he had come to know through their scent and voices were joined by another man with a guttural voice, strange footsteps, and a sour smell of garlic. A door squealed and Grey was shoved through. He barely managed to avoid crashing to the stone floor.

The gag and blindfold were jerked off. He flinched backward from the torchlight, which stung his eyes after days in darkness. The guards who had brought Grey there stood silently in the doorway while a broad man with cruel features and a wooden peg leg stood directly in front of him. The man leaned on a cane that had leather streamers falling from the brass head.

"I am Gaspard, your jailer," the man said, menace in his guttural voice. He spoke the French of Paris's worst stews. "Durand orders me to keep you alive." He gave an ugly smirk. "I fear you will not find the accommodations what you are used to, my little goddam lordling."

Grey had to strain to understand. He'd learned the French of the well born when he was a boy, but he hadn't been taught the coarse dialects of the poor and the provinces. That was changing rapidly. He wondered if he would ever hear English spoken again.

He remembered that the French had called the English "goddams" since at least the time of Joan of Arc. The name came from the constant profanity of the soldiers of the English army. Resigning himself to being a goddam, he said, "If you wish to keep me alive, food and water would be helpful."

Gaspard gave a bark of laughter. "In the morning, boy. I have other concerns now." He glanced at the guards. "Take off the goddam's coat and shirt."

The two guards silently moved forward and obeyed. Grey was too cramped and bruised to fight well, and he couldn't prevent them from stripping off his ragged, oversized coat and shirt. He'd never felt so helpless in his life.

There was worse to come. While the two guards immobilized him, Gaspard began whipping Grey's back. Dimly Grey realized that the leather streamers on the cane were the lashes of a whip and the cane itself was the handle.

After a dozen or two agonizing blows, Grey sagged to the floor between the guards. "Let him fall," Gaspard said contemptuously. "Remove the shackles. They aren't needed. There is no way the goddam will escape this cell."

Grey lay on the floor, barely aware of a key unlocking his wrist manacles. The guards rose and followed Gaspard as the jailer limped from the cell, his wooden leg tapping ominously. They took the torch with them.

After the heavy door was closed and locked, Grey was left in darkness. Even the sliver of light at the bottom of the door disappeared as his jailers walked away.

Grey felt panic rising at the thought of being trapped in darkness until he died screaming. What did the French call the ultimate prison, a oubliette? But that was a pit, wasn't it, with the prisoner at the bottom of a deep shaft? The name meant forgotten, for prisoners were forgotten and left to die.

He had the mad thought that the guillotine might be better. At least death took place in open air and was quick, if ugly.

But he wasn't dead yet. Now that he was free of gag, blindfold, and chains, he could breathe and move freely. As for the darkness—it hadn't destroyed him on the endless journey to this place, and he wouldn't let it destroy him just yet.

He pushed himself up on his knees and fumbled for his shirt and coat, which had been dropped nearby. The heavy fabric inflicted a fresh wave of pain on his lacerated back, but he needed protection against the biting chill.

Then he listened. Absolute silence except for the

faint sound of trickling water somewhere quite close. Given the dampness around him, that was unsurprising.

What had he seen of his cell before Gaspard left? Stone walls, stone floor, damp and solid. The room wasn't huge, but it wasn't tiny, either. Perhaps eight paces square, with a very high ceiling. There was something in a corner to his left. A pallet, perhaps?

Swaying, he got to his feet, then moved to his left with his arms outstretched to prevent collision. He still managed to sideswipe a wall by coming at it from an angle, but a few more bruises made no difference.

He stumbled on something soft. Kneeling, he explored by touch and found a pallet of straw and a pair of coarse blankets. Luxury compared to what he'd endured since his capture.

Standing, he skimmed one hand along the wall so he could discover the dimensions of his cell. Down the side wall to the back, opposite the door. He turned and moved along the back wall. About what he estimated as the midpoint of the wall, he stumbled on a rocky obstacle and fell heavily.

More bruises, damned painful ones, but nothing broken, he decided after he recovered his breath and tested the new injuries. He explored with his hands and identified two irregular blocks of stone.

One was chair height, so he hauled himself up

and sat, though he couldn't lean against the wall because of his injured back. As the throbbing in his knees faded, he realized he had never properly appreciated the convenience of chairs before.

The second block of stone was about a foot and a half away, roughly rectangular, and around table height. He felt positively civilized.

After the pain diminished, he resumed his exploration, moving even more slowly. At the far corner, he felt a film of water seeping down the stones. It wasn't a lot, but perhaps enough to keep him from dying of thirst if other drink wasn't offered.

There were no more stone blocks. The only other feature he located was the massive wooden door and its frame. He circled again even more slowly. This time in the back corner where the moisture dripped down, he sensed the movement of air. He knelt and found a hole about the size of two fists. The water dripped down into it and there was a faint scent of human waste.

So this is where prisoners relieved themselves. It could have been worse. He used the facilities, then made his way back to the pallet, and wrapped himself in the blankets, lying on his side to protect his back.

Despite his exhaustion, he found himself staring into the darkness wondering what lay ahead. Durand's comment that it no longer mattered what the English thought suggested that the war was about to resume after a year of truce.

Grey wasn't surprised to know that. He'd seen suggestions that the French were using the truce to regroup for another round of conquest. Since he had joined the rush of Britons to Paris when the truce began, his friend Kirkland had asked him to keep his eyes open and pass on what he saw.

Grey had used that as an excuse to seduce a married woman, and that action had brought him here. Not that Camille had required much seduction. Looking back, he wasn't sure who had seduced whom.

Dear God, what would become of him? Might Durand offer him for ransom? His parents would pay anything to get him back. But Durand wanted him to suffer. That could mean being imprisoned forever here in the darkness.

Not forever. Until he died. How long would it be until he'd be praying for death? The knowledge that he was likely to die here in the darkness, alone and unmourned, made his heart hammer with panic. Grimly he fought the fear.

Breaking down shouldn't matter since no one was here to sneer at his weakness. But it mattered to him. Everything in his life had come easily, and even when caught in mischief, he'd suffered few consequences. Until now. Resigning himself to living in darkness, he wrestled his demons until fear faded and he slept like the dead.

The next morning he awoke to find light entering his cell from a horizontal slit window near the high ceiling of the cell.

For that beautiful sight, he wept.

Chapter 5

France, 1813

In the late afternoon sun, the village of St. Just du Sarthe looked much like any other village in northern France, apart from the medieval castle rising above. As Cassie drove her cart over the hill opposite the castle, she paused to study her goal.

Locating Durand's family seat hadn't been difficult. She'd been fortunate that dry, cold weather had saved her from becoming bogged down in snow or mud. She'd moved at a leisurely speed, stopping in villages to sell her ribbons and buttons and bits of lace, along with Kiri's perfumes and a few remedies.

She'd bought as well as sold, acquiring items of clothing or handicrafts that could be sold elsewhere. In short, she'd behaved exactly as a peddler should.

Snapping the reins over the back of her sturdy pony, she made her way into the village. It was large enough to have a small tavern, *La Liberté*. Cassie halted there, hoping to find both hot food and information inside.

The taproom was empty except for three ancient men sipping wine together in one corner. A robust woman of middle years was busy behind the bar, but she glanced up with interest when Cassie entered. A female stranger traveling alone wouldn't be common here, and Cassie was moving with the deliberation of an older woman.

"*Bonjour*, madame," Cassie said. "I am Madame Renard and I hope I may find some hot food and a room for the night."

"You've come to the right place." The woman chuckled. "The only place. I'm Madame Leroux, the landlady, and I've a plain room and some hearty mutton stew and fresh bread if you're interested."

"That and a glass of red wine will suit me well." Cassie guessed that the landlady would be a good source of information. "I'll settle my pony in your stable first."

Madame Leroux nodded. "The food will be ready when you return."

The pony was as happy to be indoors and fed as Cassie was. She returned to the taproom and settled into a chair by the fire, grateful for the warmth.

She was removing her cloak when the landlady emerged from the kitchen with a tray containing stew, bread, cheese, and wine. Cassie said, "I thank you, madame. Will you join me in a glass of wine? I'm a traveler in ladies' notions, and I'm sure you will know if there might be local interest in my goods."

"*Merci.*" Madame Leroux poured a glass of wine and settled comfortably on the other side of the fire. Expression curious, she asked, "Isn't it dangerous to travel alone?"

Besides moving slowly, Cassie had grayed her hair and was wearing the antiquity scent, so she must seem worrisomely fragile. "I'm careful, and I've not had trouble."

"What do you sell?"

Cassie listed her wares between mouthfuls of the excellent stew. When she finished, the landlady said, "Our weekly village market is tomorrow. In midwinter, new goods will be welcome. I think you will find it worth your while."

Cassie sipped at her wine. "What about the castle above the town? Might I find customers there? I have some truly fine perfumes blended by a Hindu princess."

The other woman smiled appreciatively. "An intriguing description, but Castle Durand is a quiet place. The master visits very seldom, and his wife even less. There are never guests unless you count a prisoner or two in the dungeon, and I doubt they have the coin to buy."

"A dungeon?" Cassie looked properly shocked. "In modern France?"

"Men with power don't give it up easily," the

landlady said cynically. "The Durands have been lords of the castle forever. They're called the Wolves of Durand. The last Durand got chopped for being an aristo, but there's a Durand cousin up there now, not much different from the last one apart from calling himself Citoyen instead of Monsieur le Comte. 'Tis said this Durand has an English lord locked in the dungeon, but I have my doubts. Where would he find an English lord?"

"That seems unlikely," Cassie agreed, concealing her excitement. "Surely there are female servants? After the market, I could drive up there to show my wares."

"Go at your peril," Madame Leroux said. "Half the village is ill with influenza—that's why I'm so quiet here. I hear that most of the castle staff is ill, too. Not the sort of thing that usually kills, but it creates plenty of misery. Best stay away."

"I may have something for that," Cassie said. "The Hindu woman who made the perfumes also gave me what she called thieves' oil. The legend is that during the plague years, thieves used it to stay safe when they robbed the dead. I have tested it myself on this journey, and I haven't become ill despite the weather."

The landlady's gaze sharpened. "I might be interested in that myself."

Cassie dug into her bag for a sample. "Try this. A few drops in your palm, rub your hands together, then cup them and sniff the scent."

Madame Leroux followed the instructions, her nostrils flaring as she sniffed the pungent mixture. "Smells like it ought to do something! Does this remedy really work?"

"As one businesswoman to another, I will admit that I'm not sure," Cassie replied. "But I haven't had so much as a cough since I started using it."

Madame Leroux took another sniff. "Perhaps we can trade your oil for my lodging?"

After a brisk bargaining session, agreement was reached and Cassie handed over a larger bottle of thieves' oil. Madame Leroux chuckled. "If you call at the castle and fall ill with the influenza, at least you'll know it's no good."

"I hope it works," Cassie said with an answering smile. She now had a good reason to go to the castle, where she could learn if Kirkland's long-lost friend was really in Durand's dungeon. "But perhaps I will head on to the next village. This country is new to me. How far to the next village that has lodgings? In summer, I am happy to camp out with my pony, but not in February!"

"Three to four hours' drive if the weather stays clear."

"Then I shall move on after the market." Cassie mopped up the last of the stew with the heel of her bread. "But I shall make sure to stay here if I come this way again."

Chapter 6

Castle Durand, Summer 1803

By morning's light Grey saw that the heavy door to his cell had two small trap doors opened from the outside, one at head height, the other near the bottom. "Breakfast, yer lordship," a sneering voice said as half a loaf of bread and a tankard of tepid minty tea was placed through the lower door. "Return the tankard later or no dinner for you."

Because he was hungry, he obeyed. The breakfasts were usually bread with drippings smeared on and more of the herb tea. No costly China tea for prisoners.

Dinners were sparse but more varied. There might be a bowl of stew, or perhaps vegetables and a bone with meat on it. Occasionally a boiled egg. The best part was the pewter goblet of wine. It was always a coarse young table wine, but it gave him something to look forward to. He felt occasional fleeting amusement that because this was France, prison food wasn't quite as dreadful as it might have been.

Apart from meals, Grey's life was deadly monotony. He always sat in the narrow beam of light filtered down into his cell. That light saved him from madness, but not despair. Having always lived surrounded by people, he hadn't realized human contact was as essential to his life as air. Now he saw no one, not even his jailers, so he couldn't use his legendary charm to improve his situation.

He felt like a bird trapped in a small room frantically beating against the walls. But there was nothing, *nothing,* he could do to escape. The mortar that joined the stones was new and hard and impervious. The slit window that let in the blessed light was too far above his head to reach even when he jumped to try to catch the sill.

All the world was gray stone. The only features of the cell were the pallet with straw and dark blankets and the crude stone table and seat. Sometimes he caught a glimpse of a beefy hand placing the food on the floor and removing the empty bowl and drinking vessel. Occasionally Gaspard would open the upper window in the door to spew insults. Grey knew he was in a bad way when he looked forward to such interludes.

The cell warmed a little as spring turned to summer. When rain fell, the trickle of water down the wall became stronger and he could clean himself a little. He tried not to think of the magnificent new bathing rooms his father had built at the family seat, Summerhill. Tubs full of hot water large enough for a man to sink in to his chin . . .

No. He daren't think of home. Like a hibernating animal, he took refuge in sleep, spending most of the hours of the day and night wrapped on his pallet in a dark haze of melancholy. Only meals pulled him from his stupor.

That changed the day Durand visited. Floating between sleep and unwelcome wakefulness, Grey was slow to realize that the door was opening. He was still lying on his pallet when Durand strode into the cell.

"Look at yourself, Wyndham," Durand said contemptuously. "Three months' imprisonment have turned you into a filthy, dull-witted pig. What woman would let you touch her now?"

Fury slashed through Grey's lethargy and he launched himself up from the floor and straight at Durand. Like his classmates at the Westerfield Academy, he had learned the Indian fighting skills called Kalarippayattu from Ashton, his half-Hindu classmate. Surely he could break a middle-aged politician . . .

Durand slid away with insulting ease, then spun Grey around and forced him to his knees by twisting one arm excruciatingly behind his back. "You're nothing but a boy, and a weak one at that." He shoved Grey onto the floor, releasing his grip and stepping back after a parting kick in the belly. "The English are a nation of weaklings. That's why French victory is inevitable."

Gasping with pain from the kick, Grey panted, "The war has resumed?"

"Naturally. The Truce of Amiens was merely a

pause to recruit more men and build more weapons. Within the next months, we will invade England and make ourselves masters of Europe."

Grey didn't want to believe that. But it could be true. In Paris, he'd heard that the French were building boats and amassing an army at Boulogne. "Napoleon will have to get by the Royal Navy first," he spat out in a thin, rusty voice.

"We have plans to take care of your navy," Durand said confidently. His expression changed. "After the invasion, your family will probably be dead and their fortune confiscated. I wonder if it would be prudent to offer you to them for ransom now? How much would they pay for their son and heir, Wyndham? A hundred thousand pounds? Two hundred thousand?"

Grey's heart spasmed. Dear God, to be free of this place! His parents would pay any amount to get him back. They would . . .

They would beggar the family for his sake. His parents, his younger brother and sister—all would pay for Grey's stupidity. He could not do that to them.

Managing a sneer of his own, he said, "They surely think I'm dead already, and good riddance. Why do you think I spent months in France? I was an expensive, useless son. My father was furious with me and I thought it best to get out of sight. He would have disowned me if he could." Grey shrugged. "I have a younger brother who is better in all ways. He will make an excellent earl. I'm neither wanted nor needed."

"A pity," Durand said with a trace of regret. "But entirely believable. If you were my son, I wouldn't want you back, either. Then you shall stay here till you rot."

He spun on his heel and left. The locks on the door were engaged before Grey could stagger to his feet.

Had he thrown away his only chance of leaving this dungeon alive? Hard to say. Durand was a shifty devil and he might have collected a ransom and not freed his captive. Or returned Grey's dead body to England.

But Durand had been right to sneer. Grey had been wallowing in self-pity and despair, allowing himself to become weak in body and spirit. If he'd been in better shape, he might have been able to break Durand's neck. He'd never have escaped the castle, but it would have been satisfying to kill the mocking bastard.

He'd lost track of time. Three months, Durand had said. He felt as if he'd been here that many years, but from the length of his beard, three months sounded about right. It was summer, probably sometime in August. His twenty-first birthday had just passed.

If he had been home in England, his parents would have thrown a great celebration at the family seat, inviting aristocratic friends as well as all the Costain dependents. Grey would have enjoyed it enormously.

Instead, they were mourning his disappearance and likely death. He loved his family, but he'd always taken them for granted even though one couldn't have asked for better parents. He was deeply fond of his younger brother and sister, who looked up to him. He'd failed them all. The only thing he could take pride in was discouraging Durand's ransom demand.

Grey would not—*could* not—continue in this spineless fashion. First, he must begin an exercise regimen to rebuild his strength.

He studied his cell as he thought about what was possible in the space. He could run in place to build his endurance. Stiffly he began, imagining places he'd been and sights he'd seen so he could mentally leave these ugly walls.

He ran until he had a stitch in his side, then dropped to the floor and pushed himself up with just his arms. Once that would have been easy. Now he could only manage to push himself up half a dozen times before he collapsed, gasping.

Another way to build muscles was by lifting the two stones that served as chair and table. He bent to lift the smaller one. It was heavier than expected. He barely managed to raise it six inches before losing his hold. It crashed to the floor and a chip spun away from the lower edge.

Panting from his exertion, he vowed that he'd

lift that damned stone over and over until he was strong enough to carry it around his cell. Then he would tackle the larger block that served as his table.

He could and would exercise every day. What else had he to do?

Perhaps even more important, he must rebuild his mind. He'd always been lazy in his classes, able to get by with little work and the help of an excellent memory. Lady Agnes had seen to it that he learned at the Westerfield Academy, but his years at Oxford had been fairly useless. He'd attended Christchurch College, where gentlemen's sons like him dabbled in classes between social amusements. Kirkland and Ashton, characteristically, attended Balliol, the college associated with sheer brilliance.

He considered the memorizations required by different masters. How much of Caesar's *Gallic Commentaries* could he quote in Latin?

"Gallia est omnis divisa in partes tres." All Gaul was divided into three parts. He knew the Latin and English, and now he translated the passage into French. Since his voice also was weak from lack of use, he spoke the passage aloud as he exercised until he was too tired to do more.

Shakespeare. He'd studied the Bard and also performed in plays at the homes of friends. Always he was chosen as one of the leads and he learned his speeches easily. *"Tomorrow and tomorrow and tomorrow, creeps in this petty pace from day to day . . ."*

No, not Macbeth, not here and now. What did he remember from *Twelfth Night*? Yes, that was a much better choice. *"If music be the food of love, play on; Give me excess of it, that, surfeiting; The appetite might sicken, and so die."* He liked to sing and had a decent voice, so he could sing as much as he wanted to. Good for the soul and for maintaining his ability to speak.

He must keep track of time, no longer letting the days slide by mindlessly. When he'd dropped the chair stone, a small piece had chipped off. He would designate today as August 15, 1803. Using the stone chip, he scratched that on a head-high stone near the door. Every day would be marked off with a scratch.

He could hear church bells from the village. Careful listening would tell him what days were Sundays, and he should be able to determine major holidays.

From now on, his life would have purpose. He might never have a chance to free himself. But if an opportunity was presented, no matter how small, he'd be ready.

Gradually, Grey's weakened body began to strengthen. So did his mind. He was amazed at how much he remembered of his lessons. He'd always enjoyed reading, so each day he chose a book from his mental library and recalled as much of it as possible.

He didn't talk aloud to himself because doing so made him feel too close to the madmen he'd seen when one of his more rattle-pated friends had taken him to Bedlam Hospital. The friend thought watching deranged patients amusing. Grey had found it deeply disquieting. The memory of those tormented souls haunted him still, especially on those days when he wondered if he was descending into madness.

But an unexpected blessing appeared not long after Durand's visit. Though he didn't talk aloud, he had no compunctions about singing. Every day he sang several songs, and he enjoyed both the music and the way his voice was returning to normal after three months of disuse.

He'd just finished a rousing rendition of an English drinking song when a young female voice whispered in French from the slit window above, *"Bonjour*, monsieur. Is it true that you are an English milord?"

Grey leaped to his feet in excitement. Another human! And a female at that. "I was once, mamselle, but now I am a prisoner, of no importance."

The girl giggled. "A real milord! I've never met a goddam. How did you come to be here?"

"I misbehaved," he said solemnly. She giggled again and they had a brief conversation through the window, which was a foot or so above ground level. She was a castle maid and called herself Nicolette, though he suspected it wasn't her real name.

She couldn't stay long because the housekeeper was a dragon and Nicolette feared for her position if she was caught. But after that she visited once or twice a week, often with one of her friends.

Some of the girls were deliciously scandalized at the chance to talk to an imprisoned English milord. Nicolette was a kind girl with some interest in Grey as an individual. Occasionally she dropped an apple or other fruit between the bars. He devoured her offerings, amazed that he'd ever taken apples for granted.

Nicolette told him of her sweetheart and bid him a fond farewell when she left the castle to marry. He gave her his blessing, for he had nothing else to give.

None of the other maids visited as much, but he still had occasional visitors. For a time there was a boisterous young ostler from the stables who taught Grey highly obscene French drinking songs until the man was fired for drunkenness.

Grey treasured those moments of normality. They helped keep him sane.

Chapter 7

Madame Leroux was right, and Cassie did a brisk business at the small market in the village square. She rather enjoyed being a peddler. Since she didn't depend on selling to support herself, she could be flexible on prices. It was a pleasure to be able to sell a pretty ribbon to a girl who had never owned anything pretty.

The thieves' oil was popular, too. With winter illnesses rampant, buyers would try anything that might help. Customers were also interested in news, as isolated villagers always were. *Yes, the news from Russia was bad, but the emperor had escaped safely, and wouldn't this length of lace look lovely on your daughter's wedding dress?*

By noon there were no more customers, so it was time for the castle. Cassie ate a bowl of thick bean soup at *La Liberté*, thanked Madame Leroux for her help, and left St. Just du Sarthe. Instead of heading for the next village, she drove up to the castle. The narrow road was bleak and windy, and the castle was equally bleak when she reached it.

The castle proper was surrounded by a looming wall that had never been mined for stone. The massive gates stood open so people and vehicles could come and go easily, but the gates looked as if they could still be closed in an emergency.

She drove through the gates unchallenged. The walls cut the bitter wind once she was inside. Not seeing anyone, she drove around to the back of the castle and left pony and cart within the shelter of the mostly empty stables. Then she slung her peddler's bag over one shoulder and went hunting for the entrance to the servants' area.

After two locked doors, she found one that opened under her hand into a short passage leading into the castle kitchen. The long room was warm and there were pleasant smells, but there was no one in sight. Cassie called, "Hallooo! Is anyone here?"

A hoarse woman's voice replied, "What do you want?"

A heavyset woman pulled herself from a wooden chair by the fire and limped toward Cassie. Her round face looked designed for smiles, but she was wrapped in shawls and coughed every few steps.

"I'm Madame Renard, a peddler, and I see that you're a candidate for some of my throat lozenges. Here, a sample." Cassie fished a packet of honey and lemon lozenges from her bag. They tasted good and did help soothe a cough.

"Don't mind if I do." The woman removed a lozenge from the packet, then sank onto a bench. "*Merci.* I'm the cook, Madame Bertin."

"I was told most of the people here at the castle

were ill." Cassie glanced around the kitchen. A pot hung on the hob by a fire that had burned down to embers. "You look like you could use some help. Shall I build up the fire for you?"

"I'd be most grateful," the cook said. "There's chicken broth in the pot there. Could you get me some?" She coughed wrenchingly. "Everyone is sick in bed, can't even manage stairs. I've got hot food for anyone who wants it, but no one has made it this far and 'tisn't my job to wait on other servants." More coughing.

"I hope no one is dangerously ill?" A ladle hung by the fire, so Cassie scooped warm broth into a porringer on a nearby table.

"The housekeeper died early on, but she was old and sickly already. I don't think anyone else is in mortal peril, but this winter's influenza makes a body weak as a kitten for days." Madame Bertin sipped the hot broth appreciatively. "I kept the fire from dying and managed to make this broth, but now I'm too tired for anything else."

Seeing an opportunity, Cassie asked, "Would you be willing to pay a bit for some help, madame? I could carry trays of bread and broth to the servants who are ill, and perhaps do some chores around the kitchen."

" 'Twould be a real blessing. Let's see, who lives in . . ." The cook thought. "There are six maids in the attics and two men in the stables. The stairs are just through that door, but it's five

49

long flights of steps to the attic. Can you manage that much?"

"I'm spryer than I look. I'll be happy to help out. When people are ill, they need something warm." She stirred the broth with the ladle. "And I'll be glad to earn a few coins, too. Where do you keep the bread? Cheese would also be good. Strengthening."

"The pantry is there." Madame Bertin pointed. "A good thing Citoyen Durand isn't here. He'd be raging and whipping people to do their jobs even if they're too ill to stand. But what is going to happen in a quiet place like this in the dead of winter? We can all rest a day or two until we're ready to work again."

"Fortunate," Cassie agreed. She filled mugs, cut bread and cheese, and carried a tray out to the stables, where she was gratefully received. After returning to the kitchen, she prepared more trays for the maids. With six of them, she needed to make two trips up the narrow stone stairs. No wonder Madame Bertin hadn't even tried.

As the cook said, no one seemed at death's door, but all the servants lay limp in their beds, weak, tired, and very glad for sustenance. Cassie made a silent prayer that the thieves' oil would protect her. Becoming that ill while traveling would be very bad.

She returned to the kitchen, where the cook was drowsing in her chair by the fire. Cassie tucked a knee robe around her. The time had come to learn if there really was a dungeon with prisoners. "Is there anyone else I should take food to?"

Madame Bertin frowned. "There are the guards and the prisoners in the dungeon. The head jailer, Gaspard, usually sends a man up for food, but one is ill, Gaspard is off somewhere, and the one there now wouldn't dare leave his post."

"So the guard and the prisoners need feeding? How many prisoners are there?"

"Only two. With everyone ill, they're being neglected." The cook crossed herself. "One of the prisoners is a priest. 'Tis very wrong to lock up a priest, but Durand would be enraged at the impertinence if anyone told him so."

"Shocking!" Cassie agreed. "What is the other prisoner?"

"They say he's an English lord, though I've never seen him, so I can't say for sure." She shook her head sadly. "No doubt an Englishman deserves a dungeon, but surely not the priest. He is old and frail and needs hot food in this weather."

"I'll take food down to all of them." Cassie started to assemble a tray. "You say you've never seen the prisoners. They are never brought up for exercise in the yard?"

"Oh, no. Citoyen Durand is very strict about his prisoners. They are never released from their cells, and the guards never enter. Food is put through a slot." Madame Bertin crossed herself again. "The poor devils must be half mad by now."

Cassie's lips tightened as she prepared the food. After ten years of uncertainty, Kirkland's search might be about to end. But his long-lost friend might be broken beyond any chance of mending.

Chapter 8

Castle Durand, 1805

Grey regarded the sparrow that perched on his sill. "Enter, Monsieur L'Oiseau. I've kept a bit of bread for you. I hope you appreciate what a sacrifice this is." The bird cocked its head, undecided, so Grey whistled his best imitation of sparrow song. Reassured, it glided from the sill to the floor and pecked at the bit of bread Grey had saved.

He enjoyed talking to the birds. They never contradicted, and he was amused by their saucy willingness to approach. "Cupboard love," he murmured, tossing another crumb. "Not so very different from being an eligible prize in the marriage mart."

He'd been old enough to experience some of that in London before his disastrous decision to visit Paris. Kirkland and Ashton, who paid more attention to politics, had both warned him to keep his trip short since peace wouldn't last, but he'd characteristically brushed them off. He was the golden boy, heir to Costain, to whom nothing evil could happen.

Two years later, here he was, slowly going mad with boredom and grateful for the fleeting companionship of a sparrow. But at least he was stronger and more fit than before, and his singing voice had improved.

He tossed another crumb. The sparrow seized it, then cocked its head for a moment before flying up and out the window. Grey watched the bird leave with an envy so deep that it was pain. Oh, to be able to fly free! He'd wing his way over the channel and home to the beautiful hills and fields of Summerhill.

Since his company had left, he rose and began running in place, calling up images of his childhood home. Those had been happy days at Summerhill, which was blessed with a mild south coast climate. Fertile fields and plump, happy livestock. He'd loved riding the estate with his father, learning the ways of a farmer without even thinking about it. His father had been a good teacher, challenging his heir's mind and curiosity.

The earl had also talked government and the House of Lords and what would someday be expected of Grey when he became the Earl of Costain. But that had been unimaginably far in the future. His parents were young and vigorous, and

Grey would have many years to sow wild oats before it would be time to settle down.

Which was the attitude that had led him here. Tiring, Grey slowed his pace to a walk before settling on his rocky chair. He placed it so that the sunshine would fall on him. What subject would he contemplate today? Natural history, he decided. He would try to recall every bird he'd ever seen in Dorsetshire.

His list had reached twenty-three when he heard sounds in the passage. It was too early for dinner. He stared at the door, wondering if Durand was paying one of his brief visits. The minister no longer taunted his captive face-to-face, not since Grey had thrown his captor to the floor and almost inflicted lethal damage.

He'd have succeeded if Durand hadn't had a guard with him. Grey had been beaten savagely, but it had been worth it. Since then, Durand contented himself with sneering through the window in the door. The coward.

Grey prepared himself for whatever might come, but the steps stopped short of his cell. Snarling voices, a bang of the cell door next to his. Then retreating footsteps and a return to silence. Good God, could there really be another prisoner only a wall away? If only Grey could speak to him!

But the wall was too thick for sound to penetrate. Perhaps it was possible to stand at the door and shout, but the door was also thick and its two openings were covered from the outside. If Grey shouted, he would attract the evil attentions of Gaspard long before he could make himself understood by the new prisoner.

He paced the common wall restlessly, running his hands over the solid surface. If only there was some way to communicate! He wanted to howl with frustration.

He dropped to the floor, his back against the common wall, fighting the temptation to bang his head against the stone. And heard a voice, soft and low and regular. He froze, wondering if he really was losing his mind.

No! The sound came from the sewer hole in the corner of his cell. With rising excitement, he knelt beside it and listened. Yes! The words were clear now. Latin. A prayer? The cell next to him must have a similar hole that joined with his and allowed wastes to fall into some subterranean hole.

Frantic with hope, he called, "Monsieur! Monsieur, can you hear me?"

The Latin stopped and a soft, cultured voice said in French, "I can. You are another prisoner?"

"Yes! In the next cell!" Grey swallowed hard, fearing he might dissolve into tears. "My name is Grey Sommers and I'm English. I've been here over two years. Who are you?"

"Laurent Saville. I'm called Père Laurent."

Father Lawrence? "You're a priest?"

"I am." A note of dryness entered the calm voice. "My crime has been to love God more than the emperor. And you?"

"Durand . . ." Grey hesitated, uncomfortable with admitting his sins to a priest. But priests were supposed to be forgiving, weren't they? "Durand found me with his wife."

"And you live?" Laurent said in amazement.

"He thought death too merciful." Grey's words tumbled over each other. "Tell me about yourself. Where are you from? Where have you studied, what subjects do you know? Please, talk, anything!" Fists clenched, he forced himself to stop. "I'm sorry. It has been so long since I've had a normal conversation with another man."

The low chuckle was deeply soothing. "I was born and raised near here. We will have all the time we need, I'm sure. Tell me what life is like in Durand's dungeon."

The priest was right. They had plenty of time to talk. Till one of them died.

Though Grey valued the occasional exchanges with the servants, having a regular companion made a huge difference. And he couldn't have done better than Père Laurent, who was kind and wise and learned, and as willing to share his knowledge as Grey was to learn it. Sometimes they sang together.

The food improved, too. Grey guessed that

someone up in the kitchen was a good Catholic who thought a priest deserved to eat decently, and Grey benefited by that.

Laurent was older, his health more fragile. One terrible winter, he seemed on the verge of dying from lung fever. That was when Grey learned to pray.

Father Laurent survived. And together, they kept each other sane.

Chapter 9

France, 1813

Since the guard and prisoners weren't known to be ill, Madame Bertin provided a hearty sausage stew rather than broth. Carrying three meals, Cassie carefully descended the treacherous stone steps. She didn't want to break her neck when she was so close to an answer.

The stairs ended in a short corridor with a door at the other end. A locked door. Since her hands weren't free, Cassie kicked the door. "Monsieur? I have your dinner!"

A key rattled in the lock and the door was opened swiftly by a burly man. "Come in, come in! I was wondering if I'd been forgotten." Getting a look at her, he said suspiciously, "I don't know you."

"Everyone else is ill with the influenza so I'm

helping out," Cassie explained. "Shall I put the tray on your table?"

The guard nodded and stepped back, relaxing when he saw that his visitor seemed to be a fragile old lady. "Gaspard will be back soon, but we're under orders to never leave the prisoners unguarded, so I couldn't come up to the kitchen."

It said much for Durand's temper that he was obeyed even when he was a hundred miles away and his guard was hungry. As she set the tray on the end of the table, she surreptitiously studied the guardroom. There were several chairs and cards on the other end of the desk, where the guard had been playing some form of solitaire. This job must be insanely boring.

As soon as Cassie set a steaming bowl down, the guard sat and dug into the stew. She poured wine from the decanter she'd brought. "I have meals for the prisoners as well. Are they through that door?"

The guard nodded and slurped some wine. "The cells are there, but don't worry. Leave the tray and I'll take their food in after I've eaten." He wiped his mouth with the back of his hand. "If there's any left after I eat! I'm that hungry, I am."

So if he was feeling greedy, the prisoners would starve? Concealing her anger, she said amiably, "If you need more food for them, I'll bring it down when I come back for the bowls. And maybe a little more wine for you, eh?"

The guard gave her a gap-toothed smile. "You

understand what a man needs, grandmère." He ripped off a piece of the bread and dipped it into the stew.

A ring of keys hung from a nail by the door that led to the cells. Though Kirkland had sent Cassie only to verify his information, there would never be a better chance to free Wyndham if he was here. Even if he wasn't, Cassie would release any other poor devil languishing in this hellhole.

The guard was paying no attention to her, so Cassie stepped behind him and applied hard pressure to two carefully chosen spots in his thick neck.

"*Merde*!" As the blood flow was cut off, the guard jerked and started a protest, then slumped forward into his dinner. Cassie maintained the pressure long enough to ensure that he was thoroughly unconscious.

After releasing the hold, she efficiently bound his wrists and ankles and gagged him. Another moment to stow him behind the desk so he wouldn't be immediately visible if anyone entered, and then she snatched up the key ring. If Gaspard was going to be back soon, she needed to move fast.

It took a few moments to find the right key. The door swung open, and she was almost flattened by the stench in the passage on the other side. Dear God, what was it like to go ten years without a bath?

Trying to ignore the rank scent of unwashed bodies, she headed down the ill-lit passage. The right wall was plain stone; the left had four doors. Her nose confirmed that the occupied cells were at the far end. Which one held the man she sought?

As she paused, she heard the sound of a male voice behind the last door. She blinked. He was *singing!* He had a fine baritone.

She listened to the words, and smiled involuntarily when she realized that he was singing a French song so scurrilous that even she didn't know all the obscenities. Probably not the priest, then.

Now to find out if it was Wyndham. Hoping to God he hadn't been driven mad, she found a likely key and attempted to open the cell on the far end. It took three attempts to find the right key. She opened the door and found herself face-to-face with a monster from a nightmare with filthy hair and beard falling over ragged garments.

They both froze in shock, staring at each other. Was this Kirkland's golden boy? The prisoner was broad shouldered and gaunt as a starving wolf. Hard to tell what color his hair was under the filth. Not really dark, but certainly not blond. His only distinctive feature was startlingly intense dark-ringed gray eyes.

The moment of surprise ended—and he launched himself at her with murder in his crazed gray eyes.

Chapter 10

In a world of endless monotony, even small changes were instantly noticeable. Grey was running in place when a key in the lock brought him instantly alert. The door hadn't been opened since the time he'd come close to killing Durand. Ever since, Durand had spoken through the little window when he came to taunt Grey with stories of great French victories and predictions of the imminent defeat of the British.

But if Durand or Gaspard were visiting, they would know what key to use. A guard? No one else was allowed down here. Grey approached the door, every muscle in his body taut. Beside the door were ten years' worth of neat scratches to mark the days. Thousands of marks measuring endless days. If there was even the remotest chance he could escape, he'd attack.

The door swung open to reveal a woman. The shock temporarily paralyzed him. Dear God, a woman, the first he'd seen in ten years! She was old and drab and forgettable, but unquestionably female. The sheer wonder of that held him immobile.

He recovered from his surprise when he realized this was his chance to escape this damnable cell. She'd never be able to stop him, especially since she didn't even hold a weapon. He charged toward her.

He was grabbing for the keys when she tripped him, caught his outstretched arm, and used his own speed to sling him to the floor with his arm twisted agonizingly high behind his back. He lay on his belly gasping. Years of constant exercise and an old woman could flatten him?

"Are you Lord Wyndham?" she asked in a swift, low voice. "I come from Kirkland to help you."

She spoke in English. It was so long since he'd heard the language that it took him a long moment to interpret the words. Wyndham. Kirkland. Help?

She said in French, "So you're not Wyndham. No matter, if you want to escape, I'll help you if you promise not to attack me again."

He replied in the same language, "I am Wyndham. Haven't spoken English in years. Wasn't attacking you, just trying to escape. Let me up?"

She released his arm. He scrambled to his feet, feasting his eyes on the sight of another human being. Better yet, a clean, normal woman. He impulsively wrapped his arms around her and crushed her warm body into an embrace, his heart pounding.

She swore and shoved at him.

"Please," he said, his voice shaking. "I've been so . . . so hungry for touch. Only a moment. *Please!*"

She relaxed and let him hold her. Dear God, she felt good! A warm, breathing woman with a sweet old-lady scent of lavender that made him think of his grandmother. He never wanted to let her go.

After too short a time, she pushed away. "Enough," she said, her voice compassionate. "We must leave. Almost everyone in the castle is ill with influenza, so I think we can walk right out if we're careful. I have a pony cart where you can hide till we're away. Do you have anything to take with you?"

He gave a bitter laugh. "Not a single damned thing except for Père Laurent in the next cell." He took the keys from her and began fumbling through them.

"Try this." She touched a key. "It's similar to the one that opened your cell. Can the priest move quickly?"

"He's been ill. I don't know how much longer he'll last in this beastly place."

The woman frowned. "That could jeopardize our escape."

"I'm not leaving without him," Grey said flatly as he slid the key into the lock.

"Very well, then." The woman might be old and drab, but she knew when not to waste time arguing.

Grey's hands were shaking as he tried to unlock the door. Such a simple action, yet deeply unreal after ten years when he had done nothing so simple and normal. But the cold iron key was solid in his hand, and that throw to the floor had been very real.

"Who are you?" he asked as he jiggled the key in the stiff lock.

She shrugged. "I have had many names. Call me Cassie or Renard."

Cassie the Fox. Given that she'd managed to enter the castle and release him, it was a good name for her.

The door swung open and Grey finally met the man who knew him better than anyone else in the world. Laurent was lying on his pallet. On the stone wall above his head an irregular brown cross had been drawn in blood. The priest's personal shrine.

Père Laurent levered himself up on one arm as the door opened. He was thin, white haired, and ragged, but Grey would have known him anywhere by the calm wisdom in his face.

"Grey." The priest smiled luminously as he stretched out a hand. "At last we meet in person."

"Meet and escape, courtesy of this lady here." Grey took his friend's hand and pulled him to his feet. "We must move quickly. Can you manage?"

The priest swayed and would have fallen without Grey's support. He exhaled roughly. "I fear not. You must go without me. Better you escape than all of us be captured."

"No!" Grey slid his arm around Laurent's waist. The older man was just skin and bones, seeming so fragile that he might break, but once again, human touch was a pleasure deeper than words could describe. "I leave with you or not at all."

Cassie frowned. "Père Laurent is right. We must escape from the castle, avoid pursuit across France, and travel back to England. The good father doesn't look as if he can climb the stairs."

"I'll carry him!" Grey spat out.

"He is very stubborn," the priest said mildly to Cassie. "But if we can get away from the castle, I can be left safely with a niece while you two run for your lives."

"Very well." Her eyes were worried. "But we must move quickly. Sergeant Gaspard could return at any moment."

As Père Laurent reached out and touched the blood cross in a gesture of farewell, Grey hissed under his breath, "I hope the devil does return."

Luckily Cassie the Fox didn't hear him.

Chapter 11

Cassie's instincts were screaming that they must move faster as she led the way down the passage, and those instincts had saved her life several times over. But with Wyndham half carrying the priest, they moved slowly. She wondered if he'd be strong enough to carry Père Laurent up the stairs after years of abuse and inadequate food.

Her unease spiked when she heard irregular footsteps ahead. At a guess, a man descending to the guardroom. "Someone's coming," she said in a low voice.

She was reaching for her concealed knife when Wyndham said with icy menace, "Gaspard. That's the sound of his peg leg. Here, take Père Laurent."

Wyndham caught up with Cassie and transferred the priest's weight. She automatically took Père Laurent's other arm so he wouldn't fall. Which meant her knife hand wasn't free.

Before she could protest, Wyndham swept past her with an expression so savage she was stunned to silence. He moved like a wild beast that had been released from a cage, his loping stride taking him to the guardroom in seconds.

The peg-legged man appeared in the door at the bottom of the stairs. His jaw dropped as he saw a prisoner racing toward him. "*Merde!*"

Snarling curses, Gaspard pulled a pistol from his greatcoat. Before he could cock and aim the weapon, Wyndham was on him with a growl that was barely human.

There was an audible snap as Wyndham broke Gaspard's neck. The sergeant dropped like a puppet whose strings had been cut. The end had come so quickly it couldn't even be called a fight.

Cassie must have made some sound because Père Laurent said quietly, "I am not a violent man. But I will say that Gaspard got less than he deserved."

Reminding herself that Wyndham would have learned Hindu fighting skills at the Westerfield

Academy, Cassie swallowed her shock. But as she supported the priest along the last stretch of the passage, she wondered if she'd released a mad wolf to run wild.

By the time they reached the guardroom, Wyndham had pulled the dead man out of the stairwell and was rapidly stripping off his clothing. "Père Laurent, these garments will keep you warmer," he said tersely.

A practical man, Wyndham. Cassie said, "I put the guard behind the desk. He should still be unconscious. He's taller so his clothing would be a better fit for you. Just don't kill him, please."

Wyndham piled Gaspard's garments on the chair, then pulled out the still-limp guard. "You do good work," he said with approval. "First I'll help Père Laurent dress."

Cassie could understand that an aging priest might not want a woman's aid. She bent over the guard and released his bonds so she could undress him.

He was starting to stir, so she knocked him out again. She was careful not to cut the blood flow so long that his mind would be damaged. She did her best to avoid hurting or killing anyone without a good reason.

He was heavy, but Cassie was a lot stronger than she looked. By the time she had the garments off, the priest was dressed and sitting at the table gulping down a bowl of stew. As she poured wine for him, he said apologetically, "We weren't fed since yesterday morning."

"Almost everyone in the castle is ill," Cassie explained. "I volunteered to take trays around, which is how I was able to find you."

"I suppose Grey and I must be thankful that no one ever came near us, which seems to have spared us the illness." Laurent wiped up the last of the stew with a piece of bread. *"Le bon Dieu* works in mysterious ways."

Cassie had seen plenty of evidence of that, including the fact that the deity seemed to have a wicked sense of humor. She asked, "Grey?"

"My Christian name is Greydon Sommers," Wyndham said tersely. "I haven't felt much like a courtesy viscount in quite some time, so I prefer you call me Grey."

She understood that very well indeed. She poured the last of the wine into a glass for Grey, careful to keep her gaze averted as he pulled off his ragged garments. The worn, thin fabric would have been transparent if not for the layers of dirt.

"Ready," he said.

She turned and saw that the guard's clothes were loose enough to go around his waist twice but the height was close and the outfit was clean and warm compared to his old clothing. If not for the matted tangle of hair and beard falling halfway to his waist, he would look normal. Except for the chancy light in his gray eyes.

"I'll head out and bring my pony cart to the entrance," she said. "There's a landing at the top of the steps. Wait there until I come for you. I'm hoping we can get away without being seen."

Wyndham lifted a bowl of stew and began scooping it out with his bare fingers like a jungle savage. "The cart will take a few minutes, so I'll eat first."

"Just don't delay our departure." She headed up the stairs, her steps quick. She hoped the men wouldn't gulp down the food so quickly they'd become ill.

On the landing at the top of the steps, Cassie opened the door and peered out cautiously. Silence. She headed toward the back door, walking softly. She had to pass through one end of the kitchen to get outside. Madame Bertin was at the far end, snoring audibly in her chair by the fire.

Hoping that would last, Cassie left the castle and crossed the yard to the stables. The wind was sharper and even more bitter than when she'd arrived. There was a storm coming; she could feel it in the air.

Her pony waited patiently, having finished the hay Cassie had appropriated from the stable supply. She pulled off the pony's rug. It was warm and smelled horsy, but that was a minor issue compared to how the prisoners smelled.

She'd had the cart built with a false bottom capable of carrying useful cargo, and people when necessary. It was reached by a panel that opened along the side. She tossed the rug in. The compartment wasn't comfortable, but there was clean straw and the horse blanket would add warmth and cushioning. It was big enough for two men, barely.

After driving across the courtyard, she tethered the pony by the back door and went inside again. Madame Bertin still snored.

Wyndham—Grey—and the priest waited on the landing at the top of the stairs, the priest supported by his younger friend. She touched a finger to her lips in a gesture for silence.

Père Laurent looked as if he'd never make it to the cart without collapsing. She bit her lip but needn't have worried. Grey scooped the old man up as if he weighed nothing and carried him quickly and silently across the kitchen. It was like a Restoration farce, with characters tiptoeing across the stage unseen.

Wondering how Grey had maintained so much strength under prison conditions, Cassie opened the outside door and looked around. The courtyard was still empty. Giving thanks for cold winds and influenza, she held the door open so Grey could carry the priest out.

He stepped outdoors—and froze, his gaze riveted upward. A rapid pulse beat in his throat. He whispered, "I never thought I'd see the open sky again."

"It's been here waiting for you." She lifted the panel that opened the false bottom. "And the sooner we leave, the better the chances that you'll be able to enjoy it for a long time to come."

Grey stared at the compartment. He looked like a skittish colt ready to bolt. Guessing the problem, she said, "I know the quarters are tight, but it's needful."

He drew a ragged breath, steeling himself. Then he carefully laid his friend in the compartment. The priest said to Cassie in a thin voice, "Take the main road south from the village. That is the direction to my niece's farm."

"Very well. When we're safe away, you can give me more detailed instructions." She glanced at Grey. "Your turn. Does it help to know that you won't be locked in? The compartment can be unlatched from the inside."

"That does help," he said tersely before climbing into the compartment. "I always thought I'd leave this place in a bloody coffin," he muttered. "Seems I was right."

She almost laughed. It appeared he'd retained some sense of humor, so there was hope for the man. "This coffin has fresh air, and it won't be for long."

Cassie latched the long door and swung up onto the seat. The first flakes of snow were drifting softly down as she set the cart in motion.

She drove out the castle gates, hoping they'd find shelter before the snow became serious. And that the priest's niece was still alive, well, and would welcome them as he believed.

Stage one, the rescue from the castle, was successful.

Now came the hard part.

Chapter 12

Grey and Laurent slid a little toward the front of the cart as it rattled down the hill from Castle Durand. Still no shouts of pursuit, no gunshots. How long until their absence was discovered? A few hours, perhaps as much as a day.

Père Laurent murmured, "I didn't believe I would leave that place alive."

"Neither did I. Much less that I'd be rescued by Cassie the Fox."

"That is her name? It suits her. She's clever like a fox."

That she was. Grey hoped that Cassie the Fox would continue to be as competent as she'd been so far. The way she'd knocked out and immobilized the guard was impressive. He closed his eyes so he couldn't see how cramped this compartment was. It would be embarrassing to fall apart now that he was finally free.

He was grateful when the cart stopped. Sounds of rummaging above their heads, then Cassie opened the side panel. Her dark cloak was frosted with snowflakes.

Grey slid out with relief. Snow was starting to accumulate on the iron-hard ground and more was falling. Weather. Actual weather! Not just watching the light change beyond his tiny window.

As Grey helped his friend from the compartment, Cassie said, "I'll need your guidance now, Père Laurent. This has the feel of heavy snow coming and I'd like to find shelter before the roads become impassable. If your niece is too far away, we need to look for an isolated barn to wait out the storm."

Laurent gazed at the horizon, where the blurred shape of Castle Durand was still visible through the falling snow. "From where we are now, we should be able to reach Viole's farm before the roads become difficult. She married a foreigner." He gave a fleeting smile. "A man who lives more than half an hour's ride away. Romain Boyer's farm is a prosperous little place hidden well back in the hills."

"If something has happened to your niece, will her husband also welcome us?" Cassie asked. "Much has changed in France in recent years."

"We will find shelter there," Laurent said confidently. "I must ride beside you, Cassie the Fox. The way is confusing and I will have to guide you."

"Very well." Cassie lifted a pair of scissors she'd been holding by her side. "But first I'll trim your hair and beard so you'll look less conspicuous."

She began clipping efficiently at Laurent's thin white hair. After she'd cut away the tangles that fell over his shoulders, he changed from a wild-eyed hermit into a shabby old man who wouldn't draw a second glance.

When she finished, Grey lifted his friend up into the driver's seat and bundled the horse blanket around him. To Cassie, he said, "My turn. If you give me the scissors, I'll do the cutting myself so we can get moving without more delay."

"You'd have trouble with the back." She began cutting below his left ear. His hair was much thicker than Père Laurent's, so she took it in chunks. She was taller than he'd realized, average or a bit above. "This will only take a couple of minutes."

He stood still despite the closeness of the sharp blades. If he could shave his head and face completely bald, he'd be willing, just to get rid of the horrible, filthy mass of hair. During the years of imprisonment, he sometimes whiled away time by breaking off individual hairs. If he hadn't done that, the tangled mess would be past his waist.

Despite all the knots, she managed to quickly cut his hair so that it was above his shoulders, then did a beard trim. She'd left enough hair to keep his head from freezing, but removing the weight made him feel lighter and freer. Not cleaner, but that would come.

It felt strange to be so close to a female again. He wanted to wrap his arms around her and kiss her horizontal. He was embarrassed by his intense reaction to a woman older than his mother. Dear God, how long until he could find himself a willing wench?

Forcing down lustful thoughts, he stared into the snow. He might no longer be a gentleman, but at least he had enough self-control not to behave like a beast with the woman who had risked her life to save him. At least, he hoped he did.

"There." She finished trimming his beard a couple of inches below his chin, then bent to scoop up the handfuls of fallen hair. "Mustn't show our direction by leaving a trail of hair." She balled up the greasy locks and stuffed them into a corner of the cart. "Time to get back inside so we can be on our way."

"No!" The word ripped out of him. "I can't bear being closed up. There's almost no traffic in this weather. I'll lie in the back of the cart under the canvas cover."

She studied his face. Her eyes were blue and shrewd and contained unexpected depths. "Very well," she said. "Be sure to stay hidden if we pass other carts or riders."

Thank God she was a sensible woman. Sighing

with relief, he flipped back the canvas and climbed up into the cart. Given how she'd brought down both him and that great burly guard, best not to cross her. He'd had no idea how dangerous little old ladies could be. Well, there was his grandmother, the dowager Countess of Costain, but her weapons were words. With a pang, he wondered if she was still alive.

He settled in among the boxes and baskets. The space was more cramped than the lower compartment and the corner of a box stuck into his side, but he didn't care as long as he was in the open air.

A homey equine scent wafted back from Père Laurent's horse blanket. Grey didn't mind. He'd always loved riding. What would it be like to be on a horse again?

He'd probably fall off. How much of his life would have to be relearned?

The thought made him sweat despite the cold. He must proceed one step at a time. For now, it was enough that he was no longer a prisoner.

Surrendering to fatigue, he slept as a free man for the first time in ten years.

Cassie's mouth tightened as the snow became heavier. It was more than three inches deep and concealed the frozen ruts, making the ride a bumpy one. She'd slept in her cart before in bad weather, and even ridden out a blizzard once, grateful for the warmth of her pony. But she'd rather not have to do that with two men, one of them in fragile health.

The weather did have the advantage of keeping people indoors. Once a hunched rider passed them going the opposite direction, and another time she halted the cart while a farmer drove a small flock of sheep across the road. He ignored the cart and its occupants as if they were invisible.

Afternoon turned to dusk and the snow became deep enough to slow their progress. If they didn't reach their destination soon, they risked being bogged down in the empty countryside.

It was almost dark when Père Laurent said, "Turn left into that lane. It leads to Viole's farm."

Praying that farm and niece would be as he believed, she turned at his direction. The area was indeed out of the way. They should be safe here, at least for a while.

The track climbed upward and the pony began foundering in the slippery snow. Cassie halted the cart and handed the reins to Père Laurent. "Please hold these."

She climbed from the cart and went to the pony's head. Taking the bridle, she tugged the pony forward. "I'm sorry for this, Thistle," she crooned. "You're such a strong, brave pony. Soon you can rest and I'll give you some of the oats in the back of the cart. Just a little longer, *ma petite chou*."

Head down, the pony struggled forward again. At first the cart barely moved. Then it began rolling smoothly, reducing the strain on Thistle. Surprised, Cassie glanced back and saw that Grey had climbed out and was pushing the cart from behind. The man was strong. And for a British lord, fairly useful.

The last stretch of track seemed endless. Cassie was numb with cold and slipped repeatedly. She was exhausted, not just from the trials of today but because she'd been pushing herself since leaving England. She kept moving, one foot in front of the other, clinging to the pony's harness. She'd learned early that surrender was a poor choice.

She didn't notice that the track had leveled off until Père Laurent said, "We're here." His voice was warm. "It looks just as I remember."

Cassie wondered tartly if that had also been in the middle of a blizzard. She couldn't see the farmhouse clearly, but smoke came from the nearest chimney and there was light visible through the windows. Even if the priest's niece, Viole, wasn't here anymore, surely the inhabitants wouldn't turn away strangers caught in such a storm.

Shivering, Cassie made her way to the door and knocked hard. Only a moment passed before the door opened a crack, revealing the face of a wary middle-aged woman. She relaxed a little to see another female on the doorstep. "Who are you?"

"I'm Madame Renard. There are three of us, and we need shelter from the storm." When the woman nodded, Cassie continued, "If you are Madame Boyer, do you have an Uncle Laurent?"

The woman's face clouded and she crossed herself. "I did, may God rest his blessed soul."

A weary but amused voice said, "Reports of my death were exaggerated, my dearest Viole."

Cassie turned and saw the dark figure of Père Laurent emerging from the cart, supported by Grey. Viole Boyer stared in disbelief. "*Mon oncle!*"

She threw the door open and raced out into the snow and embraced the priest. If not for Grey's support, she and her uncle would have tumbled to the ground.

Père Laurent didn't mind. Tears on his face and in his voice, he said hoarsely, "My darling niece, I didn't think I would ever see you again."

The wind gusted, cutting to the bone. Cassie pointed out, "This reunion will be even better indoors."

"*Oui, oui!*" Madame Boyer took her uncle's arm and led him to the house.

Cassie asked, "Is there a stable for my pony?"

A broadly built man who must be Romain Boyer appeared, drawn by the commotion. "Père Laurent, it really is you!" After a brief, intense clasp of the old man's hand, he said to Cassie, "I'll take your pony to the stable and bed it down, madame. You and your companions need to warm yourselves by the fire."

Ordinarily Cassie would have seen to her horse herself, but this evening she was willing to turn Thistle over to someone else. "There are oats in the back of the cart," she said wearily. "Thistle has earned them."

"Indeed she has." Romain Boyer moved into the storm and took hold of the pony's bridle. "I promise she'll be well cared for."

The door opened into a large, warm kitchen with bunches of herbs and braids of garlic and onions hanging from the rafters. A fire burned on the hearth and the warmth almost knocked Cassie out. She stood, swaying, too tired to think.

A young girl and a smaller boy appeared. Seeing Cassie's condition, Madame Boyer said, "You need rest, Madame Renard." To her daughter, she said, "Light the fire and warm the extra bed in your room. This lady has brought my uncle home to us!" She turned to her son. "Fill three porringers with hot soup, André."

To Cassie, she said, "Give me your cloak. I'll dry it by the fire. Please, all three of you, sit before you fall over!"

Cassie was used to taking care of people in her charge as well as horses, but she let herself be ushered to a chair by the fire. Père Laurent sat on her right, and Grey withdrew to the corner, as far from all the chattering people as possible.

André ladled steaming soup from a pot on the hob into a wooden porringer, then hesitated, unsure whether to serve the lady or the priest first. Cassie gestured toward Père Laurent. "A priest has precedence over a female peddler."

Glad to have that clarified, the boy handed the porringer to his great-uncle, then filled another and handed it to Cassie. She cupped it in her hands, her fingers tingling uncomfortably as they warmed. She was just finishing the soup when the young girl returned. "I am Yvette. Come, madame. Your bed is warmed and ready."

"*Merci.*" Cassie set down the empty porringer and followed the girl from the warm kitchen, down a cold, drafty corridor, then into a small, warm bedroom with single beds on opposite walls.

"My sister, Jeanne, is married, so there is a spare bed," Yvette explained. "The one on the right is yours. Can I help you disrobe?"

"Thank you, but I can manage." Cassie sat on the edge of the bed and tugged off her half boots and loosened her hair. She stood to remove her sturdy gown, then crawled into the narrow but comfortable bed.

Usually in France she slept with one ear cocked for trouble. But this welcoming family and farmhouse were a haven, protected from all enemies by the storm rattling the windows and concealing the fugitives' path.

She was asleep before Yvette left the room.

Chapter 13

It was still dark outside the frost-patterned windows when Cassie woke. She had the sense she'd slept only a few hours, but long enough to cure her exhaustion.

Wondering how her newly freed charges were faring, she dressed again. Yvette had left her half boots by the small fire so they were warm and mostly dry. After pulling them on, she returned to the kitchen, which was the center of life in most farmhouses.

The long room was empty except for Madame Boyer, who was mending by the fire. She glanced up, her happiness at the reunion with her uncle still visible. "Ah, you look much better than you did, madame. Join me by the fire. Would you like more to eat? To drink? Perhaps some apple brandy, made right here on our farm?"

Cassie was about to say the apple brandy sounded good when she noticed a drying rack angled on the other side of the fire. Her cloak was draped over one end, thin tendrils of steam wisping from the heavy fabric. Hanging on the other end were the garments taken from the guard at the castle. She remarked, "Wyndham is sleeping?"

Viole made a face. "Père Laurent and my family have gone to bed, but I cannot retire before your other man—I thought his name was Monsieur

Sommers?—returns. He is bathing. In the farm pond."

"What?" Appalled, Cassie stared at her hostess. "He'll freeze to death! Surely the farm pond has iced over. How could you allow him to do such a mad thing?"

"Water flows in from a spring at one end so it doesn't freeze." Viole rolled her eyes. "I also told him he was mad, but he just asked most politely for soap and towels and a scrub brush. Uncle Laurent says he's English. That explains much." She gestured toward the fire, which was burning low. "I told him if he wasn't back by the time that log burns down, I shall send my husband out after him."

The log was almost gone. Cassie reached for her cloak. "Where is the pond?"

"Around the back of the house by the stables. It cannot be missed." Viole set her mending aside and lifted a cloak from one of the pegs by the door. "Take mine. It's dry."

Cassie donned the cloak gratefully. "May I have a blanket and perhaps some brandy in case I must pull that idiot's frozen body from the pond and revive him?"

Viole removed a small, squat jug from a cabinet, then a scratchy blanket from a different cabinet. The blanket was pleasantly warm from being kept near the fire. "If you need help removing the body, come inside and I shall wake Romain."

Cassie took the brandy and headed toward the door. "Men! It's amazing mankind has survived."

"Mankind survives because womankind has more sense," the other woman said.

"So very, very true." Cassie pulled the hood over her head. "You can go to bed now. If Monsieur Sommers is alive and in reasonable health, I'll wait with him until he's ready to come back in. If he's frozen dead in the water, I'll leave him there till morning!"

Accompanied by Viole's laughter, she headed out into the night. A foot or so of snow had fallen, making walking difficult, but the storm had mostly passed. The wind had dropped and the snow had become giant flakes, which meant the end was near.

Seething with exasperation, she followed the partially snow-filled tracks made by the foolish Lord Wyndham. The night was utterly still, and the world shimmered in a whiteness that caught all the available light and made the darkness glow.

The barn was a low stone building behind the house. Splashing sounds came from the right. Since any sensible animal would have taken shelter, it must be Grey.

One end of the pond was dark open water. As she drew closer, she saw her quarry. He was mostly immersed, only his head and shoulders out of the water as he busily scrubbed his hair.

Relief that he hadn't frozen to death flared into irritation. She marched toward him as well as a woman could march through deep snow. "I didn't go to the effort to rescue you just so you could kill yourself through stupidity, Lord Wyndham!"

"After ten years in a cell exposed to the open air, I don't notice temperature much." He ducked into the water to rinse off the soap, then emerged and pushed his wet hair back with both hands. Even in the night, it was noticeably lighter than before. "Such luxury to completely immerse myself in water! You cannot imagine."

"I love a really luxurious bath," she allowed. "But that doesn't include freezing into a solid block of ice when I take one."

"The water isn't too uncomfortable. It's the air that's bitter cold." His tone turned wry. "I'll have to move fast when I get out so no cherished bits freeze and snap off."

She suppressed a smile. "I brought a blanket you can wrap yourself in when the time comes." A log laid on the bank served as a bench, so she wiped snow off one end, set the folded blanket on the cleared area, and sat. "I told Madame Boyer she could retire since I'll stay here until you either emerge safely, or disappear into the watery depths."

"Even if I keel over from heart failure, it's worth it to be clean again." Grey used a long-handled brush to clean his back, scrubbing so hard he must be removing skin. "Not to mention the benefits of icy water on hot blood."

She blinked. "Your passions need controlling?"

His hands stilled. "For the first couple of years, I thought about women constantly. Dreamed of them. Remembered every woman I'd ever fancied in luscious feminine detail."

He soaped his hair again, hard muscles rippling in his shoulders. "Gradually that faded away. By the time you arrived, I felt like a eunuch. Now I'm a guest in this glorious farmhouse and my gracious hostess is a distractingly fine-looking woman. Her daughter is a delicious nymph who is far too young for me to be having such thoughts. So yes, ice water is useful."

"I, of course, am too old and drab to inspire unseemly lust," she said dryly.

Grey turned a burning gaze on her. She could feel the heat even on this frigid night. "I thought it best not to offend you with my improper thoughts," he said. "Particularly since you could probably defeat me in fair combat."

Remembering the desperate intensity of his embrace in the prison, she shivered, and not from the cold. "You're stronger and I presume you learned Indian fighting skills from Ashton while you were at the Westerfield Academy. I acted without thinking because you looked murderous and caught you by surprise."

"Not murderous. Merely desperate to get past

you and away from that damnable cell." He ducked under the water to rinse his hair again.

Cassie pulled her cloak tighter. The snow had stopped entirely, and the air was getting colder. "Madame Boyer attributes your mad desire to bathe outside in a blizzard to your Englishness."

He swallowed hard. "After ten years in hell, quite possibly I am mad."

She winced. Thinking he needed reassurance, she said, "Not mad, I think, though perhaps a little crazed. That will pass." She uncorked the brandy jug and leaned over the water to offer it to him. "Try the apple brandy. It might save you from freezing solid."

He took a swallow, then began coughing so hard she was afraid he'd go under. When he could breathe again, he said hoarsely, "I've lost the habit of strong spirits." He sipped more cautiously, then sighed with pleasure. "Apple fire. Lovely."

When he handed the jug back to Cassie, she sampled the contents. Though strong, the brandy was sweet and fruity, with perhaps pear as well as apple. Enjoying the slow burn, she returned the jug to Grey. "This is made here on the farm."

He took another sip. "Speak English to me," he said haltingly in English. "Slowly. After ten years of only French, I must struggle to speak my native language."

She did as he asked, speaking each word

distinctly. "Your English will return quickly once you have it in your ears again."

He frowned at the brandy jug. "I have wanted nothing more than to escape, but now that I am free, what will I find back in England?" he said slowly. "I thought I'd been long forgotten by everyone, but you said Kirkland sent you?"

"You have not been forgotten," she said quietly. "You haunt all the friends you made at the Westerfield Academy. Kirkland has searched for you for years. He made inquiries among the thousands of Englishmen interned in France when the Peace of Amiens ended. He heard rumors, and traced them all without success. Kirkland was determined to keep going until he either found you alive, or found proof of your death."

"Why?" Grey asked, surprised. "I was the very model of a useless fribble."

"But a charming one, from what Kirkland said."

"Charm is one of many things I've lost over the years." He took another sip of brandy. "Do you know anything of my family? You have called me Wyndham, not Costain. I hope this means my father is well?"

"Kirkland said all of your immediate family is in good health," she assured him. "Your father, your mother, your younger brother and sister."

The moon broke through the clouds and touched Grey's hair to brightness. Cassie was reminded that Kirkland had called him a golden boy. "If you're through washing, it's time to go inside."

"I fear emerging from the water because then the cold will be truly vicious." He handed her the brandy jug. "But I suppose I must."

"Madame Boyer said you'd brought out towels. Ah, over there." She scooped up the towels. After kicking snow off a section of the bank, she spread the smaller towel on the cleared space. "Step up here. The towel will protect your feet a bit. Use the larger one to wipe off as much water as you can, then I'll wrap you in this blanket."

"Stand back if you don't want to be splattered." He clambered onto the bank and planted both feet on the small towel as he took the larger one from her.

In the moonlight, he had a gaunt powerful beauty marred by scars and too many bones visible under his taut, pale skin. Teeth chattering, he said, "Pattens. Over there."

The wooden pattens had almost disappeared in the snow. She retrieved them and set them by his towel. Pattens were usually worn over regular shoes, but he was a tall man so they fit well enough on his bare feet.

He toweled himself off rapidly. From the little she saw of what was euphemistically called "courting tackle," the frigid water had done a good job of cooling his ardor, at least for the moment.

"Let me wipe your back," she said. He handed

her the wet towel. She swiftly pulled it down his long frame, then wrapped the blanket around him.

He pulled the scratchy wool square tight, shivering. "I knew this would be the difficult part. Where's the brandy?"

She handed it over. He swigged some as he stepped into the pattens. "Time to run for it before I end up like one of Gunter's ices. Lord, is Gunter's still in business?"

"The teashop in Mayfair?" Cassie had been there once so long ago she'd almost forgotten. But now she remembered a lemon ice, the tangy sweetness melting on her tongue. "As far as I know, it's flourishing."

"Good. I used to take my younger brother and sister there. In warmer weather!" He headed toward the house, making good time with his long legs and high motivation. Cassie followed at a slower pace, carrying the wet towels.

Though Grey had dashed into the warm house, he held the door open for her when she arrived. His gentlemanly manners hadn't disappeared entirely.

Viole had retired, but she'd banked the fire and left a lamp burning, so the kitchen was warm and welcoming. On the scrubbed deal table were eating utensils, a bottle of wine, and food covered by a light cloth. After hanging up the cloak, Cassie lifted the cloth and found bread, cheese, a small dish of pâté, and a jar of pickled relish.

Keeping her voice down so as not to disturb the sleepers, she said, "We both need to warm up by the fire before heading off to bed. Our wonderful hostess has left refreshments. Would you care for some, or did you eat enough earlier?"

"Madame Boyer wouldn't let me eat too much because she thought I might make myself ill. So yes, more food would be most welcome." He kicked off the pattens and settled into one of the cushioned chairs by the fire, the blanket wrapped closely around him. With a sigh of pleasure, he stretched his bare feet out on the hearth. "Food and freedom and a fine fire. Yesterday I could barely imagine such riches."

Cassie assembled two plates with sliced bread and cheese and mounds of pâté and relish. She was silently amused by Grey's cavalier treatment of the pattens. In his pampered youth, he would have had servants quietly straightening up behind him. In his prison cell, he'd had no possessions to keep orderly. The man needed housebreaking.

She handed him one of the platters, a knife, and a tumbler of hearty red wine. In the low light, he had become the golden youth Kirkland had described. His hair was a bright blond, his beard several shades darker and touched with red. But he was a boy no longer. Now he was a man aged beyond his years.

"Food and drink whenever I want it. What a remarkable concept." He spread pâté on a slice of bread and took a bite. He savored the taste before swallowing. "Aahhh, ambrosia."

She settled in the chair beside him with her own food and wine. She tasted cheese on bread, pâté on bread, then both plus relish. As he said, ambrosia. "How did you keep your strength up under such dreadful conditions?"

"I exercised. Ran in place, lifted the two stones that served as furniture, kept moving as much as I could." He shrugged. "At the beginning, there was barely enough food to keep a rat alive, but the rations improved after Père Laurent was imprisoned."

"The castle cook thought it outrageous that a priest was so ill used, so she sent larger servings down for you both," Cassie explained.

"I owe the cook thanks. There was never enough food to feel really full, but it was sufficient to keep me from weakening." He spread pickle relish on a piece of bread and cheese. "There was nothing better to do, so exercise at least filled some time."

"Exercise and singing?"

He smiled a little. "That and remembering poetry and the like. I was not an ideal student. It never occurred to me that an education might help me cling to my sanity."

"A well-furnished mind must be a great asset when one is imprisoned."

"Père Laurent's mind is extremely well furnished. I encouraged him to tell me everything he knew." Grey spread pâté lavishly. "Cassie, what happens next?"

"We need to stay here a day or two until the roads clear," she said. "Then north to the English Channel, where smugglers can take us home."

"Home," he repeated. "I don't know what that means anymore. I was a typical young man about town, drinking and gaming and chasing opera dancers. A useless life. I can't go back to that. But I don't know what I can go back to."

"Ten years have passed," she said slowly. "You would have been a different man now even if you'd been safe in England the whole time. You might have married and become a father. You might have entered politics since you'll be in the House of Lords in time. Many paths are open to you, and you can take your time in choosing."

"Even thinking about a night at the opera, or a boxing mill, or a gaming club frightens me," he said bleakly. "So many people! I don't know if I can bear that. That was one reason I went out to the pond. Even half a dozen kind people were too many."

"After ten years of solitary confinement, it's not surprising if you find the thought of crowds appalling," she agreed. "But you can avoid them until and unless you're ready. You're a nobleman. You can be a splendidly eccentric hermit if you like. Since you were outgoing and enjoyed people before, it's likely you will again. In time."

"I hope you're right." He glanced across at Cassie, his gaze hooded. "Do you have the apple brandy?"

"Since you're unused to strong spirits, it might be wiser not to indulge in more," she observed. "Unless you want to greet your first day of freedom with a pounding head."

He let his head rest on the chair back. "I expect you're right. Even though I didn't drink that much by the pond, I seem to be babbling away quite frivolously."

"It's not surprising you want to talk about what lies ahead, and I'm the best choice because I know England," she pointed out. "And I am safe. After we reach England, you'll never see me again, and I am not of a gossipy disposition."

"What you are is a mystery, Madame Cassie the Fox," he said softly. "What is your story?"

Chapter 14

As soon as Grey spoke, Cassie drew into herself, strength and intelligence vanishing behind the façade of a tired old woman. He wondered how old she really was. He'd first guessed her at twice his age, around sixty, but she did not move like a woman of so many years. When she wasn't trying to look feeble and harmless, she had the litheness of a fit younger woman despite her gray hair and lined face.

Wanting to hear her lovely, smoky voice, he continued, "Why are you here, looking and talking like a Frenchwoman while serving an English master?"

"I serve no master, English or otherwise," she said coolly. "Since I wish to see Napoleon dead and his empire smashed, I work for Kirkland. He shares my goals."

Grey thought about how much he didn't know. "The war. Is Napoleon winning? Durand would taunt me with news of French victories. Austerlitz. Jena." He searched his memory. "He mentioned many other victorious battles as well."

"Durand told you only one side of the story," she said, amused. "There have been great French victories, but not lately. The French fleet was destroyed at Trafalgar in 1805, and Britain has ruled the seas ever since. In the Iberian Peninsula, the British and local allies are driving the imperial army back into France."

"What about Eastern Europe? The Prussians, Austrians, and Russians?"

"The emperor has defeated the Prussians and Austrians several times, yet they will not stay defeated," Cassie said. "In an act of staggering stupidity, last summer he invaded Russia and lost half a million men to General Winter. The sands of Napoleon's hourglass are running out."

Grey exhaled with relief. "All of these years,

I've wondered if England was about to be conquered."

"Napoleon is a brilliant general," she admitted, "but even he cannot defeat all of Europe. If he had been content to stay within France's borders, he could have had his crown, but his lust for conquest is his undoing."

What else did he want to know? "You mentioned my classmates at the Westerfield Academy. What of them? And Lady Agnes?"

"Lady Agnes is well and continues to educate her boys of good birth and bad behavior." Cassie smiled. "I met her only once, but she's not a woman one forgets."

He felt a rush of relief. Lady Agnes was far from ancient, but ten years was a long time. She had been as important in his life as his own mother, and he was glad to know she was well. "What of the others? Kirkland is obviously alive and apparently active in the spying trade."

Cassie nodded. "He divides his time between Edinburgh and London as he runs his shipping company. Intelligence gathering is a secret sideline."

He thought of the friends who had become closer than brothers in his years at school. "Do you know how any of the others are doing?"

Her brows furrowed. "I'm not well acquainted with most of them. The Duke of Ashton is well, recently married, and expecting his first child.

Randall was a major in the army, but he left after becoming heir to his uncle, the Earl of Daventry."

Grey had a swift memory of Randall's taut expression after receiving a letter from his uncle. "He hated Daventry."

"And vice versa, I've heard, but he and Daventry are stuck with each other and have apparently declared a truce," Cassie said. "Randall is also recently married. He seemed very happy the time I met him. His wife is a lovely, warm person."

"I thought he'd be a confirmed bachelor, but I'm glad to hear otherwise." If ever a man needed a lovely, warm wife, it was Randall. Thinking of his other classmates, he asked, "What of Masterson and Ballard?"

"Masterson is an army major, and Ballard is working to rebuild the family wine business in Portugal." Her brow furrowed. "You must have known Mackenzie, Masterson's illegitimate half brother. He has a very fashionable gaming club in London. Rob Carmichael is a Bow Street Runner."

Grey's brows arched. "Rob would be good at that, but it must have driven his father into a frenzy."

"I believe that was part of the reason he became a Runner," she said with amusement. "Those are the only Westerfield students I know, but when you're back in London your friends will be happy to bring you up to date."

The thought of London created a knot of panic in Grey's gut. His friends' marriages also made him sharply aware of how much time had passed. They had grown up and taken on adult responsibilities. Grey had merely . . . survived.

Uncannily perceptive, Cassie said softly, "Don't compare your life to theirs. You can't change the past, but you are returning to family, friends, and wealth. You can have the future you dreamed of in captivity."

He wanted to blurt out that he was no longer capable of having the life he was born to. His confidence, his sense of himself and his place in the world, had been shattered. As a future earl, he would have no trouble acquiring a wife eager to spend his money, but where would he find a wife who was willing and able to deal with the darkness of his soul?

But whining was ugly, especially to a woman as fearless as this one. He was still amazed at how she'd come to see if he might be in Castle Durand, seen an opportunity to free him, taken down a guard, and led him and Père Laurent to safety through a blizzard. Maybe that strength was why he found her so attractive.

Madame Boyer was an attractive woman in her prime. Her daughter Yvette was a lovely girl with a face to inspire young, bad poets. Yet it was drab, aged Cassie the Fox who intrigued him. Though she might be his mother's age, she had a lovely, delicate profile, a smokily delicious voice, and a core of tempered steel.

Wanting to know more of her, he stated, "Tell me about your family."

She leaned forward to put another piece of wood on the fire. "My father was English, but we made long visits to my mother's family in France. We were here when the revolution broke out." She settled back in her chair, her face like granite. "I said we must return to England immediately, but my warnings were dismissed by the rest of the family."

"Cassandra," he said, remembering his Greek studies. "The Trojan princess who saw the future, but couldn't convince anyone of the danger she foretold. Did you choose that name for that reason?"

She winced. "No one else has ever made that connection."

"Cassandra was a tragic figure," he said softly, wondering how closely her story resembled the myth. "Did you lose your family as she did?"

Her head whipped away and she stared at the fire. "I did."

Hearing the pain in her voice, he realized that it was time to change the subject. In his younger, more gentlemanly days, he would have known better than to ask such personal questions. "What do you think is the best way to return to England? I don't even know where in France I am."

"We're about a hundred miles southwest of Paris, somewhat farther from the north coast." She frowned. "North is the obvious way to go, which isn't good if we're pursued. But any other route would be much longer."

"Do you think we'll be chased? With Gaspard dead, there might not be anyone at the castle capable of organizing a pursuit."

"His guard didn't look like the sort to take initiative," she agreed. "But once Durand learns that his prisoners are gone, he might send soldiers after you."

"He probably will." Grey flinched at the thought. "His hatred of me was very personal."

"What did you do to earn his displeasure?"

Grey disliked revealing his stupidity, but she deserved an answer. "He caught me in bed with his wife. When I came to Paris, Kirkland asked me to keep my ears open for information that might be useful to the British government." Grey sighed. "I rather fancied myself as a spy. I'd heard that Citoyen Durand was in the inner circle of the government, so I had the brilliant notion that maybe I could learn something from his wife. I met her at a salon and she made it clear that she'd welcome a bit of dalliance."

"Do you think she was trying to lure you in so you could be killed or captured?"

"I've had plenty of time to think about that, but no, I think she merely had a taste for younger men, and I was foolish enough to be caught." How different his life would have been if he'd left when she told him to. "How will we travel? The cart?"

She shook her head. "If anyone suspects that the old peddler woman with a cart had something to do with your escape, we would be too easy to catch."

"I could travel on my own," he said, hating to think that his presence would endanger her.

"Despite your ten years in France and your fluent French, you don't know what the country is like now. We need to travel together." A smile flickered over her face. "I can be your aged mother. I'll see if the Boyers want the cart. It's sturdy and well built, and it can be painted to look different. I can ride Thistle, but we'll need to find a larger mount for you. Perhaps Monsieur Boyer will know someone with a horse to sell."

"Hasn't the army requisitioned all the horses?"

"That happened in the early days of the war, but now they can draw on the resources of a continent, so the military has sufficient horses. It shouldn't be hard to find a steady, uninteresting hack for you. The sort of horse no one would look at twice."

That was probably all Grey was good for now. "If the weather cooperates, I assume a week or so to the channel coast, and that you already know some helpful smugglers?"

She nodded. "I also have forged papers for you. Kirkland provided them just in case."

Grey's brows arched. "That was certainly advanced thinking when he didn't even know if I was alive."

"In my business, it is wise to prepare for all contingencies. That leaves more time to deal with unexpected problems. And there are always unexpected problems." She covered a yawn as she rose. "I'm exhausted. At least the snow gives a good reason to sleep late. We won't be able to leave for a day or two. You have a bed prepared?"

"They made up a pallet for me in the room with Père Laurent, but I'm so comfortable in this chair that I think I'll sleep here." It was a luxury too rich for words that he had a choice of where to sleep after ten interminable years without any choices.

Going back to a complicated world, would he know how to make decisions? Or would that have to be relearned, with all the errors that implied?

Cassie added more fuel to the fire, then pulled another ragged blanket from a cupboard. She spread it over him, saying, "It will get colder toward morning."

"I'm used to the cold." He caught her hand as she started to turn. "I just realized that I haven't thanked you for rescuing me." He kissed her hand with gratitude beyond words.

A spark of electricity snapped between them.

She pulled her hand away, looking unnerved. "I was just doing my job. We were fortunate that today all went well. Goodnight, milord."

Candle in hand, she vanished into a corridor leading to the east wing of the house. He watched her go, wondering again how old she was. Her hand was strong and shaped by work, but there was none of the gnarling of age. Perhaps she wasn't so old that he need be ashamed of himself for his lustful thoughts.

He closed his eyes and slept, dreaming nightmares that he was a fly caught in a sticky web, and a spider was closing in for the kill.

Durand exploded into his castle cursing with rage as he called for his steward. A trembling maid summoned the man. Monsieur Houdin was pale when he appeared.

As he stripped his cloak and gloves off, then tossed them aside, Durand glared at the steward. "What happened to my prisoners, Houdin? Were you bribed to release them?"

The steward jerked back from his master's fury. "No, sir! No one in the castle betrayed you. But everyone here—everyone, including me—was laid low by a vicious disease that made us so ill that few could even stand. Two of the older servants died. Apparently in this moment of weakness, several men broke in and released the goddam and the priest."

"Gaspard will answer for this!" Durand said viciously.

"Gaspard is dead," the steward said starkly. "Killed in the assault. He did not betray you, Citoyen."

"Perhaps not, but he was incompetent! What of the guards?"

"Brun was sick in his bed and barely escaped death. Dupont was on duty and was injured in the raid."

Dupont would be the best witness, Durand supposed. "Where is Dupont?"

With no one to guard in the dungeon, Dupont was now working in the stables. Durand summoned him. The man showed up pale with fear.

Under questioning, he said, "There were three or four raiders at least, Citoyen Durand. I heard their footsteps, but the only one I saw was an old woman who was used as a decoy. She brought food down since so much of the staff was ill. I was attacked while I ate. They bashed me on the head to knock me out." Dupont rubbed the back of his neck. "I awoke tied like a pig for slaughter and with my clothes stripped off."

"Worthless swine!" Durand snarled. "You deserve to stay here mucking out the horses." Pivoting, he stormed back to the castle. Luckily he'd brought a squadron of his specially trained guards, all of them crack cavalrymen. He would consider the most likely routes the escaped prisoners would take, then send his men in pursuit.

He'd get that bastard Englishman if he had to send every man in the Ministry of Police.

Chapter 15

Sleeping in a chair by the kitchen fire had the advantage of letting Grey exercise choice, and the disadvantage that the kitchen became active early. When Viole Boyer bustled in, whistling, Grey came awake groggily, apologized to his hostess for being in the way, and headed off to the pallet made up in Père Laurent's room.

There he slept for hours longer, waking near noon to sunshine reflecting brilliantly off the snow. The farm occupied a lovely little valley surrounded by hills and felt safe, remote, and prosperous. Laurent was gone, and Grey's dried garments had been stacked neatly beside him.

Reveling in his freedom, he dressed and made his way to the kitchen, which bubbled with noisy life. The whole household was there, everyone happily eating and talking and celebrating the miraculous return of Uncle Laurent. Grey's pulse began hammering and he wanted to run out into the empty countryside.

"Do you wish breakfast or luncheon, monsieur?" Viole called gaily.

"Coffee and bread to take outside would be ideal," he said, managing to control his desire to bolt. "The open sky calls to me."

Viole nodded and prepared a tall mug of coffee made with honey and hot milk, and a half loaf of bread split and filled with raspberry preserves. "There will be more when you return to warmth."

Grateful she didn't try to persuade him to stay indoors, he donned a cloak and hat offered by the young son of the house and headed outside. The day was as bitterly cold as it was beautiful, and for long minutes he just stood in the yard and studied the colors and textures that surrounded him.

He didn't think he'd ever seen a sky more intensely blue. A grove of dark, graceful evergreens rose up the hillside left of the barn, the needles rustling in the wind. Flurries of snow danced silently over the smooth whiteness that covered the land.

And the tastes! The hot milky coffee warmed him, and the delicious tang of the raspberry preserves reminded him of how very good food could be. He would never take the pleasures of food and drink for granted again.

Since he was wearing the guard's boots, it was easy to plow through the snow to the pond. He cleared a place on the log that served as a bench and settled down, drinking in the scents and sounds of the countryside along with his coffee.

A hawk glided effortlessly overhead. Though he

had taken great pleasure in the small birds that visited his cell, he'd missed the sweeping power of a hawk's flight.

The world was a feast, a dizzying tumult of colors, sounds, movements, and scents, and he was a beggar who didn't know what to do with such riches. He finished his coffee and bread, but felt no inclination to go inside again.

He heard the crunch of footsteps in the snow behind him and guessed who was coming even before Cassie joined him on the log, sitting a safe yard away. He tensed, but she didn't speak, and gradually he relaxed again. She was as peaceful as the frozen pond and the sculptured drifts of snow.

She drank tea, and the herbal scent was heavenly. One of so many things he'd never appreciated when he was living a luxurious life.

Her presence was soothing, not stressful like the exuberant Boyers. Eventually, Grey felt moved to say, "Strange. I longed for company and having Père Laurent imprisoned in the next cell was the greatest blessing I've ever known. Yet now that I'm free, I find myself uncomfortable around a handful of people."

"We are social creatures. Being deprived of companionship is one of the greatest torments imaginable." She sipped at her tea. "For you to survive so many years alone required great resources of will and endurance that took you far beyond normal life. Returning will take time."

"Great resources of will and endurance?" He smiled humorlessly. "No one who knew me before would imagine me capable of either."

"Kirkland had his doubts," Cassie said with a half smile. "But that didn't mean he thought he should give up on you. Imagine the pleasure of returning to your friends and family and amazing them with your strength of character."

His crack of laughter was rusty. He and Laurent had enjoyed rich discussions, but laughter was rare. "That does sound rather appealing." He finished his coffee, wishing there was more but not wanting to go inside for it. "My wise Lady Fox, will I ever be close to normal again? Or have all the years in prison changed me into a different, unrecognizable person?"

She shook her head. "We never know our full potential until circumstances force us to meet unexpected challenges. Different circumstances would have drawn forth other aspects of your nature."

"I would have enjoyed different circumstances infinitely more," he said dryly.

"No doubt." She glanced at him for the first time. "But if you'd continued to live the life of carefree luxury, would you now find such intense pleasure in simple things? Would the sky be as beautiful, the raspberries so exquisite, if they had always been available to you?"

His brows arched. "No, but I paid a very high price for my new appreciation."

Her smile was fleeting. "Higher than anyone would wish to pay. But at least there are some compensations for what you endured." She drank more tea. "They help balance the anger."

Grey felt as if she'd struck him a physical blow. He'd been so euphoric at regaining his freedom that he hadn't really recognized the anger that seethed just below the surface of his new happiness. Now that Cassie had named it, he realized that deep, fierce anger burned inside him. Anger that was so volatile that he might do . . . anything if it was released.

Rage had consumed him when he snapped Gaspard's neck. He barely remembered doing it, apart from the vicious pleasure he'd felt in killing the bastard. He would have killed the guard if Cassie hadn't asked him to restrain himself.

Her calm request to refrain from killing had cleared his mind enough to recall that Père Laurent had benefited from small acts of kindness by one or more of the guards. Because that kindness might have saved Laurent's life, Grey had let the guard live.

Recognition of his anger was followed by two more insights. One was that his discomfort around the Boyers was not just the panic of being with too many people, but a deep fear that he might lose control and hurt one of them. Or worse.

The other insight . . . He blurted out, "You have also been a prisoner, yes?"

Cassie became very still, her gaze fixed on the dark open water where he'd bathed the night before. "For less than two years. Nothing like so severe as your imprisonment."

"Still a very long time," he said softly. "Solitary confinement?"

She nodded. "At first I was grateful not to be packed into a cell so crowded there was barely room to lie down. Within the month, I would have given everything I owned and my hope of heaven to share a cell with even a filthy, furious harridan."

"No wonder you understand what it is to be deprived of companionship. Of touch." He reached out and covered her left hand, where it rested on the log. Her fingers twitched, then clasped his. "You were eventually released?"

"I found my own way to freedom," she said in a tone that refused all questions. "Like you, I discovered potentials in myself I had never imagined." Her hand tightened on his. "Even all these years later, sometimes the craving for touch is overpowering."

Since he felt the same, he slid along the log and wrapped an arm around her. Not for warmth, but for mutual need. She relaxed against him, her arm going around his waist. He wondered again how old she was. Once more he felt shame at his lustful thoughts.

At least he knew better than to act on those thoughts. Or to ask a lady her age. "What work do you do for Kirkland? If you spend much of your time traveling through France, you're alone again."

She sighed, her breath a white puff in the cold air. "I'm a courier, collecting information and getting it back to Kirkland. Sometimes I escort people from France, as I'm doing with you. My peddler disguise allows me to go almost anywhere. Spying is a lonely trade when I'm in France, but I return to London two or three times a year. I have a home of sorts and friends there."

Though she had the satisfaction of working against Napoleon, her life sounded bleak. "Will you return to England with me, or hand me over to one of your smugglers?" His arm tightened involuntarily. He wanted her with him all the way home. With Cassie he could relax because she could flatten him if his anger erupted dangerously.

"I'll return. I have other matters of business in London." She made a face. "I need to go inside before I freeze solid. Are you considering another bath?"

"Next time I bathe will be in a tub of steaming water." He removed his arm from around her and ran stiff fingers through his beard. "I need to go inside, too. I'm hoping Romain will lend me his razor. I want to see what I look like under this thatch."

"Don't shave the beard off yet," Cassie said firmly. "We must travel inconspicuously. No one notices or remembers me, and your appearance needs to be equally drab. I have coloring to disguise your hair, and keeping a beard will add to the appearance of an undistinguished peasant."

He grimaced. "Now that a clean-shaven face is within reach, I find that I crave it, but I will defer to your judgment. Have you talked to Romain about a horse?"

"He has a decent, unmemorable hack that he'll trade for the cart," she replied. "We also discussed a route. There's an old woodsmen's track over the hills. It will be a rough climb, but once we're on the other side, pursuers will be less likely to find us."

"You really think Durand will send men after us?" Grey asked, his skin crawling at the prospect.

"I don't know the man, but my instincts say yes." She got to her feet. "We foxes survive through slyness and instinct."

He guessed she'd chosen the name Fox just as she'd picked Cassandra: because the names suited her. He wondered what her real name was. "Will Père Laurent be safe here?"

She frowned. "Reasonably so. This farm is remote, and since Madame Boyer married outside her native village, she will be hard to trace as one of his relations. Père Laurent will stay here under the guise of an elderly cousin of Romain's, recently widowed and too feeble to care for himself. He'll also keep his beard."

"That should work," Grey agreed. "Locked in that cell, no one has seen him in years, so he won't be readily recognized."

It would be hard to leave his friend after developing such closeness over the years. But even more than that closeness, Grey wanted to go home.

Chapter 16

Firmly back in her role as a sturdy countrywoman who rode astride and brooked no nonsense, Cassie waited patiently for Grey to make his farewells to Père Laurent and the Boyers. He'd endeared himself to the whole family in the days they'd stayed at the farm and waited for the snow to clear enough for travel.

She had made her appearance drab for so long that it was second nature. Grey was more difficult to tone down. Even with his worn country clothing, the rinse she'd given him to dull his hair, and the ragged cut she'd given his beard, he looked like Somebody. Ten years in prison couldn't extinguish his aristocratic bearing. She'd have to remind him to slouch wearily when they were around people.

Grey hugged Père Laurent, saying huskily, "*Au revoir, mon père,*" as if the priest truly was his father. "If I ever have a son, I shall name him Laurent."

This was the hardest farewell, for both men knew they were unlikely to ever meet again. The priest was old and frail and Grey's own return to England was far from safe. Though the war must end someday, it was impossible to predict when Englishmen could openly visit France again.

His voice thick with emotion, Père Laurent said, "Make it Lawrence, for he will be an English gentleman, like you." Ending the embrace, he said, "Go with God, my son. You are in good hands with the lady fox."

"I know." Grey swung rather warily onto his mount, a placid old gelding called Achille. The horse didn't live up to its warrior name, so it was a good choice for him now. Cassie was unsurprised to see that even after ten years away from horses, he settled into the saddle like a skilled rider.

Viole Boyer approached him. "Godspeed, Monsieur Sommers. I have your English addresses as you have ours here. When this damnable war is over, perhaps you can call again, or at least let us know how you do."

"I shall." When she offered her hand, he bent from the saddle and kissed it. "You have my eternal gratitude, madame."

"Then the scales are balanced," she said, blushing like a young girl. The fabled Wyndham charm was recovering fast, Cassie thought with amusement.

As awkward, yearning silence fell, Cassie said briskly, "Time to get moving. We have a steep ride ahead of us."

She gave a last wave and set off on a narrow path that led into the woods behind the farm, Grey following. When they reached the woodsmen's track Romain Boyer had showed her the day before, it was wide enough for them to ride side by side through the bare trees. Patches of snow lay on the ground, but there was a hint of spring in the air.

"How long will it take us to cross over the hills?" Grey asked.

"Romain told me of a hut near the summit where we can spend the night," Cassie replied. "We should reach our road on the other side of the hills by afternoon tomorrow, barring bad weather."

He studied the sky and inhaled the air. "There are no storms coming."

"You sound very sure."

"I've been studying the weather in this region for ten years. Granted, it was through a rather small window, but I had ample time to observe the local weather patterns." His mouth twisted. "Another one of those unlooked-for blessings of captivity."

"One of the more useful ones." She patted the saddlebag behind her. "Even if a late storm sweeps in unexpectedly, Madame Boyer sent us off with enough food to take us from here to the English Channel."

"She is a woman in a thousand," he said with conviction. "Unfortunate that she's already married."

"We were very lucky to have the Boyers take us in," Cassie agreed. They'd been speaking in English, but she switched to French. "We shouldn't speak English anywhere we might be heard."

In French, he replied, "That would land us in serious trouble, but I do want to continue practicing my English when we're in private. I'm still thinking in French."

"You'll find yourself thinking in English after we reach England. I find that my mind makes the switch easily when the language is all around me."

"I hope you're right. It would be embarrassing to return home speaking my native tongue like a foreigner." He frowned at the rugged hills ahead. "What will Durand do in his pursuit?"

"He'll use the fast government courier system to send word to all the gendarme posts on the roads in every direction," Cassie said. "He has very little information to go on, so odds of our being caught are slim. But not impossible."

The thought was sobering. "Then we shall have to be fast and easily overlooked."

She gave him a quick smile. "Exactly."

They fell silent for a long stretch of trail, the only

sounds the horses' hooves and the occasional cry of a bird. Halfway up the sizable hill, Grey said abruptly, "I've been thinking about what you said the other day about anger. I hadn't realized how angry I was until you said that. Now I'm afraid of what I might do if I lose control. So if I'm about to do something murderous, hit me with a rock. Break my arm. Block the blood to my brain. Do whatever you must to keep me from hurting someone."

"Very well, I will," she agreed after she got over her surprise. "Unless you're damaging someone who deserves it. Even Père Laurent thought that your Sergeant Gaspard deserved his fate."

"He did. But if you hadn't asked me not to kill the guard, I would have broken his neck as well, and I don't know if he deserved killing," Grey said flatly.

No wonder he was concerned for his sanity, but he underestimated himself. "The fact that you care whether he deserved execution bodes well for your character."

"Now I care a little," he said gravely. "But when I was in full fury, I would have killed him whether it was just or not. Ten years in hell have ruined my character."

Choosing her words, she said, "Of course ten years in prison changed you, but you had twenty years before then, and the most important were the earliest. That is when your character was formed. The Jesuits say that if you give them a boy for his first seven years, he is theirs for life. Did your parents see that you were raised well? Were you taught honesty and responsibility?"

"Yes, and kindness as well," he said slowly. "I hope you're right that my character was formed then, because I don't know whether I still have those qualities. That's why I asked you to stop me if I lose control."

"I'd rather you worked on your anger yourself," she said frankly. "With your Hindu fighting skills and strength, I would surely lose any fight unless I took you by surprise."

His brows arched. "I suspect that you've had more practical experience fighting than I, and that you know lots of wicked tricks."

She had to laugh. "You're right, I do know a number of wicked tricks. It helps that most men don't expect a woman to fight, much less fight well."

"You sound like a woman who has done a great deal of fighting."

"I've been fighting my whole life," she said, her voice flat.

Several minutes of riding later, he asked, "What will you do when peace comes?"

She shrugged. "I haven't thought much about it since I never believed I'd survive that long. Perhaps I'll find a quiet cottage by the sea and raise flowers and cats."

"In England or in France?"

"England," she said immediately, surprised by her certainty on a subject she'd never much considered. "France has too many dark memories."

He nodded agreement. Once they were back in England, he'd never have to return to France unless he chose to.

Cassie had no choice, for without her private war with Napoleon, her life had no meaning. She'd return again and again until the war ended.

Or until she died.

By the time they reached the tiny hut near the summit of the highest hill, Grey had learned two things. The first was that he hadn't forgotten how to ride despite ten years of never going near a horse. His body remembered how to sit, how to control his mount.

The second thing he'd learned was that riding required the use of muscles he'd forgotten he possessed. Despite the rest breaks, every muscle and joint in his body was complaining by late afternoon.

The track had narrowed so Cassie had led for the last couple of hours. The blasted woman seemed tireless. She had an elegant back, though, and she rode beautifully. He enjoyed watching her.

He'd stopped feeling guilty about inappropriate thoughts for a female twice his age. She was proof that a woman could be alluring no matter how many years she had. A good thing she was capable of tossing him into the nearest wall if he behaved badly.

Would he know what to do with a willing female when the time came? He supposed if he could still ride a horse, he'd be able to ride a woman. He'd find out once he was back in England. For now, he and his guide needed to concentrate on traveling quickly and not being noticed.

The hut was by a jagged outcropping of rock, just as Romain Boyer had described. Cassie halted in front. The hut was small, large enough for perhaps four people to sleep if they liked each other well. A lean-to had been added on one side for horses, and the other side boasted a pile of wood. "I'm glad to see firewood," she said as she dismounted. "It's going to be a very cold night."

Grey tried not to groan when he swung from Achille's broad back. "I don't mind the cold, but my aching body is likely to stiffen like a board by morning."

"I have some liniment that's good for sore muscles." She led her pony to the lean-to and started to bed Thistle down for the night.

"You are a remarkably useful woman to have around." He tethered Achille under the lean-to and removed the saddle. He was becoming rather fond of the old boy.

"My fairy godmother bestowed practical gifts like efficiency and endurance rather than beauty, charm, or golden hair," Cassie said dryly.

He wasn't sure what to say, so he said nothing. He doubted she would be flattered if he told her she had a beautiful back. Even though it was true.

Cassie the Fox was the perfect travel partner, Grey decided as he rolled into his blanket that night. She was relaxing to be with and fulfilled his desire for companionship while asking very little of him. Which was good, because his camping skills were nonexistent. While she prepared supper and hot tea, all he'd had to do was forage for more firewood to replace what they used from the woodpile.

On the other side of the hut, Cassie wrapped her blanket around herself. She was all of about four feet away from him. "Sleep well," she murmured. "Tomorrow's ride should be easier."

"Every day is a new adventure," he replied. "Tomorrow's will be discovering if my seat is too sore to sit a saddle."

Her laughter swiftly turned into the soft, regular breathing of sleep. He was so tired that he thought he'd sleep easily, too, but his mind stubbornly refused to slow down.

Cassie might think herself lacking in beauty, but he found her increasingly alluring. With nothing else to distract him, all he could think about was her.

He rolled onto his side facing away, but it was impossible to forget her presence. As the night wore on, he added wood to the flames in the primitive little fireplace. It barely took the chill off the air, but no matter. He was quite heated enough.

During the latter years of his captivity, passion had died and he'd felt like a eunuch. The idea had hardly bothered him when there were no women in his world except in increasingly distant memories. But now he was sharing a small space with an attractive woman whom he liked and admired, and all he could think of was how much he wanted to touch her.

He guessed it would be a long time before his craving for touch would be slaked. Greedily he remembered the hug she'd allowed when he had just been freed. She was all woman—soft and woman scented, but also strong. Efficient, but kind.

He couldn't help but wonder how far her compassion would go. Would she lie with him from pity? He was so crazed with lust that he didn't care what her motives might be. Pity would be fine if offered.

But his last shreds of sanity and honor wouldn't let him roll across the hut to wake her and beg for the sweet solace of her body. She was the bravest woman he'd ever met, his savior, and she deserved better than to be pawed by a fool like him. If he tried, she'd probably emasculate him, and justly so.

He pulled his blanket tight and ordered his mind to sleep. *Sleep.*

Chapter 17

A cold night was improved by having a warm man in one's bed. The large, stroking hand pulled Cassie from deep sleep to the edge of awareness and created a curl of desire that moved gently through her. Warm lips touched her throat and she stretched her neck into the kiss.

"Rob?" she murmured. She was wearing too many layers of clothing because of the cold, but that could be worked around. As his lips nibbled toward her ear, desire and wakefulness increased.

She turned her face toward him and his mouth covered hers hungrily. The kiss was deep and passionate. She loved the erotic brush of his beard on her face.

A *beard?* She jolted to full wakefulness when she realized that what she felt wasn't the faint bristle of an overnight shadow, but a full-blown beard. *Not* Rob.

"Damnation!" She shoved hard at the body covering hers even before she recognized that it must be her traveling companion.

Grey gasped, then swore, "*Merde!*" as he hurled himself away from her. "Dear God in heaven, what was I doing? I swore to myself that I wouldn't touch you!"

He drew a ragged breath. "I thought . . . I thought I was dreaming." There was enough light from the embers on the hearth to illuminate the genuine horror on his face.

"Your dream was an active one," she said acerbically.

"I am a *beast!*" His voice was agonized. "Please . . . please forgive me. I didn't intend such insult. I'll move outside for the rest of the night."

"Wait!" She caught his arm as he started to rise. "This was regrettable, but not entirely surprising when we're sharing tight quarters and you've been deprived of female companionship for so long. Any woman looks attractive."

"You undervalue yourself," he said tautly. "I've found you attractive from the beginning. Yes, I'm hungry for the embrace of a woman, but that alone wouldn't have led me to assault you in my sleep."

Taken aback, she asked, "How can you be interested in an old woman like me?"

"I've always liked females with something to say for themselves, and that's more common among mature women." He shook his head. "As heir to an earldom, I think I was giggled at by every brainless debutante in the *ton*. A woman like you, with strength and courage and intelligence, is a hundred times more attractive."

He laid his hand over hers where it rested on his arm. "Which is why I bathed in an icy pond my first night out of prison, and why I'd best sleep outside now. There's a reason why young people are chaperoned carefully. Being close to an attractive woman can destroy male judgment."

She hesitated, knowing she could let him go outside and they'd never refer to this awkward incident again. But did she want him to leave? Her blood hammered with rising desire. Like Grey, she yearned for touch and intimacy.

And if he thought she was attractive despite her carefully maintained guise of age and drabness . . . well, she found him attractive despite the effects of his imprisonment. Recklessly she said, "Don't leave."

His arm became rigid under her hand and the air thickened with tension. "I would like nothing better than to lie with you. I don't mind if it's from pity, but it mustn't be because I've coerced you."

"I've lain with men for worse reasons than mutual pleasure and comfort." She leaned forward and kissed him hungrily. Bedamned to restraint and good sense.

Now that they were awake and willing, sleepy fondling blazed into sharp, clear passion. His mouth was demanding, hot with need, arousing equal heat in her. Impatiently she drew him down onto her rumpled blanket.

"I may have forgotten how to do this," he said gruffly.

She laughed as he loosened the bodice of her gown. "I doubt that."

Grey might be half crazed with lust, but as with

his riding, he remembered the skills of lovemaking even after ten years of deprivation. With her gown loose, he pulled down the shift to bare her breast. Her nipple tightened in the icy air, then tightened more when his warm lips captured it.

She caught her breath and arched into his kiss, her nails digging into the hard muscles of his back. His hand moved down her body, leaving fire wherever it touched despite her clothing.

He caressed her hip and thigh, then slipped his hand beneath her gown. His warm hand on her bare flesh made a wickedly erotic contrast to the cool air that flowed over her intimate parts. Then he banished the cold with deft, heated fingers.

She pulsed against him as he brought her to swift readiness. His breathing harsh, he undid his trousers, moved between her legs and entered her with a long groan of pleasure. For an instant he was still, every fiber of his body rigid. "I . . . I can't last long."

"Of course not," she breathed as she rocked against him.

Her movement shattered his control and he convulsed, pouring himself into her in seemingly endless rapture. Chest heaving, he subsided, his bearded cheek against her forehead as he murmured incoherent endearments in French.

She brushed his damp hair, amused and frustrated. She'd known this joining would be quick. Though not how quick. "You seem to have remembered the basics."

"That was even better than I remembered," he said with a catch of laughter. "Just touching you dissolved every shred of restraint I possess." He rolled to his side and pulled her skirts down over her bare legs, then slid a hand up to her thigh under the fabric. "I also remember this matter isn't finished yet."

She gave a startled squeak when his questing fingers touched moist, sensitized flesh. Surprise dissolved into hot, pulsing sensation. She was so aroused it took him only a few skilled strokes to bring her to intense release. She buried her face against his shoulder to cover her cry of pleasure as shudders wracked her body.

She relaxed in his arms as sweet peace curled through her, content to drowse in the moment. Strange how their bodies could be in such harmony when they scarcely knew each other. Perhaps the fact that Grey would be gone from her life in less than a fortnight made this rare, startling intimacy possible.

He held her close, his hands caressing the length of her back. "I wonder if we'll have a chance to do this someplace warm enough that we can take our clothes off."

"At my age, nakedness is not always desirable," she said wryly. "It's been a good few years since I was eighteen."

" '*Age cannot wither nor custom stale her infinite variety,*' " he quoted. "You are timeless, Cassie the Fox. Now I have twice the reason to be grateful to you. You've restored not only my freedom but my manhood."

"No gratitude is needed for mutual pleasure," she said drowsily. "If you feel you owe me something, make it up in the future when you will have opportunities to help others. That's the best part of being a lord. Your power to aid the less fortunate."

"You sound like my mother." He reached for his blanket and added it to the coverings over them. "She has always been very keen on helping the less fortunate."

"And you aren't?"

He hesitated. "I was raised to have a sense of noblesse oblige, but it was just words to me. Though I assumed I'd do the right thing when the time came, I never thought much about what that meant. In the future, I shall be much more aware of how fate can be unkind, and when I might be able to help."

"Another silver lining to be found under a very dark cloud."

"I suppose." Tenderly he cradled her head. "I want to know more about you, Cassie. Have you any family? A husband, a lover, children, grandchildren?"

"If I had a husband, I would not be lying with

you," she said dryly. "I have none of the other things, either."

"Not even a lover? Any woman as splendid as you deserves a lover. Maybe several," he said firmly.

"There is a man in London," she said slowly. "More than a friend, but less than a lover. We know not to ask too much of each other." Neither of them had much to give.

His arm tightened around her. "Perhaps when this war is finally over and you find that cottage, you'll also find the companion you deserve," he said. "Someone to share your declining years."

"You're a romantic, Lord Wyndham." She smiled into the darkness, thinking there was no reason he shouldn't know the truth. "How old do you think I am?"

He frowned. "I really don't know. At first I thought you must be at least sixty, but you're so strong and fit." His fingers trailed down her cheek. "You have lovely, smooth skin, and from what I've felt of your body, your figure is one any woman would be happy to possess. Perhaps . . . you're in your midforties and descended from a long line of healthy folk who lived to ripe old ages?"

She chuckled. "I'm about two years younger than you are."

"The devil you say!" He stared at her in the dim light. "You helped me disguise myself, so presumably you've done the same to yourself. Yet still I wouldn't have guessed you to be so young."

"A friend of mine in London is a master perfumer," Cassie explained. "She created a blend she calls Antiqua. The scent is essence of harmless little old lady."

He began laughing. "That's brilliant!" Laughter abruptly cut off. "Then you are of childbearing age, and I didn't leave before I came."

"No need to worry. I use a very ancient and generally reliable method of preventing unwanted consequences." She shrugged. "Either the wild carrot seeds work, or I'm barren. I've never had occasion to worry."

"Now that we've settled that"—he nuzzled her neck—"I look forward to smelling you when you're not wearing Antiqua. I'm sure your scent is utterly alluring."

"I don't know about that, but I probably won't smell twice my age," she agreed.

"Any last guilt pangs I felt for lusting after a woman older than my mother have vanished." His nuzzling turned into a delicate tracing of his tongue around her ear. As she caught her breath, he continued, "I really must delve deeper to find the true essence of Cassie the Fox, the most delectable vixen in France."

Telling him her real age had changed things between them, she realized. He was no longer giving her the deference due a respected older woman. Instead, he was playful in a way that was new to her. "Vixens bite," she warned before nipping his ear.

He inhaled and she felt him hardening against her thigh. "So do their foxes."

He set his teeth on her nipple with exactly the right amount of pressure to excite, not hurt. She was shocked at how powerfully passion flared. She wouldn't have thought it possible so soon. "You have much lost time to make up for," she said huskily.

"Indeed I do." His palm came to rest on the juncture of her thighs, moving in slow circles as he gave luxurious attention to her breast. "And I want to make up for all that lost time with you."

She laughed, feeling like the young girl she'd never had a chance to be. Ten years couldn't be made up in two weeks. But they could try.

Grey awoke feeling like a new man. Or rather, a man reborn. The air was bitter cold, but enough morning light seeped into the hut that he could study the delicate features of Cassie's sleeping face, which was mere inches away.

Now that he knew her real age, he was amazed that he'd thought her old. She'd drawn subtle lines of age on her face, but this close he could see the smoothness of her complexion. She carried herself as a woman worn out by too many years of living when in fact she was the strongest, most physically adept female he'd ever met.

He bent the few inches forward to press his lips tenderly to hers. Her eyes flickered open. "I am in love," he breathed. "Truly, deeply, madly, intoxicated with the most wonderful woman in the world."

There was something deep and unreadable in her enigmatic blue eyes before she said briskly, "It's the passion you're in love with, not me. Don't worry, you'll recover from any infatuation that you might feel, Lord Wyndham. Now it's time we rose and broke our fast so we can be on our way."

He blinked. Even a teasing declaration should be treated with some respect. "Can't I be at least a little in love with you?"

She gave him a twisted smile. "Passion warps the mind and judgment. I merely happen to be available. That's not the same as love."

He wasn't sure he agreed with her. Love might be more than passion, but really good passion such as they'd shared through the night was surely an element of love.

He slipped his hand into the folds of her clothing and cupped her bare breast, his thumb teasing her nipple. "Available is an excellent quality and not to be wasted. Surely we can delay breakfast for a bit."

She caught her breath, her eyes turning misty. "For a few minutes, I suppose. That should be plenty of time for you."

He roared with laughter. "Is that a challenge, my delicious vixen? I shall take it as one." He wrapped his arms around her waist and rolled onto his back so that she was lying on top of him, her mischievous face above him. Her old-age perfume was wearing off, so he could inhale her natural alluring female scent. Uniquely Cassie.

There was truth in her belief that he was in love with making love. But she was far more than the nearest willing woman. He really was a little in love with her. And, he guessed as her kiss sent him spinning into rapture, he always would be.

Cassie suspected she was smiling like a fool as they set off on the rugged track that would take them out of the hills to a road that led north. Though it was hard to read Grey's expression behind the beard, she suspected he was also beaming. They'd ended up delaying breakfast for quite some time.

She'd been rather touched by his joking claim to be madly in love with her even though he was really just expressing his exuberant pleasure in his rediscovered sexuality. Perhaps she was a little bit in love with Grey. His lovemaking had a playfulness that was new to her. She looked forward to more passionate interludes between now and the time she delivered him to Kirkland in London.

Grey would return to the loving arms of family

and friends and, in time, a suitable young wife. Cassie hoped she would be sensitive about what Grey had endured.

As for Cassie, she'd return to France with blazing memories to warm her in that English cottage, if she lived long enough to retire. She'd survived more than a dozen years in the spying trade. Perhaps she'd actually live to celebrate Napoleon's death.

It was rather sweet of Grey to want her to find a companion for her old age, but also a sign of how young he was in some ways. Though he'd been born a couple of years earlier than she, most of his adult life had been spent in captivity. She'd crammed several lifetimes of experience into her twenty-nine years, while he'd had one very bad experience over and over for ten years.

That made her feel as old as her gray hair claimed she was. But the vast differences between them didn't mean they couldn't be lovers until their paths parted.

Peace disintegrated when they came out of the hills and turned onto the road north. Though traffic was light, the back of Grey's neck crawled whenever he heard hoofbeats coming toward them. Surely it was too soon for Durand to have organized a pursuit, but reason had nothing to do with his primitive fear. He wouldn't feel safe until he was back in England.

Though he couldn't make the fear and anger go away, he could at least pretend to be sane and normal. He found that it helped to concentrate on the countryside around him. Even in late winter, it was beautiful beyond belief. Dormant trees contained an infinity of subtle colors, and the wind carried intoxicating scents of life.

And he could always watch Cassie, and wait for the night.

Chapter 18

After Durand finished cursing his incompetent servants for letting the prisoners escape, he formulated plans for recapturing them. The feeble old priest should be easy. He would stay close to his old haunts, so he could be traced through friends and family.

But Wyndham would flee the country as fast as possible, so Durand must move quickly. Thank God he had the many and varied resources of the police at his disposal. There were detachments of the gendarmerie in all towns of any size. All he had to do was claim he was after English spies to mobilize them.

He would have flyers printed and send them out by the fast military couriers. The gendarmes could distribute the flyers to inns and villages along routes the fugitives might follow. A description and a reward for information would set hundreds of civilians watching any strangers who passed by.

The problem with flyers was coming up with descriptions. The only one of the raiders who had been seen was the old lady, who left no impression at all. Gray hair. Average height. Average weight. No distinguishing features. Perhaps sixty years old.

Wyndham and the priest weren't much easier. Durand knew what they'd looked like originally, but years in prison had resulted in emaciated bodies and savage beards. Coats could be padded and beards could be trimmed to change their appearances.

He had to settle for approximating the heights of the prisoners and saying that one was a feeble old man, one a young man with light hair. He added that the three people being sought might be traveling together, or separately, or with other unknown men. Very unsatisfactory.

There was also the question of which way they went. It would be clever of them to head south to Spain or east into the Low Countries or Germany, but clever was probably trumped by the fact that north to the channel was by far the fastest route to England. So Durand sent flyers in all directions, but concentrated on the roads north.

For himself, he headed to Calais. His hunter's instinct told him that area was most likely for him to find his prey. When and if he caught up with

Wyndham, he'd waste no more time on imprisonment.

This time he'd just kill the bastard.

Cassie frowned as they followed the narrow road that ran straight through the center of a small town. Until now, they'd passed through nothing larger than a hamlet and they'd slept in empty barns, but they couldn't avoid people forever. "It must be market day. Everyone in the district is in the square ready to buy, sell, and gossip."

She felt Grey tense beside her. Sharing a bed with a man made one extra-sensitive to his emotions. "Is it possible to go around?" he asked.

"I don't see any streets leading off, and if we try to circle through the countryside, we could lose half a day or more getting lost in muddy farm lanes."

"I suppose you're right." He scowled at the crowded square ahead.

"Think of this as good practice for London," she said encouragingly. "It will take only a few minutes to pass through the market and then we'll be in the country again."

He drew a deep breath, then halted his horse and dismounted. "You're right. There's no reason for me to go berserk."

Cassie swung down from Thistle. In a crowd like the one they were about to enter, it was safer to lead their mounts. "I'll buy bread if I see a

137

baker's stall, but otherwise we walk straight through. I'll call you Grégoire if a name is needed."

He nodded, tense but controlled. "What should I call you?"

"*Maman*," she said promptly. "Keep your eyes down and pretend to be not very intelligent. I'm your old mother and I take care of business for both of us."

He gave a short nod and started forward. Satisfied, she led Thistle toward the market square. This was Grey's first test among strangers, but she was confident that he could manage. At night in private, he was as amusing as he was passionate. It was clear why everyone adored him in his youth.

Though restless anger still seethed under his lighthearted charm, it was slowly dissipating, she thought. This quiet journey was gradually bringing him in tune with the world again. By the time they reached London, he should be almost normal. A new normal that was a blend of what he'd been and what he'd experienced.

At this season the market contained little produce beyond wrinkled apples and tired-looking root vegetables, but there were baked goods and cheeses and charcuterie, as well as stalls with old clothes and utensils. If she'd had her cart, she'd set up shop.

Instead she moved through the crowd as quickly

as she could without shoving and drawing attention. People were particularly jammed up around the fountain in the center of the square. Even over the noisy chatter, she could hear Grey's harsh breathing, but he kept his eyes down and moved doggedly onward.

She didn't want to stop in the middle of the market, but as they came out on the other side and the crowd thinned, she saw a bakery stall. "Hold a moment, lad, and take my reins," she said in a country accent. "I need to buy us a loaf."

"*Oui, Maman.*" He took Thistle's reins so Cassie could approach the stall. She bought bread and several tarts made from dried fruits. She liked offering new tastes to please Grey's long-neglected palate. His enthusiastic appetite was endearing.

She had just handed over her coins when shouting broke out behind her. She whipped around and saw a skinny dog running from the opposite stall with a smoked sausage in its mouth and a furious, red-faced merchant in pursuit. An onlooker called out cheerfully, "Looks like that little bitch is faster than you, Morlaix!"

"Shut your mouth, damn you!" Swearing, Morlaix cornered the dog, snatched back the sausage, and began kicking the cowering beast, which was trapped between a wall and a cart.

Grey said roughly, "Eh, sir, you shouldn't be beating the poor brute!"

He took the merchant's shoulder to pull him away from the dog. The man pivoted and swung a meaty fist at Grey's jaw. Grey dodged, but his control splintered and he pulled his fist back to strike a furious blow.

Fearing he'd injure or kill the merchant, Cassie grabbed his arm before he could throw the punch. "Steady, lad!" she cried. "Don't be hittin' the gentleman!"

She used her grip to surreptitiously jab a point above his elbow that numbed his right forearm. He swung on her, eyes wild and his body shaking.

"Steady, Grégoire!" she snapped. "Steady!"

For an instant she thought he might swing on her and she prepared to duck. Then his rage faded enough that he lowered his fist and gave her a short nod to reassure her that he'd mastered himself.

Cassie turned to the angry merchant, who smelled of beer and raw onions. Bobbing her head, she said contritely, "Dreadful sorry, Monsieur Morlaix. My boy isn't quite right in the head. He's fond of dogs and can't bear to see 'em hurt. Here, let me pay for that sausage and you can just let the poor beast go."

She pressed a generous payment into the merchant's pudgy palm. "I'll get my Grégoire out of town now, sir. 'E gets confused around so many people."

Morlaix took the money with a growl. "Get both of those beasts away from me!"

140

"I shall, sir," she said meekly. "Come along now, lad."

"Sausage," he said in a dull voice that supported her claim that he wasn't quite right. "You gave 'im money for the sausage, so it's ours."

Cassie took the damaged sausage from the merchant and gave it to Grey. He fed the meat to the skinny dog, who wolfed it down voraciously.

Swiftly Cassie collected her bread and tarts and the reins Grey had dropped when he became involved in the altercation. Lucky the horses were placid beasts that hadn't seized the chance to run off. "Leave the dog, Grégoire, we need to be on our way."

He got to his feet and took Achille's reins again. "*Oui, Maman.*" His voice was submissive, but she sensed seething anger just below the surface.

The small crowd that had gathered to watch a fight drifted off, disappointed that there was no blood. Cassie headed away from the market at a brisk pace, shepherding Grey and his horse in front of her.

When they were clear of the last of the market-goers and the main street was empty, she stopped to remount and saw that the dog was following them hopefully. "You've made a friend, Grégoire."

Grey knelt and scratched the dog's scrawny neck. She was young, medium sized, and so skinny that her ribs showed. Under the dirt, she seemed to be black and tan with white feet and muzzle. Floppy ears suggested hound ancestry.

She wasn't wild, for she licked Grey's hand hopefully. "She wants kindness as much as food," he said. "But she also needs more food. One small sausage for which you paid too much doesn't go far when one is starving. Can we spare some cheese?"

Cassie knew that feeding the scraggly little bitch was a bad idea, but she couldn't resist the dog's pleading brown eyes. She foraged in her saddlebags until she found a chunk of cheese. Breaking it in half, she handed a chunk to Grey. "You'll never get rid of her after this."

"I don't want to." Grey broke the cheese into smaller pieces and fed them to the dog one at a time. "I always had dogs. I missed them as much as I missed people." He scratched the dog's head affectionately. "If Régine chooses to follow, I won't object."

Cassie studied the skinny dog. "Naturally she should be called Queen. It will do wonders for her morale."

Grey tossed the last piece of cheese to Régine. She snapped it neatly out of the air. "I hope so. Names are important."

If Régine helped him relax and cope with the world, Cassie figured the dog was worth her weight in sausages. They proceeded out of the village side by side. A mile or so along, Cassie said, "You did well in the market. You didn't kill anyone."

Grey's lips thinned. "I would have if you hadn't stopped me. I'm not fit for civilized society, Cassie. If you aren't around the next time I go berserk, I don't know what will happen."

"I'll be around as long as you need me."

He turned and looked at her, his gray eyes stark. "Is that a promise?"

She hesitated, realizing that she was on the verge of a very large promise. But while he needed her now, that wouldn't be true much longer. Once he was back in England, there would be others better suited to helping him until the last of his demons were banished.

But for now, he did need her. "I promise, Grey."

He gave a twisted smile. "You may live to regret saying that, but thank you, Cassie. For now, you're my rock in a confusing world."

"I'm more likely to regret your adopting that dog," she remarked. "We'll have to sleep in barns for the rest of our trip."

He gave her an exaggerated leer. "As long as there is sufficient privacy to ravish you, my dearest vixen."

She laughed, glad his anger was under control again. They'd spent the previous night in a barn, and there had indeed been sufficient privacy for ravishing, though she wasn't sure who was the ravisher and who was the ravished.

Cassie glanced back and saw that Régine was following. The dog seemed to have had some training. Perhaps she was a family pet that had become lost. She'd make Grey a good companion. Cassie loved animals herself, but couldn't keep them in her traveling life. She tried not to become too attached to her horses because sometimes she had to leave them behind. Just as she had to do with men.

They were making good time and should reach the coast within a few days. She'd be glad to get her charge safely home, but oh, she'd miss the nights!

After selling out his wares, the merchant Morlaix retired to the taproom of the nearby inn. As he waited for his drink, the commander of the local gendarmerie entered and posted a flyer on the wall by the door. REWARD! shouted across the top in large letters.

Morlaix liked to practice his reading, so he ambled over to study the flyer. Fugitives were being sought. An old woman, an old man, a younger man with light hair. Maybe together, maybe separate, maybe traveling with others.

"Eh, Leroy," he said to the commander, who was an old friend. "I just saw two out of three like that in the market. The old woman and a light-haired man. But he was touched in the head and there was no old man."

Leroy, a former army sergeant, looked mildly interested. "From around here?"

"No, strangers. Heading north."

Leroy looked more interested. "The notice says they're most likely heading north. What did the old woman look like?"

Morlaix shrugged. "Nothing worth noticing. Average size, dressed one step above a rag-picker, gray hair. A man would have to be desperate to want to bed her."

Even more interested, the gendarme asked, "Old but strong?"

Morlaix frowned. "I suppose she was. She stopped her great brute of a son from attacking me."

"Why did he want to attack you?"

The merchant told the story tersely, thinking it didn't reflect well on him. The gendarme's eyes lit up. "Could he have been an Englishman? They're mad for dogs!"

"He didn't say much, but he spoke like a Frenchman. An idiot Frenchman."

Leroy tapped the flyer. "The younger man is an escaped English spy. I suppose he'd have to speak French well to be a spy. This pair may be the ones who are wanted. How long since they left town?"

"Half a day," Morlaix replied. "See here, if they're the ones, do I get the reward?"

"Maybe part of a reward, but only if they're the right villains and if they're captured. I'll send word up the road by the military mail coach." The commander spun on his heel and headed for the door.

"Don't you go forgetting my reward!" Morlaix growled. His drink was waiting, so he took a deep swallow. Damned gendarme wanted the reward for himself. France may be an empire, not a kingdom, but there was still them that had power, and them that didn't.

Chapter 19

"This looks promising," Cassie said as a small roadside inn came into view. A weathered sign proclaimed AUBERGE DU SOLEIL. Inn of the Sun.

The name MME. GILBERT was painted below. This was no bustling post house, merely a local tavern that served drinks and simple food and had a room or two for travelers. "With luck, we can get a hot meal and a bath for Régine."

"Any chance of a bath for us?" Grey stroked the dog's back. She was sprawled contentedly across his lap, having become too tired to keep up behind the horses.

"Régine needs it more," Cassie pointed out with a smile. "But if we're really lucky, there might be some hot water for us."

They rode into the small yard. It was muddy, like most of northern France now that the last of the snow was melting. Though the first welcome buds of spring were beginning to appear, there was a lot more mud.

Cassie dismounted, tethered Thistle, and entered the inn. Bells on the door rang as she entered, and a sturdy, authoritative older woman came out to greet her. "I am Madame Gilbert," she said briskly. "How may I serve you?"

"Good day, madame," Cassie said in her country accent. "My son and I are interested in a meal, a room, and perhaps a tub where he can wash his dog?"

"His dog?" The woman glanced out the window, where Grey and Régine were visible atop Achille. Grey had been trying to cultivate a vacant expression, but he wasn't very good at it. Fortunately, the beard covered most of his face.

"He found a filthy, hungry stray in the town market and wants to keep it." Cassie gave a "what's a mother to do?" sigh. "Grégoire isn't quite right in the head, and having a dog calms him."

"Is he a deserter from the army?" Madame Gilbert asked bluntly.

"No," Cassie said firmly. "He is not capable of being a soldier."

The older woman shrugged. "Best not tell me anything I might have to lie about. But as one mother to another, I'll say that the gendarmes in this district spend much of their time hunting down deserters, and they often come along this road. Most of 'em are soldiers who were invalided out of the army, so they don't like seeing anyone else escape the suffering."

"Truly Grégoire was never in the army, but he is of a soldierly age." Cassie didn't like what she was hearing. "Is there another road the gendarmes are less fond of?"

Madame Gilbert's mouth quirked up, as if Cassie had just confirmed that her "son" was an escaping soldier. "Aye, and not far away. A little muddy lane leads by my stables. It doesn't look like much, but if you follow its wandering through the fields, eventually it ends at another road that runs north. Narrow and quiet."

Curious, Cassie said, "You sound sympathetic to deserters."

The older woman's mouth hardened. "Napoleon's wars killed my husband, my brother, and both my sons. They'll not get my grandsons, and I won't help the gendarmes track down any poor devils who don't want to die in muddy foreign fields."

"I don't much care who wins." Which wasn't true. Napoleon must be destroyed. More truthfully, Cassie added, "I just want this endless fighting over."

"Amen to that. You're interested in washing the dog?"

"That, a hot meal, and permission to bed down in the stables. Grégoire will be happier if he's near the horses."

The landlady nodded, by now convinced that

Grey was a deserter. "It's a nice snug building. You'll sleep well there. As for the dog, there's a laundry shed next to the stables with a pump, tubs, soap, and brushes. The hot meal tonight is mutton stew."

"That sounds perfect, madame." Cassie pulled out a thin purse. "How much for everything?" Including information more valuable than a roof over their heads.

Régine accepted washing without enthusiasm, but she didn't bite or try to run away as Grey scrubbed her in the small washhouse. Cassie stayed out of splashing distance, admiring Grey's bare chest and the dog's increasing cleanliness. Régine would never be beautiful, but she was a happy beast who gazed at Grey with adoration. One of her parents might have been a beagle. The other ancestors were anyone's guess.

After Régine had been scrubbed and dried with rough towels, they retired to the stables, which were indeed snug. Madame Gilbert kept a pair of staid cart horses, but there was plenty of room for Thistle and Achille.

Thinking it best to keep Grey away from the landlady, Cassie carried their suppers to the stable on a tray. The mutton stew was hearty and flavorful, the homebrewed beer a good accompaniment, and there was plenty of fresh bread to sop up the last of the stew.

It was dusk when Cassie took back the tray with the dirty dishes. She returned to the stables to find that Grey had spread a blanket over a pile of loose straw and was reclining on it, Régine beside him. Grey was long and lean and glorious in the dim light of a single lantern. Though disheveled and still too thin, eating well was taking the gaunt edges off his appearance.

"This combines the informal pleasures of camping with the advantage of having a roof, a good hot meal, and an easy escape if we need to leave in a hurry." Since Régine lay on his right, he patted the straw on his left. "Come sit beside me, Cassie the Fox. Having satisfied one appetite, it's time to satisfy another."

"You are shameless," she said as she complied, happy to lounge by his warm body in the cooling evening.

"So Lady Agnes Westerfield once said. She was laughing, but she meant it. And she was right." Grey half rolled over Cassie and settled into a long, thorough kiss. "Will I have any success in seducing you?"

"I suppose I have a couple of minutes to spare," she said teasingly as the fingers of her right hand slid into his tangled hair.

"Vixen!" He kissed her throat. "You're trying to insult me into demonstrating my manly endurance."

"You have deduced my fell scheme!" she said with a gurgle of laughter. When Grey wasn't distressed, he made her laugh like no other man she'd known.

He buried his face in the angle between her throat and shoulder. "Oh, Cassie, Cassie," he said huskily. "You're the best thing that ever happened to me."

"I am merely a thing?" She nipped his earlobe, thinking how much she would miss this playfulness and laughter.

He laughed. "The *best* thing." He kissed her temple. "The *best* luck." He kissed the tip of her nose. "The *best* person." He licked her ear. "And the very best, most amazing woman." He ended his litany by bringing his mouth down on hers.

The deep, thorough kiss almost dissolved her ability to think. A long, delicious interval later, she murmured, "Your best luck was probably going to school with Kirkland. Not many men would spend so long searching for a lost friend."

"True." His hand slid down her torso. "But think of how much less amusing it would be if he'd sent one of his male agents to Castle Durand."

"Given your state of deprivation, you might not have cared who rescued you." She arched into his hand. "Any warm, willing body would do equally well."

"Wicked, wicked vixen! Even ten years wasn't enough for me to forget the differences between males and females. Though perhaps I should refresh my memory . . ."

He was reaching for her hem when shouts and the jangle of harness sounded in the yard outside. They froze.

In the quiet night, a harsh voice demanded entry to Auberge du Soleil in the name of the emperor so fugitives and deserters could be captured. Madame Gilbert replied robustly, telling the gendarmes she had no deserters in her inn, and why were the *cochons* disturbing law-abiding citizens at their dinners?

Desire and laughter vanished. Cassie swore under her breath. "Time we were leaving." She scrambled from the straw. "A good thing we hadn't unpacked."

"The *bastards!*" Grey leaped to his feet and started toward the stable doors. "I'd like to . . ."

Cassie grabbed his arm. "We are not charging out there to take on half a dozen armed men! We are going to quietly saddle up and leave by the back door and take the lane that runs away from the road and the inn."

His arm was rigid under her hand, but after drawing a deep breath, he turned away from the door and reached for his saddle. "Will they harm Madame Gilbert?"

"She's a formidable woman and she seemed experienced with such visits from the gendarmerie." Cassie tossed her saddle blanket over Thistle. "Her protests will buy us a few minutes before they search the stables. The best thing we can do for her is be gone without leaving any traces that we were here. Tell your dog not to bark."

Expression grim, Grey folded the blanket and packed it into his saddlebags. When they were ready to leave, Cassie scanned the area while Grey quietly opened the doors in the back of the stables. She'd surveyed the lane earlier. Though narrow and muddy, it ran between thick hedgerows so they would disappear from view quickly.

Cassie dowsed the lantern and they led their mounts out. Régine trotted along behind them, puzzled but cooperative. Luckily, she wasn't a barker.

They left just in time. Behind them lanterns flared and an officer ordered his men to search all their outbuildings. Giving thanks that the gendarmes were making so much noise, Cassie led the way out into the lane. A mist was turning into light rain and the damp cold bit to the bone. She hoped that somewhere down the lane they'd find shelter.

At least this time they weren't escaping through a blizzard.

He was hunted like a rabbit through the fields, hounds baying for his blood. He fell and lay panting and helpless while hunters and hounds crashed down on him. But instead of the swift death of being torn to pieces, they captured him, bound his limbs, dragged him back to prison, and dropped him into a bottomless pit, where he fell into endless night . . .

Grey woke up screaming into the darkness. He lashed out, but before full-blown panic destroyed the last shreds of sanity, warm arms embraced him and a soothing female voice said, "It's all right, Grey. We're safe here." Her soft voice and strong body were sanctuary in a black, bleak world. "We escaped without the gendarmes knowing we'd been there."

Heart pounding and fists knotted, he fought to master himself. Mind over frantic instinct. He was not imprisoned, was not trapped in a lightless eternity. "Sorry," he managed. "Knowing that we're being pursued must have triggered a bad dream."

"The first since you escaped?"

His first reaction was to say that it was, but he couldn't lie to Cassie. "Not the first, but the worst." He wrapped his arms around her, feeling his panic recede. "When you're close, they go away quickly." He frowned into the darkness. "Did I strike you when I was thrashing around?"

"No, though not for lack of trying!" she replied. "Luckily I dodge well."

Thank God for that. "Remind me where we are?"

"A shed built to protect livestock fodder," she explained. "At this season, most of the fodder has been used so there's space for weary travelers to sleep."

"No wonder it's so bloody cold," he muttered, remembering now how they'd found the lean-to after a couple of hours of wet, miserable walking. They'd led the horses because it was too dark to ride.

The sky was lightening, so dawn must be near. He rested his cheek against her hair. Régine, he realized, was the warm weight curled up against his opposite side. "How long until we reach the coast?"

"We can make it in four days if we push hard. Which we should," she said soberly. "Durand must have sent out flyers describing us as dangerous spies, likely with a reward. Anyone with even a vague resemblance to his fugitives is going to be noticed and perhaps detained."

"Should I take off my beard?" He rubbed his chin, wondering what lay beneath the whiskers. "That would change my appearance."

"They don't really know your appearance." A smile came into her voice. "I suspect that if you're clean shaven, every woman we pass will remember you, and that's the opposite of what we want."

He felt himself coloring in the darkness. When he was younger, women of all ages noticed him. He'd taken the attention for granted, vain young fool that he was. Now the thought made him

155

vaguely uncomfortable. "Any description of you would be as an old woman, wouldn't it? That's how you looked at the castle. Can you cover up the gray in your hair? Then we could travel as husband and wife."

"Changing our appearances is a good idea for both of us," she agreed. "I have some temporary brown coloring in my saddlebags."

"Nothing you pull out of those saddlebags surprises me anymore." He rubbed the lithe length of her back, wanting to touch as much of her as he could. "I half expected you to produce a four-poster bed when we stopped here."

"Nonsense. This lean-to isn't large enough for my four-poster."

He smiled and the last of his nightmare tension faded away. "I'll be glad to have you playing the role of my wife. It felt rather perverted to have you as my mother."

"That didn't stop you from behaving in a perverted way," she pointed out as she slid a hand under his coat.

He stiffened, and so did the part of his body where her hand came to rest. "I'm shameless, remember?" he said a little breathlessly. "I think we should now celebrate our new status as husband and wife."

"Well, it's a way to warm up," she said thoughtfully. "For a couple of minutes."

Joy and desire began bubbling through him

despite their precarious circumstances. "Another challenge, my lady fox?" He cupped the delicious softness of her breast. "I promise I shall warm you until the sun comes up."

And he did.

Chapter 20

Reports flooded into Durand as a result of the flyers. There were no sightings for the priest. Either Laurent Saville had gone to ground very successfully, or he was so frail that he'd died from the rigors of escape. If so, good riddance, though Durand continued searching. The old man could be useful.

But there were many possible sightings of Wyndham and an old woman. Sorting through them was the sort of work at which Durand excelled. He had an instinct for what rang true, and that instinct was triggered by the story of a minor altercation in a market town. An old woman and a man who behaved badly because of a worthless mongrel. That sounded English.

He wondered if the old woman really was female. Given the examples he'd been given of her strength and cunning, he wouldn't be surprised to learn that Wyndham's rescuer was a short man disguised as a woman. Though maybe the strength and cunning came from the men who traveled with her. There were too many possibilities. The only thing Durand had to go on was the likelihood that Wyndham was traveling north.

The pair from the market incident were heading in the right direction, but there were no convincing sightings farther along the road they'd been traveling. Durand studied alternative routes on a map. A minor road to the east looked plausible, and it ran toward Boulogne, right on the English Channel.

There were plenty of fishermen who doubled as smugglers along the coast. Which group was most likely? The Ministry of Police had files on many of them.

Map case in hand, Durand ordered up a carriage and headed north.

The next four days were plagued by the constant itchy fear of pursuit. They were also the hardest riding Grey had ever done. If he hadn't been hardened by several days of slower travel first, Cassie would have had to tie him to his mount.

Achille and Thistle were gone, traded for fresher, stronger horses. He thought he saw regret in Cassie's eyes when she sold the pony, but she was too pragmatic to complain. She was a tireless taskmistress, pushing them both with steely determination.

Some nights they were even too tired to make love. But he was never too tired to want to hold her as they fell asleep. Having her close staved off the nightmares.

Grey had enough male pride not to complain about the pace she set, though by the time they reached the seaside tavern northeast of Boulogne, he felt as if he'd been pummeled by professional boxers. It was late afternoon when the tavern came into view.

"Our destination," Cassie said. "They know me here. We're almost home."

He looked across the channel, barely breathing. "England is just across the water. It's hard to believe." Someday he'd look on this journey as a brief, improbable interlude on the way back to his real life, but for now, it was his world. The road, the travel, and Cassie. He wouldn't miss the endless fear or hours on horseback, and a return to civilized living with regular hot water and clean clothes would be welcome.

But he couldn't imagine life without Cassie.

When they reached the tavern, Cassie dismounted. "Take the horses to the stables," she said. "I'll talk to my friend Marie. She's another of France's countless war widows. With luck, we'll be able to sail tonight. The weather looks right."

"You'll miss giving me orders," Grey said as he accepted the reins of her mount.

"Very true. I adore telling big, strong men what to do," she agreed. "I'll just have to come back to

159

France and rescue some other poor fellow to order about."

Her words were teasing, but they sliced into him like knives as he headed to the stables. This journey with Cassie had been the happiest time of his life. It was jarring to be reminded that to her, he was just another job.

"I've lain with men for worse reasons." Did she lie with all the men she rescued? He hated the thought, yet he had no right to ask about her past or other men she'd known.

He bit his lip as he dismounted. Régine sensed his agitation and pressed against his leg. At least one female on this journey thought the sun rose and set on him.

As he bedded down the horses, he told himself that he should be adult enough to accept that Cassie was special to him even though he'd never be as special to her. But he wasn't sure he was that mature.

Cassie entered the tavern's taproom. The cozy room had tables and a simply built bar at the far end. A young boy sat at a table studying while a middle-aged woman with a comfortably rounded figure and a lapful of knitting sat behind the bar.

"*Bonsoir*, Marie," Cassie greeted her. "I'm glad to see you looking so peaceful."

"Cassandra! You're a welcome sight." Marie set

aside her knitting. "Do you remember my nephew Antoine?"

"Indeed I do. Don't let me interfere with your lessons, Antoine."

He stood and offered a gap-toothed smile, then returned to his textbook. Marie continued, "Are you just passing through?"

"Yes, and the shorter the visit the better." Cassie pulled out a small jingling pouch from the pocket hidden under her skirt.

"You're in luck. There's a fishing trip scheduled for tonight."

That was good news; the sooner they left France, the better. "Is there space for two passengers?" When Marie nodded, Cassie handed over the pouch. "Here's the fare."

Marie made the money disappear. "Always such a pleasure doing business with you, Cassie. Where is your companion?"

"Bedding down our horses. Two decent hacks, nothing special. I'm not sure when I'll be back this way, so use them as you need."

Marie glanced out a window. The day had been overcast, and night was falling quickly. "There's just enough time for you and your companion to have a bite before you go down to the cove. I'll send Antoine to the boat to tell them passengers are coming."

As Antoine closed his book, several horsemen arrived outside. Cassie said in a low voice, "It's possible my companion and I are being pursued."

"Or it may be customs officers arriving as they do all too often." Frowning, Marie said, "Antoine, go to the cove and tell the men there may be trouble here."

"*Oui, tante.*" Moving quickly, he went back through the kitchen and outside.

"Time for us to become two boring women having a bit of a chat." Marie poured white wine into two heavy glass tumblers and slid one across the bar to Cassie. "Will your companion know to keep out of sight?"

A good question. Grey was hard to predict. "I hope so." Cassie took the wine and settled onto a stool across the bar from Marie.

The front door was thrown open and five gendarmes swaggered in. All were armed and they had the truculent expressions of men looking for trouble.

As an experienced tavern owner, Marie recognized the look as readily as Cassie did. Her eyes were wary, but her voice relaxed as she said, "What can I do for you, Citoyens? I've some good fish stew and fresh bread in the kitchen."

"We'll be having some of that and a bottle of the best cognac in the house," the sergeant in charge said. "But what we really want is escaping spies."

He pulled a folded flyer from his coat. "An old man, an old woman, a younger English man with light hair, maybe traveling with others. Anyone like that been by here? They're running like rats for England."

Marie set five tumblers along the bar. "Can't say they sound familiar. The only old women who come by here are local." She reached under the bar for a bottle of cognac. "I've not seen any English spies that I know of."

"Bet you've seen plenty of smugglers, though," one of the men sneered. He grabbed the bottle of cognac from Marie's hand and took a swig. "How much will you give us to ride on to the next coastal tavern without searching this place?"

"Isn't it against the law to try to bribe a gendarme?" Marie asked coolly. "I've naught to fear from a search. There are no smugglers here. Only food and drink."

"And women." A tall, heavyset man who looked like a bear pointed toward Cassie. "The flyer said the old woman had no distinctive identifying marks. Neither does this one." As he gazed at her with hot eyes, the atmosphere thickened with menace.

"That's not a kind thing to say, Citoyen," Cassie said mildly, shifting on her stool so she could reach the knife sheathed on her thigh. But she hoped it didn't come to a fight. Two women had little chance against five brutal armed men. "I may be heading toward old, but I'm not there yet."

"Old enough that you should be grateful a real man is willing to roger you," the bear man said

163

with a snort. "Not that I'd touch either of you ordinarily, but for lack of anything better, you'll do."

As he moved closer, Cassie reached for her knife. Before she could grasp it, he lunged unexpectedly, crushing her in his beefy arms exactly like a bear. His breath reeked of cheap brandy.

"Let me go!" she snapped as she struggled furiously, but he had the advantages of size and strength. He shoved her down to the floor and straddled her.

The leader of the group leaned over the bar for Marie. She bashed him across the face with a bottle. Swearing, he staggered back, but a third man circled the bar to grab her and pull her into the center of the room. Her scream cut off abruptly.

If Cassie weren't pinned down, she could have immobilized her attacker, but with his weight on top of her, she was almost helpless. She hoped to God Grey didn't hear the disturbance and charge in. Though he was a fighter, the gendarmes were armed and far more likely to shoot a man than a woman.

Praying that Antoine would bring the sailors from the cove quickly, she sank her teeth into her attacker's earlobe, tasting metallic blood. He bellowed with rage and reared up to clout her on the side of the head.

She turned her head to avoid the worst of the

blow, at the same time fighting to free one arm. If she could jab his eyes . . .

A blood-chilling shout reverberated through the taproom as Grey charged through the door, eyes wild with berserker fury. In two steps he was beside Cassie and hauling her attacker off her. There was a hideous crack as he broke the bear man's neck.

Behind him, another gendarme swiftly primed and aimed his pistol. "Look out, Grey!" Cassie cried as she scrambled to her feet.

Grey whirled and dived at the man. The gun fired deafeningly but Grey didn't even flinch. He wrenched the empty pistol away from the gendarme and used the wooden hilt to club him into unconsciousness.

Since he could handle himself, Cassie turned to Marie. Her friend was pinned to the floor by a man who had one hand clamped over her mouth while the other clawed at her clothing. Cassie moved behind him and savagely jabbed her thumbs into the pressure points that would knock him unconscious in the space of a few heartbeats.

He collapsed forward with a strangled gasp. After dragging his limp body off Marie, who was shaken but seemed unhurt, Cassie turned to Grey.

He fought like a dancer, his movements swift and grimly efficient as he smashed and kicked at his opponents. But dear God, blood was pouring down the left side of his head! He must have been grazed by the pistol ball. Surely it wasn't serious or he couldn't fight so furiously? But so much blood!

Her heart constricted as she saw the last two gendarmes retreat and aim their pistols at Grey. She swore the filthiest curse she knew and hurled her knife at the closer man. It caught him dead center in the throat with a gush of blood.

As the man collapsed with a bubbling scream, his companion swung his pistol toward Cassie. "You *bitch!*"

She dived to her left, wishing for a barrier to protect her. Then Grey's broad shoulders blocked her view of the last gendarme. Growling like a wolf, he leaped at the same instant the gendarme's pistol boomed.

Undeterred, Grey clamped his powerful hands around the man's neck. The two of them went down together.

Dear God, more blood, this time streaming from Grey's right side! Yet his viselike grip didn't loosen. By the time Cassie reached them, the gendarme was dead. Grey's expression was savage, and he didn't seem to hear when she spoke his name.

Cassie caught his shoulder, her nails biting into his shoulder. "Grey, it's all right, we're safe. Let him go so I can look at your wounds."

He still didn't react, so she said more sharply, "Grey, let go!"

Long seconds passed before he released his grip

166

and sat back on his heels. The red rage fading from his eyes, he turned toward her. "Cassie? Are you hurt?"

"You're the one bleeding all over the floor," she said wryly. "I need to examine your wounds."

"Thank God you're safe!" Then he slowly keeled over.

Chapter 21

Biting her lip to keep from having strong hysterics, Cassie knelt beside Grey and did a swift examination. The head wound was bleeding ferociously into his hair and beard but didn't look deep.

The second pistol ball had raked his side. Though the ribs didn't appear to be broken, still more blood was pouring out of him. How much blood could a man lose before he died?

"Take these." Marie pressed several folded towels into Cassie's hand. "This wild man of yours is magnificent," she added admiringly. "Without fear. I could not believe how he kept fighting even when shot twice."

"Fearless or mad," Cassie said grimly. "I need brandy to clean the wounds."

Marie quickly produced a bottle of spirits. Cassie applied pressure to the head injury until the bleeding slowed, then poured a trickle of brandy over the open wound.

Grey gasped and tried to pull away. "Hold still," she ordered, thinking it was a good sign that he wasn't unconscious. "I'm almost done."

He was trembling, but he held still as she tied a crude bandage around his head. She was working on his wounded ribs when half a dozen local sailors burst into the room, the leader calling, "Marie!"

Cassie recognized him as Pierre Blanchard, Marie's brother and captain of the smugglers. He'd carried Cassie across the channel several times. He skidded to a halt and surveyed the fallen bodies. "Seems we weren't needed."

"Madame Renard's friend fought like a man possessed to save us from being raped and worse." Marie frowned at the carnage. "A great deal of cleaning will be required."

"We'll take care of the bodies and the horses," Pierre promised. "These *cochons* will simply disappear. Madame Renard, is your friend well enough to sail tonight?"

"Better that than to risk staying here," Cassie said as she bandaged Grey's ribs. He needed a real surgeon, but that could wait for England. Durand's noose was tightening, she could feel it. "Grey, do you think you can walk to the boat?"

"Yes." He drew a shuddering breath. His face was white against the bloodstains. "Will . . . need help." He pushed himself up with his right arm, giving a hiss of pain. Silently Pierre helped him to his feet.

With so many bloodstains drenching hair and clothing, Grey looked more dead than alive. Cassie moved under his arm to help support him.

"We have saddlebags in the stables," Cassie said to Pierre, not wanting to leave Grey.

As the captain sent a man to collect their possessions, Grey whispered, "Régine. Don't forget Régine!"

"A third person is in your party?" Pierre asked.

"Régine is a dog he adopted," Cassie explained.

Pierre said with amusement, "I didn't know English spies collected mongrels."

"Monsieur Sommers is not a spy," Cassie said wearily. "He was a young Englishman who bedded the wrong woman, and spent ten years in solitary confinement."

The captain's brows arched. "I hope she was worth it."

"She wasn't," Grey muttered.

Pierre gave a very French shrug. "One never knows until it's too late. But now we need to make haste or we will miss the tide."

Cassie could barely support Grey as they moved toward the door, so Pierre moved in to take her place. As soon as they stepped outside, Régine galloped up and began twisting around her master's legs, very nearly tripping Grey.

"Are you sure you can make it down to the pier?" Cassie asked worriedly. "You can be carried if necessary."

"Would . . . walk . . . on water . . ." he panted, ". . . to get back to England."

Cassie drew Régine away from Grey so they could proceed down the rocky path to the cove. At least Grey now had one possession to bring home from France.

Full fathom five thy father lies;
  Of his bones are coral made . . .

Shakespeare's words floated through Grey's misery. Drowning and suffering the ultimate sea change sounded rather good about now. He wasn't usually seasick, but he'd never crossed the channel in a small boat with two bullet holes in him, either. He wasn't sure which was worse: the pain, the nausea, or the fact that the boat was saturated with the stench of fish.

His stomach had been fairly empty to begin with, but that didn't stop the violent nausea and dry retching. He slid in and out of consciousness. Awareness was bad because he'd never felt so ghastly in his life.

Grey, Cassie, and Régine were huddled in the bow of the vessel under an oilcloth sheet, which helped keep off splashes of water, but wasn't much help against the biting cold. Sometime during the endless night, he rasped, "Toss me overboard, Cassie. I think I'd rather be dead."

"Nonsense." Her voice was brisk but her touch gentle as she wiped his damp face with a cloth.

"You have to stay alive until I turn you over to Kirkland. After that, you may drown yourself if you like."

It hurt to laugh, but he did anyhow. "My ever practical vixen. No need to worry. I haven't the strength to cast myself into the sea without help, and once I'm on dry land, the impulse will surely fade."

"Not long now," Cassie said quietly. She pulled him closer so that the unwounded side of his head rested on her soft breasts. "You're warm. Feverish, I think, but it makes you useful on a cold, wet night."

"Don't worry about fever," he mumbled. "I heal very well, or I wouldn't have lasted this long." His mind veering in another direction, he asked, "What's your real name? Before you became Cassie the Fox?"

After a long silence, she replied, "Once I was Catherine."

Catherine. It suited her, but in a very different way from how Cassie suited her. Catherine was a gentle lady. Cassie the Fox was quick, clever, and dangerous. Perhaps Catherine was who Cassie would have been if war and catastrophe hadn't intervened.

He sought her hand and held it, thinking how lucky he was to have this extraordinary woman, even if only for a while.

But God in heaven, how would he ever be able to let her go?

It was not the most comfortable channel crossing Cassie had ever made, but it was one of the fastest, with a hard wind pushing the fishing boat north. Pierre and his crew would have a much slower journey home against the wind. They were inured to the sea and its vagaries, though. Grey and Cassie were creatures of the land, and the sooner they returned to solid ground, the better.

After endless miserable hours, she saw a faint white line gradually forming on the horizon. She waited until she was sure before saying softly, "The white cliffs of Dover, Grey. Home."

He jerked out of his doze and pushed himself up to stare over the gunwale. "Home," he said in a husky voice. "I never thought I'd see England again."

His eyes glinted with unshed tears. She blinked back some of her own. Even after all these years, the sight always moved her.

Together they watched the approaching shore, the white cliffs a beckoning ribbon of hope. Dawn was breaking when Pierre brought them into a sheltered cove with a weathered pier. The cove belonged to an English seafaring family named Nash, and there was a long and profitable relationship between them and Pierre's family. Cassie knew both families well.

Pierre sent a man to the nearby Nash house to

gather help in unloading the illicit cargo. He personally helped Cassie get Grey out of the boat and onto land.

Grey was weaving but grimly determined. Once they were ashore, he shook off his helpers, then alarmed Cassie by falling to the ground.

Her heart clenched until she saw what he was doing. Incredulous, she asked, "Lord Wyndham, are you kissing the ground?"

"Damned right I am." Grey struggled to rise again. "Both because it's solid land, and because it's England."

The French captain asked with interest, "What does English sand taste like?"

"Much like French sand, I suspect." He turned to Cassie, his face ablaze with joy under his bloodstained bandage. "I'm never leaving England again!"

"Won't you want to travel to Rome or Greece or some such place when the wars are over?" she asked.

"I reserve the right to be inconsistent." Grey wrapped an arm around Cassie's shoulders, sagging against her. "What next, milady vixen?"

Several Nashes were heading down to the cove to help with the contraband. Cassie said, "We go to the house and ask Mrs. Nash if she has any broth to feed you. Then we hire one of their sons to drive us to Dover, where we'll find an inn and call a surgeon for you."

"Please," he said in a rough whisper. "Take me home."

She frowned. "Your family seat is in Dorsetshire, isn't it? That's too far. You need treatment before then."

"Not Summerhill," he said with effort. "The Westerfield Academy. It's not far, just off the London road."

She hesitated, thinking it would still be several hours of travel, and the sooner she got him into a clean bed and called a surgeon, the better.

"Please!" he said, his voice raw.

The school had been his home for years, she realized. A place where he'd made lasting friendships, and where Lady Agnes welcomed all her wandering boys, no matter what sort of trouble they'd been in.

"Very well," she said. "We'll go to Westerfield."

The coach Cassie had hired in Dover rumbled to a wet stop in front of Westerfield Manor. Grey had been silent on the ride, suffering stoically. As the coach driver opened the door and let down the steps, Cassie said quietly, "We're here. Are you awake?"

As he ground out an affirmative, Régine leaped out, ready for a new adventure. She'd put on weight even better than Grey had.

Cassie descended and helped Grey out of the coach into a rainy and very English night. "Can you manage him, ma'am?" the driver asked.

"We're fine," Grey mumbled. As Cassie paid the coachman with the last of her money, Grey headed unerringly toward Lady Agnes's door. He'd told Cassie that Lady Agnes used one wing of the sprawling manor-turned-school as her private quarters, so there should be room for unexpected visitors.

Saddlebags over one arm, Cassie caught up with him as he wielded the large brass knocker. Grey swayed while they waited for the door to open, so she moved beside him, an arm around his waist. The end of this mad adventure had arrived.

The door was opened by Lady Agnes herself. She wore a practical but elegant gown that was perfectly suited to a headmistress of noble blood.

Her brows arched when she saw the ragamuffins on her steps. "If you go around to the kitchen door in the back of the house, someone will give you food."

"What, no fatted calf?" Grey said unevenly. When Lady Agnes gasped, he said with a crooked smile, "The prodigal has returned."

Durand reached Boulogne to find the district commandant wondering what had happened to a squad of his gendarmes. Five experienced men, all former soldiers, had been patrolling the coast looking for smugglers as well as Durand's runaway spies.

The patrol had vanished without a trace. It was

hard to know how far they'd traveled on their route since the folk who lived along the coast were a closemouthed lot whether they were farmers, fishermen, or smugglers.

Perhaps the gendarmes had run afoul of smugglers and their bodies were now feeding fishes in the channel. But Durand's intuition said that that devil Wyndham had had something to do with the disappearance. By now, he was probably back in England, beyond Durand's reach.

If ever Wyndham returned to France, he was a dead man. And Durand had come up with a plan to lure the bastard back to France.

Chapter 22

"Dear God in heaven," Lady Agnes whispered. "Grey, it really is you!" Ignoring his wet, filthy, and bloodstained garments, she gave him a bone-bruising embrace.

Régine waited politely on the doorstep and Cassie stayed in the background, the unremitting tension and wariness of the last weeks dissolving in a rush of relief. Grey was home, back in the arms of those who loved him. Cassie would spend a fortnight or so in London recovering, then be off to France again.

She hoped her next mission wasn't a rescue. The strain was much greater when she was responsible for people beyond herself.

Tears running unabashedly down her cheeks, Lady Agnes stepped back and waved them inside. Surveying her prodigal, she said, "It looks like you've had a rough passage, my lad, but you can tell me about it later. For now, you need a bath and a bed."

"Not necessarily in that order," Grey said. Now that he'd reached his destination, he looked ready to collapse. Even with Cassie's help, he stumbled crossing the threshold.

"That is one of the less impressive dogs I've met," Lady Agnes said as Régine trotted by her.

"But she has a sterling heart," Cassie said. "Grey rescued her in France."

"Don't worry, I'd never dream of separating a boy and his dog." Lady Agnes's brow furrowed as she studied Cassie. "We've met, but I'm having trouble placing you."

"We were introduced briefly at the wedding of Lady Kiri Lawford and Damian Mackenzie," Cassie said. "No reason you'd remember me."

"Miss Cassie Fox," Lady Agnes said as she pulled the bell rope to summon a servant. "One of Kirkland's dubious associates."

"Very dubious indeed," Cassie agreed as she steered Grey to a chair set in a corner of the small vestibule. Wearily she deposited their saddlebags on the floor.

"Sorry, I meant no insult," the headmistress said, her gaze sharpening. "Kirkland's associates tend to have exceptional abilities, which is surely why Wyndham is here. Thank you, Miss Fox, from the bottom of my heart."

"He was imprisoned in a private dungeon in France," Cassie said succinctly, thinking that was sufficient explanation for now. "I'll be out of your way soon, but for now, add a surgeon to the list of Lord Wyndham's needs. He was grazed by two bullets and needs treatment before the wounds turn septic. And send a message to Lord Kirkland. He's been waiting for this news for a very long time."

Lady Agnes nodded. "I'll notify Wyndham's family as well. They'll be overjoyed."

"Not . . . my family." Grey's head was tilted back against the wall and his eyes were closed. "They would come thundering down here and be horrified by my present condition. The news of my miraculous survival can wait until I'm more restored."

"As you wish," Lady Agnes said with reluctance. "Can you manage the steps up to a guest room?"

He thought a moment. "With a strong railing and Cassie's help, yes."

A capable-looking housekeeper arrived in the vestibule. By the time Lady Agnes gave orders for food, drink, and hot water to be sent to the blue bedroom, Grey was halfway up the stairs, doggedly hauling himself up by the railing one step at a time.

Cassie shadowed him in case he stumbled, but he made it to the top without help. Lady Agnes followed two steps behind, a lamp in her hand.

"To the left," the headmistress said, moving ahead to light their way to a room down the corridor. She opened the door. "Note the richly patterned coverlet on the bed, designed not to show blood or mud stains."

If Cassie had been less exhausted, she would have laughed. "Obviously Lord Wyndham is not the first wounded prodigal to arrive on your doorstep. But even so, you might want to put a dark blanket over the coverlet."

"I've had other students return from the dead, but miracles never grow old." Lady Agnes pulled a navy blue blanket from a chest and spread it over the bed. "But you're right that Wyndham is quite exceptionally filthy. He never did things by halves."

Grey was the next thing to unconscious when Cassie guided him onto the bed. As Régine jumped up beside him, Cassie squeezed his hand. "You're safe now, my lord. It's been quite an adventure, hasn't it?"

He tightened his grip when she tried to pull away. "You aren't leaving now, Cassie. You *can't*."

"Of course she isn't leaving now," Lady Agnes said briskly. "She looks almost as close to collapse as you, so she'll be staying here also. There will be plenty of time for a proper goodbye

179

when you've both recovered from your journey."

Several servants bustled into the room with steaming canisters and trays. Leading them was an older man of military bearing and a woman about Lady Agnes's age, but shorter and softer in appearance. Cassie guessed that these were General Rawlings and Miss Emily Cantwell, Lady Agnes's colleagues in running the school.

Face working, the general clasped Grey's other hand. "By God, boy, you've taken your time getting out of whatever trouble you found!"

Grey gave a breath of laughter. "I should have listened better to your lectures, sir. I had to be rescued by this lady here, Cassie Fox."

The general turned to Cassie, his eyes gimlet gray. "Rather more than a lady, I think. You're one of Kirkland's lot, aren't you? I look forward to hearing the tale."

"Later," Miss Emily said firmly. "These young people need rest and a good wash first. I also want to see what's under those bandages." She made a shooing motion at Lady Agnes. "Show Miss Fox to her room. We'll take care of Lord Wyndham."

Cassie was happy to transfer responsibility to these capable hands, but she felt oddly empty as she followed Lady Agnes into the room across the corridor. Two of the servants followed with hot water and a tray of food and drink.

Lady Agnes said, "I could order a tub, but my guess is that you prefer a quick wash, an even quicker bite to eat, and a very long rest. You'll find a nightgown in that wardrobe. If you leave what you're wearing outside the door, I'll have the garments cleaned and pressed."

"Most excellent." Cassie buried her face in her hands for a few moments as she tried to collect her scattered thoughts. "The dye on Lord Wyndham's hair will wash out with vinegar. The injuries are less than a day old. He says he heals well, but he was a little feverish on the channel crossing. The wounds need cleaning."

"Anything else can wait till tomorrow. Rest now, child," Lady Agnes said softly. "Your job is done." Briefly she rested a hand on Cassie's shoulder before leaving.

As Cassie stripped off her filthy clothing, she understood better why Lady Agnes's lost lords loved her so much. No doubt Wyndham's family loved him deeply, but that kind of love came with hopes, fears, and expectations. Lady Agnes offered love, warmth, and acceptance. And it even extended to dogs.

Limbs leaden and mind numb, Cassie folded her bedraggled clothing and set it outside the door, did a quick but much appreciated wash at the basin, then pulled on a soft cotton nightgown. After eating a piece of cheese on bread, followed by a few sips of wine, she crawled under the covers.

The mattress was soft and comfortable, but the bed was far too empty. She thought, with a sharp pang, that holding Grey in the fishing boat as they crossed the channel would be her last night with him. Viscount Wyndham, heir to the Earl of Costain, had been returned to his rightful rank. There was no place in his life for a spy with no name or reputation.

She must be grateful for what they'd shared. For Cassie the Fox, there was more work to be done.

Suffocating, falling into endless night . . .

Grey jerked awake, heart pounding. "Cassie, Cassie? Where are you?"

A wet tongue slurped his face. Shaking, he reminded himself that he was safely back at Westerfield. He'd been well taken care of and left to sleep, but now he wanted Cassie. She wasn't far away, but he wasn't sure where, and he was too exhausted to wander till he found her.

Besides, she deserved her rest, too. She'd practically carried him most of the last stretch of their journey. He must settle for Régine, who was burrowed under his right arm.

He forced himself to relax, not easy when he was craving Cassie. He'd known she was his shield and defender as he adapted to the world outside of prison, but he hadn't realized just how much he needed her strength and calm intelligence.

He was weak and wrong to need her so much. But that didn't stop him from wanting her.

Chapter 23

Grey was jarred awake by screaming. It took a moment for him to remember where he was, and to recognize the cries as boys shouting while playing some game outside.

He relaxed, remembering when he'd shouted on those same playing fields. Lady Agnes and General Rawlings were firm believers in young males burning off their energy in sports. There was a place for everyone on the teams, even the least athletic, and no bullying was allowed, ever, which made it better than any other school in Britain. Those had been good days.

He ached all over and the bullet wounds in his head and side throbbed painfully, but that was mitigated by the comfort of a soft bed and safety. He allowed himself to luxuriate even though the warm weight against his side was Régine, not Cassie. Ideally, they'd both be here; the bed was large enough.

He'd missed animals for so long that he'd almost forgotten the pleasure of their company. Perhaps he'd buy a small cottage like the one Cassie wanted and live there with numerous animals. And her.

He sighed, knowing the dream was impossible. Eventually he'd have heavy responsibilities that couldn't be ignored. Worse, someday all too soon she'd vanish back into her mysterious, dangerous world. But not quite yet.

Régine made a small canine noise that made it clear that she needed to go outside and then eat and no shilly-shallying. "Soon, my furry little queen," he said as he ruffled her ears. He was so tired that he could barely move. Partly relief at the end of his long journey, he supposed. Not to mention the amount of blood he'd lost. It would take time to recover from that. He'd have to eat plenty of beef.

Like Régine, he required both bodily relief and food, so he swung out of the bed. The long mirror on the wardrobe reflected a complete savage.

He vaguely remembered arriving at the manor, struggling to this room, then sliding into unconsciousness. Efficient hands had cleaned him up and dressed his wounds, and damned painful it had been, too. After the superficial blood and dirt were gone, they'd managed to get clean drawers on him.

He was otherwise naked except for neat bandages around his head and ribs. His hair and beard were matted disasters, and far too many bones were visible under his pale English skin.

Giving thanks that a razor and hot water were only a bell pull away, he lurched to the wash-stand, which was to the left of the door. He was pouring water into the basin when the door opened and a deep male voice said, "Breakfast, Lord Wyndham."

The unexpected, startlingly familiar voice was such a shock that Grey dropped the pitcher. As the china shattered, he instinctively jerked away from the opening door. He banged into the solid wing chair behind him and lost his balance. As he pitched to the floor, he swore, "*Merde!*"

The elegant, dark-haired man who entered with a large tray of covered dishes and a steaming teapot breathed an oath of his own as he set the tray on a small table. "Sorry, I didn't mean to startle you, Wyndham. Are you all right?"

"Of course I'm not all right!" Grey pushed himself up on all fours, shaking. He'd thought he was becoming used to the normal world, but apparently not. Humiliating. "I have two bullet holes in my hide and I'm near as dammit to feral." Trying for lightness, he added, "You've come down in the world if you've hired on as a footman, Kirkland."

"I thought I might be more welcome if I arrived bearing food." Kirkland offered a hand. "Shall we start over again?"

Grey pulled away from the proffered help until his back was against the wing chair. "I'm not ready for this," he blurted out, heart pounding. Kirkland was getting a damned poor return on the time and effort he'd put into Grey's rescue.

Kirkland dropped his hand, his face ashen. He

looked much older than his years. "I'm sorry," he said again. He reached for the doorknob. "I should have known you wouldn't want to see me. I swear that you won't have to again."

Grey frowned, surprised. "Why wouldn't I want to see you in particular? It's the whole world I'm having trouble with."

"Because of me, you spent ten years in hell," Kirkland said, his eyes bleak. "You'd be entitled to call me out."

Grey blinked. "That is the most idiotic thing I've ever heard." He'd forgotten how bloody conscientious Kirkland was. Too much Presbyterian responsibility and guilt. "The ten years of hell were because of my own stupidity. I never blamed you."

He'd have been happy to stay on the floor because he felt weak as a kitten, but speaking to Kirkland's kneecaps was a further embarrassment. He grasped the arm of the wing chair behind him, hissing at the pain that blazed through his injured side.

Seeing him struggling, Kirkland again offered a hesitant hand. This time Grey took it, shaken by nerves, emotion, and physical weakness.

As Kirkland lifted Grey to his feet, he said in a low voice, "Dear God, I'm glad to see you alive again!"

Swaying, Grey steadied himself with his other hand on Kirkland's shoulder, and suddenly they were hugging each other. Very unlike an English gentleman, Grey thought, but he was no longer a gentleman, so he appreciated the warmth and strength Kirkland was wordlessly offering. Kirkland had always been ironic, cerebral, and frighteningly intelligent, but one couldn't have asked for a better or more loyal friend.

"Forgive my strange behavior," Grey said as he ended the hug. A warm banyan had been draped over the chair, so he put it on before sagging wearily into the chair. "It doesn't take much to set me off these days."

Kirkland efficiently moved table and tray in front of Grey's chair, then brought the wooden chair from the desk and set it on the opposite side of the table. As he took silver covers from the dishes, he said, "I wouldn't have recognized you under that facial thicket. Do you intend to keep it?"

"Lord, no. I would have cut it off by now, but Cassie thought it a useful disguise." Grey discouraged Régine from putting her paws on the table. Not that he blamed her. The English bacon smelled like heaven. "How did you get here so quickly?"

"I left London as soon as I received Lady Agnes's message," Kirkland said simply. He set a couple of pieces of ham on a bread plate and placed it on the floor for Régine. "Help yourself. There's enough food for both of us and a hungry dog as well."

If Kirkland had spent half the night traveling, it was no wonder he looked tired. Grey served himself bacon, ham, fried potatoes, and eggs scrambled with cheese.

Eating was easy, but being with an old friend was unnervingly awkward. Before becoming imprisoned, he'd never been ill at ease with other people, but he wasn't that relaxed, confident young man anymore. He'd desperately wanted to return to Westerfield because Lady Agnes was like a beloved, tolerant aunt. She was sanctuary.

Old friends with ten years of complicated living behind them were different. He settled for, "After ten years, you could have slept another few hours before charging down here."

"Seeing is believing." Kirkland looked down at the toast he was buttering. "I needed to see that you were really alive."

Grey guessed that he'd also needed to learn if Grey hated him. "Why did you think you might be an unwelcome sight?"

"Because I asked you to keep an eye out for information in France, and it cost you ten years of your life." Kirkland's expression was bleak. "Bad years, judging by all the bones and bandages. As you said, you look feral."

"Only half feral, thanks to Cassie. She's been slowly reintroducing me to the world." Wanting to know more about her, Grey continued, "She's an amazing woman. Where did you find her?"

"Cassie found me. She's one of my most valuable agents." Kirkland poured two steaming cups of tea. "Do you still take milk and sugar?"

What a memory the man had. "Just milk now. I lost the habit of sugar."

Kirkland poured in milk and handed over the cup. "Can you tell me what happened? Or would you rather not?"

Grey stared into his milky tea. "I don't even know where to start. Ten dreadful years of nothingness. I don't recommend it. And I don't know where to go from here."

"You take it one step at a time," Kirkland said. "I've brought my valet, who can give you a clean shave and a haircut. Since we used to be about the same size, I brought some of my clothes. They'll be loose on you but at least you'll look like an English gentleman again."

"Is that what I want?"

Kirkland hesitated. "I have no idea. Do you know what you want?"

Cassie. But he couldn't say that. Not only were their paths about to diverge, but why on earth would a strong, independent woman like her want a man who was as needy and confused as Grey?

"I wanted freedom. I never looked beyond that." He gave a twisted smile. "I don't really have much choice, do I? My path was laid out the day I was born heir to Costain. I inherited wealth and privilege and great responsibilities. I can use those things well or badly, but I can't really walk away from them. They're another sort of prison."

"Though a much more comfortable one than the dungeons under Castle Durand," his friend observed.

"More comfortable, but much more demanding. In prison, the only requirement was to survive."

Grey had attempted lightness again, but Kirkland was not fooled. "You don't have to do anything you're not ready for," he said quietly. "Though I hope that you'll let me tell your family soon."

"I will," Grey promised. "Soon. After I've recovered some from the blood loss. I feel as weak as a day-old kitten."

"I almost bled out once," Kirkland said. "In a fortnight or so, you should be in much better strength. In the meantime, I'll send up a bath, my valet, and the clothing I brought for you. After you're clean and shaved and dressed like a gentleman, you'll feel more the thing."

Grey hoped so. It would take all his strength to face his family's loving excitement. And once they knew he was alive, the whole world would know. Life would become enormously complicated and stressful.

A year from now, he'd probably be so settled back into his existence as Viscount Wyndham that he'd hardly be able to remember the vapors he was experiencing now. But just now, the vapors were winning.

Chapter 24

The sun was high when Cassie finally woke. Lady Agnes's guest beds were very comfortable, though she'd have slept well on broken rocks. She stretched luxuriously and wished Grey was beside her. But he was no longer her lover Grey; he was Lord Wyndham, restored to his proper station and the people who loved him.

Usually when a mission ended successfully, she felt satisfaction. Triumph, even, for she'd struck another small blow against Napoleon's tyranny.

This time, she felt . . . empty. She made a brief, doomed effort to convince herself that she was only regretting the loss of a superb bedmate.

Scowling, she swung from the bed. Bedamned to her rationalizations. She wouldn't have survived so many years as a spy if she'd been prone to self-delusion. With Grey's combination of wry charm, vulnerability, and desperate strength, he had touched her as no other man had. She wasn't sure whether to be grateful or irritated.

She tugged on the bell pull. Her suspicion that Lady Agnes's household was exceedingly well run was confirmed by the rapid appearance of a maid. Fifteen minutes later, Cassie was drinking delicious hot chocolate while immersed in a perfumed hot bath. ("Her ladyship told us to have lots of hot water ready, miss.") She didn't emerge until the water cooled and the chocolate was long gone.

A lavish breakfast was delivered on a tray, along with her shabby but now clean gown. After she'd eaten, dressed, and pulled her hair back into its usual unflattering style, she went exploring.

Grey wasn't in his room, so she headed downstairs. Since Lady Agnes was busy running her school, Cassie waylaid a passing maid. "Do you know where Lord Wyndham might be found?"

"He might be in the conservatory, ma'am," the maid replied. "I saw him heading in that direction."

"I didn't know Lady Agnes had a conservatory," Cassie remarked.

"It's rather new," the maid explained. "A gift from the Duke of Ashton to remind her ladyship of India. Shall I take you there? It's built off the sitting room in the back of the house."

"Thank you, I'll find it on my own." Cassie set off in the direction indicated. Lady Agnes's private quarters were only one wing of the sprawling manor, but even so this was a gracious and sizable home.

She reached the drawing room and saw that the conservatory had been cleverly designed to open off the farthest right French door so it didn't obscure the sitting room's view of the well-tended grounds. This side of the house faced south, so the conservatory would get the maximum possible sunshine and warmth.

She opened the door, then stepped into a tropical paradise. She stopped short, delighted by the warm, humid air and the lush fragrances of flowers and plants. The perfect antidote to an English winter.

The structure was so crowded with flowers and trees—and was that a pair of brilliantly colored birds flashing by?—that it was impossible to judge its size or see if anyone else was inside. She set off on a flagstone path that wound between palm trees and flowering bushes. It passed a clearing with small tables, a loveseat, and several chairs. A perfect place for tea or a meal.

A twist in the path led her by a small shrine containing a stone statue of an elephant-headed being. A Hindu god, perhaps? She continued, making a mental note to ask for a guided tour of the conservatory.

Another turn of the path, and she discovered the most beautiful man she'd ever seen. With shining golden hair, sculpted features, and an impeccably tailored navy blue coat, he was the model of an English gentleman. He stood by a bush covered with scarlet blossoms, his eyes closed as he raptly inhaled the spicy scent of one that he'd picked.

Cassie held her breath as if he were a wild creature who might take wing if disturbed. One of the school's old boys, or perhaps the father of a prospective student.

The man turned and she saw a neat white head bandage on the left side of his head, almost hidden under the golden hair. *Grey.*

She froze as visceral shock blazed through her. She'd known all along that their affair would be brief, that they could have no possible future. But seeing him now, indisputably Viscount Wyndham, the golden heir to the Earl of Costain, underlined their differences with vicious clarity.

She had just an instant to bring her shock under control. As soon as he saw her, his pensive face lit up. "Cassie! I was tempted to wake you, but managed to control the impulse. Yesterday was far too exciting for both of us."

He moved forward with swift strides and enveloped her in a hug. Desire flared as soon as he touched her. Whatever else he might be, Cassie thought wryly, Greydon Sommers was no snob. He didn't seem to have noticed that he'd transformed into a glittering aristocrat while she was still a drab, aging spy.

As she slid her arms around him, he gasped, "Oww!"

"Sorry!" She stepped out of his embrace. "I forgot your wounded ribs."

"So did I." He smiled ruefully. "I'm healing well enough that mostly I don't feel either of the bullet wounds. Except when they're touched." He felt gingerly around the head wound. "Another few days and I'll be fine."

"A good thing you kept the beard till now, my lord. If you'd shaved in France, every female we passed would have remembered you."

He made a face. "It's strange to look into the mirror and see a man who looks so much like the young idiot I used to be." He delicately tucked his scarlet blossom behind her left ear, then cupped her face between his lean, strong hands. "Now to see what I can do that won't hurt my ribs."

He leaned into a kiss, his lips moving tenderly over hers. His face might not be familiar, but his mouth was. As exotic floral fragrance wafted around her, she closed her eyes and reveled in how he gave so much of himself. Perhaps prison had stripped away the armor most Englishmen used to bury their emotions.

She stroked his lips with her tongue. Such sweetness in the moment. So few moments left.

Remembering she shouldn't carry on with him under Lady Agnes's roof, she broke the kiss. "You smell of vinegar," she said teasingly. "Like a particularly handsome pickled onion."

He laughed, so lighthearted that she could imagine how he'd been as a youth. "The consequences might be onionish, but vinegar did a good job of washing out that brown hair coloring. Kirkland's valet found me an interesting challenge."

Her brows rose. "Kirkland is here already?"

"Apparently he set off for Kent in the middle of the night as soon as he received Lady Agnes's message. He provided the clothing as well as the valet," Grey explained. "Now where was I?"

He resumed kissing her, and this time sweetness deepened into fire. Her resolve to behave dissolved. She wanted to pull him down into the tropical flowers and rip off those well-tailored garments so they could take advantage of what little time they had left.

"Excuse me if I'm interrupting," Kirkland's dry voice said. "I'm glad to see you're undamaged, Cassandra."

Cassie jumped as if she'd been caught in adultery rather than sharing a private, if indiscreet, kiss with her lover, while Grey turned rigid. "Did my faithful hound track me down?" He bent to ruffle Régine's ears as she bounded from Kirkland's side and began twining between Grey and Cassie.

"She did, though I wouldn't want to wager what percentage of her is hound." Kirkland's cool gaze met Cassie's. "Shall we adjourn to the sitting area near the entrance so we can relax and discuss what comes next?"

"There's a way to ruin a previously good day," Grey said with brittle humor. He rested his hand on the back of Cassie's waist and ushered her toward the sitting area. "But the sitting part sounds good since I'm fatigued again."

"You were shot twice yesterday," Cassie pointed out. "You are entitled to take things slowly for a while. If Lady Agnes summoned a surgeon, he probably told you to spend several days in bed."

"Indeed he did, the tiresome fellow. I ignored him, of course. How can one rebuild one's strength without exercise?"

"I see your natural disdain for authority hasn't changed," Kirkland observed.

"Disdain for authority is the bedrock of my character." They reached the sitting area set among the palms and cascading blossoms. Grey folded into the loveseat, tugging Cassie down beside him.

When she was settled, he took firm hold of her hand, lacing his fingers between hers. She wasn't sure whether to be pleased or irritated at his blatant proclamation that they were lovers. Not that it mattered, since Kirkland had already figured it out.

Grey's tenseness made Cassie uneasy. He'd been fine until Kirkland appeared. Was he angry with his old friend? Or uncomfortable with everyone but her?

Willing to delay the discussion about his future, Cassie said, "This conservatory was a magnificent gift. Ashton must have enjoyed his years here."

"He did. We all did. Lady Agnes does more than teach Latin, rhetoric, and mathematics," Kirkland said. "She helps boys fit into their lives."

That was a gift far beyond the ability to conjugate Latin verbs. Cassie wondered how Kirkland had ended up at Westerfield. She didn't know the reason even though she'd worked closely with him for years. Kirkland's reserve didn't encourage questions.

The other man continued, "Wyndham, have you changed your mind and decided to go to Summerhill right away?"

"I have not," Grey snapped. "I have no idea how long it will take to screw my courage up. At the least, weeks. Perhaps months."

Cassie stared at him. "You want to delay seeing your family for that long?" She'd give anything to be with her family again for a single hour. "I thought you got on well with them."

"I do," he said starkly. "But I don't want to return to Summerhill until I'm more like the Greydon Sommers they remember."

She understood his reluctance, though she suspected his mother would want him back right now no matter what condition he was in. Seeing his agitation, she kept her voice neutral as she asked, "Have you any plans for how to make that happen?"

"None at all." His hand tightened on Cassie's. "But I will manage. In time."

"Do you want to stay in a quiet country cottage somewhere until you get used to England again?" Kirkland frowned as he sought a solution.

Grey gave a twisted smile. "Sounds delightful, but I'd probably never leave. Maybe I should stay here at Westerfield? I don't think Lady Agnes would mind."

"She would love it," Kirkland said, "but you'd run the risk of being seen and identified before you're ready. Do you think you could stand London? My house is comfortable and you'd be more than welcome."

Grey shook his head. "Kirkland House is in a fashionable neighborhood. Every time I went outside, I'd run the risk of being identified by my mother's second cousin or my godfather or someone else who has known me since I was in the cradle."

"That would be true anywhere in Mayfair," the other man agreed. "I imagine you don't want to be cooped up in a house."

"Or anywhere ever again," Grey said, his voice edged.

His words gave Cassie an insight as to why he was so skittish about returning to his own world. As heir to an earldom, he'd have wealth and a great deal of freedom, but he'd also be trapped in a gilded cage of responsibilities and expectations. When he was younger, he hadn't recognized the bars.

If he couldn't face an immediate return to his family, what would be a good alternative? "You might be better off in London, but living anonymously. You can become accustomed to people while having a safe retreat whenever you need quiet. No one will flutter anxiously outside your door if you go to ground. When you're ready, old friends can come by one at a time."

"Exeter Street," Kirkland said instantly. "That's brilliant, Cassie. The house was designed to be a sanctuary, and that's exactly what is needed."

"What is Exeter Street?" Grey asked warily.

"The location of a house Kirkland owns near Covent Garden. It's a boardinghouse for his agents when they're in London," Cassie explained. "It's the closest I have to a home. The neighborhood is busy but not fashionable, so you're unlikely to meet anyone from your former social circles."

Grey exhaled with relief. "Perfect, if you'll be there."

She bit her lip, thinking it would be wiser to disappear now that Grey had been delivered to Kirkland. He needed to manage without her—and she needed to consign him to the past so she could continue her work without distracted thoughts about passionate nights. It was most unfair that he was so meltingly attractive!

But apparently it wasn't yet time for her to move on. And she wouldn't mind a little more time with him. Not at all. "I'll be at Exeter Street for a fortnight or so."

Grey relaxed. "Good. I'm used to having you around." Releasing her hand, he got to his feet.

"I'm tiring far too fast today, but tomorrow I should be fit for the trip up to London. Are you going upstairs now, Cassie?"

Before she could respond, Kirkland said, "If you have a few minutes, Cassie, I have some questions about what you learned in Paris before going to Castle Durand."

Such sessions were normal after a mission, though this time the questions would be more complicated. "Of course. I have a message from one of your agents in Paris."

"I'll see you later, then," Grey said with a touch of acid. "Feel free to talk about me. I know you will as soon as I'm out of earshot."

Kirkland looked uncomfortable, but Cassie said tartly, "Of course we'll talk about you. You're so utterly fascinating."

"More of a nuisance than fascinating." His smile was twisted. "You would have been wiser to have left me to rot in France."

Chapter 25

Grey stalked off, Régine on his heels, leaving Cassie shaken. Kirkland looked equally uncomfortable.

When Grey was safely out of earshot, she said in her driest voice, "Leaving him in France wouldn't have been wiser, but he's right that we're going to talk about him."

"Of course we are. He's the reason we're both here." Kirkland leaned forward, his expression worried. "Can you tell me more about his . . . his mental state?"

Hearing what wasn't being said, Cassie said reassuringly, "Wyndham's not mad, though he worries that he might be. His moods can be volatile, his temper can be dangerous, and groups of people upset him badly. But he isn't broken beyond repair. He just needs time." Surrendering to curiosity, she added, "What do you think? Is he so different from the way he was?"

"No. Yes." Kirkland ran stiff fingers through his dark hair. "I've been trying to imagine what it would be like to spend ten years locked in a cold stone cell, and—it's beyond my imagination. I want to help, and I don't know how."

"He just needs time," Cassie repeated. "He's strong, Kirkland. Much stronger than you or he or anyone else expected."

"He must be, or he really would have run mad." Kirkland frowned. "I'm grateful for all you're doing for him, Cassie. But I'm concerned as well."

"Because of my services above and beyond the call of duty?" she said, her voice edged. "You've always known I'm a slut."

Kirkland's eyes flared with rare temper. "You know damned well I've never given you reason to think such an appalling thing. I've never known a woman I've respected more."

"Perhaps for my spying skills," she retorted. "You're good at concealing your true thoughts, but I know that I don't conform to your priggish Scottish morality."

His expression turned to ice. "Remind me never to be feverish and hallucinating around you again."

She winced. "I'm sorry, I shouldn't have referred to that. But I'm in no mood for a lecture on how inappropriate it is for me to be lying with Wyndham. You have no need to worry. Once he's ready for normal society, I shall quietly disappear, the way a woman of no reputation is supposed to. I won't be an embarrassment to the golden boy."

She rose and turned to leave, but Kirkland caught her wrist. "I'm not worried about you being an embarrassment, Cassie! Wyndham obviously needs you. You freed him, you know what his prison was like, and he trusts you. You can help him heal from the damage he suffered in prison as no one else can."

She jerked her wrist free. "Then what are you concerned about? Most men are happy when they have warm and undemanding women in their beds, and I'm fulfilling that role competently."

"I'm worried about you being hurt. Worse than hurt. Devastated, because you've already lost more than anyone should lose in a lifetime." He stood, looming over her. She tended to forget how tall he was. "People have been falling in love with

Wyndham since he was in the cradle. Even now, when he's angry and suffering from the effects of imprisonment, he has that magnetic charm. But there can be no future for you with him."

"You think I don't know that?" she snapped, glaring up at him. "Don't worry, James. I've survived worse." She stalked away, fuming at his words even though they were true. She had indeed survived worse than losing a lover.

But she'd never had a loss like this one.

Temper simmering, Cassie swept out of the conservatory and headed up to her room. She and Kirkland had never quarreled before. And all because the damned man was right. Even damaged and struggling to recover from ten years of hell, Greydon Sommers was far too easy to love—and she could have no real place in his life.

If only her father had listened when she'd begged him to take the family back to England! But she'd been only a child so he'd laughed off her frantic warnings of imminent disaster. At the time she'd not understood why she was so convinced of approaching doom. She'd just known that they should leave France immediately.

In the years since, she'd realized that she had a powerful instinct for danger. That had kept her alive, against all the odds, for a dozen years of perilous work. In the process, she'd been transformed from Catherine, a well-behaved and well-brought-up girl, to Cassandra, a haunted and ignored prophetess and instrument of revenge against the revolution that had destroyed her family.

Her life would have been unimaginably different if they had left France in time. She might have met Grey when they were both young and whole. They might . . .

She halted at the top of the stairs, startled by the recognition that if they'd met then, he'd never have noticed her. There was nothing special about young Catherine that would have caught the notice of the golden heir to an earldom who was happily sowing wild oats in all directions. She was no more than passably pretty, and as a girl she'd possessed no special charms or talents. The only thing out of the ordinary about her now was her fierce, charmless ability to gather information and survive.

Oddly, that recognition calmed her. She'd have been no use to Grey when she was seventeen, but the woman she was now had been able to free him and get him safely out of France.

She was also in the best position to help him recover from his harrowing experiences. So much more useful than if she were just another girl hopelessly besotted with young Lord Wyndham.

Instead of going to her own room, she tapped on his door. No response. She tried the knob and found the door unlocked. He probably didn't like being behind locked doors. Or perhaps he wasn't here at all and had gone for an angry walk across the estate.

She entered the room quietly and saw his long form sprawled across the bed, all angles and gaunt strength. He lay on his side and hadn't even removed his shoes.

Régine lay beside him, but her head popped up when the door opened. The dog was looking round and well fed.

She jumped down, trotted to Cassie for a head scratch, then left the room. She was probably heading for the kitchen to beg for a handout, or anxious to go outside. She'd taken easily to housebreaking after Grey had adopted her in France.

Cassie moved closer to the bed. Grey looked like a ravaged angel, his face lined with exhaustion. Not just physical fatigue and the aftereffects of being wounded, but the drain on mind and spirit of being back in a world where people had expectations of Greydon Sommers, heir to the Earl of Costain. He'd tried his best to conceal that strain, even from her, but now it was carved into those sculpted features.

She locked the door so no one could enter, then lit the fire laid in the fireplace because the room was chilly. As in her room, the wardrobe held a folded quilt, worn but clean and scented with lavender. She shook it over him, then crawled underneath and lay behind him, molding her body to his and wrapping an arm around his lean waist.

Grey didn't wake, but he exhaled softly. His hand moved to cover hers where it rested on his chest.

Tension from the difficult scene in the conservatory began to fade as the world narrowed down to this man and this bed and this moment. She was tired, too.

And nothing would soothe her more than sleeping with Grey.

Chapter 26

Grey woke slowly, tired and not happy about the scene with Kirkland. But he was relaxed now. He was safe in England and Cassie was cuddled around him. Peace.

Limited peace. From the angle of the sun, he judged it was late afternoon. Soon he'd have to rise and prepare to dine with Lady Agnes and her friends, and tomorrow he would travel to London. An intimidating thought.

He rolled onto his back, pulling Cassie close against his side. Her eyes blinked sleepily, then opened, blue and hazy and deep with acceptance. She smiled up at him. "Régine was here, so I changed places with her."

"A good trade." He tightened his arm around her, grateful that she'd joined him. "It appears that you're the only person I'm really comfortable with. You, and Régine, and perhaps Lady Agnes. In that order."

"An interesting list. The only thing we have in common is being female."

"There's a reason for that. Females tend to be more forgiving."

"They certainly are forgiving of handsome men." She slid her fingers into his hair. "But don't forget Père Laurent."

Grey thought of his friend's infinite acceptance, which was very like Cassie's, now that he thought about it. Grey needed a lot of acceptance. "It's a good thing you're forgiving, my lady fox. I'm asking you to do far too much for me."

"Never too much," she said quietly. "London and your old life might seem overwhelming at the moment, but it won't be long before your wings are fledged and you take flight again."

He wished he had her confidence. Best to take this reemergence into the world one step at a time. And the present step was to appreciate the woman in his arms.

"I've wanted to see you naked in daylight," he said thoughtfully. "And here we are, nicely private and with late afternoon sunshine pouring in the window. I must take advantage of this situation." He untied the drawstring at the throat of her ghastly shapeless gown. Opening in front, the garment was intended for a peasant woman who had to be able to dress herself without assistance.

"It isn't the situation you're taking advantage of," she said tartly as she batted away his hand. "It's me. I rather like being safely blanketed by darkness. Night covers my deficiencies."

He pulled pins from her hair and combed the thick waves around her shoulders with his fingers. What color was it under the dull gray and brown? A nice glossy brown, he guessed, with a shine reflecting her age and good health. She'd washed the lines of age from her face, revealing a complexion with the transparent purity of porcelain. "You underrate your charms, Cassandra. I may not have been able to see you, but I've touched as much of your delicious body as I could, and all of it has been first rate."

He started on the buttons that closed the front of her bodice. "Your bare skin will certainly be lovelier than this appalling gray gown. An uglier garment I've never seen."

She laughed. "That's rather the point. No man would look at me twice. Not even once if he could help it."

"Yet you look astonishingly attractive even so," he mused. "It's a great mystery."

She made a face. "Very well, but you must bare yourself as well." She tugged at his crumpled cravat. "The only time I've seen you with your clothes off was when you were shivering in an icy pond at midnight. I was too afraid you'd freeze to death to admire your manly charms."

"You don't really want to see me unclad," he assured her. "Despite your best efforts to feed me up, I'm still more scarecrow than not."

She grinned wickedly. "Now you know how I feel about my imperfections. Are you willing to forgo mutual nakedness?"

"I am not," he said firmly. "It's worth revealing my bony carcass to see your much more pleasing form."

"Ah, well," she said philosophically. "If only beautiful people mated, the human race would have died out long since. We must accept each other's deficiencies."

She was opening his shirt when he parted her bodice and chemise, laying bare her lovely breasts. Feeling stronger by the moment, he lapped her nipple with his tongue.

She sucked in her breath, eyes widening. "You intend more than looking?"

"I'm not sure how much more," he admitted. "I may not have recovered enough for what I would dearly like to do." He rolled her other nipple between thumb and forefinger. "Shall we see how far I can go? I promise you won't be left unsatisfied."

"By all means continue," she breathed. "But undressing will be easier if we stand."

"You are a natural leader who always has excellent ideas." He slid from the bed and took the opportunity to toss more fuel on the fire and kick off his shoes. Then he offered his hand with a courtly gesture. "Join me, my lady, in the prelude to seduction?"

She grasped his hand and alighted from the bed with a smile that made her seem decades younger than her appearance, even younger than he knew her to be. "I look forward to removing your garments one by one, my Lord Wyndham."

She started with his coat, then attacked his shirt. He knew he was showing too many bones, but there was admiration in her eyes and sensuality in her touch as she skimmed her palm over his bare chest.

"My turn now," he said with a catch in his breath as she pressed her lips to the hollow at the base of his throat. "That gray gown must go."

"Resist the temptation to burn it," she warned. "It's all I have till I return to London."

He tugged the coarse garment over her head, making a silent vow to buy her silk in the city. She emerged from the gray folds laughing and luscious in her stays and chemise. The more she removed, the lovelier she became.

Garment by garment, they peeled off each other's clothing with kisses and laughter. When he removed the worn white chemise, leaving her bare and golden in the late afternoon light, he said huskily, "You are even more beautiful than I realized."

She tugged his drawers down from his hips with

a passing caress that temporarily paralyzed his simple male brain. "Lust is warping your judgment." Wistfully she added, "Though it's a lovely lie to hear."

"I can't deny the lust, but it's not warping my judgment." He removed his drawers entirely. "At least, not about how desirable you are."

"I'm boringly average," she protested.

"Not average. Quintessential." He cupped her breasts in his hands, caressing the warm weight. He moved his hands in a slow circle, feeling her nipples harden against his palms. "Every part of you is exactly right. Your breasts are neither too large nor too small, but a perfect handful."

He kissed the shadowed cleft between them. "Your skin is remarkable. Smooth and almost luminescent, like a sun-touched marble statue by Michelangelo."

"You . . . look . . . better than you claimed, also. Too thin, but such splendid shoulders!" She ran her hands across them to demonstrate.

She was being kind. He knew his ribs were showing and he'd picked up some ugly scars after his capture in Paris. He wished they'd met when he was young and at his best, but as she said, one didn't have to be perfect to mate. Fortunately.

"You really are perfect," he said as he skimmed his palms over her hips and thighs. "Like Botticelli's Venus born of the sea, your proportions are exactly right. Slim but round in all the right places. Beautifully fit and strong." He kissed his way down the gentle curve of her belly, becoming more aroused than he would have thought possible. She was deliciously feminine and edible.

She gasped as he swirled his tongue around her navel. "Time to go from vertical to horizontal," he said in a thick voice. Catching her up in his arms, he laid her onto the bed and came down beside her, resuming his kisses down toward the tantalizing mysteries between her thighs.

She cried out and her fingernails bit into his shoulders hard enough to draw blood when his lips and tongue reached her most sensitive, secret places. Her responsiveness was intoxicating, sending fire through his blood.

She shattered around him, her ecstasy driving him to urgent need. He moved between her legs and joined their bodies, merging them so they were as close as man and woman could be. She gasped. "I see you've recovered fully, my lord."

"You are better than any surgeon for healing, my sweet vixen," he said breathlessly as he rocked into her.

Laughing, she drew him down as they moved together into bliss. This was even better than his first fierce coupling when he was mad for the solace of her female flesh. This was a joining of spirit as well as bodies beyond anything he'd ever known. "Cassandra," he gasped. "Catherine . . ."

Perfection.

• • •

Even though that evening's dinner was in the small family dining room, it was the most watchful meal Cassie had ever consumed. Lady Agnes, General Rawlings, and Miss Emily watched Wyndham, the two women also watched Cassie, and Kirkland watched everyone. Grey was worth watching. Golden haired and with the ability to make his borrowed clothing look custom tailored, he was the model of an English gentleman. He spoke little but was effortlessly magnetic.

No one watched Régine, who'd slipped into the dining room and was resting under the table with her muzzle on Grey's foot. As long as no one took official notice of the dog, she didn't have to be ejected. She'd fattened up noticeably since they found her.

The tightness around Grey's eyes made it clear that he wasn't comfortable with all the attention, but he bore up under it well. Cassie thought she deserved some credit for having relaxed him so thoroughly that afternoon. Her gaze dropped to the braised beef at the thought. If she'd relaxed him, he'd made her feel desirable.

At the end of the meal, Lady Agnes rose. "Miss Fox, Emily, let us withdraw to the morning room and leave the gentlemen to their port."

Seeing Cassie's expression, Lady Agnes said, "You're surprised that I'm so conventional?"

214

"Yes," Cassie admitted as she got to her feet. "I thought you only conform to customs when they suit you."

Lady Agnes grinned. "You're very perceptive. Sometimes it suits me to withdraw, and when I do, I have a decanter of the same excellent Ballard port in the morning room."

Cassie glanced at Grey. He looked wary but resigned to being left with the general and Kirkland. After he gave her a small nod of reassurance, she left with the two older women. Closing the morning room door behind her, she said, "I'd like some of that port to support me in the upcoming interrogation, please."

Lady Agnes poured three glasses of tawny port and distributed them. "I want to know more about Wyndham's captivity and rescue. If I ask him directly, he'll get all stiff and stoic and claim that all is well."

"Perhaps," Emily Cantwell said thoughtfully. "But he was always better at speaking his mind than most of our boys."

"Then, yes," Lady Agnes agreed. "But he was in reserved English gentleman mode this evening." She fixed Cassie with a gimlet gaze. "I won't ask you to violate his privacy, but"—her face tightened—"will he ever . . . be himself again?"

"He is himself, though it's a self formed by traveling an unexpected path," Cassie said gently. "He will become more relaxed in society, I'm sure. But he will never be that uncomplicated golden boy again."

Lady Agnes exhaled. "I knew that, of course, but it helps to hear it from the woman who knows him best. Of course he's been changed by his experiences. But I pray that in time he'll be whole and happy."

"I always thought he'd be a wonderful father," Miss Emily said. "He was so patient with the younger boys." Both women turned assessing gazes on Cassie.

"Are you planning on giving me the lecture about not developing expectations of Wyndham?" she asked with acid sweetness. "No need, Kirkland has already done so."

Lady Agnes winced. "I didn't intend a lecture. You're a woman of the world and you understand the situation. But I do want to thank you for all you've done. For rescuing him, for being there as he recovers from all he's endured. I suspect the price for you will be high."

"As you say, I am a woman of the world. I have no illusions." Cassie sipped the excellent port, thinking that Lady Agnes's comment was another oblique reference to Grey's general lovability. "Since we are hinting around the subject of Wyndham's future, I will give you my private opinion. I wouldn't be surprised if he never marries. Or if he does, it would be far in the future."

Miss Emily's brows arched. "You can't convince me that he has lost his appreciation of women!"

No one knew better than Cassie how much Grey liked women, but this conversation had crystallized an insight. "He likes women very well, but after ten years behind bars, he hates being trapped by society, by responsibility, by other people's expectations. He will not shirk those responsibilities, but I think that he will see marriage as one set of bars that he can avoid."

After a long silence, Lady Agnes said, "You're remarkably clear-sighted, Miss Fox. As a woman who has avoided the bars myself, I can understand that."

"But it will be a waste of a good father," Miss Emily said with a sigh.

Grey and Cassie had agreed that afternoon that for discretion's sake, they should sleep in their separate rooms. But in the dark hours after midnight, Grey's resolve snapped when a nightmare of darkness and desolation yanked him awake.

Shaking, he crossed the corridor to Cassie's room. She woke instantly, as a good spy needed to do, and equally swiftly recognized her visitor. Silently she extended a hand. He took it gratefully and slid into the bed next to her.

In her arms, he slept.

Chapter 27

With a groan, Grey sat up in bed. "It's almost dawn. I'd better slink back to my own room."

Cassie wrapped an arm around his waist. "This doesn't seem like the sort of household where anyone is easily shocked."

"Perhaps not, but I don't want to put Lady Agnes in an awkward situation." He kissed her forehead. "Don't complain. You get to stay in this nicely warmed bed."

"It just got a great deal colder," she sighed as he stood up.

"We have a cozy journey to London ahead of us. By the time we reach there, you'll be bored with me." He opened her door, checked that no one was in sight, and slipped back to his own room, thinking there was a reason people got married. Sharing a bed legally would be much more pleasant than tiptoeing through icy corridors.

He wasn't going to sleep again, so he dressed and headed downstairs in hopes of acquiring a cup of tea since the kitchen staff started early. He found not only a friendly cook and tea, but toasted bread with honey. He was happily consuming a second slice when Lady Agnes appeared fully dressed and with amusement in her eyes. "Good morning, all."

As Grey murmured a response, the cook poured

a cup of tea, added honey and milk, and handed it to the headmistress. After a deep swallow, Lady Agnes said, "Complications have arisen, Wyndham. Come with me and I'll show you."

"Yes, ma'am." It was easy to fall back into schoolboy mode. Though Lady Agnes didn't seem upset, he was curious, so he swallowed the last of his toast and honey and followed her upstairs. To his surprise, she led him to her private rooms and threw open the door to her dressing room.

"Behold the complications," she said with a laugh.

Curled up on an expensive velvet cloak were Régine and three fat little puppies who were blindly nursing. "Good heavens!" Grey knelt to examine the new arrivals, keeping a careful distance away. "Aren't you looking proud of yourself, Régine. Apart from eating enough for three horses, you kept your secret well. I wonder what the father looked like? The puppies look even more mixed than their mother."

"They're adorable," Lady Agnes said firmly. "Lineage doesn't matter."

Grey grinned. "There speaks a woman with some of the bluest bloodlines in Britain."

"I didn't choose my ancestors any more than these puppies chose their father." Lady Agnes swallowed more tea. "I rather like mixed breeds. More surprises."

Régine briefly looked up from licking the pups,

then returned to her washing. Grey got to his feet. "I have no idea how she got in here, Lady Agnes. I will replace the cloak when I have money again."

Lady Agnes made a dismissive gesture. "No need to worry about that, but you can't take a new mother and her puppies in a carriage to London."

He laughed at her expression. "You aren't the least bit sorry, are you?"

She grinned. "I've a weakness for all young creatures, whether children, kittens, or puppies. I'd love to keep one of these. My old dog died a few weeks ago, and I've been thinking it's time I looked for a new pup. There are boys here who would like puppies, too." She looked thoughtful. "There is one lad in particular who really needs a pup of his own."

"You can give away the puppies, but I'll be back for Régine when her offspring are old enough to do without her." He extended one hand, and when Régine didn't seem inclined to bite, he scratched her head. "I'll miss her, though."

"You'll just have to keep your Miss Fox close then," Lady Agnes said blandly.

Grey certainly intended to try.

After a fast trip up to London, the luxurious coach rumbled to a halt in front of Kirkland House. As the footman lowered the steps, Kirkland offered his hand to Grey. "I'll call in Exeter Street tomorrow. If you need anything, just send word."

"I'll be fine." Grey shook his friend's hand. "When I feel ready to return to the bosom of my loving family, you'll be the first to know."

"More likely the second to know." Kirkland inclined his head to Cassie, then climbed out of the carriage.

After the door was closed and the carriage resumed its progress across the city, Grey settled back in the seat and took Cassie's hand. "Was London always this crowded, smelly, and noisy?"

"Yes, which is probably why you've buried those memories." She laced her fingers through his. "Does London make you want to run screaming?"

"Somewhat." His smile was twisted. "I'm doing better than I would have even a week ago. But I'm glad to be heading to a cave where I can hide for the rest of the day to recover from the journey."

"For the rest of today, you can relax. But I warn you that as of tomorrow I'll be marching you out to sample the delights of London," she said. "Starting with the Covent Garden market. It's so close to the house that if you run screaming, you won't even be out of breath by the time you return to your cave."

"Very thoughtful of you. But I think that if you're with me, I should be able to control myself under most conditions." He dropped a quick kiss on her forehead. "I don't know why I find your presence so easy, but I'm grateful for it."

"I may be easier because I didn't know you before Castle Durand," she said thoughtfully. "I don't expect you to be the same as you were at twenty. And because I know you're not broken beyond repair, I'm not hovering and worrying and missing the glittering Lord Wyndham of fond memory. I'll settle for seeing you happy as the man you've become now."

He waggled his eyebrows. "The fact that I'm an amazing lover isn't part of your calculations?"

She laughed. "That belongs on a different set of scales, my lord."

"Scales of solid gold, I'm sure." His smile faded as he gazed out the window. "My parents might be in London waiting for Parliament."

"Perhaps. Even if they're here, you needn't see them until you want to."

"I do want to see them. Just . . . not yet." He made an effort to lighten his tone. "I'd rather visit Astley's Circus or some other entertainment. I assume the Theatre Royal is still in Covent Garden?"

"Yes, though the theater you knew burned down several years ago. A new one was built in the same place, so the shows carry on," she replied. "Perhaps tomorrow we can go by the theater and look at the playbills to see what's being performed."

He hesitated. "I like the theater, but I'm not ready to be part of a rowdy theater crowd, and I can't sit in a box without the risk of being recognized."

"Maybe in a week or two," she said peaceably.

They fell silent, but their hands remained locked together. Grey's gaze was riveted on the city that was the beating heart of Britain. Cassie thought he was handling the crowds and confusion well. Every day, he became stronger. Better able to manage.

Dusk was approaching when they arrived at 11 Exeter Street. "It's bigger than I expected," Grey said as he helped Cassie from the carriage.

"This area was once fashionable and the large houses remain." She produced her key and led the way up the front steps. "There are enough boardinghouses in the neighborhood that our comings and goings aren't noticed."

She opened the door to the small foyer and she and Grey entered, his arm slung affectionately around her shoulders. Inside was a tall, lean man on the point of departure. Cassie stiffened as she recognized the whipcord strength and brown hair.

As he saw her, his serious face lit with a smile. "Cassie! Since I'm leaving for Scotland tomorrow, I stopped by on the off chance you might have just returned."

Rob Carmichael. Cassie froze as he moved toward her. Then Rob stopped dead, his gaze moving from Cassie to Grey.

"My God, Wyndham, you're back from the grave!" Rob said with amazed pleasure. His expression changed as he saw and correctly interpreted the casual intimacy between Grey and Cassie. His voice hardened. "You seem to have come out of France smelling of roses, Wyndham."

"Hardly," Grey said, frowning as he looked from Rob to Cassie and back.

"I thought you had better judgment than to fall for cheap charm," Rob said to Cassie, his voice brittle. "Or is it for his money? Wyndham certainly has more than I do, and he had a reputation for being generous to his mistresses."

"Watch your tongue, Carmichael!" Grey removed his arm from Cassie's shoulders and stepped forward, his hands tightening into fists. "Apologize to her!"

"For speaking the truth? Not bloody likely!" Rob also moved into a fighter's stance, his jaw set with fury.

"Stop it, both of you!" Cassie snapped in a voice that could have cut glass. "You're behaving like children!"

Mrs. Powell, who ran the house with her husband, had been drawn to the foyer by the sound of voices, so Cassie continued, "Mrs. Powell, this is Mr. Sommers and he'll be staying here for a while. Please take him up to a room."

When Grey opened his mouth to protest, Cassie gave him a glance that said *Go!* He didn't look happy about that, but he followed Mrs. Powell up the stairs.

"No need to send him off," Rob said, his voice harsh. "I'm leaving. I doubt our paths will cross much in the future, Cassandra."

"You are not leaving until we talk, Robert," Cassie said firmly. "In the drawing room." She grabbed his arm so he couldn't escape without shaking her off.

After a moment of boulder-like resistance, he accompanied her into the adjoining room. In the better light, Cassie saw pain in Rob's eyes. Her annoyance evaporated. "I'm sorry, Rob. I didn't intend that you find out in such a difficult way."

"I don't think there is any good way to dismiss a lover," he bit out.

"You and I weren't lovers, Rob. We were friends and occasional bedmates when it suited us. We swore no vows of love or constancy."

"Did you intend to tell me that you were with Wyndham? Or did you hope I wouldn't find out?"

She sighed. "You and I have never talked about other lovers, though since I'm in France so much, I've assumed you don't always sleep alone when I'm not here."

"Oddly enough, I have." His mouth twisted. "I thought we were more than merely convenient bedmates."

"Yes, but the true bond has always been friendship, not romantic love." She caught his

225

gaze with her own, wanting him to believe her words. "The friendship and caring and trust have been real, Rob. I would hate to lose that."

A muscle in his jaw jerked. "Why *Wyndham,* Cassie? His legendary charm? It was hard to hate him even when I wanted to."

She frowned. "Why did you want to hate him?"

He shrugged. "Merely because I was jealous that everything came so easily to him."

And nothing had come easily to Rob. "Perhaps it will make you feel better to know that Grey spent ten years in solitary confinement in a castle dungeon," she said tartly. "I assure you that surviving that did not come easily."

"Ten years of solitary confinement?" Rob exclaimed, looking appalled. "Poor devil. You helped him escape?"

She nodded. "We've only just returned to England." Wearily she unfastened her cloak. "I was looking forward to a quiet evening."

"With Wyndham." Rob shook his head. "I have trouble imagining you with him. Is it because he needs you for now and you feel bound to help him?"

Why Wyndham indeed? "Perhaps," she said thoughtfully. "You never let yourself need anyone or anything, Rob. I'm the same. Both of us are experts at asking for nothing. So self-sufficient that we can't connect deeply with another human

226

being. With Grey, I . . . I become someone else."

Rob's gaze was searching. "Are you in love with him?"

"A little, I suppose." She hesitated, not sure how honest she could let herself be. But Rob deserved honesty. "With him, I *feel* again. It hurts, but it's . . . rewarding."

"Ah, Cassie, I didn't know you had a shred of romance in your soul." Rob pulled her into a swift, hard hug. "If you want more than you had with me, I hope you find it. But it won't be with Wyndham. He'll never marry you."

Recognizing that this was an embrace of friends, she relaxed against his hard, familiar body, tears stinging her eyes. Though they might save their friendship, any chance of becoming more was gone. "If I ever had such illusions, I've been sufficiently warned by any number of people eager to explain how that will never happen. When Wyndham and I go our separate ways, I won't be surprised or devastated."

She was very good at moving on alone.

Rob's anger was gone, but he sounded wistful when he said, "I thought that someday the two of us might retire to a quiet village where we could bore each other with our old war stories. But that isn't going to happen, is it?"

"Highly unlikely," she agreed. "But . . . Rob, can we be friends again? Please?"

"We can." He ended the embrace. "But I'm glad

227

I'm off to Scotland. I should be sufficiently busy that I won't pine."

"You won't pine," she said with a touch of amusement. "I was just a habit."

"Perhaps, but a good one," he said quietly. "Take care, my dear girl."

She watched him leave the room, taut and always ready for trouble, and wished they'd been able to love each other.

Girding herself for another difficult discussion, Cassie headed upstairs. She met Mrs. Powell at the top of the steps.

"I put Mr. Sommers in the room at the back of the house where it's nice and quiet," the older woman said. Though she was middle-aged and known for steady good sense and discretion, she gave a girlish giggle. "He's quite the handsome fellow, he is! How long will he be staying?"

Grey's charm was obviously recovering along with the rest of him, Cassie thought acerbically. "Several weeks, perhaps. He's an old friend of Lord Kirkland's."

"A lord himself, I'll be bound," Mrs. Powell said as she turned to descend the stairs. "I'll make sure he's comfortable."

Cassie headed down the long corridor to the Blue Room. After knocking on the door as warning, she entered before Grey had time to tell her to go away.

He stood at the window watching night fall on London, the dome of St. Peter's silhouetted against the skyline. He was cool and remote and very much Lord Wyndham.

"I'm sorry for that scene," she said without preamble. "It was the purest bad luck that Rob Carmichael happened to stop by as we were arriving."

"Bad luck indeed," he said, not turning to look at her.

"You knew I was no innocent virgin," she said with exasperation.

"Neither was I, but my dalliances are all ten years in the past." After a long silence, he said haltingly, "And . . . there's a difference between abstract knowledge and knowing that you've been with a man I know and always found rather intimidating." In a softer voice, he added, "A man who seems very much your sort."

"Intimidating is a useful trait for a Bow Street Runner," she agreed, interested in how the two men saw each other. "Will you please stop staring out the window?"

Grey turned, though it was hard to read his expression in the fading light. "I owe you an apology for damaging your affair with Carmichael. While I knew you were a woman of the world, I didn't realize you had a lover waiting in London."

"I just had this conversation with Rob," she said dryly. "He and I have been friends and partners and have shared danger. But though we sometimes shared a bed, that was never the most important part of our friendship."

His eyes narrowed. "Is the bed the main point of our friendship? Or just part of the nanny service you offer when you rescue fools from captivity?"

She resisted the urge to throw something at him. "I should have let you and Rob break each other's necks!" She spun on her heel and headed for the door, thinking that Grey was becoming a detached, ironic gentleman all too quickly.

He swore and caught up with her before she reached the door, wrapping his arms around her from behind and pulling her tight against his chest. "I'm sorry, Cassie," he said intensely. "I didn't know I had a possessive streak, but with you, I'm different."

"Circumstances are different," she said, trying not to melt back into him. "Don't worry, you'll recover soon from any mild possessiveness and return to casual affairs where it doesn't matter who else the lady may be keeping company with."

His arms tightened around her waist. "A casual affair is not what I want, Cassie."

"Then what do you want?"

"I want to be special to you, Cassandra," he said starkly. "At the beginning I didn't care if you lay with me from pity or duty, but now I do care. I . . . I want to be more than just another assignment."

She swallowed hard. "You are, Grey. Despite

what you might think, I've never lain with men casually. Certainly not with men I'm escorting to safety."

"I'm glad to hear that." He kissed the top of her ear. "But . . . the first time we came together, you said you'd lain with men for worse reasons than comfort and friendship. I wasn't sure what that meant."

He didn't say the words as a question, but she knew it was one. "I've told no one my past," she said in a low voice. "Not the whole sordid story."

"Perhaps if you do tell someone, the burden will lessen." His warmth was taking the chill off the evening. "Cassie, you know everything of importance about me, and I know so little about you." He stroked his hand down her right arm. "Only that you are kind, sensual, dangerous, and fearsomely competent."

She almost laughed at his list, but her smile faded. She'd locked the past away for so long that it was hard to imagine speaking. Yet he was right. He knew little about her while she'd seen vulnerabilities of his that no one else ever would.

She'd spoken truly when she told Rob that he and she were both too self-sufficient, too unwilling to need or be needed. Her relationship with Grey was different, and much of the reason for that was because he'd been willing to let her see his pain and fears and weaknesses. She owed him the same.

"Very well," she said wearily as she moved out of his embrace. "But this will take time. If you open the door on the left side of the wardrobe, you should find various drinks to soothe the savage agent."

Grey whistled when he opened the door and saw shelves of bottles and glasses. "Kirkland knows how to make guests feel welcome. What would you like?"

If she drank brandy, she'd pass out before she got through her story. "Port."

"Then port you shall have." As he pulled out the bottle, she folded into a chair and wondered bleakly if she was capable of unveiling the shadows of her past.

But if she could tell anyone, it was Grey. He'd also lived seasons in hell.

Chapter 28

When Grey handed Cassie the glass of wine, she asked, "Where should I start?"

"At the beginning, of course." He knelt to start the fire laid on the hearth, then settled in the chair opposite her, close enough to touch. The firelight burnished his bright hair and sculpted the strong planes of his grave, patient face.

Cassie stared down into her wine, turning the glass around and around. "My father was English, my mother French. We made long visits to France to stay with her family. My nurse was a Frenchwoman because my mother wanted her children to speak French as well as we spoke English."

When the silence became too long, he asked, "Children?"

"An older brother and sister. I was the pampered youngest." She closed her eyes, remembering her father's warm hug, her mother's firm but gentle discipline. Her teasing big brother, her beautiful older sister, who had been excitedly planning for her debut.

"We were visiting France when the Reign of Terror began. The adults were concerned and the French relatives were debating whether they should leave the country. But most of the turmoil was in Paris and the Montclair estate was outside Reims, a safe distance away. There was time to decide the best course."

"But you knew better, young prophetess," he said when she fell silent again.

"I felt a terrible sense of approaching doom." Cassie sipped numbly at her port, needing the sweetness and the fire. "I played with local children and overheard their parents' talk. In the village, I saw radical speakers from Paris who ranted against the rich. I heard my mother's family accused of vague 'crimes against liberty.' I tried to explain all of this to my parents, but because I was only ten, they wouldn't listen. *They*

233

wouldn't listen!" Even after so many years, fury and anguish pierced her heart.

"It's a tragedy that they didn't listen to you," Grey said quietly. "But not a tragedy of your making."

Perhaps not, but she'd never stopped wondering if she'd spoken differently, given her warnings better, she would have been heard. "My father laughed and said soothing words and told me that in a month we'd be home again. By then, it was too late. The Terror had already reached out to destroy us."

Once more he coaxed her when she fell silent, asking, "How?"

"I didn't learn this till later, but a band of Parisian sans-culottes was traveling through the village on their way to join the army. They had a barrel of cheap spirits and shared their drink freely. The result was a great drunken riot with the sans-culottes whipping everyone into a frenzy. When their rage became murderous, they marched out to my mother's family home." She squeezed her eyes shut. "And . . . and they surrounded the house and set it afire."

He caught his breath. "Were you inside?"

Cassie shook her head. "Josette Maupin, a young nursery maid from the Montclair house, often took me to visit her niece, who was my age and a great friend of mine. While I played with my friend, Josette would flirt with her young man.

This wasn't in the village, but a farm in the opposite direction."

She drank more wine, her gaze on the past. "We went to the farm that day and stayed longer than usual. Coming back, we didn't know there was trouble until we saw smoke rising. We both began to run. When we reached the edge of the lawn, we saw the house ablaze and surrounded by howling men who shouted insults at the filthy aristos. Anyone who tried to escape the house was shot."

She swallowed hard, barely able to keep speaking. "My uncle tried to break out. He was carrying a child, my youngest cousin, I think. They were both killed. An old Montclair aunt jumped from an upper window to escape the flames. Even if she survived the fall, she couldn't have survived the beating after."

His face reflected her horror. "All of your family was inside?"

"*Oui*," she whispered, slipping into French like the child she'd been. "I started to run screaming toward the house, but Josette stopped me. She had friends in the house and was crying as hard as I was. We stayed there in the ornamental shrubbery clutching each other as the house burned. She said we should leave, but neither of us could move. We stayed and watched as the house burned and burned and burned. It lit up the night sky for hours."

"A funeral pyre," Grey said softly. "With luck,

many of the people inside died quickly of the smoke rather than the flames."

She hoped so. Dear God, she hoped so. "Finally the burning house collapsed into embers and we crept away. Josette took me to her family, promising that I'd be safe. My expensive garments were burned and I was given a plain gown that belonged to one of her nieces. Her family was . . . so kind."

That was Cassie's first experience of disguise, for not only was she given a peasant girl's gown, but Josette had used a color rinse to dull her distinctive hair.

"Josette married her sweetheart and moved to his family's farm, which was still farther away. I went with her under the name Caroline Maupin and was described as an orphaned cousin. Catherine St. Ives was dead."

"How long did you live as Caroline?"

"Almost six years. I never forgot that I was English and I planned to go back to England when the fighting finally ended, but most of the time I was just a girl busy with day-to-day life on a farm very like that of the Boyers. They treated me as a member of the family, for there was always work for a pair of strong hands." She finished her port and set the glass aside so she could rub her cold hands together.

Quietly Grey leaned forward and took her hands in his warm clasp. "What happened then?"

She drew a ragged breath. "There were people in the area who knew I was Catherine St. Ives, but they didn't report me because I was only a child. That protection disappeared when I grew up. I don't know what happened. Perhaps there was a promised reward for information about enemies of France. Perhaps I slighted a potential suitor.

"For whatever reason, I was reported to the local gendarmerie as an English spy." She gave a burst of near hysterical laughter. "I was *fifteen!* I lived on a farm and milked cows and made cheese. What did I know of spying?"

"Facts don't matter where there is fear and hatred," he said, his hands tightening over hers. "You were arrested?"

"In the village square on market day. I was selling cheese and eggs." She drew a shuddering breath, barely able to speak, then spat out the words in a torrent. "I was taken to Reims, judged and condemned, raped by two guards, and thrown in a cell to rot."

"Dear God in heaven." Swearing in two languages, Grey scooped her from her chair and cradled her shaking body on his lap, his body the only warmth in a world of cold, bleak memory. "How did you escape?"

She buried her face against his shoulder, struggling not to dissolve into tears. If she started to cry, she feared she'd never stop.

"After a year or so, a new guard arrived who

rather fancied me. He'd talk through the grill in the door. When he was sober, he'd promise me special treatment if I was kind to him. When he was drunk, which was more common, he threatened to take what I wouldn't give him." His foul breath had seemed to fill the whole cell as he described all the things he wanted to do to her.

"I'd reply that I'd be sweet as marzipan if he'd let me out of the cell. He laughed at that. I knew his patience was running out, so one day I accepted his offer. He waited until it was after midnight, then came into my cell. I let him have his way with me." She gagged at the memory before finishing in a raw whisper, "When he was done and sweaty and half asleep, I killed him with his own knife and escaped."

Saturated by unbearable memories, she dissolved into wrenching, uncontrollable sobs. She was barely aware when Grey lifted her from his lap and transferred her to the bed. Lying alongside her, he wrapped his warm body around her cold, shaking limbs, her back tucked against his front as he murmured soothing words into her ear.

She cried until there were no more tears left and she felt as dry as dust. But as she finally fell into the sleep of utter exhaustion, she realized that in Grey's arms she felt safe for the first time since her father died.

• • •

Grey held Cassie close as the last light faded from the sky and the fire burned down into embers. His muscles were stiff from not moving, but he didn't want to disturb her. Didn't ever want to let her go.

He'd taken her strength for granted, drawing on it as if she had limitless reserves. He never once thought of how that strength had to be hard won. He was a selfish fool.

Finally, she stirred in his arms. "How are you?" he asked softly.

"Water?" she asked for in an almost inaudible whisper.

He rose and fumbled his way across the room. After lighting a lamp, he filled a glass with water from the pitcher and carried it to the bed, then raised her to a sitting position so she could drink. When she'd emptied the glass, she lay back on the pillows again, dark shadows under her bleak eyes.

Since the room was cold, he rebuilt the fire. Then he found a folded blanket in the wardrobe and spread it over her. Sitting on the edge of the bed, he stroked her back. She looked like a crumpled child, not a supremely capable woman. "I'm sorry I pressed you to talk about your past."

"I'm not sorry," she said unexpectedly. "Speaking of what happened released some of the pain. Put more distance between then and now."

"Then I'm glad you told me." Though her memories would give him nightmares. "Some-

239

times I'm ashamed of my sex. You've been treated abominably by men."

"Yes, but I've also been treated very well by other men. Kirkland has been a combination of friend and brother, almost a father sometimes. There have been others." She sighed. "Women can also behave very badly."

"I'm amazed you will allow any man to touch you." His hand came to rest on the curve of her hip. "Grateful, but amazed."

"I had a craving for touch just as you did." She laid her hand on his. "It took a long time, but I found that with a man I trusted, I could tolerate the intimacy because I needed the warmth. With time and kindness, I came to enjoy the intimacy as well."

He looked at her tired eyes, realizing that there were mysteries in her past that he'd never know. That he had no need, or right, to know. Softly he said, "You are the most remarkable woman I've ever known."

"Merely good at surviving." Her lips curved in the faintest hint of a smile. "I was once told that I didn't have a shred of feminine delicacy."

Grey was surprised into a laugh. "I hope you took it as a compliment. How did you find Kirkland?"

"I wanted to return to England, and since there was no legal way to cross the channel, I looked for a cooperative smuggler," she explained. "It took time. I worked at different jobs along the coast, usually as a barmaid, until eventually I found Marie.

"When we came to trust each other, I told her I wanted to go to England and learn to become a spy against Napoleon. After she discussed me with her brother, Pierre delivered me to the Nashes in England on his next crossing. They sent me on to Kirkland, and three days later I was in London telling him he needed me as an agent."

"And he was wise enough to take you on." Grey studied her weary face. He'd thought her plain when he first saw her, but he had long since stopped judging her appearance. She was simply Cassie, unique and unforgettable. A woman who made him feel both desire and tenderness. "Are you hungry?"

She frowned. "I do believe I am."

He rose from the bed. "I'll find my way down to the kitchen and steal some food."

"No need to steal. There will be soup on the hob and cold meats and cheeses and bread in the pantry. If Mrs. Powell is there, she'll flirt with you."

"I should hope so." He ventured a smile. "I shouldn't like to think I've lost my touch. I'll bring up a tray, we'll eat, we'll sleep properly, by which I mean not fully dressed, and tomorrow we'll decide how to amuse ourselves in London."

"I shall like that." She caught his hand, her gaze

241

intense. "But before we sleep, I want you to help me forget, if only for a little while."

He never received a greater honor in his life. He suspected he never would. "It shall be as you wish, my lady vixen. Tonight we give each other the gift of forgetting." He kissed her hand before reluctantly releasing it. "And tomorrow, we will each be another day further from our demons."

Chapter 29

Cassie woke with a smile the next morning, Grey's golden head on her breast, and his arm around her waist. He'd done his generous, passionate best to separate her from her tormented memories, and he'd succeeded. She felt lighter and freer than she had since her childhood. The past couldn't be altered, but now it felt more like . . . the past.

Their night hadn't involved large amounts of sleep, but Cassie and Grey were both in a good mood for carefree roaming across London. The sun had even come out for them, which Cassie privately thought a good omen.

They set off early to nearby Covent Garden market. There they drank steaming hot tea and ate sweet buns from a stall while they watched carts of fresh foods rattle by to feed the city. The bustle was cheerful, the scents of vegetables and early flowers a pleasant contrast to the usual city smells. Spring was arriving, and the market grew steadily busier and brighter.

When they'd seen enough of the market, they boarded the plain carriage Kirkland had provided. The driver drove them west through the city by a twisting route that took the coach past many of London's great landmarks, from churches and palaces to the quiet squares of wealthy residential Mayfair.

As he gazed at buildings lining the Strand, Grey said, "I've ridden or walked down here countless times, yet it seems new and wonderful all over again. The Strand reminds me that I've come home. I've always loved London."

"Then you've come to the right place," Cassie said with a smile. "I know a pleasant waterside tavern down in Chelsea. I thought we might dismiss the carriage and eat very English food at the tavern, then hire a boat to take us downriver again."

"I like that idea." He looked thoughtful. "I think I'll ask the driver to take us past Costain House to see if the knocker's up and my family is in town."

"If they're in residence, will you want to climb the steps and rap on the door?" she asked. "Return of the prodigal?"

His face shuttered. "Not yet."

The knocker at Costain House wasn't up, which spared Grey any second thoughts, but Cassie thought it was progress that he was interested in

243

his parents' whereabouts. After traveling through Mayfair, they headed down to Chelsea, where they consumed good British ale and hot meat pies with flaky crusts.

As Grey finished his third pie, he said, "If I had any doubts, this beef and onion pie would prove I'm home." He brushed crumbs from his lap. "I'm looking forward to seeing the city from the water."

"If you like, tomorrow we can go east to the Tower of London and the great shipping docks." Cassie got to her feet, feeling full and satisfied. "What do you think of that skiff down there? The one painted yellow."

"The boatman looks sober, and I like the cheerful color," Grey replied. "Let's see what outrageous amount he'll try to charge us."

The amount quoted was indeed outrageous, but it didn't take long to bargain down to a rate that satisfied everyone. As the boat skimmed along the river, Grey said, "Much more comfortable than the last boat ride we took."

"So true." Cassie shuddered at the memory of their fraught journey across the channel. "Look, here comes a chicken boat!"

They sailed by a dinghy filled with cages of screeching, indignant chickens. A small red feather blew into Cassie's hair. Grey removed it and tucked it in his pocket, saying playfully, "A token of my lady! I shall cherish this chicken feather forever."

The comment dimmed Cassie's mood a little as she wondered if he actually would keep the silly feather. Probably not. She didn't think she'd leave many traces in his life. No matter. They were enjoying a lovely day now.

After the boatman set them off, they walked the rest of the way back to Exeter Street. As Cassie pulled out her key, Grey said, "I'm tired and looking forward to dinner and a quiet evening."

She guessed that being around so many people had caused the fatigue. "You did well," she said as she inserted the key in the lock. "You didn't run screaming once."

"Male pride is returning," he explained. "The desire to run screaming is surpassed by my desire not to look like a complete coward in front of a lovely woman."

She rolled her eyes. "Your gilded tongue has certainly recovered."

They were both chuckling as they entered the foyer. The door that led to the drawing room on the right was open, and Cassie heard a familiar female voice inside. Pleased, she called, "Kiri, is that you?"

"Cassie!" Dark haired and stunning, Lady Kiri Lawford emerged from the drawing room and enveloped Cassie in a hug. "Since we're going to the theater and were in the neighborhood, I decided to drop by some new perfumes for when

245

you returned, but I didn't expect to see you. I'm so glad you are safely home again!"

Cassie laughed and hugged her friend with care, since Kiri was dressed in a dashing green evening gown. "I am a woman of mystery, my movements never to be predicted." Then she registered the fact that Kiri had said "we."

"I'm glad to see you've cheated the devil again, Cassie," a deep voice said.

Cassie looked over Kiri's shoulder as a tall, powerfully built man entered the foyer from the drawing room. Damian Mackenzie was smiling and more than handsome in formal evening wear.

Cassie's first reaction was pleasure. She always enjoyed Mackenzie, and it was hardly surprising to see him with his new wife.

Her second reaction was, *Damnation!* But it was too late for retreat. Mac's gaze moved behind her and he stopped dead. "Ye gods, is that you, Wyndham?" he breathed. "Or am I hallucinating?"

Even without looking, Cassie sensed Grey tensing, but his voice was steady as he stepped forward. "It's early in the evening for hallucinations, Mac." He offered his hand. "So I think I must be real."

Mackenzie's face lit up. "Kirkland would never admit you were dead, and damned if he wasn't right again." Exuberantly he seized Grey's hand in both of his. "I've never been so glad to be wrong in my life!"

Seeing Grey next to Mackenzie's broad, athletic figure made Cassie realize how thin Grey still was. But he smiled with genuine pleasure as he shook Mac's hand. "I'm rather pleased about it, too." He bowed to Kiri. "And surely this magnificent creature is your wife, Ashton's sister?"

"You're as good at flattery as Mackenzie, Lord Wyndham." Kiri's shrewd gaze moved from Grey to Cassie. "You must be tired, so we won't keep you with questions about what happened." She glanced at her husband. "We need to be on our way to the theater. Cassie, may I call on you tomorrow to catch up on the gossip?"

"I'd love to see you, but not before midafternoon since we'll be out earlier." Cassie caught her friend's gaze. "Don't tell anyone we're back."

"So you're not yet officially returned, Wyndham?" Mackenzie commented. "I imagine adjusting to London takes time after ten years abroad."

"Especially after ten years in prison," Grey said tersely. He and Cassie had discussed what he would say about his long absence, and he'd decided to keep the explanation as simple as possible. Kiri and Mac were in the inner circle who might be told more, but the details could wait.

"Then we'll not speak of it until the miracle is official." Mac hesitated. "Is there any single-sentence explanation you can give to assuage my curiosity?"

Grey's mouth twisted. "I was a fool, and paid for it with ten years of my life."

"Was a woman involved?" When Grey nodded, Mackenzie said, "Some night when we're drunk enough, I'll tell you how being foolish about a woman got me flogged, almost hanged, and tossed out of the army."

Grey's smile turned genuine. "Good to know I'm not alone in my foolishness."

Kiri shot her husband a curious glance. Cassie had the sense that Kiri knew the story, but was surprised that Mac was willing to talk about it. Mackenzie must have guessed that sharing his failings would make his old friend feel better.

Mac laid his hand on the small of Kiri's back to usher her out. "If there is anything I might do to ease your return, Wyndham, Cassie knows where to find me."

When they were gone, Grey wrapped his arm around Cassie and drew her close. "Obviously this house is not as private as you and Kirkland thought. I wonder what old schoolmate will pop in next?"

"I didn't give enough thought to the fact that this is a center for Kirkland's work," Cassie said apologetically. "I can't think of any other old schoolmates who might appear, but that may be lack of imagination on my part."

"Will Mackenzie or Lady Kiri tell others that I've returned from the dead?"

She shook her head vehemently. "Absolutely not. The first thing Kirkland's agents learn is discretion."

"That gorgeous creature Mac married is another agent?" Grey asked, surprised, as they headed up the stairs side by side. "For that matter, I didn't know that Mackenzie dabbled in the murky undercurrents of intelligence work."

"That wasn't very discreet of me to reveal that," Cassie said ruefully. "Though you would have figured it out quickly enough."

"Lady Kiri was an unlikely visitor to a spy house," Grey agreed. He was looking drained by the day's activities.

"A pity so many people liked you," she said as she opened the door. "It makes for very energetic celebrations of your return to life."

Grey's expression eased. "Mackenzie was always energetic. Rather like a large and likable puppy. Now that I see Mac again, I realize that there must have been more going on under his surface than I realized when I was a callow youth."

"Isn't that true for everyone?" She unfastened her cloak. "More under the surface than is visible?"

"Not me. I was entirely on the surface." He hung their cloaks in his wardrobe. "No more substance than a sparrow."

"Not a sparrow. A glittering golden finch."

He laughed. "I am correctly classified. Thank you, Catherine."

His brows drew together when he saw her shiver at his use of her real name. "I won't call you Catherine if it bothers you. I've always thought it a lovely name, and it suits you. But if it calls up too much pain . . ."

"The name does call up deep feelings, but it's not all pain." She considered. "I wouldn't want the whole world to call me Catherine, but I don't mind if you do sometimes."

"Very well, Catherine." He brushed a kiss on her hair. "Cassandra. Cassie. The names suit different aspects of your personality."

She narrowed her eyes and said mysteriously, "I am a spy, a woman of a thousand disguises. With whom will you sleep tonight?"

Laughing, he drew her into his arms. "All of you!"

Chapter 30

Cassie and Grey were discussing a boat ride down to Greenwich when Kirkland appeared to ruin their breakfast. "What's wrong?" Cassie asked as soon as she saw him.

"Am I that obvious?" he said tiredly.

Cassie's "Yes" clashed with Grey's "No."

"I'm glad I can still mystify some people."

Kirkland accepted the cup of steaming tea that Cassie poured for him. After a deep swallow, he said, "I'm afraid I'm the bearer of bad news, Wyndham. I've just learned that your father is critically ill."

Grey's face paled. "At Summerhill?"

Kirkland nodded. "I don't know any details, but . . . I'm told his life is despaired of. You might want to reconsider visiting your family as soon as possible."

"I'll go tomorrow. Can you arrange a carriage?"

"I'll have one here first thing in the morning."

Grey turned to Cassie, his gaze stark. "Will you come with me? I can't manage this on my own."

She gasped. "I can't go with you to your family estate!"

Grey caught her hand. "*Please,* Cassie! I need you."

"If you need support, take Kirkland." Cassie shot a burning glance at the other man. Wyndham was supposed to be Kirkland's project, not hers!

"It isn't me he needs, Cassie. But you've already done more than enough." Kirkland rose from the table. "I need to speak with the Powells, so I'll leave the two of you to sort this out."

"Tactful of Kirkland to let us argue in private," Cassie said after the door closed. "But the answer is the same. Taking your mistress to your family home would be scandalous under any conditions, much less when your father may be dying." Her

251

mouth tightened. "Nor will anyone believe a man like you with a woman like me."

Grey looked blank. "Why not?"

"Look at us! A gentleman and a washerwoman." Furiously she stood and yanked on his arm, pulling him to his feet so they could see their reflections in the mirror above the sideboard. Grey was not only strikingly handsome, but in an aristocratic way. Cassie looked like an aging peasant, not fit to be even his servant. "Unattractive men with money can easily find a beautiful woman, but handsome men with money don't choose plain, aging women."

He studied their images in the mirror. "Strange. I see a fractured man who can barely manage day to day, and a woman with the heart of a lion and more beauty than she allows the world to see."

She bit her lip, fighting an urge to weep. "You may believe that, but no one else will look at us as you do."

Turning from the mirror to her, he said, "I agree that you can't go as my mistress. That would be most improper. You must go as my fiancée."

Cassie thought she was beyond shock, but at that, her jaw dropped. "I told Kirkland that you weren't mad, but apparently I was wrong!"

He smiled. "When you're better dressed, no one will question us being together."

"But there isn't time for new clothing!" she said with exasperation as she thought of her wardrobe.

There wasn't a single item suitable for wearing at a nobleman's country estate. The plain dark clothing she kept here in London would have suited a middle-aged widow of modest means. Not a single garment could claim to be fashionable or flattering. "Old gowns from a rag shop will not turn me into a plausible fiancée and there's time for nothing else."

Ignoring her comment, he said earnestly, "You don't have to marry me. Why on earth would you want to? Just pretend to be my intended bride for a week or two until I've come to terms with my family. Then you can end the engagement and return to London."

"You don't know what you're asking." She shook her head, her throat tight. "My family was not of your rank, but I was raised to be a lady. I was a child when that life ended. I've lived as a farm girl, a prisoner, a peddler, a spy, a dozen other things. I would be as out of place at your home as that washerwoman."

"I don't believe that," he retorted. "You have played many roles convincingly, and this one you were born to. It will only be for a few days, a fortnight at most. I hate that you will be uncomfortable, but I know you can do this."

Perhaps. But the idea of acting as a lady terrified her, and pretending to be Grey's betrothed was even worse. "The risk is too great for you," she argued. "What if I want to become a countess and claim that the betrothal is real? You'd either be stuck with me or caught in a dreadful scandal."

"You wouldn't do that." His dark-edged eyes turned thoughtful. "Though I wouldn't object if you held me to it. I just can't imagine that you'd want to."

Not want to marry him? Dear God, even thinking of the possibility muddled her mind. The fact that he still needed her so much that he was willing to obliquely suggest marriage was the wickedest temptation she'd ever known.

But if she took advantage of his present weakness, they'd both regret it. "It would be so much easier if you'd just trust your family, Grey," she said, trying to sound calm and reasonable. "You don't need a stranger at Summerhill at such a difficult time."

"I don't need a stranger, but I do need you, Cassie," he said quietly. "And you promised not to leave me as long as I need you. I swear I'll never ask anything of you again, but please come with me. You were right that it will be difficult with my father's life in doubt. If . . . if the worst happens, a great deal of responsibility will come crashing down on me. I'm much less likely to break under the strain if you're with me."

She swore to herself, knowing that it had been a mistake to make such a sweeping promise. But she'd given him her word. Even if she hadn't, she couldn't abandon him now. "Very well, but I'll need to find some fashionable clothing very quickly."

A knock sounded on the door of the dining room. "Is it safe to come in?" Kirkland asked.

"Come in. The golden boy has prevailed again," Cassie said tartly. "I'll go with Wyndham to Summerhill."

"I'm glad you're willing," Kirkland said, relieved. "Tomorrow, not today?"

Grey nodded. "We need time to get ready. Also, the extra day allows time for a message to be sent to my mother so she'll know I'm coming. She can decide whether or not to tell my father. I wouldn't want to kill him from shock."

"I'll take care of it," Kirkland said. "What else can I do to help?"

"I'll need some more of your clothing." Grey grimaced. "Black. Just in case."

Kirkland nodded. "What do you need, Cassie?"

"Can you take me to Kiri Mackenzie's house when you leave?" Cassie asked. "She's the most fashionable woman I know, and I'm praying she can render me respectable by tomorrow."

"Of course. Anything else?"

Grey shook his head. "I'm going for a long walk so I can think myself into the proper state of mind."

Cassie's brow furrowed. "Shall I go with you?"

His gaze was hooded. "No, you need a wardrobe and I . . . need to be alone."

That made sense, given that they'd been together day and night since Castle Durand, but it felt strange not to be watching out for Grey. Kirkland, more pragmatic, pulled a sleek little pistol from under his coat and offered it to Grey. "I trust you remember how to use one of these?"

"I do." Grey studied the weapon without enthusiasm. "I suppose I could use this if necessary, but the real purpose is that you'll feel better knowing I'm armed."

"Exactly right," Kirkland said. "I'd also suggest a less expensive coat and hat."

"Disguising myself even in my native land," Grey murmured. He gave Cassie a swift kiss on the cheek. "Don't worry. I'll be fine."

She said lightly, "Can't I worry just a little?"

"If you find it entertaining."

Watching him go, Cassie thought wryly that if he got himself killed in the streets, at least she wouldn't have to go to Summerhill.

Impatiently Grey changed into a nondescript coat provided by Mr. Powell, added an equally shapeless hat, and headed east. He wanted to stretch his legs, see more of London. Pull his cracked self together so he could be the son who was needed at Summerhill.

And somewhere along the way, he wanted to find a good fight.

Cassie had never visited Mackenzie's house, and it proved to be a handsome building right next door to his club, Damian's. As she waited for a footman to announce her to Kiri, she studied the furnishings, seeing attractive Indian accents that must have been added by the new mistress of the house.

"Cassie, what a pleasure!" Lady Kiri swept into the entry hall and hugged her guest. "I was writing letters, very tedious. Much better to hear of your adventures!"

Cassie gave her bonnet and cloak to the footman and followed Kiri to the pleasant morning room, which included a desk with papers and pen. "Adventures can come later," Cassie said. "First I must throw myself on your mercy, for I'm in dire need of your services."

"Perfume? Of course." Kiri settled gracefully into the chair by her desk and gestured for Cassie to sit opposite.

"Much more than perfume is required," Cassie said grimly as she took the chair. "Tomorrow I must accompany Wyndham to his family seat in the guise of his betrothed, and I need to be transformed into someone whom he might plausibly wed."

Kiri's eyes widened. "You are to be a false fiancée? Why?"

Cassie explained tersely. When she was done,

Kiri said, "This is a difficult mission for many reasons, yes? Because this time it is more than playacting."

"You have put your finger on my uneasiness," Cassie said slowly. "I am too involved with Wyndham for this to be easy. Also . . ." She looked down at her knotted fingers and realized she was feeling an anxiety very different from the straightforward fear of death or imprisonment that was a constant threat in France.

"Also . . . ?" Kiri prompted gently.

"For the first time, I must enter the world I was born to, but lost," Cassie said haltingly. "I survived by accepting that that world was lost and moving forward, always forward. Now I must pretend to belong in that lost life, and the thought is . . . terrifying." Her throat closed.

"I'm trying to imagine myself in your situation, and I can't. But I see it would be deeply unnerving." Kiri's eyes narrowed. "Might this be easier if you look in the mirror and see a stranger instead of yourself? That would be more like playacting."

"Perhaps." Cassie bit her lip as she recognized another possibility. "I don't want to lie to Grey's family since he'll have to live with them, so I should use my real name. That way if an old aunt asks about my family, I can give a real answer rather than make something up and possibly be caught out."

Kiri noted her use of Grey's personal name without comment. "I can have cards printed for you today so you'll have them to support your role."

"You can get cards made in a day?" Cassie asked incredulously.

"There are many advantages to being daughter and sister to a duke," Kiri explained. "Here's pencil and paper. Write down what the cards should say."

Cassie wrote out her birth name for the first time in almost twenty years. "This feels strange. I am no longer Catherine St. Ives."

"Part of you is, despite all that has happened. It may not be a bad thing to become better acquainted with Catherine." Kiri's brows arched when she saw what Cassie had written. "Next, appearance. Can that hair coloring you use be washed out? Not only is the color ugly, but it dulls your hair."

"The color can be washed out with vinegar, but I don't want to go to my natural color." Cassie made a face. "It's a violent red that was the bane of my childhood. I was happy to have a reason to dye it brown. I haven't seen the original color since I was a child, and good riddance."

The color had worn off when she was in prison. After her escape, she'd worn a head scarf and avoided mirrors until she could make and apply a batch of the coloring.

"If you wish to create a role that is not you, what better place to start than with Catherine St. Ives's hair? It will have darkened over the years so it will be a less alarming shade of red now." Kiri made a note on her list. "Clothing. You will need at least two good day dresses, another for evening wear, and a riding habit. Plus the undergarments and shoes and cloaks and other accessories."

Cassie sighed. "Which will be impossible to obtain by tomorrow. At least, not clothing of the quality the role requires. Even more middling garments will be difficult on such short notice."

"Nonsense. My sister, Lucia, is close to you in size. I shall ask her to send over several gowns she can spare that will suit your coloring. I shall also summon the splendid Madame Hélier, modiste for all the women in my family. She may have partially completed garments that would suit you, and she has seamstresses who can do quick alterations." Kiri grinned. "This will be such fun!"

"I'll wager you liked playing with dolls when you were a girl," Cassie said dryly.

"Indeed I did. I turned them into beautiful warrior queens."

Cassie had no trouble imagining that. "Like you? But I am neither beautiful nor a warrior queen."

Kiri's eyes gleamed. "You will be when I'm finished with you."

Cassie rolled her eyes. "I'm beginning to think coming here was a mistake."

"I promise you'll thank me for it later." Kiri's eyes narrowed. "Might you be ready to wear the perfume I created for you?"

Cassie's heart clutched as she thought of roses and frankincense, lost dreams and darkest night. Was she ready for that much truth? Haltingly she said, "Perhaps . . . I am."

"Truly you will not regret it," her friend said quietly. "Now let me send off these notes to summon my troops, and then we'll go to work on that hair!"

Chapter 31

Grey headed east across London at a ground-eating pace. He needed to burn off the seething anxiety induced by his imminent return to his family home.

After years of captivity and weeks of travel by horse, boat, and carriage, it felt good to stretch his legs. He also discovered a new kind of freedom in having no one know where he was.

To his surprise, it even felt good to be alone. After ten years of solitary confinement, he'd been hungry for human contact only to find that crowds sent him into a flat panic. Only with Cassie was he truly comfortable, though he could manage a few friends like Père Laurent or Lady Agnes or Kirkland.

He hoped he'd be able to retrieve Régine soon.

He'd need her company because soon he wouldn't have Cassie. The thought of living without her was a pain so deep he didn't have words to describe it. But even her superb kindness couldn't hide her impatience to be free of her nursemaid duties so she could return to her real work.

He was a little ashamed of invoking her promise to stay with him as long as she was needed so that she'd come with him to Summerhill. Though not ashamed enough to wish he hadn't done it.

With his father critically ill, of course he must return home. The prospect had been paralyzing even before he'd learned of his father's illness. Now it was worse.

He didn't doubt that they'd welcome him. The problem was facing them. Even more than his lifelong friends, his family had expectations and memories of him. They were the people he'd hurt the most. He couldn't bear the thought of hurting them more by being so different from what they remembered.

The situation was made much more difficult by his father's critical illness. If Lord Costain died . . .

Grey shuddered, not wanting to think of it.

He suspected that once his family's initial shock was over and all the explanations had been made, he'd be able to manage, with Cassie's help. Then he'd prepare himself for the even more devastating challenge of saying goodbye to her.

He set aside his worries about returning home

and concentrated on London. He'd reached the busy stretch of the Thames called the Pool of London, which stretched east from London Bridge. There was a forest of masts from the sailing ships moored two and three deep at the public quays. Sailors of many nations walked the streets and exotic scents and accents overlaid the usual smells of London.

He found that the crowds didn't bother him much as long as he stayed on the edges. Apparently his fear of crowds was diminishing.

He paced along the quays, studying the ships. Once he'd dreamed of boarding such a vessel and sailing to distant lands. France had been his first venture from England's shores. It had not turned out well.

He wondered if he'd ever regain that desire to travel. At the moment, the idea of never setting foot out of Great Britain was immensely appealing.

He walked and explored for hours. It was well into the afternoon before he realized that he really should eat. He was walking past a tavern called the Three Ships, which seemed as good a place as any. Grey entered, inhaling the tang of hops and good English ale mixed with the scent of fish and meat and baking. England. Home.

Eight or ten men were clustered in small groups in the taproom. Stevedores by the look of them. Kirkland had given Grey cash to tide him over until he had his affairs sorted out. In a mood of reckless generosity, Grey called to the landlord, "I'm just back to England after too many years abroad, so I'll stand every man here a drink. Including one for you, sir." He laid coins on the counter.

That raised a murmur of approval from the other patrons. A grizzled older man raised his refilled tankard. "Here's to your health, sir, and welcome home!"

Most of the customers collected their drinks with thanks, but good will wasn't universal. A particularly burly stevedore sneered, "What's a flash cove like you doing in our tavern?"

So much for the disguising effects of a shapeless coat and hat. "Buying beer for my fellow Englishmen," Grey said mildly. "Would you like one?"

The man spat. "I don't need nuthin' from a so-called gentleman like you."

"What kind of fool doesn't want free beer, Ned?" the grizzled man asked indignantly. "I'm happy to drink the gentleman's health."

The significant glance he cast at his tankard had Grey putting more coins on the bar. "Seconds all around for those who want them."

This suited everyone except Ned. He swaggered up to Grey, smelling like sour gin. "Don't need you here, puttin' on your airs!"

Using his most supercilious voice, Grey

drawled, "I do believe that you are looking for a fight. Am I correct?"

"Bloody right I am!" Ned swung a furious punch.

Fierce joy coursed through Grey's veins. He'd been spoiling to smash his fists into someone, and finally his opportunity had arrived.

He dodged to one side so he wouldn't be trapped against the bar. Ned was taller and three or four stones heavier, but his fighting was based on strength, not skill. Grey easily blocked or avoided his punches while landing several good hits himself.

When Ned swung a particularly wild blow and became unbalanced, Grey caught his wrist, then flipped the man onto his back. Ned landed with a mighty "Ooof!"

"Take it outside!" the landlord barked.

Grey balanced lightly on his toes, ready to move in any direction. "Had enough?"

"No, by God!" The stevedore lurched to his feet. "No skinny gent like you can lick Ned Brown!"

"Then let us move outside." Grey made a sweeping bow that he knew would irritate the stevedore, then exited before Ned could attack again.

They resumed their fight outside on the windy street. The patrons from the Three Ships followed, beers in hand and placing bets on the outcome. Ned was apparently a well-regarded street fighter and he was favored at first over the "skinny gent."

But Grey had been trained well at Westerfield, where sparring with other boys was the favorite sport. Later he'd had boxing lessons at Jackson's Saloon before traveling to France. His muscles remembered the feints, strikes, and kicks.

He reminded himself that this was no fight to the death, just a tavern brawl as an outlet for his churning emotions. Though he was careful not to cause real damage, he gloried in the physical release.

Ned managed to connect with a few glancing blows that would leave bruises, including one across Grey's cheek, but Grey was faster and more agile. When Ned started wheezing dangerously, Grey decided it was time to end the brawl.

He threw Ned onto his belly, put a knee in the stevedore's back and twisted the man's arm up behind his back. "Well fought, sir!" he panted. "Shall I break your arm, or buy you a drink in the Three Ships?"

After a startled pause, Ned chuckled hoarsely. "You're the damnedest fellow, but you sure as bloody hell can fight. I'll go for the drink."

"You're likely right about the damned part." Grey released Ned. When the big man got up, the two of them led the parade back into the tavern.

The older man asked, "Where were you in foreign parts?"

"France." Grey took a swig of ale, testing how

he felt about saying more. Since these men were strangers, he decided to continue. "Ten bloody years in a French prison."

The grizzled man gave a low whistle. "No wonder you're so glad to get home! Here's to a healthy future here in England!"

Even Ned drank to that. Grey bought several more rounds, downing his share. He'd always been good at talking to men from every station in life, and he found that he hadn't lost the knack.

When his head started feeling disconnected from his body, it was time to leave. Evening was coming and he wanted to get back to Cassie. He emptied his tankard, then called out, "My thanks to you gentlemen for helping me celebrate my homecoming."

He left the tavern followed by a chorus of invitations to return to the Three Ships any time. Maybe he'd do that, too. It had all been blessedly uncomplicated.

Summerhill would not be uncomplicated.

Grey took the direct route home, but it was nearly dark when he reached Exeter Street. Even though his feet were sore, he was whistling and pleased with life. By most standards, it had been a wasted day—but he felt better able to face Summerhill.

His step quickened as he went up the steps to the front door. Surely Cassie would be back by now.

It was absurd to yearn for her company so much when it had been only a few hours, but the world felt right when she was near.

He had to fumble a bit to find the key to the house. He probably should have stopped a drink or two earlier. He finally managed to open the door and he stepped into the lamp-lit foyer.

Grey was removing his coat when he heard light steps coming down the staircase. The steps sounded like Cassie's, so he looked up hopefully, but the woman was a stranger.

Granted, she was a stunner, with bright auburn hair and a splendid figure. Even though Grey was out of touch with current fashion, he recognized that the elegant blue-green gown had to have come from one of London's best modistes. It took talent to make a woman look ladylike and deeply provocative at the same time.

She must be one of Kirkland's agents. If so, that décolletage made clear how she coaxed information from the enemy. Trying not to stare too obviously at her neckline, he bowed as well as he could without falling over. "Good evening, mademoiselle."

She stopped three steps from the bottom of the stairs and said in an icily aristocratic voice, "I beg your pardon, sir, but have we been introduced?"

That voice . . .

He gasped. The perfect height and proportions, the delicate, vulnerable features, the blue eyes with unknowable depths. "Cassie?" he asked incredulously.

"I'm surprised you recognized me, given where you were looking," she said with tart amusement.

"Cassie." He moved forward and embraced her. Since she was standing on the stairs, his arms went around her waist and he rested his head on the delicious softness of her breasts. Lilac and rose blossoms and other scents he couldn't identify, all of them adding up to make her smell even more like Cassie. "I've missed you."

Smiling, she looped her arms around his neck. "It's only been a few hours."

"Too many hours." He slid one hand over her perfectly curved backside. Yes, everything was just as it ought to be.

"What do you think of my fine feathers?" she asked shyly.

He pulled back and surveyed her from bright hair to slipper-shod feet, missing nothing in between. "I have an intense desire to make mad, passionate love to you," he said with complete sincerity.

"You do that even when I look like a washerwoman." Her brow furrowed. "Seriously, do I look fit to be your fiancée?"

Seeing her concern, he forced himself to concentrate. Perhaps some would not call her a beauty because she didn't have classically perfect features and that spectacular red hair looked distinctly naughty. But she was allowing her strength and warmth and intelligence to show, and to him, she was the most beautiful woman he'd ever seen.

Beautiful, and more. "You are every inch a refined lady," he said seriously. "You've always been beautiful. Letting the world see that beauty must make you feel more confident, and that makes you even more beautiful. But I am a bit jealous because now everyone will see you as I do."

"I'm glad I look sufficiently ladylike." She brushed her fingers through his hair, very much his Cassie despite her new appearance. "Though otherwise you're not making a lot of sense, and you smell of beer. Are you drunk?"

"Yes," he said meekly.

She touched his bruised cheek. "Were you in a fight?"

"Yes. But I won."

"What did you win?"

"The right to buy the fellow a beer."

"I suppose that makes sense to males." Her laughter was soft. "Are you happy?"

He sighed and pulled her closer. Lovely décolletage. Lovely gown. He wanted to take it off her. "Yes. Especially now that you're here. Would you like to go upstairs so I can make mad, passionate love to you?"

"Later, perhaps, but at the moment, I wish to feed another appetite," she said. "The Powells serve supper to anyone in residence and Kirkland intended to stop by if he had time. Join me, for you need some food and some strong coffee."

"I expect you're right. I believe that I forgot to eat."

"It's good that you're a happy drunk rather than a mean one." She descended the last few steps. "My lord, will you give me your arm to take me into dinner?"

"Let me see if I remember how to be gentlemanly." He made a sweeping bow without falling over, then straightened and offered his arm. "If you would do me the honor . . ."

As she stepped toward him, he stroked her hair, enjoying the silkiness and bounce. The bright auburn had to be natural, for it suited her complexion much better than the dull brown. "How did you manage to transform yourself so quickly?"

"Kiri did it all. I just obeyed orders. Kiri's sister is near my size and she contributed several lovely gowns. Kiri's own modiste came personally with some partially made up garments, plus seamstresses for instant alterations. Kiri even managed to get cards engraved and printed for me." She pulled a card from her dainty little reticule and handed it to Grey. "The ink is still damp, but they look very proper."

"I'm surprised to see you carrying a purse too small to conceal a weapon," he remarked as he took the card.

"I've weapons concealed elsewhere," she assured him, amusement in her eyes.

He glanced at the card, then read it again, startled. "The Honourable Catherine St. Ives. Your father was a peer? You've always implied that you're from a lower order of society. In fact, you said your family was not the rank of mine."

She shrugged. "My father was a mere baron, the third Lord St. Ives. We're merchant stock, not old and prestigious and wealthy like the earldom of Costain."

"Close enough. You come of noble blood." It was another piece of the puzzle that was Cassie Fox. Or rather, Catherine St. Ives. Returning to her childhood station after spending a lifetime as peasant and peddler had to be . . . supremely disorienting.

"That meant nothing when I was cleaning out chicken coops in France," she said dryly. "And it means even less now."

"Your brother would have been the heir," he said. "Who inherited instead? Or were there no heirs so the title went into abeyance?"

"My father had a younger brother, and he had three sons. The two oldest were around my age." She made a dismissive gesture. "There was no shortage of heirs."

"Haven't you ever written your cousins?" he asked. "Surely they would be glad to know that you survived."

"Catherine St. Ives *died,*" she said impatiently. "She would have stayed dead except that resurrecting her for the next week or two will make me a more convincing fiancée. When I leave Summerhill, she will return to her French grave, this time for good." She turned on her heel. "Enough of this nonsense. I'm hungry."

As she headed toward the dining room, Grey slipped the card into his pocket. She might not be interested in her family, but he was. He'd have a word with Kirkland.

He caught up with her and offered his arm again. She laid her hand lightly on his forearm and they progressed to the dining room as if they were entering a grand ball. Kirkland, Mr. and Mrs. Powell, and a nondescript young woman Grey hadn't met were eating family style around the table.

Everyone glanced up as Grey and Cassie entered. There was a stunned silence as everyone, particularly the men, stared at Cassie.

Kirkland was first to rise to his feet. "Miss Fox." He inclined his head and permitted himself a small smile. "I always knew you were brilliant at disguise, but I didn't recognize that your greatest disguise was concealing your natural beauty."

"Flatterer," she said without heat. "The credit goes to Lady Kiri and the helpers she summoned to transform me." As Grey pulled out a chair for her, she continued, "I am not Cassandra Fox at the moment. I decided using my birth name will best suit this particular charade." She gave Kirkland a card.

His face became very still. "Your father was the third Lord St. Ives?"

She nodded, her expression opaque.

When she didn't say more, Kirkland continued, "Since you're traveling to Dorset as a lady, you need a maid, so one of my associates will take that role." He gestured to the girl next to him. "Miss St. Ives, may I present Miss Hazel Wilson? I think you'll find that she has the usual skills of a lady's maid's, and a few more as well."

"I'm pleased to meet you, Miss Wilson," Cassie said formally. "Thank you for taking this position on such short notice."

"Call me Hazel, miss," the girl said with a London accent. She stood and curtsied. She had brown hair and a pleasant if unremarkable face. Her blue eyes showed humor and intelligence. "This would be Lord Wyndham, I presume?"

Grey bowed with the respect due one of Kirkland's agents. "Indeed I am, Hazel. Thank you for your willingness to leave London for the wilds of Dorsetshire."

Hazel bobbed her head. "I look forward to dressing your beautiful hair, miss!"

Cassie blushed. "I hated my red hair when I was a girl. I was called the Carrot."

"Any girls who teased you then are now envious, and the boys will be languishing for your smiles," Grey said as he took his own seat.

"Your gilded tongue is in good working order," she said with amusement.

"He's right, miss!" Mr. Powell blurted out.

"I think the lass is more interested in shepherd's pie than flattery," Mrs. Powell said, giving her husband a stern glance. "If you pass your plates, I'll fill 'em up."

Grey and Cassie obeyed. As he smelled the steaming-hot pie, Grey realized he would enjoy this common fare more than the elaborate meals served in his parents' homes.

Though his appearance was once more that of a gentleman, he was a very long way from the young Lord Wyndham who had left Summerhill ten years earlier.

Chapter 32

London was dark when they left the next morning. The journey from London to Summerhill could be made in a day if the roads were dry, but it was a long day with numerous changes of horses. Cassie and Hazel spoke occasionally, but Grey mostly gazed out the window, disinclined to talk as he watched the familiar landscape go by.

How often had he made this journey? Very often. He knew every town and village, every posting inn, and he'd known a few friendly barmaids on this route as well.

He liked seeing landmarks like the spire of Salisbury Cathedral, but his tension grew with every mile. If his father died when Grey might have been there at the end if he hadn't taken an extra day to mentally prepare for the trip . . .

But he and Cassie had needed that day in different ways, and his family would benefit by the advance notice of Grey's return from the dead. Though his mother might choose to keep the news from his father, she would tell Peter and Elizabeth. They must be grown by now, but in his mind, they were still children.

His family would welcome him even if they were also disappointed in him. Once he got beyond the first few days, it would be all right. So he told himself repeatedly. In between prayers for his father's survival.

It was dark again by the time they finally reached the estate. As the carriage turned in at the gate, his heart was pounding and he realized he was clenching Cassie's hand. *Summerhill, Summerhill, Summerhill!*

The long, tree-lined drive up to the house wordlessly declared the long history of Costain wealth and power. He took comfort in the thought that he was merely one slightly bent twig on an otherwise healthy family tree.

As the carriage halted under the porte cochere

on the east side of the house, Grey said tersely, "This house is fairly new, less than a hundred years old. Far more comfortable than the rambling original building."

"I'll take comfort over historic drafts any day," Cassie said lightly as he helped her from the carriage. He felt tension in her gloved hand, but she concealed it well.

Now that she wanted to look fashionable, she had the superb French sense of style. She looked every inch the sort of aristocratic beauty a man like him would be expected to marry. Yet she was so much more.

"*Courage, mon enfant,*" she whispered in French under her breath.

"And you also, *mon petit chou,*" he whispered back. "At least here our lives aren't threatened. Only our pride and sanity."

Her face brightened with suppressed laughter. "Since you put it like that . . ." She took his arm and they walked to the door, where he wielded the massive brass knocker. It was shaped like a dolphin, a sign of the sea that lay on the other side of the hill.

There was a long wait and Grey knocked again, all too aware that the death of the master of the house would cause this kind of disruption. Finally, the door was opened by a flushed young housemaid. Her gaze passed over the visitors with no recognition beyond seeing that they were obviously well born. She bobbed a somewhat ragged curtsy. "Are you expected, sir? Madame?"

"We are," Grey replied. "Lady Costain has been notified of our visit. Please tell her we have arrived."

"Very good, sir. If you'll wait in the small salon just over here, I'll inform her ladyship." The girl bobbed another quick curtsy and darted off without asking his name.

The salon was cold and ill lit. Too restless to sit, Grey took the tinderbox from the mantel and started a fire. "Housekeeping standards have slipped," he said. "That child has not been well trained."

"Obviously receiving guests is not her usual job." Reassuringly composed, Cassie settled on a brocade-covered chair.

He straightened as the fire caught and small flames appeared. "Do you think that means my father has . . ." His throat closed and he couldn't continue.

"There is no reason to believe he's gone," she said swiftly. "And no point in worrying. We'll find out soon enough."

Another wait. Grey was tempted to go in search of his mother, but before the last of his patience vanished, the door swung open and he heard her voice saying, "You should have taken their names, child!"

Lady Costain swept into the room, followed by the maid. She was still tall, blond, and beautiful though she looked strained, as if she'd been carrying too many burdens.

Grey had believed he'd never see her again, and the fact that she was *here, now,* paralyzed him. Half afraid she was a dream and would disappear, he managed to whisper, "Mother?"

She said brusquely, "My apologies for . . ." Her gaze reached Grey and she stopped dead in her tracks. Color drained from her face. "No, it's not possible!" she whispered. Then she crumpled to the floor in a dead faint.

"Mother!" Horrified, Grey rushed to her side and dropped to his knees, cradling her in his arms. "Mother, it really is me, not a ghost!"

"Bring smelling salts quickly," Cassie ordered the housemaid. "Are there any other members of the family available?"

"Lord Wyndham is here," the girl replied.

Lord Wyndham? Peter must have assumed the title when Grey had been given up for dead. Grey snapped, "Send him here immediately. Tell him his mother is ill."

Tenderly he carefully lifted his mother onto the sofa, then spread a knitted knee robe over her. She looked so tired, with lines in her face that hadn't been there ten years before. But it really was her. His wry, patient, loving mother. He blinked back tears.

Lady Costain's eyes fluttered open to see Grey bent over. She made a choked sound and raised a shaking hand to touch his cheek. "You . . . you're real?"

He caught her hand and held it. "I am." A pulse beat hard in his throat. "Didn't you get the message Lord Kirkland sent yesterday? I wanted to avoid shocking everyone like this."

Her gaze searched his face, as hungry as his. "A message arrived, but I didn't bother to open it. He writes now and then to say he has found no information about you, but continues to search. With your father ill, I couldn't be bothered to read that."

"So much for my good intentions," he said ruefully as he helped her sit up. "I'm sorry, I wanted to spare you this."

"When I saw you here, I . . . I had the horrible superstitious thought that you were a ghost come to guide your father to heaven." She pulled him into a hug as tears ran down her cheeks. "Of all the times to ignore a message! Oh, Grey, Grey!"

Pounding feet could be heard and a distraught young man burst into the room. "Mother, are you all right?"

Grey straightened and saw . . . himself at twenty. Or close enough. Peter had reached his brother's height and was blond and heartbreakingly handsome. His face looked designed for laughter—he'd always been a cheerful child—but he was haggard, worried now for his mother as well as his father.

Peter skidded to a halt, his astonished gaze going from his mother to his long-lost brother. "Grey?" he asked incredulously. Disbelief on his face, he stalked closer, his gaze searching. "You must be an imposter! My brother has been dead these ten years."

"Sorry to disappoint you, Peter," Grey said with a twisted smile. "I would have written to disabuse you of the notion, but the prison where I resided was shockingly short of amenities such as paper and pen."

"My God," Peter breathed as he studied Grey's face. "That scar on your left eyebrow, from that time you fell on broken stones and cut yourself. It really is you!"

Grey touched the faint mark. "The scar I acquired when you shoved me down at the pond, if I recall correctly."

They'd been playing by the water on a hot summer day and Peter had gleefully caught his older brother off balance, only to be horrified when the cut Grey received had bled copiously. In retrospect, it was a happy, playful memory. Grey offered his hand hesitantly. "You apologized for days."

"I'll apologize again if you like." Peter caught his hand with both of his and pumped enthusiastically. "Prison, you say?"

Grey started to explain, then couldn't. His return home had released a torrent of raw emotion. If he tried to explain Castle Durand, he'd fall apart entirely. He managed, "For ten years. Later, I'll tell you more, but not tonight. Please, tell me about Father! What happened? How ill is he?"

His mother joined her sons, composed again. "Costain fell when he was hunting and his horse balked at a high fence. He broke a bone or two, but the real danger is a head injury. He . . . he's been unconscious since the accident."

Several days then. That was bad, very bad. Grey closed his eyes for long moments as he battled despair that he might have arrived too late. "Can I see him?"

"Of course. Your sister is with him now. We've been taking turns sitting with him." Lady Costain's eyes narrowed as she registered Cassie's presence for the first time. "Please introduce your friend to me, Grey."

He turned to Cassie, who had stayed tactfully in the background. Taking her hand, he drew her forward. "Allow me to present my affianced wife, Miss Catherine St. Ives." He whispered a silent "Thank you" that his family couldn't see. "Cassie, my mother, Lady Costain, and my brother, Peter Sommers."

His mother's gaze intensified as she studied Cassie. "St. Ives. Are you one of the Norfolk St. Ives?"

Cassie's fingers tensed, but she said with the confident calm of a born aristocrat, "I am, Lady

Costain. But I met Lord Wyndham in France."

"Where she saved my life." As Grey spoke, he saw a shadow flicker across Peter's face. He'd been happy to find that his brother was alive, but now he was recognizing that the title and inheritance he'd come to regard as his own had been snatched away. It was a complication Grey hadn't considered, but should have. Peter was no longer a child, but a man. He'd not welcome being superseded.

Grey buried the thought for later since he could handle no more anxiety. Not tonight. Taking Cassie's arm, he said, "I assume Lord Costain is in his usual rooms?"

When his mother nodded, he set off, grateful to have Cassie at his side to keep his nerves steady. Bad enough that his family was staring at him, but servants were peering from behind doors and around corners. The attention made him twitch, but he couldn't let that show. This was home. He must appear sane, no matter how difficult it was.

There was something deeply unreal about striding the familiar corridors, climbing the marble steps with one hand on the polished railing he used to slide down. Yet at the same time, Summerhill seemed eternal, the ten years in France scarcely more than a bad dream. This disorientation must be one of the reasons he'd been reluctant to return. If not for Cassie, it would be easy to drown in the depths of his own mind.

His parents had a massive suite of rooms in the center of the house. Grey entered his father's bedroom with Cassie beside him. Lamps cast soft light on his father's still form. The earl looked lost in the large bed, his powerful figure diminished.

His father's longtime valet, Baker, sat on the near side of the bed. He glanced up, barely noticing Grey as his admiring gaze went to Cassie. Then he saw Peter enter and his jaw dropped as he looked from Peter to Grey and back again.

Grey nodded to him and circled to where a lovely young blond woman was sitting, head bent and golden hair tied back. Lady Elizabeth Sommers. His little Beth.

He rounded the bed, then halted in his tracks. Elizabeth was nursing a baby.

It was Grey's turn to be shocked. His little sister, a mother? Yet she was twenty-three now. Certainly old enough to have a husband and child. He fought for composure, for nothing else had made him as aware of how much time had passed.

His sister looked up from her baby and her gaze made the same journey from Grey to Peter and back again. In the dimly lit bedroom, it would have been possible to assume that Grey was Peter returning to the sickroom, but since they were together, the conclusion was obvious.

Elizabeth's mouth formed an O of surprise. She breathed, "Grey?"

"None other. Like a bad penny, I have returned." He was proud of himself for keeping a light tone as he brushed a kiss on her forehead.

The baby was blond and cherubic. Grey was no expert on babies, but he was pretty sure that compliments pleased doting parents. "Who is this lovely creature?"

"My daughter. Your niece." Elizabeth's expression blazed with excitement. "I named her for you. Grace."

He was touched and rather awed by this tiny perfect being. "A better name for a daughter than Greydon. Who is your husband? Someone worthy of my sister?"

She smiled. "Johnny Langtry."

The Langtry family's estate marched with Summerhill. As the two highest-ranking families in this part of the shire, there had always been easy communication between the households.

John Langtry was a couple of years younger than Grey, and his father's heir. Solidly built and with an infectious smile, he was a thoroughly good fellow. Far more reliable than Grey. "Minx! You had your eye on him since you were in the nursery."

Elizabeth grinned. "Johnny never had a chance. Not that he's complaining!"

Grey studied his sister and her daughter, the images of a blond northern Madonna and child. "He's a very lucky man."

"He is indeed," his mother said as she joined them, putting her hand on Grey's arm as if fearing he'd vanish. "You must be tired if you came from London today, Grey. Let's adjourn to the morning room for refreshments. Baker can stay with your father. We all want to know what happened to you for all these years." Her gaze went to Cassie. "And I wish to become acquainted with my future daughter-in-law."

Grey guessed Cassie cringed inside to hear that, but her face remained calm. Of course his family was wild with curiosity, but he couldn't answer their questions. Not tonight. Some questions he'd never answer.

His gaze went to the earl's still face. "I want to sit with Father. There are things I need to say to him." He gave a humorless smile. "Even if he can't hear me."

"Maybe it's better if he can't talk back," Peter said with a note in his voice that made it not quite a joke.

Cassie asked quietly, "Do you want me to stay?"

"Thank you, but no." Grey drew a deep breath. "Some things must be done alone."

Chapter 33

"Please ring if there is anything lacking in your room, Miss St. Ives," Lady Costain said as she ushered Cassie into a guest room. "I'm sorry I didn't read Kirkland's message yesterday. I would have had time to prepare for you properly."

"No need to worry, Lady Costain." Cassie had excused herself from the family supper as quickly as possible to avoid more questions. It had been a tiring day, and facing the Sommers family without Grey beside her had been a strain.

She stepped into her room, which was immaculately clean and warmed by a quietly crackling fire. The rose floral draperies and bed hangings glowed in the lamplight and a vase of out-of-season flowers sat on the desk. "This is lovely. I've stayed in much humbler accommodations." An understatement of massive proportions. "Does Grey know where his room is, or are his old rooms available?"

The countess frowned. "I'd forgotten about that. Peter moved into those rooms when . . . when we gave up hope that Grey would ever return. I'll have another room prepared for Grey to stay in tonight. It's too late to move Peter's things."

"Is it necessary for Peter to move?" Cassie asked, surprised.

The older woman looked puzzled. "Peter has

been living in the heir's suite. Now that Grey is back, it belongs to him."

Cassie hesitated before saying, "Surely in a house this splendid, there are other suitable quarters. Even happy news can be disruptive. Since Peter will have other major changes to adjust to, perhaps moving isn't essential?"

The countess frowned. "I take your point. I shall discuss this with Grey before any plans are finalized. He has the right to request his old room back." Lady Costain's scrutiny turned to Cassie. "I didn't wish to have this discussion in front of Peter and Elizabeth, but I do wonder about your background. The St. Ives family doesn't mingle much in the beau monde, but I had the impression that there are only sons."

Her tone equally cool, Cassie said, "Your real question is whether I'm a fortune hunter taking advantage of Lord Wyndham's vulnerable state." Her head was aching, so she began pulling pins from her hair. "I am who I claim to be. I'm not a scheming slut sinking my greedy claws into your son."

Lady Costain drew a sharp breath. "You believe in directness."

"When appropriate." Cassie's lips twisted. "But I lie well when that's required."

"And I have no way of knowing which you are doing now." Lady Costain sighed. "I'm sorry for my bluntness, but surely you can understand that

I'm concerned for my son's welfare. I never thought . . ." She bit her lip. "You aren't making this easy for me. You were remarkably evasive when we talked over supper. Is there anything you're willing to tell me that might soothe my maternal concerns?"

Cassie moved to the dressing table. The image in the mirror was of a red-haired temptress. A sophisticated and ruthless woman of the world. No wonder Lady Costain was worried. If Cassie had a son, she'd want to keep him out of such a woman's clutches.

"Grey's story is his to tell, and I will let him decide how much he wishes to say." She picked up the silver-backed brush and began brushing out her hair. "The current Lord Ives is my father's younger brother, and indeed he has only sons. My mother was French. All of my family except me died in a massacre during the Reign of Terror. It was many years ago, so it's not surprising you were unaware of what happened to them."

The countess gasped. "Your whole family was killed? How horrible! How did you survive?"

Cassie continued brushing. Her natural hair color might be outrageous, but it was rich and beautiful in its way. "My nurse had taken me out for the afternoon. Of course, I could be lying and the real Catherine St. Ives died with the rest of her family. As it happens, I'm telling the truth." Wanting to ease the countess's concerns, she added, "The betrothal will be a long one. I will not hold Grey to his word if he changes his mind."

After a long silence, the other woman said quietly, "I believe you. What have you been doing these many years?"

"Surviving." Cassie gazed at her reflection, seeing circles under her eyes. She'd known that coming to Summerhill would be difficult, but she'd only be here for a few days. Telling Grey's family some truth about herself meant they'd be happy to say goodbye when the time came.

"Are you Grey's mistress?" Lady Costain asked.

Mistress. Such a simple word for such a complex relationship. "Yes." Cassie removed her small gold earrings.

"It didn't take him long to find one," his mother said disapprovingly. "I hoped he'd outgrow his womanizing by this age."

Suddenly furious, Cassie spun away from the mirror. "Imagine ten years in solitary confinement, Lady Costain. Ten years of never seeing or touching another living being. No hugs, no kisses from your children or granddaughter, no husbandly pat on your derriere when no one is looking. No scent of another human, no sight of a human face. Imagine all that—and don't you *dare* criticize your son!"

For a moment the countess looked ready to explode. Then her expression changed. "You're in love with Grey."

Throat tight, Cassie turned and pulled the bell to summon Hazel, which would end this painful conversation. "That is between Grey and me. But I assure you that I'm not here to cause trouble for the Sommers family."

"I shall take you at your word." The countess turned to leave. "And . . . thank you for bringing my son back to me."

Cassie closed her eyes in exhaustion. She didn't need Lady Costain's thanks. Everything she'd done had been for Grey.

After the family and his father's valet left, Grey settled down in the chair his sister had occupied. His father's still face showed more wrinkles around his eyes and mouth and there were silver strands visible in the Sommers blond hair. But the strong features hadn't changed. Lord Costain looked ready to wake at any moment.

Grey took his father's hand. It was limp, neither warm nor cold. "I've come home, Father," he said softly. "I'm sorry for all the worry I caused you. You did your best to train me to be a strong, compassionate earl who knew about farming and law and everything else a peer of the realm should know. You were a good teacher so I couldn't help learning, but I know I'm responsible for a good number of those white hairs."

He thought he felt the barest squeeze of his father's hand, though it was probably his imagination. "Let me tell you about how I came to be imprisoned in France. If I'd had a whit of sense, I would have come home before the Truce of Amiens ended, but no, I was the golden boy to whom nothing bad could happen."

He continued talking, his words sometimes halting and painful as he described the imprisonment, the near madness, the blessed company of Père Laurent. Everything he'd been unable to say to the rest of his family. "Père Laurent was my second father. You would like each other if you ever met."

Grey smiled as he tried to imagine such a meeting. "Though he's a Catholic, he didn't seem at all disposed to invade England and convert all us heretics by the sword." That ambition belonged to Napoleon, and there was nothing religious about it.

Several times he halted until he regained his composure, but he needed to say all this to his father even if he was too late for a real conversation. When he finally ran out of words, he said softly, "I really wish you wouldn't die, Father. I'm nowhere near ready to become the next Lord Costain. I need you. We all need you."

His words choked off. Trying for a lighter note, he said, "But I've done one thing right. You wanted me to marry and secure the succession, so I've brought my fiancée to Summerhill."

"Is she pretty?"

The whisper was so thin that Grey was sure he'd imagined it. Bending over his father, he asked in a hushed voice, "Did you say something?"

The pale eyelids fluttered open. "Is she *pretty?*"

Stunned, Grey choked out, "She's beautiful. A redhead."

"Redheaded grandchildren?" The earl sounded disapproving. "Tell . . . more."

"Her father was Lord St. Ives. She's the most incredible woman I've ever met, and she saved my life several times."

His father blinked. "Sounds . . . too good for you."

"She is." Grey wanted to stand up and shout his exhilaration at his father's improvement, but that seemed disrespectful for a sickroom. "You'll get to meet Cassie, but now you should rest."

"Tired of resting." The earl's eyes closed. "Could hear people talk, but couldn't answer. Till you came. Had to tell you you're a damned young fool."

"Yes, Father. I have been. I'll try to do better." Silent tears were sliding down Grey's cheeks. "I'll get Mother. She'll want to talk to you."

A faint smile softened the earl's face. "Need my Janey."

Jubilant, Grey squeezed his father's hand. "She'll be here soon."

Outside the room, he was unsurprised to find Baker quietly waiting to return to his master's bedside. "Good news! He woke up and was talking to me. Entirely coherent, too." Grey grinned. "Called me a damned young fool."

"Sounds like he's in his right mind," the valet said with a glimmer of humor. "Shall I go in?"

Grey nodded. "He wants to see her ladyship. I'll tell her."

Despite the late hour, he found his mother in the morning room. She was sitting by the fire, neglected needlework in her lap as she gazed into the flames. Looking up at Grey's entrance, she asked, "Did you make your peace with your father?"

"I hope so, but if not, I'll have other chances later. Mother, he woke up! He's weak, but he spoke clearly. He wants to see you. I think he's going to be all right."

The countess stood, her face luminous as her embroidery fell to the floor. "Thank God!" She hugged Grey, clinging to him as she struggled to control herself. "What a day of miracles this has been!"

"It has indeed." He held her a moment longer, remembering how she held him and sang lullabies when he was very small. He'd given up hope that he'd hold her again like this. "I'm sorry for all the trouble and grief I caused you."

"Children exist to cause their parents trouble and grief," she said wryly. Releasing him, she added, "But they also give life's greatest joys. You were sometimes too heedless, but there was no malice in you. Being caught in France when the truce ended . . ." She shrugged. "It was abominable luck, but not a sin on your part."

He didn't agree, but he was too tired to discuss that. "What did Cassie tell you about my time in France?"

"Very little. She said the story was yours to tell."

That was his Cassie. Discreet to the bone. He wasn't sure himself how much he wanted to say, but knew he'd avoid details. He hoped his father didn't remember them.

His mother said, "Why do you call her Cassie? Is it a nickname for Catherine?"

He nodded, since the real reason was too private to reveal. "I think it suits her."

"What an extraordinary young woman she is." His mother's voice was neutral. "Formidable, even."

Formidable. A perfect description. "She is, isn't she?" Grey agreed. "Now go to Father. He'll be looking for you, if he hasn't drifted off again."

"He was in his right wits?" she asked, looking younger than when he'd arrived.

"Yes. I think he was on the verge of waking up on his own, and hearing my voice made him curious."

"I prefer to call it a miracle." She gave him a radiant smile. "I half expect to wake up in the morning and find you're a dream."

"If I were to appear in your dreams, I probably wouldn't be as thin and eccentric," he said wryly.

She studied him more critically. "Definitely thin, but your usual elegant self."

"Thanks for the elegance are owed to Kirkland, who lent me decent clothing."

"I hope you start patronizing his tailor!" Her face sobered. "Have you become eccentric, Grey?"

"That might not be the right word." He studied her beloved face and knew that she could never really understand. "I just . . . I'll need time to become used to normal life. I require more peace and quiet than when I was younger."

She laughed and patted his arm. "We all do when we grow up. Good night, my darling. Sleep as late as you like in the morning."

"I intend to." He watched her leave, wondering what room Cassie was in. He could have asked his mother, but it seemed a rather indelicate question.

He considered. As Grey's fiancée, she would have been put in one of the best guest rooms. Probably the Rose Room, which was discreetly distant from Grey's suite.

He set off for the Rose Room, desperate to find his thorn among the roses.

Chapter 34

The hour was very late, after midnight, so Grey saw no one as he climbed the stairs in search of Cassie. There was light visible under his father's door, and the soft murmur of his mother's voice. He passed by and headed down the corridor. Summerhill was shaped like a shallow U, with wings coming off each end of the main block. He turned right into the short passage at the east end.

Yes, a faint line of light under the Rose Room's door. Probably a low-burning night lamp. He turned the knob, glad the room wasn't locked, and stepped silently inside. The dim lamplight revealed Cassie's sleeping form. She lay on her side, a thick braid of hair falling over her shoulder in a rope of dark molten copper.

She was so beautiful his heart hurt. He quietly closed the door behind him.

Before he could announce himself, Cassie woke and hurled herself off the far side of the mattress with amazing speed. A knife appeared in her hand as she took cover behind the massive four-poster bed and evaluated the threat.

He held absolutely still. "Sorry. I should have known better than to startle you." After she relaxed and the knife disappeared, he said, "From your reaction, I'm guessing that Summerhill feels dangerous to you."

"Apparently so," she said ruefully as she circled the bed. The nightgown she wore was thick and warm, but it couldn't conceal the lithe grace of her movements. "I was feeling rather . . . alone and vulnerable."

He winced. "I'm sorry, I should have stayed with you rather than leave you to carry the full weight of my excited relatives."

She shook her head. "It would have been nice to face their curiosity together, but you needed to talk to your father while he's still breathing."

Reminded of the miracle, Grey exclaimed, "He woke up! He spoke to me quite coherently. I think he'll be all right. My mother is with him now."

"That's wonderful news!" She caught his hands in delight. "And not only because it means you don't succeed to Costain for a while."

"I'm hoping my father is good for at least another twenty years," he said fervently as he wrapped his arms around Cassie.

She melted into him with a welcoming sigh. "I'm so glad you came. I'll sleep better for seeing you and getting a good hug."

"I need a good deal more than a hug." Hungrily he bent to her mouth, wanting to draw her essence into himself. "Cassie, Cassie . . ." He peeled off her nightgown, then walked her back to the bed.

"Should we be doing this under your mother's roof?" she asked uncertainly, but her hands were pulling at his coat.

"It's my roof, too." He swept her onto the bed, then tore at his garments with no thought for Kirkland's expensive tailor. "I need you far more than I need propriety."

Cassie lay on her side watching him strip, a cream and copper goddess in the dim light, her haunted blue eyes as hungry as his own. When he was down to skin and too many bones, she pulled him onto the bed, saying huskily, "You're as powerful a drug as opium, my lord." Then they spoke no more.

His demands were met by her strength, but also a vulnerability he'd never felt in her before. He poured everything he had into her, wanting to return the priceless gifts she'd given him. And together, they found fulfillment.

After the shattering culmination, they lay limp in each other's arms. Her braid had come undone and her hair lay in a shimmering veil over his chest. "Catherine," he murmured, as he twined a strand around his fingers. "You have the most beautiful hair I've ever seen. Coloring it might have been essential for your work, but it's a crime to deprive the world of such splendor."

"No carroty little girl would ever believe that. And for a full-grown woman, the color is considered vulgar. Sluttish, even." Her voice turned wry. "Not that that doesn't fit me, since I am a slu—"

"Don't!" he said sharply. "Don't *ever* say

anything like that about yourself! You are the finest woman I've ever known, true and generous and strong. Don't look at yourself as narrow minds would."

"It's hard not to, especially here," she pointed out. "Your mother and sister are good women in every sense of the word. I . . . am not."

"Have they been rude to you?" he demanded. "I will not allow that!"

"You're fitting back into your lordly role very quickly," she said with amusement. "Your sister was charming and happy to meet me because she assumes we'll be neighbors and she wants to be friends. Your mother . . ." Cassie hesitated. "She wasn't rude, but she is naturally concerned for you and wanted to assure herself that you hadn't fallen into the talons of a fortune-hunting harpy."

"How dare she!" he said angrily. "I shall speak with her."

"No," Cassie said firmly. "Your mother's concerns are legitimate. I'm no one's idea of an innocent virgin bride."

"Why the devil would I want one of those?" he retorted. "Sounds deucedly dull."

"Many men worship the purity of innocence. I'm glad you're not one of them," Cassie said with a laugh. "But any mother would worry when her long-lost son shows up with a strange woman."

"You're not strange." He cupped her breast with one hand. "You're magnificent."

Cassie gave him an intimate, teasing smile. "Your return has gone better than expected, hasn't it? With your father recovering, you can take your time rather than being forced into major responsibility before you're ready." She brushed her lips on his cheek in a feather kiss. "I'm not needed here, so I can return to London right away."

Her words were like a drench of ice water. "No! You can't leave, you just got here." He drew a deep breath as he struggled with his panicky reaction. "Of course you want to return to your real life, but no urgent mission awaits you. Stay a week or two. Relax, ride good horses, let yourself be cosseted and treated like a fragile flower. You deserve that."

He held his breath as he waited for her response. He knew she would leave, but please God, not immediately!

"Very well," she said. "I'll stay a week." Her hand began to wander down his body. "I shall certainly miss this."

She cupped him and pure fire shot straight through his veins. "So will I," he said raggedly. As he bent to the rich nourishment of her mouth, he wondered if he could survive without this sweetness and fire.

Despite her fatigue, Cassie lay awake for a long time after Grey fell asleep in her arms. She wanted to cherish every remaining moment with him. She'd been too weak to refuse to stay longer, but a week must be the limit. Lady Elizabeth had been so friendly and welcoming that Cassie was ashamed of being at Summerhill under false pretenses.

There was also the stark fact that the longer she stayed with Grey, the harder it would be to leave. She'd never felt such closeness with another man. He was willing to open himself to her as no one else had.

As she thought back to the night's intense lovemaking, she realized that there had been a shift in the balance between them. At the beginning, he'd needed a woman, any woman, and she had accepted that in return for the simple delights of passion.

That had changed as they'd grown to know each other better. She'd become special to him, and he'd become special—incredibly so—to her. In the past, she'd given him healing intimacy in return for pleasure. Tonight, he'd returned healing and wholeness to her. It was time to leave. While she still could.

Much as Grey would have liked to sleep until noon with Cassie, he'd regained enough gentlemanly discretion that when he woke and saw the first faint light of dawn, he groaned and swung himself out of the bed. "Time to leave."

He leaned over and kissed Cassie's bare shoulder. He noted with amusement that she was now so relaxed that she only made a sleepy sound of acknowledgment rather than leaping from the bed with a knife in her hand.

He pulled the covers over her bare shoulder, then dragged on enough clothing to be decent. Carrying his shoes in one hand, he slipped out into the corridor. It was still very dark inside the house, but it wouldn't be long before busy maids were stirring.

Now that he was back at Summerhill, his profound reluctance to return had almost vanished. Before, facing the demands and commotion that would be aroused by his return from the dead had seemed an insurmountable barrier.

He'd been right about the commotion. His return would have been easier if his mother had opened Kirkland's message and been prepared for him. But now that was over, and he was feeling . . . like himself.

That self wasn't the callow Lord Wyndham who had flitted off to Paris for amusement, but an older, knocked-about, and hopefully wiser man. A man who belonged here at Summerhill. This house, this land, these people were *his*. He felt like a flower that had been jerked from its native soil and withered away in the rubbish for years. Now he'd finally been replanted where he belonged.

He felt strong enough that for the first time, he dared wonder if there was any chance of persuading Cassie to stay. He'd wait a few days until she'd had time to experience the beauty and peace of Summerhill.

And then, they'd talk. He was no longer willing to let her go without at least trying to change her mind.

Chapter 35

Grey's rooms were at the opposite end of the sprawling house, but he was able to reach them unseen. Feeling happy over his decision about Cassie, he opened his door, then halted at the sight of his brother sitting in front of the fire.

Fully dressed except for his coat, which he'd replaced with a casual banyan, Peter was sprawled in a wing chair and holding a drink as he stared into the flames. He looked like the careless, drunken Grey of a dozen years before.

"Peter?" Grey asked, surprised. As he glanced about, he saw that some of the furnishings and decorations had been changed.

"Ah, the young lord and master has arrived to claim his property!" Peter rose and made an exaggerated bow, sloshing his drink and almost falling over. "I'm surprised you didn't throw me out of here earlier, but I suppose you were too busy rogering your doxy."

Fury blazed through Grey. "Don't you dare talk about Cassie that way!"

"Why not?" Peter opened a cabinet that contained glasses and bottles. "Damned bad form to bring your mistress to your family home, but you never did care for anyone but yourself." He pulled out a brandy bottle and tilted it back to drink directly. "How much does she charge? She looks expensive, but during my years as heir apparent, my allowance was substantial. I should be able to afford a night or two."

Grey launched himself at Peter, so enraged he was barely aware of how he punched and threw his brother, then pinned him to the ground. Nothing mattered but destroying the man who'd said such vile words.

He was dragged back to awareness by a hoarse whisper, "Grey! Grey, in the name of God, stop!"

Yanked from his killing rage, Grey realized that he had pinned Peter to the floor and was choking him. His brother's face was darkening and he could barely gasp out his plea.

Grey wrenched himself away and buried his face in his hands as he gulped for breath. He thought he'd mastered his furies. Instead he'd almost murdered his brother. An unspeakable crime that he'd rather die himself than commit.

A few feet away, Peter lay on the floor retching out his guts on the priceless Chinese carpet. The effects of too much brandy and being strangled, no doubt.

As Peter pulled himself to a sitting position and leaned against a wing chair, Grey rose and dipped a towel in the water pitcher, then handed it to his brother. Wordlessly Peter wiped his mouth and face, then drank the glass of water Grey had poured.

"Dear God, Peter, I'm so sorry," Grey said, sickened by himself. "You shouldn't have spoken so about Cassie, but nothing can justify almost killing you."

"I shouldn't have said such vile things about your guest," Peter replied, sounding more sober. He folded the wet towel and pressed it against a rapidly developing black eye. "Where the devil did you learn to fight like that?"

"The Westerfield Academy." Still shaken, Grey poured himself two fingers of brandy, then sank down on the carpet a yard from his brother and leaned back against the sofa. "Ashton is half Hindu, and he taught his classmates a fighting technique he'd learned in India. It's become a school tradition."

"I should have gone there instead of bloody Eton," Peter muttered.

"You were less worrisome so it wasn't considered necessary." Grey exhaled roughly. "Say anything you like about me, but I won't hear a word against Cassie. She's the finest woman I've ever met."

"Then it's a pity she looks like the very best grade of Bond Street ware." Seeing Grey's thunderous expression, Peter said hastily, "I believe you that she's no whore, but she is . . . not what one would expect of your bride. Why did you bring her to Summerhill when Father is dying and you're returning from the dead? Not exactly ideal circumstances for introducing a new member of the family."

Grey said, "The good news is that Father isn't dying. He woke up and spoke to me. Mother is with him now."

Peter's face brightened. "Wonderful!"

Grey took a sip of his brandy. It was tempting to get drunk, but he and Peter wouldn't have fought if his brother hadn't been drunk enough to ruin his judgment. Or perhaps his temper. Peter was obviously not happy about losing his expectations.

"Cassie is here to keep me sane." Grey's laughter was bitter. "I thought I was making progress on that front, but apparently not. If she'd been here, I wouldn't have come so close to fratricide."

"She can stop you when you run mad like that?" Peter asked skeptically.

Grey smiled fondly. "She certainly can."

"You seem sane enough now," Peter said hesitantly.

Grey realized he needed to explain more. "Cassie went alone into the castle where I was imprisoned and freed me and the priest in the next cell, who had become my only tie to reality. She got us to sanctuary and guided me out of the country, lending me her strength and sanity when I had none. Believe me, I am much improved. I owe her more than I can ever possibly repay."

Peter frowned. "She sounds admirable, but is it reason enough to marry her?"

Choosing his words carefully, Grey said, "I want to marry Cassie, but she hasn't said yes yet. She wants to wait and see how things develop." He drew an uneven breath. "She'll leave soon. I may never see her again." Saying that aloud was agonizing.

Hearing the pain in his brother's voice, Peter said awkwardly, "I'm sorry. Can you . . . manage without her?"

"I'll have to, won't I?" Grey said brusquely. "What about you, Peter? I thought you were happy I'm alive, but when I came in, you acted as if I was your worst enemy."

"I am happy you're back. Truly. And I rather like Cassie, from what I've seen of her. But"—his brother ran stiff fingers through his tangled blond hair—"I looked up to you so much. When you disappeared, it was . . . it was the worst thing that had ever happened to me. I spent years waiting and hoping. We all did."

Grey winced. "If only I'd had the sense to return to England when I was warned to do so!"

"That would have made all our lives easier, but you couldn't know the consequences. If you'd been interned, we'd have learned of it and could have settled down and waited for you to come home. As it was . . ." Peter shrugged. "Of course we assumed the worst."

"From what Cassie tells me, being interned isn't bad. Boring, but living a fairly normal life." And not being driven mad by isolation. "Of course, if I'd been interned, I'd still be in France, waiting and wondering if this bloody war would ever end."

"But we would have known you were alive." Peter sighed roughly. "Instead, without anyone quite admitting you must be dead, people started treating me as the heir. Seven years after your presumed death, the earl said it was time I styled myself as Lord Wyndham. Mother moved my things in here when I was at university. I began to think of myself as the next Earl of Costain. I learned how to run the estate, started paying attention to Parliament. And now"—he spread his hand in a hopeless gesture—"you come back and it's all snatched away. All that effort and planning for nothing."

Grey glanced around the sitting room, which was easily ten times the size of his cell in France. And the suite had a bedroom and dressing area as well. "You can have these rooms. I don't need them and it hardly seems fair to drive you out. But

I can't let you have the title and the entailed property. The law doesn't work that way. As long as I'm alive, I'm the heir."

"I know." Peter struggled to his feet and poured more water before sinking wearily back onto the carpet. "I've spent the night drinking and wondering what to do with my life. I've no taste for becoming an idle wastrel."

"The traditional occupations for a younger son are the church, politics, or the military. None of them interest you?" When Peter made a face, Grey asked, "Is there something less traditional you'd really like to do?"

Peter hesitated, his expression torn. "The theater. I want to be an actor."

"An *actor?*" Grey asked incredulously.

His brother's expression closed. "You see why I don't talk about it. Not that I ever thought the theater was possible. Until you returned, Summerhill was my fate."

Grey studied Peter's handsome, youthful face. His first reaction on meeting his grown brother the day before had been how much they resembled each other. It was true that they had similar height, build, and coloring, and anyone seeing them together would immediately know they were related.

But they'd always had very different temperaments. Grey was outgoing, interested in people and in solving problems. Peter had been more of a dreamer, enjoying art and music and, yes, the plays that were occasionally staged during house parties. He said slowly, "I remember that even as a little boy, you enjoyed taking part in plays. The adults always found your earnestness rather charming. But your interest was serious even at that age, wasn't it?"

Peter nodded. "I fell in love with acting the first time I stepped onto an improvised stage. I love the language, the drama, the larger-than-life characters. It's . . ." The flow of words cut off and he sank against the chair behind him. "It's impossible."

"Have you had the opportunity to act in recent years?"

"Not as much as I'd like," his brother admitted. "But last summer I stayed with a friend up in Yorkshire. There's a good-sized theater there, and the company manager did a special production of *As You Like It* with local people acting in many of the roles. That's the play with the "All the world's a stage" speech. The idea was to get friends and neighbors buying tickets to see the show. I auditioned and was cast as Orlando."

Orlando was the romantic lead, if Grey remembered his Shakespeare. With Peter's looks, he was a natural for such roles. "Did the play do well?"

"Most of the acting was dreadful, but the manager, Burke, made pots of money." Peter paused, then said shyly, "After the last show, Burke took me aside and said that if I ever wanted to act professionally, there would be a place for me in his company. He knew I was a gentleman, but I auditioned as Peter Sommers so he didn't realize that I was heir to an earldom." His mouth twisted. "At least, I was then."

"Which would you pick if you had a choice?" Grey asked. "The earldom or being a successful actor?"

"Acting," Peter said instantly. "I wouldn't even have to be well known. A journeyman's career with steady work would be beyond my maddest dreams."

"Then do it," Grey said flatly. "The parents won't be best pleased, but I will support you in this. And if they cut off your allowance, I'll see you don't starve."

His brother's jaw dropped. "You'd do that? You wouldn't be ashamed to have your brother become a common player?"

"I think you'd be an uncommon player." Grey smiled ruefully. "Ten years in a dungeon strip away a lot of ideas about what is proper. You were willing to do your duty as heir to Costain when that seemed necessary. Now that it isn't, I think you should do what you love. Even if you fail, better to try and fail than to spend your life wishing you'd tried."

"I won't fail," Peter said intensely. "I'm good,

Grey. And I'll do whatever is necessary to succeed."

Grey grinned. "Am I forgiven for surviving?"

"Now I have even more reason to be grateful you're alive!" Peter was bubbling with delight. "I'll write Mr. Burke and tell him I'm taking him up on his offer. It will be small roles, I'm sure, but a start."

"I'm glad. Today Yorkshire, tomorrow London!" Grey set aside the rest of his drink since it was now daylight, and brandy was a damned odd breakfast. "I suggest you wait a few days till Father is stronger before announcing your plans."

"I'll wait until I hear from Mr. Burke before I speak up. And if he's changed his mind, well, I'll find another theater manager to approach." Peter cocked his head to one side. "What about you, Grey? Have you ever had secret dreams of what you want?"

Grey had never thought about it, but his answer was immediate. "This." He made a sweeping gesture with one hand. "Summerhill. For as long as I can remember, I've known that I am Summerhill, and it is me. The land, the people, the responsibilities of the earldom. I'm even looking forward to sitting in Parliament and helping to steer the ship of state. There's nothing else I've ever wanted." Except Cassie.

"Then it's a damned good thing you've returned

from the dead," Peter said with a grin. "Because you'll make a much better earl than I would."

Perhaps, perhaps not. But like Peter, Grey was determined to do what was necessary to succeed.

Chapter 36

Cassie was awakened by a maid with a small pitcher of hot chocolate and a note from Grey. *"Would you like to go for a ride after breakfast? It's a perfect day to see Summerhill."*

She glanced out the window and saw the pale, clear sunshine of early spring. He'd promised her fine horses. She scribbled, *"Yes, please!"* on the note and directed the maid to take it to Lord Wyndham. A good thing Kiri had found a riding habit, golden with dark brown trim, for Cassie's hastily assembled wardrobe.

After donning the dashing habit, Cassie headed downstairs for a proper breakfast. News of the earl's recovery had lightened the atmosphere. Lady Elizabeth had been staying at Summerhill since her father's injury, but now she looked forward to going home. Peter positively beamed at Cassie, and Grey greeted her with proper formality while his eyes made wicked suggestions.

Lady Costain had been with her husband, but she came down to the breakfast parlor to say, "Costain wants to meet you, Miss St. Ives."

"Is he strong enough for visitors outside the

family?" Cassie asked, hoping she didn't have to meet him.

"He is much stronger, and quite firm about meeting you," the countess replied.

No escape there. "Then it will be my pleasure," Cassie murmured.

As she rose, Grey said, "I'll go with you. I haven't seen him yet this morning."

Cassie headed for the steps, grateful for Grey's company. As they climbed the wide steps side by side, he said, "You look very lovely in this gold habit."

"Lady Kiri's sister has enough red in her hair that we can wear similar colors," Cassie explained. Dropping her voice, she asked, "How should I act with your father?"

He gave her a warm smile. "Just be your lovely self, Catherine."

She supposed calling her Catherine was a strong hint. They entered the master's bedroom. For a man who had been tossing the dice with St. Peter the day before, the Earl of Costain was looking very well. He was propped up in bed by pillows and dictating instructions to his secretary.

He was also a remarkably fine-looking man, with the family good looks molded by years of authority. There was humor and intelligence in his eyes as he dismissed the secretary to concentrate on his visitors. Grey would look very like his father someday.

"Come closer to the bed," Lord Costain ordered. "So it really is you, boy. I wondered if I was hallucinating last night."

"Not at all, sir." Grey took his father's hand with heartfelt, wordless emotion. "I surprised myself with my tenacity."

"I can't recall all you told me last night, so I'll hear more about what happened later." There was a glint of moisture in the earl's eyes as he held his son's hand. His gaze moved to Cassie. "But now I wish to meet your future countess. You're right, she's pretty despite the red hair, but you didn't tell me her name. Introduce us."

"Sir, allow me to present Miss Catherine St. Ives." Grey smiled at Cassie. "I'm sure you've deduced that this is Lord Costain, Cassie."

Before she could respond, Costain exclaimed, "Good God, surely you must be Tom St. Ives's daughter?"

She inhaled sharply. "You knew my father?"

"Indeed I did. We became friends at Eton, and remained so until his untimely death." The earl shook his head. "I was there the night he met your mother. What a stunner she was. We were all madly in love with her." He looked nostalgic for a moment before adding, "Of course, that was before I met my wife, who drove all other women from my mind."

Cassie pressed her hand to her chest as her breathing constricted. She hadn't expected her distant, half-forgotten past to come to shocking life. "Did you hear what happened to my parents and the rest of my family?"

The earl nodded sadly. "A great tragedy. Damn the French revolutionaries! I knew some of your Montclair relations, too. Fine people even though they were French. By what miracle did you survive?"

"I was out with a nurse when the house was burned down," she explained. "But I could be an imposter, you know."

Costain laughed. "Nonsense. You've got the St. Ives red hair, and you have a great look of your mother, too." He offered her his hand. "Well done, Grey. I'm honored to see the St. Ives blood joined with the Sommers family. I'm even reconciled to redheaded grandchildren."

Cassie took his hand as she fought back tears. She barely managed to say, "Thank you, my lord."

"There now, I've made you cry." Costain released her hand and settled back in his pillows, looking tired. "Grey, take her off and make her smile again. And send your mother in. I miss her."

Eyes concerned, Grey offered Cassie his arm and led her away. Outside the room, he ordered the secretary to send for his mother. Then he led Cassie downstairs and into the empty salon. As soon as the door closed, he wrapped his arms around her. "Damn, Cassie! I'm sorry you were upset like that. I had no idea my father had known your parents."

"It was . . . a shock," she said unsteadily as she buried her face in his shoulder. "I feel like . . ." she searched for words. "Like my arm was amputated and now it's been reattached. Only this is my life, not my arm."

"Like a foot that's gone to sleep and is beginning to wake up," he murmured as he stroked her back. "Alive but very uncomfortable."

"Exactly." She closed her eyes as she struggled for composure. "My family has been dead to me for so long that it never occurred to me that there were other people who remembered them."

"Maybe it's not a bad thing to be reminded that this is the world you were born to," he said softly. "Your father went to Eton, your mother was an enchanting woman who captured the hearts of young Englishmen. You belong to the *ton* every bit as much as I do, even though we've both spent years in exile."

"The reminder isn't bad, but it is very uncomfortable." She sighed. "I felt like such a fraud when your father talked about redheaded grandchildren."

"We could make it a reality," Grey said hesitantly. "Or at least try."

She jerked away from him, even more shocked than by his father's reminiscences. "What on earth does that mean?"

He was watching her with enigmatic gray eyes. "You're here as my fiancée, so we could go ahead and get married. We get on well and it would save me having to brave the Marriage Mart."

She rolled her eyes, needing to turn the issue into a joke. "That is the laziest reason for marrying that I can imagine. Let's go for that ride. It's a lovely day and I could use some fresh air."

He smiled, unperturbed by her rejection of his proposal. "And I'm anxious to see Summerhill. I can't tell you the number of hours I spent visiting the estate in my mind."

"And I'm anxious to ride one of those good horses you promised me." She caught up the skirts of her long riding habit and led the way to the door. Life was complicated. Riding was simple.

She wanted simple.

"Race you to the top of the hill!" Grey called.

Cassie and her mount took off like lightning, her laughter floating behind her. Grey was hard pressed to keep up. She rode as well sidesaddle as astride, and in her flowing golden riding habit, she was far more alluring than as a peddler on a pony.

They reached the hilltop in a dead heat, both of them laughing, and pulled in their horses. "I've saved the best for last," Grey said. "This is the dower house. Sea Grange." He gestured at the hollow below, where a sprawling stone house overlooked the sea.

Cassie caught her breath. "Look at that river of daffodils pouring down the hill! They're just starting to bloom everywhere else."

"Flowers always bloom here first because the house faces south and it's protected on three sides." He nudged his horse down the hill. "Other flowers come later, but there's nothing to match the daffodil glory of spring."

Cassie started down after Grey. "The house looks older than Summerhill."

"It is by a couple of centuries. It was a farmhouse originally." He feasted his eyes on the familiar weathered walls. "I don't think anyone has lived here since my grandmother, the dowager countess, died three years ago. I wish I'd seen her again."

"What a waste of a beautiful house."

"I've always thought that when I marry, I'd live here until I inherit," Grey said. "It's only a few minutes from the main house, but it has more privacy. And the view!"

"Wise to put a bit of space between a lord and his heir," she agreed. "The estate seems as well run as it is beautiful. No wonder you love it so much."

"Though I thought of Summerhill every day of my captivity, I'd still half forgotten just how . . . connected I feel to this land." Grey struggled to find the words to explain. "Being here repairs some of the holes in my raveled psyche."

Cassie gave him a warm, intimate smile. "I can see the difference. You're acquiring more confidence by the hour."

"As long as I also acquire more sanity," he said wryly. "I almost killed Peter this morning. It was horrifying for us both."

Cassie gasped. "What happened?"

"I'll explain over lunch. I had the kitchen pack food and drink. I don't have a key to the dower house, but there's a porch at the far end where we can eat."

She nodded agreement and didn't ask questions until they'd tethered the horses and he brought their picnic to the side porch. A massive stone table and benches sat there, sunshine pouring over them, and there was a splendid view of the sea.

Cassie sighed with pleasure as she brushed dust and a few leaves from the bench, then sat in a cloud of golden skirts. "I love that the sea is so close. Did you sail as a boy? Dream of being a ship's captain and seeing the world?"

He laughed and handed her a cup of wine. "My dreams were land bound."

"Tell me what happened with Peter."

The memory was painful so he kept his explanation terse. Cassie listened while she ate a ham, cheese, and chutney sandwich. When he finished, she said thoughtfully, "So he's going to try for a career in the theater. Your parents won't disown him, I hope?"

"No, though they won't be pleased. But they have me back as heir, and they want their children to be happy. Elizabeth could have had a far grander marriage than Johnny Langtry, but he's the one she wanted. If Peter prospers as an actor, they'll probably buy him his own theater."

She laughed. "I can imagine someone making a cutting remark about Peter's acting and your father staring him down with an 'I am Costain' expression on his face."

Grey grinned. "You took his measure well. We Sommerses have our share of pride. The House of Hanover is a collection of upstarts by comparison."

"Pride, yes, but not arrogance," she said. "You'll make a very fine earl, Grey."

"I hope so. It's the only thing I've ever really wanted." Except Cassie, and he knew better than to say that out loud. Not after she'd recoiled at the suggestion that they could make their betrothal a real one.

He watched the play of light on her richly colored hair, aching to keep her close always. He needed to change her mind. But time was running out.

After a lazy meal in the sunshine, they headed back to the main house. Cassie had loved the ride, the horse, and the beautiful spring day. Most of all, she loved the feeling of wholeness she sensed in Grey.

Though his captivity had been beastly, she suspected that some of the ways it had reshaped his life were good. Certainly any tendency he might have had toward arrogance had been knocked out of him.

The emotional damage would take more time to heal. She guessed that large groups of people would continue to distress him for some time to come, and the incident with Peter proved that his temper was still dangerously close to the surface.

But the foundation of his character was being rebuilt into a structure that was so solid that she need no longer worry about him. Not much, anyhow.

They emerged from the woods and saw a crowd of people gathered in the courtyard outside the entrance to the house. "Those are tenants and neighbors," Grey exclaimed. "Good God, my father!"

Chapter 37

Grey kicked his horse into a blazing gallop toward the house. Cassie followed only a couple of strides behind, knowing he was right to be afraid. Head injuries were unpredictable, and even though the earl had seemed to be recovering, he might have taken a lethal turn for the worse. This sort of gathering is exactly what might happen when word went out through the neighborhood that a great and beloved man had died.

Thirty or forty people had gathered, but as Cassie drew nearer, she saw that the mood was festive rather than solemn. Yes, it was an impromptu party, with tables holding refreshments set up below the portico. Two men, one of them Peter, were dispensing tankards of drink from casks.

"Here he is!" A cry went up as Grey was spotted racing toward them. "Hip, hip, hooray! Hip, hip, hooray! *Hip, hip, hooray!*"

Cassie and Grey realized at the same moment that it was a welcome home party for the long-lost heir to Costain. Waving, Grey slowed his mount to a walk. When Cassie drew up beside him, he said quietly, "News of my miraculous return obviously spread fast. Most of the tenants and local villagers are here."

His jaw was tight and she guessed that he was feeling crowd panic. "You could ride around the back and go into the house that way," she suggested. "Then you could call out a greeting from one of the front windows."

He shook his head. "Sommerses don't do things like that. If they came here to show that they're glad I'm alive, I can't hide away. But please . . . stay close, Cassie."

"Are you going to introduce me as your fiancée?" she asked warily. "This lie is spreading faster and faster."

"I won't if you'd rather I didn't, but I'd be amazed if everyone here hasn't already heard that my beautiful redheaded companion is the next Countess of Costain." He gave her a lopsided smile. "For someone who has survived on quick wits and guile, you're remarkably attached to the truth."

She had to laugh. "Living a life of deception is the reason why I draw a very clear line between truth and lies whenever possible."

People were pressing forward toward the riders, calling greetings to Grey. Cassie said under her breath, "You'll feel less overwhelmed if you remain on horseback."

"True," he agreed, "but I can't."

He dismounted and took the hand of a broad, grizzled farmer who had tears in his eyes. This wasn't a lord greeting a peasant. This was living proof of a community where the Sommerses of Summerhill were part of a greater fabric. The community had mourned Grey's apparent death, and now the people celebrated his miraculous return.

The farmer said, "I knew those damned frogs couldn't kill you!"

"They came very close, Mr. Jackson!" Grey called back.

A heavyset older woman enveloped him in a fierce hug. "Don't you ever frighten me like that again! You're not too old to be spanked, young man!"

"And you're just the woman to do it," he said with a grin as he hugged her back.

Despite Grey's warm responses, Cassie saw that he was strung as tight as a harp string. She slid from her mount and moved to stand at his left shoulder. Two young boys emerged from the crowd and took the reins to the horses and led them away.

As Grey had requested, Cassie stayed close, but people were closing in around them, pressing closer and closer. Though the mood was happy, even Cassie grew nervous at the crowding. Concerned for Grey, she grabbed Peter's arm when he joined them. Under her breath, she said, "Crowds upset him. Take his other side and keep people from getting too close."

Peter's brow furrowed. "Grey seems fine."

"He isn't!" she retorted. "Please, help him get more space."

Accepting her word, Peter moved to Grey's other side to form another barrier to the jostling crowd. Cassie took Grey's arm. She whispered in his ear, "You need to help your frail fiancée into the house!"

"You, frail?" he said incredulously, but relieved. "A good excuse, though."

He began to walk through the crowd, shaking hands and accepting hugs with his free arm as he continued to exchange greetings. On his other side, Peter intercepted well-wishers and deflected some of the excitement.

They reached the steps and climbed up to the portico. At the top, Grey turned and raised both hands for silence.

When the hubbub died down, he said in a voice that filled the courtyard, "I can't describe how much it means to be welcomed home like this. For ten long years, I've dreamed of Summerhill. Of my family"—he clapped Peter on the shoulder—"and of my friends. Like you, Mrs. Henry, who made me work in your garden if I was to earn your wonderful gingerbread."

The crowd laughed while a large woman called back, "Just this once I'll send a batch to the big house to celebrate your homecoming!"

"If you forget, you'll find me on your doorstep, hungry," he promised. His gaze moved across the upturned faces. "I'd think about all the pretty Lloyd daughters. I see that there are two more now than when I left." More laughter. He added, "Before I forget, I want to say that my father is recovering well from his accident, so you won't have to deal with me for some time."

More cheers and laughter. Cassie watched admiringly as Grey continued talking to his friends and neighbors with wit and charm. He truly was born to Summerhill. These people were proof of how generations of Sommerses had cared for their land and their tenants. How they loved, and were loved in return.

Her eyes stung from a mixture of emotions.

Pride in Grey. Envy of his powerful sense of belonging. And regret that she would never see this connection between Grey and his community again, because it really was time for her to leave. Grey had everything he needed right here.

A voice called out, "Tell us what happened, Lord Wyndham, or we'll make up stories that will curdle milk!"

"Can't have that." Grey hesitated. "The story is simple, really, and I have every intention of forgetting the details, so don't ask me more. Ten years ago I was in Paris and I offended a high government official just as the Truce of Amiens ended. It was a chaotic time, so the official threw me into his own private dungeon out in the country. Ten years of one boring day after another, so there isn't much to tell. When I finally escaped, I headed north and found a smuggler to bring me home. And here I am."

"Who's the lady?" a woman called. "Is she the next countess?"

Grey took Cassie's hand and drew her forward with a whispered, "Sorry." Turning to the crowd, he said, "This is Miss Catherine St. Ives of Norfolk, who helped me escape. I hope to persuade her to stay. Will you give her a Dorsetshire welcome?"

The crowd burst into roars and applause while Cassie blushed bright red. Damn her pale redhead's complexion!

Grey waved a farewell. "Miss St. Ives is tired so I'll say goodbye and thank you. I shall never forget this day."

As soon as they were inside and the door closed behind them, he crushed her in his arms and shook. She felt his hammering heart against her breasts. "Thank you for rescuing me once again," he said roughly. "The welcome was wonderful in theory, but I wouldn't have lasted much longer without behaving badly."

"I think you would have lasted as long as necessary." She stroked a calming hand down his back. "But you've been tested enough for one day."

Peter followed them in, closing the door behind him. "People obviously prefer you to inherit rather than me," he said cheerfully. He sobered when he saw his brother's strained face. "That really was hard on you! I thought Cassie was exaggerating."

"She's very good at keeping me from falling apart," Grey said wryly, not letting Cassie go. "All those people just showed up? I was afraid it meant that Father had died."

Peter winced. "That would look similar, wouldn't it? When Mother saw tenants arriving, she sent me out to play host while she arranged for refreshments. I think half the reason people came was because this is the first real spring day we've had, and everyone wanted an excuse to celebrate."

"So my return was the excuse." Grey relaxed enough to end the embrace, though he kept an arm around Cassie. "And by coming here, they had a good shot at Summerhill cider and ale and probably Summerhill hams and cheeses as well."

"An opportunity they took full advantage of," Lady Costain said from above. She glided down the stairs, one hand on the railing and looking every inch a countess. "I was about to send out grooms to find you, Grey. But when you did return, you handled it all well. Your father was watching from his room."

"He must be much stronger," Grey said. "Which probably means he'll be down for dinner tonight."

His mother laughed. "Indeed he will. Since we have so much reason to be grateful, I decided that tonight we'll have a special celebration feast just for the family. Elizabeth and her husband will join us. Catherine, do you have a favorite dish I should ask the cook to prepare?"

Cassie blinked. Apparently she was no longer a fortune-hunting slut. After a moment's thought, she said, "There's a sweet I loved when I was a child, an apple tart made with a handful of currants that have been soaked in brandy. It was served warm with custard or cream on special occasions."

"Apple with currants soaked in brandy?" The countess looked intrigued. "That sounds excellent, and well within my kitchen's capacity. Grey, I imagine you would still enjoy Mrs. Bradford's special roast lamb?"

"Oh, yes," he said fervently. "With mint sauce."

"I shall see you at dinner then." With a gracious nod to her sons and Cassie, Lady Costain sailed off for the kitchen.

"My mother now thinks of you as part of the family," Grey observed.

"She could hardly forbid me the table when I'm your guest," Cassie pointed out. "I need to examine my wardrobe to see what will suit a family celebration in the country when half the guests have titles."

"You could wear that habit and look beautiful," Grey assured her.

"But not appropriate! I'll see you later." She caught up her skirts and climbed the stairs. When she reached her room, she rang for Hazel, who appeared promptly. "You're the perfect maid," Cassie observed. "Good at all the maidly skills, but since you're one of Kirkland's people, we can gossip as equals."

Hazel bobbed a very proper curtsy. "I've much experience as a maid. It's a good way to gather information without being noticed."

Cassie nodded. Maids, like old peddlers, were usually invisible. "I need something very nice but not too flamboyant to wear for dinner tonight. The earl will come down for the first time since his accident, and they want to celebrate Lord

Wyndham's return as well. Two escapes from death." Cassie grinned. "Lady Kiri threw this wardrobe together for me so quickly I'm not sure what I have."

"There's a green satin gown that will look a treat with your red hair," Hazel said. "It's not as full or long as a ball gown and the neckline isn't as deep, but it's handsome enough for a special dinner. It might need a bit of altering, so you'd best try it on after you're out of the riding habit."

"I'm really fortunate that Lady Kiri's sister is so close to me in size and has such a generous nature." Cassie turned so Hazel could unfasten the back of her habit. "Are you bored here with no spies or indiscreet government ministers to watch?"

Hazel laughed as she undid one of the ties. "It's been very restful. This is the rarest of places, a happy household."

"Unusual indeed. What do the servants think of Lord Wyndham's return?"

"Everyone is delighted, particularly the older folks who knew him better. They say he's very like his father, and that's good for Summerhill." Hazel tugged the gown over Cassie's head. "The more thoughtful folk recognize that ten years in prison change a man. They hope he hasn't changed too much."

"He's remarkably resilient, so I think they have no reason to worry about their future here." Cassie raised her arms so Hazel could drop the green satin gown over her. "What do they think of Peter? For years he's been considered the heir."

Hazel smoothed the fabric over Cassie's figure. "He's well liked and people thought he'd have done a decent job if he'd inherited, but they think his elder brother will do the job best."

"I'm sure they're right. Grey truly loves this estate and all the responsibilities that go with it." As Hazel pinned the gown in several places, Cassie tried not to think about the perfect lady needed to match Grey's perfect lord.

Chapter 38

Grey's eyes widened as Cassie descended the staircase in a shimmer of green satin. "You look splendid. The gown is perfect for tonight."

Though she laughed, she was pleased by his warm admiration. "Since you were happy with my riding habit, I don't know how much I should trust your judgment."

He offered his arm. "I assure you that I've always had impeccable taste when it comes to dressing women." His voice dropped to a whisper. "And I'm equally good at undressing them."

"Shhhh!" she said with a blush as they entered the small salon where the family was gathering for pre-dinner drinks. Lord Costain was seated on a sofa rather than standing, but he looked very well.

His wife was beside him, and they held hands like besotted newlyweds.

Cassie made a deep curtsy in front of them. "I am glad to see you so well, my lord. I thank you both for your courtesy to an unexpected guest."

Lord Costain smiled benevolently. "Very prettily said. My wife and I could not be happier to meet our son's future bride, and to find her so suitable." A glint in Lady Costain's eyes suggested that she wasn't entirely in agreement with her husband's statement, but her smile was gracious.

Peter entered the salon followed by his sister and her husband. John Langtry was pleasant looking rather than strikingly handsome like the Sommers men, but he had an appealing smile and he and Elizabeth clearly doted on each other.

Cassie was pleased to see how relaxed Grey was with his family now that the initial hurdles had been cleared. He talked easily, shared reminiscences with his brother-in-law, and was attentive to Cassie so she didn't feel like the odd woman out.

After half an hour of relaxed conversation, Lady Costain got to her feet. "Shall we adjourn to the dining room?"

"An excellent plan," Grey said. "I hear a roast lamb calling my name."

Cassie smiled, looking forward to Grey's lamb and the St. Ives apple currant tart. As she stood, the butler appeared in the door. "There are two gentlemen here to see Miss St. Ives."

Hard on his heels were two well-dressed young men around Cassie's age. They were of similar height and build, though one was a bit taller and broader. The men were clearly related by blood—and they had auburn hair the exact shade of Cassie's.

"Look at the hair! It has to be her!" the leaner one hissed to the other. Raising his voice, he asked eagerly, "Catherine? Are you our Cat?"

Cassie's wineglass dropped from nerveless fingers and smashed on the floor as she stared at the newcomers. When she had known her cousins, they'd all been children with faces not yet fully formed, but in the features of these grown men she saw echoes of her dark-haired, long-dead brother, Paul.

Rushing memories tightened her throat so she could barely speak. Gazing at the leaner man, she breathed, "Richard?" Her gaze shifted to the other. "Neil?"

She swayed until Grey put a steadying hand on her shoulder. "You are Cassie St. Ives's cousins?" he asked.

"We certainly are!" Richard drew Cassie into an exuberant hug. "Cat, dear God, it's a miracle! We thought you were dead." He pulled back without letting go of her and asked hesitantly, "Did . . . did anyone else survive?"

She shook her head, tears running down her face. "Only me."

The other young man moved his brother aside. "Being the heir doesn't mean you get all the hugs, Richard." His embrace was rib bruising. "You'd better remember me also, Cat, or I'm going to put frogs in your bed!"

"If you do, you'll find one in yours, too!" she said with a catch of laughter. She leaned into her younger cousin's embrace. He was tall and strong, a man now. The three of them had been close in age and they were a large part of the childhood she'd buried in the depths of unbearable memory. "You've grown, Neil. I used to be able to defeat you when we wrestled."

"And didn't our mothers hate when we did that!" he chuckled.

Richard turned toward the fascinated gazes of the Sommers family. Bowing to the earl and countess, he said, "Lord Costain, Lady Costain. Please accept my apologies for intruding on a family occasion. My only excuse is that once we learned that our cousin might be alive, we were desperate to learn the truth."

"We above all can understand what it is like to experience this kind of miracle," Lord Costain said. "Our prodigal son was missing for only ten years. Your prodigal cousin has been lost for nigh on twenty years."

"Exactly, sir." Richard's smile lit up the room.

"The lost has been found, and we couldn't be happier."

Lord Costain studied the newcomers. "I know your father, and your uncle was a good friend of mine. I'm glad to meet the next generation of St. Iveses."

Lady Costain glanced at the butler. "Set two more places at the table and prepare rooms for our guests."

"That isn't necessary, Lady Costain," Richard protested. "We'll stay in the village inn. We should have waited until tomorrow to call, but . . . we couldn't." He swallowed hard. "Catherine's brother and sister were dark haired like their mother and too old to be playmates for us, but Cat was our age and a true redheaded St. Ives. More like a sister than a cousin."

"Of course you'll stay here," the countess said briskly. "Our families are soon to be connected, so you are very welcome under our roof. Tonight is a celebration of my husband's recovery from a serious accident and my son's return from France. What could be more fitting than for you to join us in celebrating your cousin's survival?"

Neil said, "You are gracious, ma'am."

"I am known for it," the countess said with a sparkle of amusement. "Would you gentlemen like to have a drink before dining?"

The brothers exchanged a glance. "It appears that you were on the verge of going in to dinner,"

Richard said. "Give us a moment to wash up, and we'll be happy to dine now if you don't mind our travel dust."

That was agreed to. In the following flurry of activity, Grey murmured to Cassie, "You have no doubt of their identities?"

"None at all," she replied. "Their father was vicar of the St. Ives parish church, so Richard and Neil and I grew up together." She gazed after them as they left to wash up. "After my family was killed, I closed the door on my childhood. Now they've opened that door and I find so many bright, clear memories."

"I'm glad," he said simply.

He was, she realized, but there was another emotion in his eyes. One that she couldn't read.

With twice as many males as females present, Cassie was able to sit next to Grey and opposite both her cousins. She asked them question after question about the family. Their parents were well, and George, the brother who'd been only a baby when Cassie last saw him, was now a student at Oxford and planning to follow his father into the church. The three of them ate and laughed and sighed happily over the apple currant tart.

When Lady Costain rose to signal the end of the meal, she said, "Rather than separating the males and females for port and tea, I suggest that perhaps Catherine and her cousins might like time together to talk since they have much to catch up on."

Cassie, feeling awkward, glanced at Grey. After he gave her a slight nod, she said, "I'd like that very much if it's agreeable to Richard and Neil."

They said they'd like nothing better, so the St. Iveses were escorted to the library, where both port and tea were available. Feeling reckless, Cassie poured three glasses of port and settled down in front of the fire with hers.

Her cousins sprawled opposite, visibly fatigued from their long journey, but deeply content. Richard remarked, "I noticed Lord Wyndham called you Cassie. Do you prefer that to Cat?"

"Either will do. I haven't been Cat in almost twenty years. I rather like hearing it again." Cat had been a happy, mischievous child. Very different from serious, haunted Cassie, but both of them were real. "Do your parents know about me, or are they in Norfolk?"

"They're in London, but we didn't tell them," Richard said. "I know Kirkland slightly and he gave me the information about you so I could choose how to handle it."

"Kirkland," she said wryly. "I should have known. Why didn't he tell your father since they were both in London? I'm sure they know each other."

Neil grimaced. "About ten years ago an

imposter showed up. It was very painful for the family, especially my parents."

"Someone was impersonating me?" she asked, startled. "Why?"

"Not you. Paul, since he was the heir to St. Ives," Richard explained. "Like Paul, the imposter had your mother's dark hair, and he looked quite a bit like Paul. Like a St. Ives. And he'd gathered enough information about the family to be moderately convincing, too."

"If only it had been Paul," Cassie said sorrowfully. "But I'm sure I was the only survivor." Tersely she described the fire and how she'd been saved by her nurse, Josette. The story hadn't seemed suitable to tell during a celebratory dinner.

"At least it was quick, not months of misery in a dungeon waiting for execution," Neil said, repressed savagery in his voice. "Your family's deaths changed everything and not just because Father inherited the title."

"Though going from the vicarage to St. Ives Hall was a considerable change, and not always as amusing as one might think," Richard observed.

Neil gave a nod of agreement. "If your family had died of fever or smallpox, it would have been tragic but could be considered God's will. Being murdered because you were English in the wrong place at the wrong time was utterly, infuriatingly wrong."

"We both wanted to go into the army and kill Frenchmen," Richard said bluntly. "But since I'm the heir, I accepted that my responsibilities lay in England."

"So I got to be the dashing hero," Neil said with a grin. "I'm a captain in the Life Guards."

"To be fair, he's probably better at mayhem than I."

"I look better in the uniform, too," Neil said smugly.

Cassie laughed at the brotherly teasing. "Tell me more about the imposter. How did you find he wasn't Paul?"

"My mother had always doted on Paul, and she embraced him wholeheartedly. She wanted him to be Paul. My father wasn't so sure," Richard explained. "He'd never expected to become Lord St. Ives and he was shattered when your family was killed. But he'd had ten years of being a lord by the time the imposter showed up. He found that he liked it. So when he had doubts about the imposter, he wasn't sure if they were genuine, or if he didn't want to believe for selfish reasons."

"My father said his brother was the most honorable man he knew," Cassie said softly. "No wonder he was torn. How was the imposter exposed?"

"I could see that Richard had some of the same conflicts as Father," Neil said. "It was easier for me since I wasn't the heir and didn't have as much

341

to lose. Faux Paul was fairly convincing, but I didn't have the sense I'd ever known him before. He felt like a stranger. After I talked it over with Richard, we started setting traps. Pretending we remembered doing things with him that never happened and the like. He was good at being evasive, but eventually we had enough evidence to support our belief that he was a fraud and we presented it to our parents."

"Mother didn't want to believe us," Richard said, continuing the story. "Father frowned and called Faux Paul in and demanded he take off his shirt."

Cassie blinked. "Why?"

"Apparently when Paul was very small, before you were born, he fell against a piece of jagged wood and was badly injured. He almost died and was left with a huge scar on one shoulder. Few people knew about that, but of course my parents did."

Fascinated by the story, Cassie asked, "Did Faux Paul try to escape?"

"Very briefly, but Richard and I were both there," Neil said grimly. "I pinned him down and cut off his shirt. No scar. That was enough to convince even my mother."

"What happened to him?"

"We conducted a family court right there," Richard said. "His name was Barton Black and he's actually a first cousin of ours. His mother was a bastard daughter of our grandfather, who seems to have been a lusty old goat. When Barton learned of the deaths in France, he began studying the family. When enough time had passed to blur memories, he showed up and claimed to be Paul."

"I think this is one cousin I'm glad I haven't met," Cassie said, bemused. "What did the family court decide?"

"My father hadn't known about Barton's mother, and he thought she and Barton had been treated very shabbily. He made Barton sign a detailed confession with all of us as witnesses, then said he could go free." Richard laughed. "Barton was a cheeky devil. Said he wanted to leave England for warmer climes and asked for the fare to Botany Bay because he'd heard there were great opportunities there."

"Father agreed and we escorted him to the docks and put him on a ship. We'll not see him again." Neil grinned. "I rather liked him even if he wasn't Paul. But you can see why when Kirkland said Catherine St. Ives was alive, Richard decided to look you over before we told our parents. Since I was in London, he roped me into coming."

"You'd not have forgiven me if I hadn't asked," Richard pointed out.

"You had no doubts of my identity?" Cassie asked curiously. "Twenty years is a long time. Two thirds of our lives."

"You had the hair," Neil explained. "Also,

Kirkland said he'd known you for years. Since you'd never announced yourself to the family, it didn't seem as if you were after anything."

"Why didn't you tell us?" Richard said, his voice low and laced with pain. "Did you think we didn't care?"

Cassie looked down at her port and realized that she'd drunk it all. She rose and poured more, topping up her cousins' glasses as well.

When she resumed her seat, she said, "I was an orphaned child in France, lucky to be alive. My English life seemed very distant, no more than a dream. With a war going on, it wasn't a simple matter of writing a letter. By the time I was old enough to return, too much time had passed. I didn't think anyone would remember or care who I was."

"You should have known better, Cat," Richard said. "I meant what I said to the Costains. You were like a sister. How could you imagine Neil or I would forget you?"

As she gazed into her wine, she realized there was another reason. "I needed to believe that . . . that your family was well and happy," she said haltingly. "If I'd found that one of you had died, I wouldn't have been able to bear it."

Neil leaned over to give her shoulders a brotherly squeeze. "We were well and happy, Cat. But we would have been happier to know you were alive."

"What have you been doing all these years?" Richard asked. "Did you marry? Have children? How have you survived?"

She hesitated, wondering how much to say. But Richard and Neil were family. They deserved some truth. "I've spent much of my time in France, but I return to England regularly. I do work that the British government considers useful."

"You're a spy," Neil said with dawning understanding. "Damn, Cat, but you always were the gamest girl I ever knew!"

"I think I better understand why you didn't write us," Richard said soberly. "The work you've been doing must be very dangerous."

Cassie shrugged. "There was no reason to disrupt your lives, and if something happened to me, you wouldn't have the pain of losing me a second time."

"Actually, you had a very good reason to let us know you were alive, Cat," Richard said. "Didn't you know that you're an heiress?"

Chapter 39

"An heiress?" Cassie echoed, startled. "My parents' marriage settlements would have specified portions for each child of the union, but surely that went back into the St. Ives estate after our deaths were reported. Why would there be any money due to me?"

Neil grinned. "You tell her, Richard. You're the one who spends all the time with the estate lawyers and bankers."

"For my sins." Richard rolled his eyes. "You're still eligible for your portion since you are alive, but that's just the beginning. Your mother had a substantial fortune, and the settlements divided it equally among her children. Since you're the only surviving child, her entire fortune comes to you, along with your portion from the St. Ives estate."

Still doubting, Cassie said, "The Montclairs were well off, but I assumed all their wealth was confiscated by the French government during the revolution."

"Perhaps. I have no information about that," Richard replied. "But since your mother married an Englishman, her fortune was transferred to England, where it's been growing very nicely ever since."

"We St. Iveses are businessmen at heart, you know," Neil said with a grin. "We're much better at making money than the average aristocrat."

It was more than Cassie could grasp. "So now I can afford to buy myself a cottage by the sea."

"You can buy a castle by the sea if you like," Richard assured her.

Cassie shook her head, having trouble grasping the magnitude of this news. "I never thought I'd live long enough for money to matter. My expenses have always been reimbursed by the people I work with, so I've had salary to spare." There was no point in buying clothing or jewels when she could almost never wear them. "I've never worried about the future because I never expected to make old bones."

"Enough of that nonsense, Cat," Neil said, his voice stern. "As a soldier during war, there are any number of ways I might come to a premature end, but I jolly well intend to retire as a crusty old colonel and live till I'm ninety. There's no point in assuming one will die young."

Cassie had assumed that. But now she was discovering reasons for living.

"Enough talk of death," Richard said. "Cat, come back to London with us. My parents will be overjoyed to see you."

Leave Grey? Leave Summerhill? But she must, and soon. Stalling, she said, "I must think about it. This is all so sudden."

"The world turned upside down," Richard agreed. "Bring Wyndham along. He should meet your family. I'd like to get to know him better. See if he's good enough for my almost sister."

"He's just returned to Summerhill and he won't want to leave again so soon."

Her cousins nodded with understanding, then began to fill her in on family news of the last couple of decades. She felt as if a bright, shiny new world was being created right before her very eyes.

It would replace the bright world she'd glimpsed here that could never be hers.

By the time Cassie and her cousins ran out of conversation, the rest of the household had retired. When she became too weary to continue, Cassie hugged them both good night. "I'd forgotten how wonderful it is to have a family."

"There's nothing more important," Richard said as he released her so Neil would have his turn. "Now that we have you back, you'll never lack for family again."

"Do return to London with us, Cat," Neil added. "I'm leaving for Spain by the end of the week, and I feel like we still have years of conversation to catch up on."

"I'll consider it." With a last smile, she returned to her room, feeling lightheaded from all the port she'd drunk. She'd never forgotten Paul and Anne, her true brother and sister, but she should have remembered that she had other brothers as well.

A crack of light showed under the door of her room, so a maid must have left a lamp for her, and perhaps a fire to warm the chilly night. With a sigh, Cassie realized she must ring for Hazel to help her out of her gown.

She stepped into her room and was unsurprised to see that she was not alone. Grey was lying stretched out on the bed, his hands folded under his head and his gaze on the ceiling. He'd shed his boots and coat and was all lean, pantherish power, his hair golden and his masculine frame etched by firelight.

When she entered, he turned his startling dark-rimmed eyes to her. "You're going to leave, aren't you?" he asked quietly.

She closed the door and leaned back against it, her decision made. "Yes."

"I can see how much it means to you to have a family again. Your cousins seem like good fellows. Nonetheless . . ." In one smooth movement Grey was off the bed and across the room to stand an arm's length from her. "Don't go, Cassie. Please."

She wanted to walk into his arms, hold him and never let go. She wanted to learn ever deeper mysteries of his soul, to be intertwined as closely as two humans could be.

But she couldn't. "It's time for me to leave, Grey," she said, fighting to keep her voice steady.

"Why?" he asked fiercely. "Don't you think we could have a good life together?"

"I don't know. Neither do you." She shook her head. "You've been free only a few weeks. We've been together constantly ever since, facing danger and sharing passion. I've been the one constant as you've reentered the world. But that's not a good enough reason to marry." She made a sweeping gesture that encompassed her surroundings. "You don't need me anymore, Grey. Everything you really need is right here at Summerhill."

"I'm not asking you to stay because I need you, but because I want you," he said gravely. "Does that make a difference?"

She shook her head again. "Desire is powerful, but it shouldn't be allowed to overcome judgment."

"No? You think this is so easily dismissed?" He moved forward and trapped her against the door with a searing kiss. His hands slid over her with heat and promise, bringing her body to yearning life.

Resistance and judgment vanished as she gave herself to the passion that bound them. They drew together, writhing with the need to join, yet too impatient to undress.

Breathing harshly, he drew her green satin gown up till it crushed around her hips. Then he delved into moist silken heat with unerring skill.

She gasped, pulsing against his hand. She wanted to melt into him. Equally she wanted to tear off his clothing. Mayhem won and she yanked his shirt from his trousers so she could slide her hand over the taut warmth of his belly.

When she found hot, hard flesh, his whole body jerked and a low moan escaped him. He ripped open his trousers while she raised one leg and wrapped it around his hips. When he sheathed himself inside her, they merged with panting breath and fierce rightness, male and female finding wholeness together.

"Catherine," he breathed hoarsely as his hands tightened on the perfect curves of her derriere. "Cat. *Cassie!*" He shattered, tumbling into the abyss and taking her with him. She bit his shoulder to stifle her cries as he filled and fulfilled her, dissolving the pain that had shaped her life and leaving only sensation.

Yet it wasn't enough. Not when passion faded and left her with gasping lungs, weakened muscles, and regret.

She might not have made it across the room if he hadn't half carried her. Once they were standing by the bed, he deftly unfastened the ties and hooks of her satin gown. As he removed her layered garments, she wondered if the gown could be saved.

She supposed it didn't matter since she could now buy any gown she wanted as a replacement. But Cassie was the product of too many years of frugality to not care if a beautiful garment had been wantonly destroyed.

And she was too much a product of danger and deception to give herself entirely to a man who wanted her now, but would not want her forever. That was the crux of it, she realized, as she slipped under the covers, then watched him strip off his clothing.

He was beautiful, all hard muscles and strong

planes. He was a man who loved and liked women, and when the passion that joined them now faded, he would find fresh passions elsewhere.

Grey wouldn't be unkind. He'd do his best to keep his affairs hidden from her to protect her feelings and her dignity. But she'd know. An expert spy was impossible to deceive about a matter so close to her heart.

In a year or two, when the fractured parts of his character had healed into a new shape that couldn't yet be known, he might be ready to find the next Countess of Costain. She'd be a beautiful, sophisticated virgin who would be content with what he had to offer, and perhaps enjoy the freedom to take lovers of her own after passion faded and they had the heir and the spare his position required.

But Cassie the Fox would never be such a woman. She had no desire to share. She must leave now, before she was too deeply in love with him to leave.

As he held her close, he said with sad resignation, "You're still going to leave, aren't you, my lady vixen?"

"Yes," she whispered. "There is attraction between us, and the bond created as we escaped from France, but that's not enough to build our lives on."

"I rather think it is, but if you disagree, I don't know how to change your mind." His caressing hand moved down from her shoulder, warming and shaping the soft flesh he found along the way. "I want to give you everything, yet there is nothing you need from me. You've found your way back to the life of wealth and position that you were born to, so I can't even give you that."

"You've given me something more valuable than a title and a fortune." She turned her face to kiss his lips with lingering tenderness. "You've opened my heart in a way that makes a different kind of future thinkable. If I survive this war, and I'm beginning to believe that perhaps I will, I'll be able to live a better life than if I hadn't known you."

He cupped her breast. "I'm glad you value the time we've been together. I thought all the benefit had been to me, and I'm not so selfish as to prefer it that way."

"You're not selfish." She kissed him again, tenderness sliding into heat. "You're generous in ways none of the other men I've known can match."

He rolled so he was above her, supporting his weight so that his body barely skimmed hers. "You're right that recovering from hell will take longer than a month. Will you think me a better, saner prospect a year from now? When you're in England, can I take you for mad, passionate holidays by the sea?"

"No!" she said sharply. "We must end this *now.*

You mustn't wait to see if I'll change my mind, and having an affair will only prolong the pain. Find joy in all the things you were deprived of. A year from now you won't be interested in an aging spy."

"I'm tempted to spank you," he said with exasperation. "You worry about my state of mind, yet you're so daft that you don't recognize what an extraordinary and beautiful woman you are." He began kissing his way down her throat, stirring sensations she'd thought exhausted. "Can I at least convince you that you are incredibly desirable?"

She opened her legs and he settled between them, his hardening length sliding along her exquisitely sensitive flesh. As she rocked against him, she said huskily, "You make me feel like the most desirable woman on earth."

"Because you are." He buried his face in the angle of her shoulder. "Ah, God, Cassie! If we only have tonight, let us spend every moment of it well."

"We will," she breathed as she drew him into her. "We will."

When passion and words were exhausted, Grey cradled her spoon style, her back against his chest so she could feel the strong beat of his heart. She wondered if she'd ever feel so close to another man again.

Perhaps. Her time with Grey had changed her in fundamental ways. She could now imagine a life beyond war. If she survived, she'd buy a home in Norfolk to be near her family. Perhaps she might even marry someday. But just now, it was impossible to imagine loving any man but Grey.

She was half asleep when Grey began to sing, the soft words and melody barely audible. She hadn't heard him sing since finding him in the dungeons of Castle Durand. She'd been surprised as much as by his strong, rich voice as by the amazing bawdiness of his song.

His voice was still rich, but this time he sang of love, or rather lost love. Her throat tightened as she recognized the haunting song from her childhood.

Are you going to Scarborough Fair?
Parsley, sage, rosemary, and thyme.
Remember me to one who lives there
She once was a true love of mine.

The verses continued in the series of challenges to accomplish impossible tasks before love could be achieved. Aching, she closed her eyes against the sting of tears.

Remember me to one who lives there
He once was a true love of mine.

Chapter 40

Grey had faced more difficult challenges than bidding Cassie a civil farewell as she left him forever, but he couldn't offhand remember when. He prayed that he would be able to maintain his composure rather than break down and confirm her worst suspicions of his mental stability.

The whole Sommers family had gathered in the front hall to say goodbye to Cassie and her cousins. She wasn't dressed for glamour this morning, but the rich dark brown of her beautifully tailored morning gown was a perfect complement to her glorious auburn hair and porcelain complexion. When she turned to him to make her farewell, she looked more regal than the queen of England. It was hard to remember that they had lain naked and passionate in each other's arms the night before.

While Richard and Neil gave effusive thanks and farewells to the earl and countess, Grey took the opportunity for a few last private words with Cassie. Close up, he saw shadows under her eyes. Not surprising, given how little sleep they'd had. He probably looked much the same.

"If I can get through this without breaking down into strong hysterics, surely I'm cured of my prison madness," he murmured, trying for a light note. "Though, to be honest, the only thing preventing me from sweeping you away and locking you in the attics is the knowledge that you'd break my arm or something even more valuable."

Her eyes lit with wry amusement. "I don't doubt that you're well on the way to recovery, Grey. Soon you'll be breaking every female heart in the beau monde."

"Oddly enough, that's not my ambition." He studied her face with such desperate ferocity that his gaze should have scorched her pale redhead's complexion. In a remote corner of his mind, he understood why she believed they must go their separate ways. An even smaller part of him agreed. But his heart, body, and soul believed otherwise.

"Time to go, Cat!" Neil called.

"Goodbye, my lord and companion in adversity." Cassie raised her hand and brushed Grey's cheek with feather lightness. "I shall never forget you."

His control snapped and he crushed her into a desperate embrace. "Don't go, Cassie!" he whispered into her ear. "Stay."

For an instant she hugged him back just as hard. Then she broke away, her face flushing. "Live well, Grey. Be happy." She turned and walked out of Summerhill.

Taking his heart with her.

Cassie didn't relax until the coach was well away from the estate. Not that she expected Grey to come galloping after her and sweep her onto his horse. Surely he knew better than to try. But with him, she could never be quite sure.

When they reached the main road east toward London, she finally settled back. Four people in the coach meant they were warm, so she removed her bonnet. Richard sat beside her. The facing seat held Neil opposite Cassie, while Hazel, looking invisible as only Kirkland's agents could manage, sat across from Richard.

Richard had been silent until now, but he said abruptly, "I saw what Wyndham did as we were leaving. Has he behaved dishonorably to you, Cat?"

"Dishonorably?" she asked incredulously. "What do you mean?"

Looking embarrassed but ready to call Grey out, Richard asked, "Did he lead you to have expectations that he didn't fulfill?"

Caught between amusement and irritation, Cassie said coolly, "If you're practicing to be head of the family, don't. I am quite capable of taking care of myself."

"But is he doing right by you?" Richard persisted. "I'm serious, Catherine."

She studied her cousins for a dozen turns of the carriage wheels, wondering if they could understand the reality of a spy's life. They'd probably be shocked—they were the sons of a vicar, after all. Better not to try to explain the complexities of her situation. "Wyndham wanted to marry me. Most people would consider that honorable behavior."

"And you didn't want to?" His voice was puzzled. "I don't understand. You seemed very fond of each other."

"It's complicated." She closed her eyes, cutting off discussion. She didn't understand, either. But she knew she was right. Grey was not yet ready to take a bride. When and if he became ready, it wouldn't be her.

Once more the trip to London was made at the quickest pace that a hired coach and frequent changes of horses could manage. Even so, it was midevening by the time they reached London. At her request, Hazel was set down near Kirkland's office. Cassie suspected the agent would report about Wyndham's return home.

As Hazel climbed from the coach, Cassie said, "Many thanks. You made my visit to the West Country much easier."

Hazel smiled. "I enjoyed it. Perhaps we'll meet again at Exeter Street."

When the coach began moving again, Neil observed, "Not the usual lady's maid."

Cassie smiled. "I'm not the usual lady."

St. Ives House was only a short ride away. As Neil helped her from the coach, she studied the façade. This block of houses was handsome and well proportioned. As a child, she hadn't been brought to London often, but she remembered the house well.

"Is it difficult to be here again?" Richard asked as she took his arm.

She nodded. "I stayed here only a few times, but I have fond memories of the place. So I've avoided it."

"You never came by when you were in London?" Neil asked, surprised.

"Never." Her mouth twisted. "I buried everything to do with my childhood, and never looked back."

"That's not going to happen again," Neil said firmly. "We won't allow it."

"Bossy brothers," she said with a smile. "Even when I was eight years old, I didn't take orders well."

Richard grinned. "Can't I briefly hope that you've become more biddable?"

"A waste of time. Best turn your thoughts to not shocking your parents too much," she advised. "When Lady Costain saw Wyndham without warning, she fainted."

"Good point. I'll go in and prepare them. Neil, give me a couple of minutes to set the stage before you bring in Cat."

"Shall do."

The footman who admitted them gave Cassie a curious glance, but he was too young to have known her. "Welcome home, sirs. If you wish to pay your respects to Lord and Lady St. Ives, they're having tea in the salon."

"Send up a supper for three people," Richard ordered. His step quick, he climbed the stairs to the salon.

Neil took Cassie's cloak and bonnet, adding, "Prepare a room for our guest." When the servant bustled off, he asked Cassie, "Ready to meet more relatives?"

She smiled crookedly as she took his arm. "I now have more sympathy for Wyndham's nerves about going home after long absence."

"Since you weren't expecting Richard and me, you didn't have to worry first," he agreed. "But this won't be bad. Now march lively!"

She laughed and obeyed. As they climbed the stairs, she tried to remember her cousins' birthdays. Richard was about a year older than she, Neil a year younger. Close enough that the three of them had run around together like a pack of heathens. The vicarage was much more relaxed than the manor house, and Cassie had spent much time there, sitting in on lessons taught by her uncle.

The house appeared similar to the way she remembered it, with a number of furnishings that she recognized. Yet there were enough changes, particularly new artwork and upholstery, that it no longer felt like her parents' house. She was glad of that.

When they entered the drawing room, Lady St. Ives was saying placidly, "How long must we wait for this happy surprise, Richard?"

"Not long," her son replied. "Behold!" He made a sweeping gesture toward Cassie and Neil, then moved to join them. With the three of them next to each other, the family resemblance was undeniable.

Cassie's aunt and uncle gaped at her. The passing years had added pounds and wrinkles and gray hair, but they were still the easygoing aunt and uncle she'd adored. She gave a deep curtsy. "It's been a long way, Uncle Vicar. Patient Aunt Patience." She used the nicknames deliberately as a way of verifying her identity.

"Catherine?" her aunt gasped.

Her uncle swiftly crossed the room to look at her more closely. John St. Ives resembled her father, but he was softer and wider and two decades older. "Catherine." He squeezed her hands, his face beaming. "My dear girl! This is no imposter, Patience!"

The reunion that followed was much like the one with Richard and Neil, but with more people, more food, and more overlapping voices. As midnight approached, Cassie began to yawn. "I'm sorry," she apologized. "It's been a long day."

"I should have asked for a room to be made up!" her aunt exclaimed. "I was so busy talking that I forgot."

"I didn't forget," Neil said fondly. "The room will be ready when Cat is."

"Which is now." Cassie smothered another yawn. She was tired not only from travel, but so much social interaction. She was used to a quieter life.

"What are your plans now, Catherine?" her uncle asked. "This is your home while you are in London, of course. But would you like to go to Eaton Manor? With spring coming, Norfolk will be particularly lovely."

The thought produced a stab of pain. Cassie had spent most of her childhood at Eaton Manor, and there would be more memories than she could bear to face now. "Perhaps later," she replied. "For now, I have business in London."

After goodnight hugs, she retreated gratefully to an attractively furnished and comfortable room warmed by a briskly burning fire. Her clothing had been brushed and hung in the wardrobe.

A maid arrived moments after Cassie. The girl was there to help her with her gown, and she also brought a posset of warm spiced milk to aid sleep. Tears threatened when Cassie held the gently steaming mug. She could tell from the scent that the posset was her mother's French recipe. She'd drunk it often as a child.

After the maid unfastened her gown, Cassie dismissed the girl. Changing into her nightgown and robe, she took the mug and moved to the window to gaze out over sleeping London. A sip of the posset showed that in deference to her mature years, a fortifying dose of rum had been added.

What was Grey doing now? Better not to think of that.

Much as she loved her rediscovered family, she'd been independent for too long to allow them to take her over. They had the best intentions in the world, but she'd been Cassie the Fox, sworn to work toward Napoleon's defeat, for all of her adult life.

Yet though she wasn't ready for Eaton Manor, she would enjoy spending time with the St. Iveses and being a woman of means. She owed Lady Kiri Mackenzie and Lucia Stillwell a really splendid shopping spree as a thank-you for their providing her with a wardrobe overnight.

She realized that since she now had assets, she should make a will. She'd never needed one before.

She also wanted to bare her teeth at Kirkland because he'd informed Richard St. Ives that she was alive, and he'd done it without her permission. The fact that it had turned out well just meant that Kirkland was his usual irritatingly right self.

After she chided him, she'd ask him for another mission. Her life might have changed dramatically in the last weeks, but there was still a war going on in Europe. And she wouldn't be satisfied until Napoleon was destroyed.

The fox hadn't finished her run.

Grey took up running. He had run in place for countless hours during his years in prison, imagining that he moved through green, open landscapes. Often he mentally visited his home on those runs to nowhere. Now he really could run through Summerhill. He needed the exertion because he wasn't burning up energy in a bed with Cassie.

He quickly realized that running up and down hills was different from running in place. Though he discovered some new muscles that hadn't been needed on the flat, he loved the freedom of running whether it was in sunshine or rain or on misty mornings. And he would never tire of Summerhill's beauty.

Though he loved riding, being on foot showed new aspects of Summerhill. The local cobbler made him a pair of lightweight, comfortable half boots that perfectly suited his new passion. He felt himself growing stronger emotionally as well as physically. This lovely ancestral land healed him in ways he couldn't describe.

He tried not to think of Cassie. His maturing

might have been stalled by his years in prison, but dammit, he was an adult. He should be able to accept that a woman had good and sufficient reasons not to want him.

Unfortunately, he was reminded of her every time his parents gave another small dinner party for the neighbors. He'd agreed to the gatherings because he knew people were curious about the prodigal son, and he needed to become part of his community again.

But he hated being eyed like a beefsteak thrown into a pack of hungry dogs. He'd had to tell his family that Cassie had ended their betrothal, though he refused to answer questions. The fact that he was available, however, meant that every eligible young lady in the neighborhood was studying him and evaluating her chances.

Those who weren't ladies evaluated him in different ways and made a different kind of offer. He became an expert at politely disappearing. So much nubile femininity emphasized how unique and special Cassie was. He missed her intelligence, her warmth, her hard-won wisdom. He also missed her deliciously rounded and sensual body.

Whenever his thoughts moved in that direction, it was time to start running again.

After a fortnight at home, he was beginning to relax and feel like Lord Wyndham again. Then he received a letter that turned the world upside down again.

Grey went in search of Peter and found him in the library, which was his brother's particular haunt. Peter looked up from a letter with a beaming smile. "This is from Mr. Burke, the theater manager! He says his company needs a young actor to make the ladies swoon, and since I show signs of acting ability, he'll give me a chance."

"Wonderful!" And now Grey had to destroy his brother's happiness. "But don't tell the parents yet." Grimly he held up his own letter. "I must travel to France. If I don't return, you'll be heir to Costain again."

Chapter 41

Samuel Johnson said that a man who was tired of London was tired of life. Perhaps that didn't apply to women, because after a fortnight of shopping and socializing, Cassie was restless. She was used to living a life of purpose. Choosing ribbons for bonnets didn't seem very important compared to working toward Napoleon's end.

It was a relief to receive a message from Kirkland requesting that she pay him a call. She'd visited earlier to chastise him for telling her cousins of her identity, but neither of them took her scolding seriously since the results of his meddling were good.

This was different. As she wielded the dragon's head knocker, she remembered the January day when she'd called on Kirkland and been asked to determine if the long-vanished Wyndham was alive. The intervening months had been so eventful that the time seemed much longer.

Once more she was admitted by the butler and made her way back to Kirkland's study. He rose courteously when she entered.

"What do you have for me today, James?" she asked lightly. "Information to be moved from England to France or vice versa? Scouting, assassination?"

"I have information for you," he said somberly. "What you choose to do with it is up to you."

She took a seat at his gesture. "This sounds serious."

"It is." He settled back in his chair wearily. "You know that the French and the British governments have hidden ways of communicating with each other?" At her nod, he continued, "I received a message sent by Claude Durand. It came through many hands before reaching me. He has recaptured Père Laurent, Wyndham's companion in captivity. And he also arrested the people who were sheltering the priest."

"The Boyers." Cassie's stomach clenched so badly that she was almost physically ill. Bad enough that Durand had recaptured Père Laurent, but Viole and Romain Boyer as well? "The priest's niece and her family. They gave kindness and shelter when we were in dire need of it. Did Durand arrest their children as well?"

"Apparently. He said he's imprisoned four members of the Boyer family."

Durand probably hadn't bothered with the older married daughter, but that was small comfort. Cassie swore with words that Catherine St. Ives wouldn't have known. "That devil!" Understanding settled over her in an icy wave. "Durand sent the information to bait a trap, didn't he? He wants Wyndham to return to France."

"It's the only reason why he'd go to the considerable effort of sending this information to the English," Kirkland agreed. "And I'm afraid he's going to get his wish. Wyndham is preparing to leave for France right now."

She gasped. "Why the devil did you tell Wyndham? Rescuing the Boyers would be almost impossible even for trained agents. If he goes to France, he'll be killed!"

"I hope not. As for why I told him about Durand's message . . ." Kirkland grimaced. "Despite your not unjustified comments about my meddling, I don't like making decisions for people. How would Wyndham feel if he learned later that Père Laurent had been recaptured and died in prison? And the Boyers? They sound like good people whose only crime was offering sanctuary to Madame Boyer's uncle."

369

"You must have known Wyndham would feel compelled to go back to France." She winced. "I can imagine him bargaining with Durand, offering himself in return for the freedom of Père Laurent and the Boyers."

Kirkland toyed with his quill pen with tense fingers. "It would be devilish unwise to bargain with a snake like Durand, but I can imagine Wyndham doing that if he thought it was the only way."

Calm settled over Cassie. "You must know that I won't let Grey go alone."

"I considered it likely that you'd insist on going with him," he admitted.

"Do you ever tire of playing God, James?" she said in an edged voice.

"Frequently." The quill snapped in his hands. "If Wyndham goes alone, he's unlikely to survive, much less succeed in his mission. If you go with him, the odds of success increase, but still aren't good, and I've endangered your life as well. What would you do in my place?"

She considered. "The same as you're doing. But I need to be angry at someone, and you're nearest."

"Feel free to curse me. I'm used to it." He gave her a twisted smile. "Here you are with a new life. A loving family, a fortune, a return to the station you were born to. And I'm dragging you back into the murky and dangerous world of spying."

"If it's any comfort, I was becoming bored with

the fashionable life and was ready to return to work." Her eyes narrowed like the Cat of her childhood nickname. "I'm sure you know how I'd react if you let Wyndham go to his doom without telling me."

"I'd be in fear of my life," he said promptly.

"Wise man." She stood, knowing what she must do. "Do you know where Wyndham is?"

"Upstairs in my guest room. I invited him to stay here while he's in London."

She spun on her heel and headed toward the door. Behind her, Kirkland said, "Second floor, all the way to the back."

Not that she needed directions. Now that she knew Grey was near, she'd find him. And God help anyone who got in her way.

Grey was writing one of several difficult letters that he hoped would never need to be sent when the door to his room opened soundlessly. He glanced up, thinking it was one of Kirkland's soft-footed maids, then froze. Cassie.

She looked composed and quietly elegant in a dark blue morning dress. This would be her style as an English lady, he realized. Impeccable tailoring, beautiful fabrics, and a rather conservative cut to balance the sensual magnificence of her flawless figure and bright auburn hair.

She closed the door and leaned back against it, one hand on the knob as if she was ready to bolt.

Heart pounding, he got to his feet, thinking it was damned unfair of Kirkland to send Cassie. The atmosphere turned thunderous with tension. He wanted to cross the room and wrap his arms around her and drag her to his bed.

Instead, he forced himself to stay behind the desk. Skipping the preliminaries, he said flatly, "I'm not going to change my mind."

She regarded him with a cool, assessing gaze. "So you think you can make your way across the channel and through France and rescue five people, at least one of them in poor health, from Castle Durand?"

"I don't know," he said honestly. "But I have to try. I owe Père Laurent and the Boyers too much not to do what I can."

"You're sure?" she asked. "You spent ten years in hell. Now you have regained everything. Your family, your wealth, your station in life. Are you prepared to throw it all away in an impossible quest?"

"I am." Despite his spells of anger and wildness, life had been almost unbearably sweet since Cassie rescued him. After searching for words, he said haltingly, "I need to do this. I've had so many blessings from the accident of my birth, and I've never been required to do anything difficult in return. I've never risked myself on behalf of anyone else. I . . . I need to prove to myself that I'm a man, not a callow boy."

She nodded as if his words confirmed her thoughts. "I'm not here to waste my breath trying to change your mind. I knew you couldn't turn your back on them."

"I have years of frivolousness to make up for. So"—he eyed her warily—"if you aren't going to try to change my mind, why did you come? To tie me up and lock me in a wardrobe so I can't leave London?"

Her brows arched. "To take charge of this mission, of course. Left to your own devices, you'll get yourself killed and waste all the time and effort I put into you."

He was torn between laughing and swearing. "No. You've already risked far too much for me. Père Laurent and his family are my responsibility, not yours."

"That's arguable since I drove us straight to the Boyers' farm and benefited by their generosity," she retorted. "What isn't arguable is that you haven't the experience and skills needed to make it safely into France and have a chance of coming out alive again."

"You underestimate me," he said shortly, knowing she was right. "I speak French like a native, and having traveled with you across France, I have some idea of how such things are done. Kirkland has also promised me a new set of papers."

"Can you find transportation across the

373

channel? Given that you were suffering from two bullet wounds when we reached England, I suspect you'd have a hard time finding your way back to my English smugglers."

She was right that he'd been hazy from his wounds and seasickness, but he'd thought about this. "Their name is Nash and I have a fair idea of where we landed. I'll find them, and offer to pay so much that it would be bad business to refuse me."

"You might be able do that," she agreed. "You could also probably make your way to Castle Durand, given the right papers, though some people might question a healthy young male who isn't in the army. But what about when you reach the castle? Are you planning a one-man invasion?"

"I'll think of something, and it won't be straightforward assault. I may be inexperienced, but I'm not stupid."

"Not usually, but refusing my help is profoundly stupid. Together, we have some chance. On your own . . ." She shook her head. "You told me that Peter didn't want to inherit the earldom. Are you going to force the title on him?"

"Tactfully put," he said with exasperation. He covered the distance between them in two long strides and kissed her with the passion that had been building since their last night together.

Touching her simultaneously soothed and

inflamed. Her mouth was sweet and hot and her breasts crushed against him as she responded, her fingers digging into his back. Dimly aware that this wasn't what he'd expected, he broke the kiss and retreated, breathing hard. "Do you seriously think we can travel together and keep our hands off each other?"

"Obviously not." Her face was flushed and auburn hair tumbled to her shoulders. She gave him a ruefully mischievous smile. "That's why we must travel as husband and wife."

Chapter 42

Grey had to laugh. "Is sharing a bed my reward if I let you come with me?"

"Probably more of a rationalization. We're both mad to attempt a rescue from Castle Durand." She stepped forward and kissed him as she tugged at his cravat. "But I'm serious about the fact that I won't allow you to go alone. If you try, you might find yourself locked in a wardrobe after all."

Reason dissolved as he unfastened her gown, then her corset. He needed to see and touch all of her, to absorb her wonderful Cassieness into every fiber of his being.

She must have felt the same for she tore at his garments with a fever that equaled his. Though it had been only a fortnight since they'd been together, it seemed like years. He wanted to devour her, to delight in shimmering coppery hair and subtle scents and powerful woman.

When they were finally skin to skin, they fell onto the bed, kissing and touching with frantic need. When he could wait no longer and buried himself in her, he groaned with pleasure and held very still, knowing how quickly this might end. Wanting to prolong their union, he rolled over so she was on top of him.

"Yesss," she breathed as she adjusted, finding a rhythm that suited them both. But she was equally impatient, equally needy, and all too soon she convulsed around him.

He culminated instantly, clutching her tight as he surged into her. *Cassie, Cassie, Cassie . . .*

With passion exhausted, he stroked her back as he struggled for breath. When he could speak coherently, he said, "I'd considered traveling as a priest, but I don't think that will work."

"Definitely not," Cassie said with a choke of laughter. She slid off him and lay on her side along his left flank, her hand resting warmly on his midriff.

"Any moment, you'll explain to me that this doesn't alter the long-term situation and we have no future," he murmured. "But that if we're traveling together, it's more sensible to behave as husband and wife than to try to keep apart."

"Sensible," she mused as she traced a finger around his navel. "That's us."

He grinned as he toyed with a glossy lock of hair. "Maybe that's not quite the right word."

"Probably not." Voice sober, she said, "Our chances of successfully rescuing Père Laurent and his family are even odds at best. That makes the pleasures of the moment worth the possible pain of the future."

"So if we fail, we won't be alive to endure the pain of separation? That's sensible, in a morbid sort of way." He caressed her bare shoulder, thinking this intimacy was worth a very high price. Even years of his life.

She cuddled under his arm, all warm, soft curves. "How were you doing at Summerhill?"

"I've taken up running for amusement since it feels good and it's healthy. I've also been riding out to visit tenants to remind them who I am and assure them I'm reliable." He chuckled. "There are still some doubts, but I've been pretending to be gentlemanly with some success. My mother has also been inviting the gentry over one family at a time so I can renew my acquaintance with the neighbors."

"Wise of her to keep the entertainments small," Cassie observed.

"Her first event was a tea where she invited about two dozen guests despite my request to avoid large groups," he said dryly. "When I walked in the door and saw the number of people in the drawing room, I bowed politely and left. That convinced her I was serious in my request."

"But overall, you're feeling better?"

Hearing the concern in her voice, he said reassuringly, "Much better. I might be up for the autumn social season in London." If he was alive and back in England then. "What about you? Were your aunt and uncle as welcoming as your cousins?"

"Oh, yes. My Aunt Patience always wanted a daughter. I was a tomboy as a child, but now I rather enjoy being a surrogate daughter."

And having a surrogate mother, he suspected. "Cassie, you asked if I was really sure I wanted to risk losing so much. I have to ask you the same question. You have rediscovered a life that you thought was gone forever. Are you really sure you want to risk losing it for a cause that isn't really your own?"

"I'm sure." She rested her forehead against his arm. "One rule I've lived by is that you don't abandon people who helped you. The Boyers helped us. It's damnable of Durand to use them to lure you back to France. I can no more stand back and say, 'How unfortunate, but it's no matter of mine' than you can."

He'd made the decision to go to France knowing the chance of success was negligible, but with Cassie at his side, he felt a stirring of optimism. "Since you're the expert agent, how do you think we should proceed?"

"I started thinking as soon as Kirkland told me of your mad scheme." She pulled the covers over them, which improved their comfort and reduced distractions. "How far had you gone with your ideas?"

"I was planning on coloring my hair and maybe growing a moustache to disguise my features, but that takes time. Can I attach a convincing false moustache?"

"False moustaches look false and they're hard to attach for any length of time." She ran a light fingertip along his upper lip, feeling the almost invisible pale hairs growing there. "In a couple more days, this hair can be colored. It will be a short moustache, but enough to distract attention from the rest of your face."

"What about you? Will you be a gray old lady again?"

"I need to look different from before. Besides, I don't think you can be made to look like a gray old man who would be a convincing mate." She pursed her lips thoughtfully. "We should travel as a boring middle-aged couple of modest income. You can be a clerk or a low-grade government official. I will be prim and humorless. Monsieur and Madame Harel. People will avoid us."

He studied her lovely face. "I'm having trouble remembering that I thought you old and plain at first, but if you did it once, you can do it again."

She gave him a flat stare and . . . faded away. She hadn't moved, her features and coloring were the same, but she was duller and less interesting. "How do you do that?" he exclaimed. "It's like you had a candle burning inside, and then you pinched it out."

"I can't really describe how. I just think myself plain." She gave a half smile. "I've spent most of my adult life as a plain woman unworthy of any man's notice. It comes naturally to me."

"I shall want you just as much even if you're disguised as the drab wife of a boring official." He chuckled. "Think how amusing it will be to peel away the drab layers to reveal the delicious mysteries hidden beneath."

She smiled agreement. "Just remember that in public, we need to look like we haven't touched each other since our wedding night."

"Difficult, but I'll try my best." Having settled that, he moved to the next question. "How shall we travel once we reach France? A cart like you had before?"

"As boring Monsieur and Madame Harel, we can travel by public coaches, which will be much faster. We'll take a different route, too. Come at Castle Durand from a different direction."

"Shall we get a couple of good riding hacks when we get close?" he asked. "We'll need transportation of our own, and horses can go places carriages can't."

She nodded. "I hope we don't have to spirit the whole lot of them out of France, though. That would be much, much more difficult. We'll need to arrange some sort of safe house before we move in. Kirkland will also need to get his fine forger to make papers for the whole family, just in case."

They hadn't even climbed out of bed, and already he was impressed by the advantages of working with an experienced agent. "Durand hates me and wants me dead, or he wouldn't have gone to such lengths to lure me within his reach. If at all possible, he'll want to be at Castle Durand, but he can't be sure when or even if I'm coming, and surely he has responsibilities in Paris. So my guess is that he's hired a number of men to guard the castle, and they'll have orders to capture rather than kill me if possible. Does that make sense to you?"

"Yes, but he might be in residence since he can deduce when you're most likely to show up." She frowned. "He might be able to convince his superiors that he's investigating a ring of traitors near Castle Durand and must be based there so he can find them all."

Grey hoped so. He wanted the bastard to be at Castle Durand so Grey could kill him with his bare hands. Which wasn't likely since all the advantages were on Durand's side, but a man could dream. Voicing his worst fear, he said, "Do you think that Durand has already killed Père Laurent and the Boyers?"

"It's certainly possible," Cassie said, her voice grave. "But I think it unlikely. France is a nation of laws, and since the revolution, many of those laws are designed to protect the weak from the strong."

When Grey snorted, Cassie said, "Don't laugh. The Code Napoleon is the only thing I give the emperor credit for. Before the revolution, the country was an impossible patchwork of feudal and church laws, with mandated privileges for the nobility and the clergy. The Code Napoleon specifically forbids privileges based on birth."

"Durand's behavior has been very close to the edge, hasn't it? He may not have a title, but many of his actions are not unlike those of his aristocratic ancestors."

"Exactly. He's been able to get away with a private dungeon within the walls of his castle, particularly since he was holding a priest and an Englishman. But murdering a respected local property owner and his family would get him into serious trouble." Cassie's brow furrowed as she thought. "Most likely he's had Père Laurent charged with treason and is investigating the Boyers as possible traitors. That allows him to hold them for some time while he investigates. He may release them if he has you."

"Dear God, I hope so." Grey's words were a real

prayer. "If you're right, so far he hasn't really done anything to get himself into serious trouble with his superiors. As you say, the revolution always hated priests and the power of the church, and no one would question killing an English spy. So the Boyers may be safe."

Cassie caught his gaze and said with icy precision, "You will not, under any circumstances, offer yourself to Durand in exchange for their freedom. I will not allow you to do that."

Grey's eyes narrowed in response. "Do you think you could stop me?"

"It would be an interesting battle, wouldn't it?" she said softly. "Let's hope it doesn't come to that."

Grey agreed. The last thing he wanted was to be at odds with Cassie. Changing the subject, he said, "Your marching into Castle Durand when everyone was ill was a miraculous fluke. We won't be so lucky again. You probably had a better look at the castle walls than I did. Will I be able to scale them with the right equipment?"

"We both can, and will. We'll need to take dark garments to help conceal us if we go over the walls." Cassie gazed at the ceiling as she thought. "Is it a fair assumption that prisoners would be put in the dungeons where you and Père Laurent were held?"

"I think so. They're impossible to escape without outside help."

"As I recall, the cells had slit windows high up

on the wall. Too high and narrow for anyone to escape that way, but still, windows. Do you know where they opened?"

"On a quiet back courtyard between the castle and the stables, I think. There was very little noise or traffic. The windows are just above ground level. Occasionally castle maids would come by and chat a bit, so I don't think the courtyard was used much."

She laughed. "You were able to carry on flirtations even in durance vile?"

He thought of the curious girls who would sometimes stop by and exchange a few words. "I was so hungry for people that I'd have welcomed any voice. On some occasions, if I was really fortunate, a maid might toss down an apple. Heaven."

Her amusement vanished. "It's amazing that you came through such an ordeal as well as you did."

"If not for Père Laurent, I would have been fit only for Bedlam," he said, equally sober. "I can't bear to think of him dying back in Durand's dungeon."

"We'll do our best to see that doesn't happen." She bit her lip in a way he found very distracting. His body must be recovering from their passionate encounter.

Her mind still on business, she said, "We must do some careful scouting around the castle. Local help will be invaluable if we can find it."

"That might be difficult to find."

"We can start at the Boyer farm. If there's anyone there, they might have information about the Boyers and Castle Durand."

"More likely Durand gave the farm to some crony," Grey said pessimistically. "If we ask for help, we'll be arrested as spies."

"Remember what I said about France being a nation of laws," she said. "If Durand confiscated the property and the Boyers have yet to be charged with any crime, someone in the community would go to a magistrate and complain."

"So he would probably not take over the property himself. Might the farm be sitting vacant?"

Cassie shook her head. "A farm can't be neglected, especially not in springtime. There is a married daughter. My best guess is that she has returned to the farm with her husband to take care of the animals and the planting. She's probably praying that her parents will be released. If they aren't, or they're executed, presumably she is the heir. If we can find her, she'll be a source of information and aid."

"I hope you're right. We're making a lot of assumptions."

She smiled wryly. "Call them deductions. It sounds better."

He began stroking her under the blanket. Discussions in bed had much to commend them. He stroked her nipple with his thumb and she caught her breath. "We need an army," he muttered. "One with artillery."

"I was thinking along those lines myself." Cassie's hand moved to his thigh.

"What?" He pushed himself up on one elbow and stared down at her. "I'm the one who is supposed to be mad here!"

"Whatever gave you a foolish notion like that?" She laughed with wicked amusement. "We're both mad to attempt this, so let's not waste a moment of madness." She looped her hands around his neck and pulled him down for a kiss.

In mere moments, sanity was forgotten.

Chapter 43

Against the night sky, Castle Durand loomed stark and impregnable, looking much as it must have in the fifteenth century. Cassie and Grey, dressed in black and with faces mostly covered with dark scarves, had come to scout.

The journey to France had gone so smoothly that Cassie found herself superstitiously expecting disaster to strike. Grey had made it across the channel in rough seas without getting ill, though he was a little green when they disembarked. Their guise as a drab, humorless couple had been very effective. They were never challenged, and few people wanted to talk to Monsieur and Madame Harel.

But the easy part of the journey was over. The previous night they'd stopped in a sizable town a dozen miles from St. Just du Sarthe, the village below Castle Durand. Grey bought sturdy riding horses while Cassie played the role of submissive wife.

After riding toward the village as the conventional Harels, they'd found an abandoned barn nearby and well off the road. Silently they'd settled the horses and changed into the dark clothing of thieves and burglars. It was a sign of Grey's tension that he hadn't made a single suggestive remark about Cassie's trousers.

From the barn, it was only half an hour's hike through the woods up to the castle. The night was raw and windy, with clouds scudding across a waning moon. She sensed that Grey was winding tighter and tighter, like a violin string. She couldn't even imagine what it felt like to return to the place where he'd endured ten years of imprisonment.

When the castle came into sight, they lingered in the shadowed woods to study it. Unlike during Cassie's first visit, the gates were closed and there was a guard in the small gatehouse. The crenellated walls must have been at least twenty feet tall. They surrounded the square castle grounds, with a cleared strip perhaps thirty feet wide at the base.

On top of each corner was a guard turret. Dim

glows from braziers showed they were occupied. The guards were probably bored, but they had clear views of the walls, should anyone attempt to climb into the castle.

On the shadowed back wall opposite the main gates, they found a small postern gate. Cassie investigated, using a couple of thin metal picks on the lock. It seemed to be rusted shut. Opening the door would be neither easy nor quiet.

To her left, Grey was studying the stone wall itself, running his hands over the surface to check the condition. He found a toehold and began to climb the wall by touch. He was halfway up when Cassie gave a small, fox-like yip to catch his attention.

He halted. After a half-dozen heartbeats, he quietly dropped to the soft ground. Cassie touched his arm and gestured for them to withdraw to the woods on the other side of the cleared zone.

When they were safely back in the shadows, she asked quietly, "Are you all right?"

"I wanted to keep climbing." He stared at the massive bulk of the wall. Voice thick with emotion, he said, "I wanted to get inside and kill Durand with my bare hands and then blow the whole place to bloody hell."

She locked a hand around his wrist, her grip hard. "Understandable. But you *must* control yourself when the time comes to go in! If you run berserk, you risk everything. Everyone."

He drew a shuddering breath. "I know you're right. I swear I'll not do anything that will endanger you, Père Laurent, or his family."

She released his wrist, hoping he'd be able to keep his vow. He was far more stable than when he first escaped the dungeon, but an extreme situation could kick him over the edge again. Focusing on the business at hand, she said, "Tell me about the wall. It looked like you were climbing easily."

"The mortar between the stones is crumbling in many places. It wasn't hard to climb even in the dark. What about the postern?"

"The door is heavy and hard to move and the lock is rusted shut. The wall might be a better way to get in without being noticed. But we'll need to blast the postern open to get our people out."

He nodded. "We should go around the castle once more."

Agreeing, Cassie set out and he followed her. Tonight, scouting. Tomorrow they would seek assistance.

After a good night's sleep in the old barn, they dressed as the conservative Harels and set off for the Boyer farm. The trip by horseback was faster than driving a cart through a blizzard, and the road up to the farm was much prettier now that it wasn't scoured by blizzard winds and snow.

Cassie prayed silently they'd find the Boyers'

married daughter at the farm. She could be a valuable resource. Without her, their odds would become even worse.

No one was visible in the farmyard, but smoke trickled from the kitchen chimney. The house was not empty.

As aware of the stakes as Cassie, Grey swung from his horse, tossing her the reins. As the traditional Harels, Grey took the lead in everything, while Cassie rode sidesaddle and kept her eyes cast demurely down.

Grey knocked on the door. Several dogs began barking crazily inside. They sounded as if they were slavering to get out and rip the stranger to shreds. The horses twitched nervously but Grey stood his ground.

A few moments passed quietly except for the barking dogs. Then a small window at head height opened and a woman asked suspiciously, "What do you want?"

Cassie couldn't see the speaker, but the voice was young. Grey said peaceably, "I'm an old friend of Monsieur and Madame Boyer and was near. Are they home?"

"No," was the snapped response. "Go away!"

Grey held the window open when she tried to close it. "What about Père Laurent? Is he still here?"

"Who are you?" This time, the voice sounded frightened.

Judging it was time to be honest, Grey replied,

"I am Monsieur Sommers. I was your great-uncle's companion in adversity."

The young woman sucked in her breath. "The Englishman?"

"The same. Are you the Boyers' married daughter?"

"Yes, I'm Jeanne Duval." The voice was uncertain. "Why are you here?"

"To free your family," Grey said softly. "Can you help?"

Another long pause. Then a key scraped in the lock and the door swung inward. Jeanne Duval couldn't be more than twenty, and her bright brown hair and hazel eyes would be pretty if not for her worried expression. She had gathered the dogs around her as if they were a weapon ready to strike.

Grey bowed with aristocratic elegance. "It's my pleasure to meet you, Madame Duval. I spent only a few days here with your great-uncle, but it was long enough to develop the highest esteem for your parents."

Tears sprang into her eyes. "Do you really think you can free them?"

"I don't know, but I will certainly do my best." He gestured toward Cassie. "Allow me to introduce Madame Renard. It was she who freed Père Laurent and me. May we come in?"

Jeanne fidgeted with the edge of her apron. "Why do you want to talk?"

391

"If we are to have any chance of freeing your family, we need as much information about their captivity as possible," Grey said patiently.

Jeanne gave a jerky nod. "Madame Renard can come in while you take the horses to the barn. I'll call my husband to join us."

Grey offered Cassie his hand to dismount from her horse, then led their mounts off to the stable. Jeanne rang a sizable bell that hung by the door, using three sets of three rings each. Cassie was quite sure the bell hadn't been there on their earlier visit. Another sign of how stressed the household was.

They moved into the kitchen. The furnishings and broad fireplace were familiar, but the house was too quiet, no longer bustling with a whole family. As Jeanne shooed the now well-behaved dogs into the backyard, Cassie noticed that the young woman's crisp white apron covered the gentle curve of midpregnancy.

"You are with child?" she said sympathetically. "How exhausting on top of the worry for your family!"

Jeanne promptly burst into tears. Alarmed, Cassie guided her to a chair by the fire. A blanket was folded on a bench, so she shook it out and tucked it around the girl. "Would you like something? A glass of water?"

Jeanne said in a barely audible whisper, "I want my mother."

Collecting herself, she produced a handkerchief, blotted her eyes, and blew her nose. "I'm sorry, everything makes me cry now. It was Père Laurent who first told me I was with child. I wasn't sure myself, but when I came to visit my parents and found him here, he took one look at my face, smiled, and said that soon he would become a great-great-uncle." More tears appeared.

"He can see that?" Cassie said with surprise.

"Oh, yes, he was famous for it. When he had a parish, young wives would come from miles around to see if he could confirm their hopes. I never heard him to be wrong, either." She put a protective hand over the modest curve of her belly. "He thinks I shall bear a son, though he isn't so accurate predicting whether it will be a boy or a girl."

Cassie had heard of midwives who were very good at identifying pregnancies. She supposed that a wise and observant old priest could have similar talents.

A tall, broad young man with dark hair and a missing left hand swung into the kitchen, his expression ready for trouble. "Jeanne!"

He moved behind her and put his right hand on her shoulder. "Is this female upsetting you?" Jeanne's husband wasn't much older than she, but he looked capable as well as protective. The missing hand explained why he wasn't in the army.

Jeanne laid a hand over his on her shoulder, but before she could reply, Grey arrived. Cassie studied him, thinking how very good he looked, even with the narrow moustache. He was still lean but he no longer looked bony, and he had an air of authority that was real, not the officiousness of Monsieur Harel.

"It's all right, Pierre," Jeanne assured him. "This fellow says he's the Englishman who was imprisoned beside Père Laurent, and that he's come to free my family."

"Madame Boyer said the Englishman had golden hair," Pierre said suspiciously.

"I dyed my hair brown to be less conspicuous." Grey smiled a little. "There are parts of my body where the natural hair color is visible, but we'll have to withdraw to another room so I can show you without offending the ladies."

Pierre flushed. "Say something in English," he ordered.

Not missing a beat, Grey switched to English and said, "Père Laurent is the wisest, kindest man I have ever known. I would not have survived ten years in a dungeon if not for him. I needed him far more than he needed me."

Pierre recognized the sound of English even if he didn't speak it, so he gave a short nod. "What makes you think you can free Jeanne's family from Castle Durand? The castle alone is difficult, and Durand has brought in guards for protection."

Speaking for the first time, Cassie said, "We saw the guards last night when we scouted the castle. It would be useful to know how many there are."

Pierre's wary gaze moved to her. "Who are you?"

"I am called Madame Renard."

Jeanne nodded recognition, but remarked, "My mother said you were older."

"I have some skill in changing my appearance," Cassie explained. "Have we convinced you we are who we say? I don't blame you for being cautious."

Jeanne glanced up at her husband, their gazes meeting. After a moment of silent communication, Pierre said, "You seem genuine. But what do you think you can do to rescue five people from a well-guarded castle? It would take an army to break in!"

"We do have a plan," Grey said. "But we need more information. First, are you sure they're being held there? And if so, are they in the dungeons?"

Jeanne got to her feet, looking strong, hopeful, and quite like her mother. "If we are to discuss such matters, it should be over food. Your dinner waits, Pierre. I have soup, so there will be enough for us all."

Grey's stomach noisily agreed with the suggestion, which broke the tension. Though Cassie's stomach was more discreet, she was also hungry. Their breakfast that morning at the barn had been bread, cheese, and water.

Jeanne proved herself her mother's daughter by producing thick bean soup, fresh bread, cheese, and a pork pâté. Cassie tried not to gobble greedily.

Even if the Duvals ended up telling their visitors to go away, at least Cassie and Grey would be well fed when they left.

Chapter 44

When appetites had been satisfied, Jeanne pushed her plate away and fixed her gaze on her guests. "You want to free my family. What can we do to help?"

"As I said earlier, we must be sure they are alive and held at Castle Durand," Grey said seriously. "Have you been allowed to visit your parents?"

She shook her head sadly. "I have not seen them, but Pierre has a cousin who works in the castle. She says they are there and she has spoken with them through the windows, which are very narrow and near the ground. She said they are in two cells, my mother and sister together, and right next to them my father, Père Laurent, and my brother. Not happy, but not unwell, though it is hard on Père Laurent."

Grey felt almost dizzy with relief at the knowledge that his worst fear, that they were already dead, hadn't happened. "Have they been charged with a crime?"

"My father and I went to speak with the local magistrate about them," Pierre replied. "Père Laurent had been charged with treason, and the Boyers are being investigated as partners in his crime." The young man snorted with disgust. "It is absurd and the magistrate knows it, but he said that so far, Durand hasn't broken the law."

Again, this was as Cassie had speculated. Giving thanks that he was partnered with a woman who really understood France, Grey asked, "Did your cousin say how many guards have been brought in to protect the castle?"

"A dozen and a sergeant. They are privately hired guards, but all were soldiers, my cousin thought." Pierre's expression was skeptical. "You think you can challenge and defeat so many? Do you have a squad of English soldiers hidden nearby?"

"No squad, and no straightforward attack." He nodded toward Cassie. "My lady fox will explain."

"We intend a diversion to draw the attention of the soldiers," Cassie said. "While they are busy with the diversion, we'll climb the castle wall and go to the dungeon windows. With the right tools, we should be able to open one of the windows and help the prisoners out."

"I will skip most of the questions your statement raises and ask what diversion you have in mind,"

Pierre said tartly. "It will have to be substantial in order to draw more than a dozen men away long enough to break into the castle dungeons."

"Explosive grenades," Cassie said calmly.

Pierre and Jeanne gaped at her. His, "Have you grenades with you?" clashed with his wife's, "Aren't they dreadfully dangerous and unpredictable?"

"They are indeed dangerous," Cassie admitted, "but that's why they're useful. I brought with me enough black powder and fuse to make a couple of dozen grenades about the size of a large apple." She demonstrated with one hand.

Pierre looked dubious. "Will they be strong enough to breach the castle wall?"

"We don't want to take down a wall, just the two gates, and we certainly don't want to hurt any of the castle servants like your cousin," Grey explained. "But if a dozen or so are tossed over the wall at different places, they will create a diversion."

Beginning to look intrigued, Pierre said, "Grenades are gunpowder packed in a metal casing, aren't they? Did you bring the casings?"

Cassie shook her head. "They would be too heavy, and far too conspicuous. When we were here before with Père Laurent, your mother gave me apple brandy from a sturdy little pottery jug. My hope is that you have more such jugs that can be used as casings. Pour in gunpowder, add a fuse, cork the jug, and voilà! A diversionary weapon."

By this time, Pierre was staring at Cassie with open awe. But his brain hadn't stopped working. "Can the two of you throw enough grenades over the wall quickly enough for the effect you want? Much running and throwing will be required if the grenades are to explode about the same time."

The young man had put his finger on one of the plan's weaknesses. Cassie replied, "I'll aim to make the fuses last about ten minutes. Timing grenades is difficult, though."

"What if a fuse goes out, or the guards see them burning and realize what is happening?"

She shrugged. "That might happen. We must hope that enough grenades will go off about the right time to create the confusion we need."

"You need more grenade throwers." Pierre grinned. "I throw very well."

"No!" Grey exclaimed. "You can't help us."

Pierre flushed. "Because of this?" He held up the stump of his left arm.

"Of course not. That won't interfere with you throwing," Grey said. "But it's vital you not be associated with this in any way since you are the first people who will be suspected of helping them escape."

"He is right." Jeanne laid a hand on his right arm. "We must be above suspicion. I have an idea for that. The magistrate is a cousin of my mother's." She grinned. "We are all related hereabouts. He has been advising us about the legal situation. On the night of your plan, we can ask him to meet us at the tavern in St. Just du Sarthe. We will buy him one of Madame Leroux's fine dinners and he can tell us if he has had any luck inquiring of his superiors about the legality of arresting my family."

"That is another question," Pierre said. "Even if you free them, where will they go? They cannot return here as long as Durand is after them."

"I know. We have found a temporary place for them to stay while we decide what is best. After that . . ." Grey spread his hands in a very French gesture. "If necessary, I will take them all the way to England. This war will not last forever."

He avoided Cassie's worried gaze. They had discussed this repeatedly on the journey. Getting the two of them out of France had been a challenge. Seven people would be far more difficult. But he would damned well do his best to ensure that his friends were safe and free.

"I suppose you are right that I shouldn't be part of your raid on the castle," Pierre said with regret. "But I can find other men who will be happy to help you."

Grey caught his breath. "That would be very helpful, if they can be trusted."

"Durand is not well liked," Jeanne said. "There was outrage when his men arrested Père Laurent and my family."

"There are also many royalists in this area," Pierre added. "We do not discuss such things. And we do not turn each other in to police informers." He held up his stump. "I lost this fighting for France and my family, not Napoleon nor a fat, stupid Bourbon king. Any man I recommend can be trusted. There is a man who works on this farm whom I would trust with my life."

Grey's smile was wry. "I hope I can trust him with mine." And Cassie's.

Jeanne had slipped out, and now she returned with a squat little jug and four small ceramic sipping cups. She set the jug in front of Cassie. "My mother is known for her apple brandy. We sell it in the town market. Will it make a good grenade? There are a couple of dozen more jugs in the pantry."

Cassie hefted the jug to feel the weight and took out the cork to check the thickness of the walls. "These should work. We need to make and test some sample grenades to be sure."

"Then we should empty the jug." Jeanne poured a little into each of the small cups and passed them around the table. She raised hers. "Liberty for my family!"

Grey was happy to drink to that. The apple brandy was just as fragrant and fruity as when he'd first sampled it in the icy farm pond.

And it had just as much of a kick.

· · ·

When Grey and Pierre left the house to bed down the horses and find a good place to test a grenade, Cassie sat down at the table with Jeanne to make their test weapons. She'd brought several pounds of gunpowder and yards of fuse with her. Jeanne watched warily as Cassie made a paper funnel to pour the powder into the first jug.

"That isn't going to explode and blow up my kitchen, is it?"

"No, gunpowder is very stable. The grenade won't explode without the lighted fuse." After Cassie poured in the powder, she cut a length of fuse and slid it through the mouth of the jug, then corked the bottle very tightly. It looked quite innocent when she was done. A small brandy jug with a cord running out of it. "I'll make a couple more with different fuse lengths and amounts of gunpowder."

As she started on the second, Jeanne asked, "How soon will you raid the castle?"

"As soon as possible." Cassie delicately funneled the gunpowder into a jug. "Preferably within the next two or three nights. The moon is waxing, and each night will be brighter." Frowning, she cut a length of fuse. "Plus, my instincts are saying that the sooner this is done, the better. For all your family's sake, but especially Père Laurent's."

Jeanne nodded gravely. "He had become

stronger while here at the farm, but he is frail. Imagine the horror of being back in the cell where he spent so many years!"

"I'm trying not to think of it." Cassie bit her lip as she made a third test grenade. This would be a chancy operation, with far too many variables. She hoped Père Laurent was on good terms with the divine, because they were going to need all the help they could get.

That night they all tromped into the forest to test grenades. Even Jeanne came, not wanting to miss the action. Grey and Pierre had found a test site on a wilderness slope opposite the village and the castle. Even though they were miles away, sound traveled, and they didn't want anyone to be alerted to the use of explosives.

A light rain was falling, which meant the explosions would sound like thunder. As Cassie picked her way through the woods with a shielded lantern, she gave thanks for such ideal test conditions.

After half an hour of hiking, they reached the site. A pair of rocky outcroppings had a pocket of soil between them where several trees about the height of the castle walls grew. Not only could they practice their throwing, but they could see how much damage the grenades did to the rocks on the other side while taking shelter behind the outcropping on their side.

Cassie eyed the trees. "Shall we start by tossing stones about the same weight to test our throwing abilities?"

Grey nodded. "Earlier Pierre and I collected some that seem about the right weight. They're piled over there."

He set his lantern on the ledge of rock behind him and hefted a stone. After tossing it up and down a couple of times, he hurled it over the trees. The stone cleared with space to spare and clattered against rock on the other side.

"Not bad," Pierre said as he chose a stone. After testing the weight, he threw. It cleared the trees by a huge margin. He hadn't been lying about his good throwing arm.

Cassie was next. Her stone didn't clear the trees by much, but it was an adequate throw. Next came Jeanne. Determination on her face, she wound up, threw—and the rock crashed into the tree's budding branches.

"I think it's good you'll be dining with the magistrate," Grey said with a grin. "Are we ready for live ammunition?"

Cassie produced three grenades that she'd packed in a canvas carrier bag with towels for padding. "I've put different-length fuses in these. I think they will explode in about five, three, and two minutes, but I'm guessing and want to test my guesses."

She lifted the one with the shortest fuse. "This is

another test—less gunpowder. A smaller charge will be useful for blowing in the postern without attracting as much notice as the explosions in front. We'll also need one if we must blast our way into the cells. I don't want to kill the people we're trying to save. Pierre, since you have the best arm, you can throw this one with the shortest fuse after we've tested the other two."

Pierre nodded, pleased. Grey started by lighting the longest fuse with the lantern flame, then tossing the grenade. They joined Jeanne behind the rocky outcropping and covered their ears while Cassie counted down the time mentally.

KABOOOM!!!!!!!! The ground shook and air and sound battered them even behind their barrier.

After the rattle of falling debris ended, Grey said, "Let's look at the damage."

They found that the grenade had left a small crater, tossing earth and stones away and cracking the stony outcropping. Grey put a warm hand on Cassie's shoulder. "Is this what you expected?"

"Yes, though the fuse burned faster than I expected. I'll have to cut longer fuses." Cassie threw the next grenade, which had about the same amount of explosive power. Pierre's low-gunpowder version seemed to have the right power for use on the windows. As they studied the smaller crater it made, Grey said, "We have our arsenal."

Voice throbbing with excitement, Jeanne said, "Your plan seems more real now. Perhaps my family will be free in a few days!"

Cassie didn't bother to say that grenades were the easy part.

Chapter 45

Two days later, all the arrangements had been made and the raid was set for that night. Pierre and Jeanne had already left in a cart to meet the magistrate, and Grey and Cassie were in their small bedroom preparing the equipment they might need. Ropes; a short, heavy crowbar; weapons. Grey frowned, wishing they were better armed.

He would carry the heavier equipment and most of the grenades in a pack they'd devised to sling over his back, leaving his hands free. He double and triple-checked the contents, his nerves taut even though he and Cassie had had endless discussions about the possibilities and refining their list of materials. "Is this kind of tension like going into battle?" he asked. "How long does it take to become used to it?"

Cassie hadn't yet changed into her black male clothing, but even with drab hair and a plain brown gown, she was lovely. Calm, sure of herself. He missed the red hair.

"We *are* going into battle, so tension is normal,"

she replied. "Though you're twitchy now, as soon as the first grenade explodes, your nerves will steady and you'll be fine and dangerous. We've planned as much as we can. Now it's in God's hands."

"I hope God wants to save one of His better priests, and us along with him." Grey surveyed his pack. "I wish we had firearms."

"We discussed that," she said patiently. "We couldn't have carried a rifle through France without being noticed, and one rifle wouldn't have been much use against a squad of soldiers. Pistols aren't very accurate, especially at night when we're moving as fast as we can. I have a knife, and I know how to use it."

"Firing a weapon can make the enemy take cover and buy time even if one has only one shot," he pointed out.

"True." She patted her smaller bag, which held the rest of the grenades. "But we do have explosives, if not firearms."

He looked out the window at the darkening sky. "Is it time to go yet?"

She laughed. "Not yet. You're as impatient as a child who has been promised an ice at Gunter's."

"I've never done anything like this." He perched on the small bed opposite Cassie's. Jeanne and Pierre had made it clear that they didn't mind what sleeping arrangements their guests made, so he and Cassie were sharing the room that had belonged to the two Boyer daughters. They'd used only one of the narrow beds, which was crowded, but they'd wanted to be as close as possible. A single bed was sufficient for making love.

"One's first experience of war is difficult," she observed. "But everyone has a first time. At least you're no green seventeen-year-old soldier who has never faced the enemy before."

"I'm not so much afraid of being a coward," he said slowly as he puzzled out his concerns. "But the stakes are so high! I'm afraid I'll fail and it will hurt others."

"Life and death are the highest stakes there are," she said calmly. "But we all die eventually. I hope it's not tonight, but would either of us choose not to be here?"

"As I said in England, this is something I must do." He scowled at her. "But you don't have to. You could be safe and learning how to spend money in London. Haven't you ever thought of retiring from this most dangerous game?"

"I have," she said, to his surprise. "When I visited Kirkland to chastise him for letting my cousin know I was alive, he told me it was time to leave spying behind. I've done noble work and helped my country, but Napoleon's doom is inevitable." She smiled a little. "Though he was very complimentary, he made it clear that my services were no longer needed."

Grey's brows arched with surprise. "Interesting.

Even more interesting that you didn't mention this to me earlier."

"I'm torn," she admitted. "Though I still want Napoleon dead and his tyranny ended, I no longer feel as much need to do it personally. But what will I do to fill the time if I'm not skulking around France and sleeping rough and wearing terrible clothes?"

He chuckled. "I'm sure you'll find worthwhile activities soon enough."

After a silence, she said hesitantly, "I've considered buying an estate in Norfolk near my family and managing it myself. Looking out for the welfare of my tenants, perhaps starting schools—that's work worth doing."

Before he could suggest that marrying him would give her a chance to perform such services, she continued, "What about you? God willing, it will be years till you inherit the earldom. Will you spend them in wine, women, and dissipation?"

He shuddered. "I had enough of that when I was young. Actually, I've been thinking of Parliament. My father controls a number of seats and one of his MPs is in poor health and considering retirement."

"That might keep you out of mischief," she said thoughtfully. "And it would be good experience for when you inherit and take your seat in the House of Lords."

"Exactly!" He couldn't keep the excitement

from his voice. "I want to be involved with things that matter. I want to forge relationships with MPs that I can use later when I'm in the Lords. The world is changing, Cassie. This is an age of revolutions. If Britain is to avoid having one, we must change the system in ways that benefit the average citizen." He grinned. "One of the things that needs changing is the way noblemen like my father control multiple seats in Parliament."

Cassie laughed. "So you'll become a reformer! I take back what I said about you keeping out of mischief if you go into politics. But I agree with your goals, and I can easily imagine you as an MP."

Perhaps. He wondered if either of them would survive to fulfill the goals they were discussing tonight. Feeling tense again, he stood. "Since it's still too early to leave, I propose we spend the time in a way guaranteed to relax us." He held out his hand.

Her eyes sparked. "An excellent plan."

Cassie rose lithely and flowed into his embrace. His kiss was fierce, hungry, hers equally so as the tension simmering inside them exploded into annihilating passion. He needed to worship her, possess her, bind her to him through eternity.

Passion burned even brighter when it might be their last time.

The night sky mixed clouds and moonlight with a hint of possible rain in the air. Though Grey and

Cassie had aimed at being early at the rendezvous below Castle Durand, two men were already waiting. The recruits wore dark clothing and had covered their faces, as Grey and Cassie did. Safely anonymous. They moved out from the shadows when Grey and Cassie dismounted.

"*Liberté*," a burly man said in a husky voice.

Grey responded, "*Égalité*."

"*Fraternité*." Having completed the code, the burly man offered a hand. Grey shook it, giving silent thanks for Pierre's help in recruiting their grenadiers. A half dozen had agreed to participate, and Pierre attested that they were trustworthy and experienced country men. If trouble overflowed the castle, the men should be able to get away safely.

The second grenadier, slighter and quicker in his movements, said, "Just after we arrived here, a fancy coach drove up the road and into the castle."

"Durand?" Grey said, heart quickening.

"Mebbe. The guard opened the gates right quick."

Grey wanted Durand to be there so they could have a confrontation and he could break the devil into small pieces. But would having the master of the castle present make the guards more alert? Or would they be distracted by Durand's arrival?

Impossible to know. Either way, there was no help for it. The mission had begun and they must carry on.

The other recruits arrived in quick succession. When everyone was present, Cassie gathered them around and explained the use of the grenades.

"You'll each have several grenades with different-length fuses," she said in a low voice that disguised her gender. "If a fuse burns too quickly, throw the grenade or pull out the fuse! Our mission is to save lives, not blow up our friends."

"How do we light the fuses?" a grenadier with a youthful voice asked.

"With these." Grey produced three very small closed lanterns. Using a tinderbox, he lit one, then the others. With the doors slid shut, almost no light escaped.

"One for each three of you, the last for us. Remember how far light and sound carry at night, and conceal both as much as possible. We'll be at the back wall and plan to escape through the postern gate, so you need to be bombing the front part of the castle. A grenade for the main gate and then over the walls on both sides. Any questions?"

There were none. One fellow said, "I've wanted to bomb Durand for years."

"I'd like to kill 'im myself," the burly man said wistfully.

The bastard really was unpopular. Grey said warningly, "We aren't even sure Durand is here. Remember that our main mission is to free Père

Laurent and the Boyers, and do it without any casualties."

"A night of good fun and grenades," one of the volunteers said cheerfully. "Takes me back to me army days. Are we ready?"

They were ready. Only Grey and Cassie had horses. They led their mounts through the woods toward the castle. The ground was soft enough from the previous night's rain that there wasn't much sound. When they were just below the castle, Grey said softly, "Give us time to get around the back of the castle. *Bonne chance, mes amis*, and my thanks." He offered his hand to the nearest grenadier.

Shaking hands, the fellow said, " 'Tis my pleasure!"

There were handshakes all around. Then Grey and Cassie circled around the castle in the woods. They tethered their mounts in the shadows, but not too far from the castle, in case they were needed.

Then they waited. Grey's pack was much lighter now that most grenades had been distributed. He planned to put the small dark lantern in a pocket when he climbed, and hoped to God the flame didn't go out. He was fast with a tinderbox, but any time lost could be the difference between success and disaster.

The wait seemed interminable. On their scouting trip, they'd chosen a particularly rough patch of wall that was halfway between the postern and the left corner guard tower. It should be a safe place to climb while the guards were distracted by grenades. They'd come down close to the dungeon windows.

KABOOOM!!! The first explosion shattered the night air. Mere moments later, another. Then another. The grenadiers were doing a good job on their timing.

Cassie was right. As soon as the grenade exploded, Grey's nerves steadied down to cool, focused necessity. He lit a grenade with a short fuse and tossed it to the foot of the postern. Then he and Cassie bolted toward their chosen area of wall.

More explosions and shouts rose from the front of the castle precinct. Flames flared, probably a wooden shed that had been struck by a grenade. More shouting.

The postern door exploded, shaking the ground and rattling loose stones from the castle wall. Not waiting to see if any guards were drawn to the postern, Grey and Cassie started climbing. The wall was weathered enough to supply hand- and toeholds, but feeling their way in the darkness seemed horribly slow.

Light and agile, Cassie reached the top before Grey. He was nearing the top when a hold crumbled under his foot. The pack he was carrying affected his balance and he almost fell. He flung a hand upward and caught hold of the edge of an embrasure and managed to save himself from tumbling to the ground.

Heart pounding, he pulled himself the rest of the way and crouched in the embrasure as he gasped for breath. Cassie knelt beside him and he took her hand as they studied the chaos they'd caused.

Though the castle blocked some of their view, they could hear a leather-lunged sergeant bellowing to gather his troops by the shattered front gate. Flames illuminated running men, and there seemed to be efforts to contain the fire. Not very successful ones, because the light from the fires was growing.

"Perfect," Cassie breathed. "Time for us to go in."

Grey pulled a long coiled rope from his pack. One end was looped. He tossed the loop over the crenellation and let the other end drop to the ground.

As he lowered himself swiftly, he saw that his grenade had smashed the postern wide enough to allow people to pass through the hole. Mercifully, the blast had drawn no attention because the guards were gathering in front of the castle, where the main attack was taking place.

As soon as he touched down, Cassie swung onto the rope and walked down the wall. He was male enough to notice that she might be dressed as a man, but she wasn't shaped like one. As soon as she was beside him, he spared an instant for a kiss

415

before they ran around the back of the castle to the quiet yard between dungeons and stables.

No one was in sight. Enough light came from the burning shed in the main yard to show four horizontal slit windows for the dungeon cells. Grey dropped down by the nearest slit, which he guessed was for his old cell. "Père Laurent?" he called, keeping his voice low. "Madame Boyer?"

"Grey, can that be you?" the priest replied in a startled voice.

"It is, and we're here to get you out." As he spoke, Grey tested the bars. They were set too solidly to be worked loose. "You're there with Romain and André?"

"We're here," Romain said softly. "Viole and Yvette are in the next cell."

Cassie had been investigating the other slit windows. To Grey, she said, "We'll never loosen these bars in time. We need to blow up this window, which is farthest from the prisoners."

Knowing she was right, he said to the men, "Protect yourselves. We're going to use a grenade to enter the farthest cell."

"A grenade?" It was Viole's voice from the next window. "So that is what we've been hearing! Come, Yvette, we will burrow into a corner like foxes."

Another round of explosions was coming from the forecourt as Grey lit a reduced-powder, short-fused grenade Cassie had built for this purpose.

Luckily, the flame in the lantern hadn't gone out during their exertions.

As soon as the fuse was burning, he set the grenade by the fourth window, which led to an empty cell. Then he and Cassie withdrew behind a nearby stone buttress.

The grenade went off between the explosions of two others in the main yard. Though theirs was modest compared to the others, there was still an ear-numbing blast and debris rattled all over the yard.

"I should have used less gunpowder!" Cassie said with mad humor as they raced to the blown-out window. There was now a pile of rubble and a gap wide enough to admit Cassie, though without much room to spare.

Grey had another rope. He wrapped it around his waist several times, then dropped the other end through the hole. Cassie crawled backward through the shattered window. When she was inside with one hand on the rope, he handed her the lantern. "I'll work on widening the hole."

"Right." She disappeared down into the dark, dank cell.

Grey pulled the short crowbar from his pack and went to work prying loosened stones from around the window opening. So far, everything was going according to plan.

It couldn't last.

Chapter 46

Cassie landed on loose rubble below the blown-out window, twisted her ankle, and almost fell. Grey's strength on the rope kept her upright.

She tested her ankle, decided there was no real damage, and opened the lantern door to release some light into the Stygian darkness. She crossed the cell to the door and was glad to find it unlocked.

Breathing thanks that she wouldn't have to pick the lock, she stepped into the corridor. Light came from the slit under the door to the guard's office. She raced down and tried the door. Locked, no sound audible from the other side. Praying that the guard had gone outside to deal with the attackers, she pulled out her lock picks.

The lock was old and simple, and it took her less than a minute to open it. Nerves taut, she opened the door cautiously in case there was a guard waiting to shoot her. The room was empty. And blessed be, the key ring hung on the wall! She grabbed the keys, along with the larger lamp that had been left burning on a hook.

It took three attempts to find the right key to the men's cell, but finally it swung open. "Madame Fox?" Romain said, startled. Beside him was his wide-eyed young son and Père Laurent, looking less frail than the last time she'd rescued him from

418

this hellhole. Both the men needed a shave, but on the whole, they looked to be in good shape.

"None other," Cassie said, realizing that her dark scarf had fallen down around her neck to reveal her features. "We'll leave from the cell at the end where the window has been enlarged and there's a rope. André, you're the lightest. Your father can help you up and out. Then you and Sommers can pull out Père Laurent."

Romain looked stubborn. "I won't leave without my wife and daughter!"

"By the time André and Père Laurent are out, your womenfolk will be free, too. Now *move!*"

She handed Romain the larger lantern, then went to work on the door to the women's cell. Again, it took excruciatingly long moments to find the right key. As soon as the door opened, Viole and Yvette tumbled out. Viole hugged Cassie. *"Mon ange!"*

"I'm no angel!" Cassie briefly hugged back, relieved that her friends seemed to have survived captivity well. "Come along now. The sooner we leave, the better."

They moved to the escape cell and found that Père Laurent was being bodily lifted by Romain and dragged from above by Grey. It had to be painful and difficult, but the priest doggedly contributed what strength he had and didn't complain.

As Père Laurent disappeared above ground, Romain grabbed his wife and daughter in a fierce embrace. "Yvette, you first," he said huskily. "I'll help you up. Then take the rope and let Sommers and André pull you through."

"*Oui*, Papa." The girl picked her way through the rubble, then reached up as high on the rope as she could. Romain boosted her so that her hands were almost to the opening. A moment of scrambling, and she was through.

"Viole, you next," Cassie ordered.

She was heavier than her daughter so Cassie helped with the lifting. Viole's pleasantly rounded hips barely made it through the expanded gap. "You now, milady fox," Romain said. "It will take everyone's strength to get me up."

Knowing he was right, she let him lift her. The relief on getting outside and not seeing armed guards pounding down at them was enormous. She squeezed Grey's arm with heartfelt relief. "Do you think Romain can make it through that space?"

"It will be tight, but he'll fit." Grey unwound the rope from his waist and held it out to the others. "Everyone who feels strong enough can help."

Cassie and all the Boyers grabbed on to the rope. Père Laurent said ruefully, "All I'm fit for is praying."

"Pray away, Father!" Cassie felt Romain's weight on the rope. He had to be lifted from the bottom of the cell, and his broad frame and farmer's muscles made him heavy.

Romain's head appeared, then his shoulders. A very tight fit indeed, but as he worked his way through the ruined window, Cassie gave a sigh of relief. Almost here . . .

Relief was premature. Romain had just crawled onto solid ground when a booming voice echoed off the walls. "Wyndham! I knew you'd come!"

Cassie looked up to see Claude Durand swaggering toward them, his dark cloak flaring against the torches of the half-dozen armed guards he led.

Cassie and Grey had run out of time.

Grey hissed to Cassie, "Get everyone else out the postern while I distract him!"

She made an anguished sound but didn't argue. "You be careful, damn you!"

"I'd much rather be a live coward than a dead hero," he assured her. But as Grey turned to Durand, he realized that he might not have a choice. Fate had turned full circle and brought him back to this place and this enemy.

Grey guessed that the darkness behind him prevented Durand and his men from seeing the escapees. If he could keep their attention focused on him, they might not notice Cassie shepherding her charges to safety.

Time to provide that distraction. He pulled down his scarf, revealing his face. As retreating footsteps sounded behind him, he strolled toward Durand with the arrogant confidence of an aristocrat, guessing that would focus the man's attention.

"Of course I'm here, Durand," he drawled. "Very bad of you to imprison innocents to lure me back to France. You could have killed me anytime during the ten years I was here. Better that than play these childish cat-and-mouse games."

"That's a mistake I'm going to rectify!" Durand raised a pistol and cocked it, his hands trembling from rage.

What were the chances that the pistol would misfire or Durand would miss his shot? Didn't really matter since Durand was backed up by half a dozen soldiers carrying rifles, and they were professionals, not crazed amateurs.

"Why do you hate me so much?" he asked in a conversational tone. "I could have understood if you'd shot me at the beginning. A crime of passion, very traditional. But why throw a foolish boy into a dungeon for ten years?"

"I wanted you to *suffer!*" Durand looked more than a little mad, and he was gripping his pistol as if savoring the moment, not wanting to shoot too soon. "Spoiled, selfish aristocrats like you brought France to ruin. I would have sent you to the guillotine, but that would have made death too easy, and everything in your life had been easy. You deserved to die a difficult death."

"You're right, I was spoiled and selfish, but at least part of that was simply being young, not my most noble blood." Grey halted twenty paces from the other man. He was trying to think of a really good insult so he could go down like a fearless, insouciant Englishman. Strange that events had brought him back here to die. But he'd had the best weeks of his life since Cassie rescued him.

That gave him an idea. Instead of an insult, he said lazily, "It will horrify you to know that I'm not only a much better man for my imprisonment, but in the months since I was freed, I've had a lifetime's worth of happiness."

"You'll have no more!" Durand stared down the barrel of his pistol with narrowed eyes. "Shall I shoot you in the knee so it will take you days to die in screaming agony? Or should I put a bullet in your heart and end this nonsense?"

"You're giving me a choice? How gentlemanly of you." Grey gave a brief, ironic bow. "I'll have to think about this. Though I might survive being shot in the knee, if I don't, it's a nasty way to die. But being shot in the heart is so very final."

"I'm not giving you a choice, you bloody Englishman!" Durand snarled.

He was steadying his aim when a dark figure walked past Grey. Dear heaven, Père Laurent! The old priest looked disreputable, but his head was high.

In a rich voice that could fill a church, he said, "Don't kill another innocent man, Claude. You have enough sins on your soul."

Durand's pistol began wavering. "Get away from me, you vile old man! You are not my judge!"

"I was merely your confessor," Père Laurent said calmly as he stepped between Durand and Grey. "God is your judge, but a merciful one. Redemption is possible even for the great sinners if there is true contrition. Repent before it is too late."

"I am damned already!" Durand squeezed the trigger. At the same instant, a dagger flew out of the darkness behind Grey and sliced into Durand's hand. Cassie.

Durand swore and his hand jerked as the pistol fired. The blast echoed between the walls as Père Laurent crumpled to the ground.

Père Laurent! Feeling as if the dagger had struck his own heart, Grey hurled himself past the priest and tackled Durand before the devil could reload his pistol. Grey and Père Laurent might be doomed, but Grey would damned well take Durand with them.

They flailed across the ground in a tangle of fists and thrashing limbs. As the sergeant yelled at his men not to fire because they might kill the wrong man, Durand hissed, "You stupid decadent goddam! Do you think you can escape alive?"

"Probably not." Grey remembered the time they'd fought before when Grey had been weakened from his imprisonment. Durand was still surprisingly strong for a man his age, and a tough, dirty fighter, but now Grey was stronger and in a killing rage. "But I'm not going alone!"

He locked his hands around Durand's throat, cutting off a stream of obscenity. From the corner of his eye, he saw the soldiers approaching to pull the fighters apart. It was time to end this. "In the name of justice, I execute you, Claude Durand!"

He twisted the older man's neck. There was an audible snap, and the light of life vanished from Durand's eyes.

A moment later rough hands seized him and dragged him to his feet. The sergeant flung up his rifle and aimed at Grey's chest at pointblank range. Grey felt no fear, and only one regret. *I should have told Cassie I love her.*

The sergeant was cocking his rifle when a powerful woman's voice called, "Halt! Do not shoot this man!"

Grey and Durand's soldiers all snapped their gazes toward the voice. A tall, full-figured woman was rushing toward them, a cape billowing around her. A dark angel silhouetted against a burning shed.

She stopped ten feet from Grey, panting for breath. "No more shooting, no more violence! Not if you and your men wish to be paid for your work here. I'll add a bonus for everyone if you obey now."

The sergeant sputtered, "Madame, this pig

murdered your husband! A government minister!"

"The man was acting in self-defense." Camille stared at her husband's body. Crossing herself, she added, "Durand shot a priest. He refused God's mercy, and received God's punishment."

Grey was released, though he heard muttered cursing. But since these men were mercenaries, the promise of money was enough to buy their cooperation.

"Sergeant Dupuy, gather your men to fight the fire," Camille ordered. "This castle has stood for five centuries. I don't want to see it burn tonight." She swallowed convulsively. "Tell the castle steward to take my husband's body to the chapel and have the estate carpenter make a coffin."

Scowling, Dupuy gathered his men with a glance and headed toward the fires. Grey bowed deeply to his savior. "My most profound thanks, Madame Durand."

"Grey. It's been a long time," she said quietly. "I prefer you call me Camille."

"You look well, Camille." And she did. Fuller of figure, touches of silver in her dark hair, but still a handsome woman. "I'm sorry you had to see your husband killed."

"I'm not." Her face worked as she struggled to maintain her composure. "There was . . . much between us, but he was a monster."

Grey caught a motion from the corner of his eyes and turned to see Cassie helping Père

Laurent to his feet. "Père Laurent, you're alive!"

"Indeed I am, and barely touched by the bullet." He patted Cassie's supportive hand. "Madame Renard's knife ruined Durand's shot, but because I am old, a grazed shoulder was enough to knock me down."

"God be thanked!" Camille caught hold of the priest's hands. "I swear I didn't know what Durand did to you and Lord Wyndham. He never told me, and I never came to the castle because I dislike it."

"This has not been a happy place," Père Laurent agreed.

She surveyed the bleak stone walls with a shudder. "I much prefer Paris. But Durand insisted I come this time because there was something here to amuse me."

Durand had wanted her to see Grey and Père Laurent die. It sounded like the man was deeply twisted, and he compelled his wife to witness his mad whims.

"I never believed that you condoned his behavior," the priest said soothingly.

Camille released the priest's hands and turned to Grey. "I'm sorry, my golden boy. I never thought a bit of amusement would have such terrible repercussions." Her mouth twisted. "Durand was aroused by my indiscretions. But I should have known not to take an Englishman to my bed. That he could not bear."

It was altogether too French for Grey. He took her hand and bent to kiss it lightly. "There is no need for apologies. We both erred. That is the past. What matters is the present. Can Père Laurent's niece and her family go home safely with no repercussions?"

"Of course. They never should have been imprisoned. You may borrow a carriage to get them home. Père Laurent, will you stay till morning? Your wound should be seen to, and I am in dire need of confession." Camille's gaze moved to Durand's body again. "Also . . . there is a funeral to be arranged."

"Of course, my dear girl." The priest, who had knelt to close Durand's eyes, moved forward to take Camille's arm and they headed toward the castle entrance.

Grey's gaze returned to Durand's body. He didn't feel triumphant. He didn't feel guilty for killing a monster. He felt shaken and tired and glad that the long nightmare was over, and he and his friends had survived.

Cassie had been standing quietly in the shadows, but now she moved to Grey's side. "You have interesting taste in mistresses, and I thank God for it."

He put an arm around Cassie, so tired he could barely stand. "Perhaps Père Laurent's prayers brought her here in time for a miracle. Now we need a good night's sleep, and a safe journey home to England. It would be far too ironic to survive this and get ourselves killed on the way out of France."

"That won't happen," Cassie said confidently. "Soon we'll be safe in London and Kirkland will heave a great sigh of relief."

Dragging his mind back to the present, he asked, "The Boyers escaped safely?"

"They wouldn't leave in case you needed help."

He turned and saw Viole and Romain and their children hastening toward him. They were in dire need of baths and fresh clothing, but they wore beaming smiles.

Viole came right up to Grey and kissed him on the cheek. "You have the courage of ten lions, Monsieur Sommers!"

He gave her a tired smile. "Then your uncle has the courage of a hundred lions."

"I think he prayed us a miracle." She slid an arm around Romain's waist, holding tight. "It's a long walk back to the farm. Where might we find that carriage ride that Madame Durand offered?"

"At the stables." Grey wrapped an arm around Cassie's shoulders and led the way. "My lady fox and I will ride. May we rest at the farm for a day or two before leaving?"

"You can stay as long as you desire, *mon heroes*," Romain said fervently.

As they moved into the main courtyard, Grey saw that two sheds were burning, but the flames were under control through the efforts of the soldiers and some of the castle servants.

No signs of their grenadiers. The men must have faded back into the woods to watch from a distance. Though there were numerous grenade craters dotted irregularly inside the walls, he didn't see any bleeding bodies.

Viole was right. There had been a miracle.

Chapter 47

It was very late when Cassie and Grey arrived back at the farmhouse. They pushed their narrow beds together and slept in each other's arms despite the awkward gap between the mattresses. Cassie was so tired she could have slept on a bed of nails.

It was nearing midday when she woke. She drowsed a little, not opening her eyes. She'd had grave doubts about whether she'd see another day, yet here she was. And she'd have another fortnight or so with Grey before they reached England and said their farewells.

"You're smiling like a happy cat," Grey murmured in her ear, his breath warm. "Shall we get up and find something to eat? I'm ravenous."

"Life-threatening adventures do work up an appetite." She debated seducing him—it was never difficult—but she was hungry and also wanted to affirm that everyone really was well.

She swung from the bed, did a quick wash at the basin, and donned her boring Madame Harel gown. She was going to burn the beastly thing when she reached England.

They followed the sound of laughter to the kitchen. Cassie and Grey entered to find the Boyers and Duvals and incandescent happiness. She and Grey were greeted with welcoming cries and seated at the long table opposite Père Laurent, who had just returned from his duties at Castle Durand. Cassie felt quiet satisfaction that Grey didn't flinch at the number of people.

"You're looking well, Father," Cassie said. The priest was clean and relaxed as he dug into a large herb and cheese omelet. "The graze on your shoulder wasn't deep?"

Père Laurent smiled mischievously. "People have predicted my imminent demise since I was a sickly toddler, yet I'm still here. The bullet barely touched me. I think it knocked me down more because it caught the fabric of my coat."

Grey shook his friend's hand fervently. "I couldn't believe it when I saw you confront Durand! It was the bravest thing I've ever seen."

Père Laurent shrugged. "The worst he could do was kill me, which is not a disaster for a man of faith. But I'll be pleased to return to a church and a congregation." He eyed Grey sternly. "I wouldn't have wanted you to risk your life for an old man like me, but for the sake of my Viole and her family, you have my deepest gratitude."

As Grey looked uncomfortable with the thanks, Viole set steaming mugs of real, expensive coffee in front of Cassie and Grey. "Isn't it fine how much we're in charity with each other?"

"Proof that the French and the English can be friends given half a chance." Cassie added cream and sugar to her coffee and took a deep swallow. It was delicious, hot and invigorating. Warmth and energy curled through her weary body.

"May the future hold peace, and soon." Grey raised his coffee mug to Cassie in a toast, his eyes warm. As a woman both French and English, she couldn't agree more. She'd never wanted war between her two homelands.

As Cassie started in on the omelet Yvette placed in front of her, Père Laurent said thoughtfully, "Your natural hair color is red like your fox namesake, isn't it?"

She swallowed before replying. "More like a fox and less like the carrot I resembled as a child."

He chuckled. "I wonder if your child will have red hair?"

Her coffee cup froze in midair as she stared at him.

His bushy white brows arched. "You didn't know you were with child? Of course, it's very early yet and you've been busy with other matters."

Cassie felt her fair complexion turning violent

red as everyone gazed at her with deep interest. Beside her, Grey got to his feet, clasped her upper arm in a firm grip, and said pleasantly, "If you'll excuse us, my betrothed and I must talk."

He marched her out of the kitchen and back to their room. After settling her trembling body on one of the beds, he knelt and built up the fire. She was grateful for the warmth since she was in shock.

He stood and regarded her intently, looking very tall and very broad shouldered. "I gather that's news to you?"

She nodded, her stomach roiling. "Jeanne told me that Père Laurent is famous for being able to tell if a woman is with child. I . . . I've been feeling a little off, but thought it was the worry and danger."

"You said you had a reliable method of prevention?"

"Wild carrot seeds. They work fairly well, but no method is perfect." She gave him a twisted smile. "Heaven knows we've been giving the wild carrot seeds quite a lot of challenges."

"I am . . ." He shook his head, groping for words. "I am awed. Amazed. Delighted. I never thought I'd live to become a father." He sat on the bed opposite her, his knees only a foot from hers, his gaze intent. "But how do you feel about this sudden change in circumstances?"

She hesitated, her mind churning. "Delighted

because I never thought I'd have a child, either. Dismayed because the timing is . . . awkward." She scowled at him. "And really irritated because now you'll feel you have to marry me."

"Wrong."

She blinked. "You aren't going to become all gentlemanly and honorable and insist that we marry because of the baby?"

"No, I'm not." He leaned forward and caught her hands. "The baby will be a joy, but in terms of marriage, it's irrelevant. I already had every intention of persuading you to marry me. We're just having this discussion a little earlier than I expected."

She tried unsuccessfully to tug her hands away, but his grip was gently implacable, and it didn't seem appropriate to start a wrestling match. "Unless my memory is failing, we had a conversation where I explained that needing me was no basis for marriage and that in a year you'd want something different from what you want now," she said, exasperated. "I thought you agreed with me."

He grinned, looking so attractive she almost melted. "I only agreed with part of it. At the time, I thought you'd have to be mad to take on a semi-crazed fellow like me. But I've improved. I haven't tried to kill anyone without a good reason for almost a month."

She rolled her eyes. "I've heard more convincing arguments."

"Very well." He leaned forward, his gaze on her, his dark-edged gray eyes vivid. "I've changed a great deal in the last two months, but so have you."

She thought of the hardened, wary spy she'd been when Kirkland had sent her to Castle Durand and nodded agreement. "Your legendary charm works even when you're half mad."

His turn to roll his eyes when she mentioned legendary charm. "There is nothing wrong with needing another person," he said firmly. "My parents need each other every hour of every day because they're devoted. They're happiest when they're together."

"They do seem very fond."

He must have heard a note of doubt in her voice because he said perceptively, "Are you concerned that because I've always liked women I'm incapable of being faithful? There you're wrong. My father was much like me, I'm told. Quite the young gallant, including great admiration for your mother. Then he met my mother. He hasn't looked at another woman since. I am very like him. I sowed my share of wild oats until I met the right woman. You. I love you, and that is not going to change if we wait a year."

She stared at him helplessly, wanting to believe. Unable to.

He lifted her hands and kissed the back of one, then the other. "I love you, Cassie Catherine Cat," he said softly. "I've never met a woman with your strength and grace and utter trustworthiness. Nor can I imagine a wife who will better understand me, and there's a lot to understand."

She hadn't thought of that. What would a sheltered young lady make of the scarred, complicated man he'd become? Her hands curled around his protectively as she realized she didn't want to leave him to the tender mercies of someone who couldn't fully appreciate his hard-won strength and resilience and courage.

Seeing her expression change, he said soberly, "I'm functioning reasonably well, but I'm not yet anyone's idea of normal. I might never be able to tolerate crowds, my temper may always be chancy. Are you willing to take me on? I was prepared to wait a year if you insisted, but the situation has changed." He gently rubbed her flat abdomen with a large, warm hand. "I'd prefer our child be legitimate."

She caught his hand and pressed it to her, thinking of the baby they'd made together. As soon as Père Laurent had said the words, she'd known in her marrow that he was right. Didn't she owe her child a father?

And yet . . . "I've seen too much, experienced too much," she said haltingly. "I don't want you to regret that someday."

"What will it take to convince you that I'll never want a boring innocent?" he asked with exasperation. "It's your experience that makes you what you are. A woman of irresistible strength and wisdom."

He suddenly lunged the distance between them and pinned her down on the narrow bed, kissing her throat and sliding a scandalous hand up her thigh under her very respectable Madame Harel skirt. "The fact that you are also the most deliciously attractive female I've ever met is not the most important thing about you."

He raised his head a moment and thought. "Though it's close." He captured her mouth for another kiss.

She began to laugh as belief and desire pulsed through her. "What if I'm a shallow, lustful female who would only agree to marry because of your magnificent face and body and . . . and advanced amatory skills?"

"That's all right, too." He looked at her hopefully. "Do you really want to marry me for my looks and use me shamelessly? I like that much better than being stalked for my wealth and title."

Her throat tightened and she brushed at the dull brown hair that should be golden. They had changed each other, and for the better. She'd rescued him, nurtured him, taught him how to live in the world again. He'd taught her to open her heart. To give love. Even more difficult, to receive love.

Voice husky, she said, "I don't want to marry you for your looks and passion, or your position and wealth." She swallowed hard before she could get the words out. "Only because . . . I love you."

His face lit with a joy that matched her own. "That's the best reason of all, my lady fox." His eyes crinkled with laughter. "Can I use you shamelessly now?"

She wrapped her arms around his broad chest. "Oh, please do!"

They came together with a sweet carnality where all the barriers to intimacy of mind and soul dissolved. Passion was swift and satisfying beyond anything she'd ever known. From the words of love Grey sang softly into her ear, the same was true for him.

As they lay tangled together in the too small bed, she said dreamily, "Will Père Laurent marry us without bans? It will make the child's birthday look less irregular."

Grey kissed her temple. "I'm sure he will, though I guarantee our families will want a second, entirely proper Church of England marriage as well."

"I won't mind. If wedding once is good, twice should be better."

"That's not the only thing that's good once and twice is better." He stroked suggestively down her torso.

Even as desire curled through her, she said a

little breathlessly, "If you're thinking what I think you're thinking, I'm impressed by your stamina!"

He grinned down at her, eyes alight with mischief. "Shall we ask Viole for a second cup of coffee?"

Epilogue

"I pronounce that they be man and wife together."

With the marriage ceremony complete, Grey escorted his radiant bride down the aisle of his family's parish church accompanied by jubilant organ music. Indeed, wedding once was good and twice was even better.

Père Laurent had married them first in the Boyer farmhouse the morning after the raid. Grey hadn't really thought that Cassie would change her mind, but he didn't want to take any chances.

After sharing danger, the Boyers and Duvals felt like family, and Grey had thought he couldn't be happier than when Père Laurent had pronounced him and Cassie man and wife. Cassie had glowed and Grey had beamed like the summer sun. The regular breakfast was easily converted into a wedding breakfast with the addition of a bottle of fine wine the Boyers had been saving for a special occasion.

The bride and groom stepped out onto the church porch. As guests tossed handfuls of flower petals, Cassie leaned up to whisper, "This wedding is even better because we have our natural hair colors."

Laughing, he brushed a kiss on her shining dark copper hair. In the fortnight since their return to England, spring had arrived in full force and the air was filled with birdsong and the scent of blossoms. "You smell of roses," he murmured.

Cassie's Aunt Patience had stepped into the role of mother of the bride and helped with a trousseau, starting with a bronze gown that emphasized Cassie's coloring with breathtaking richness. Grey took care of the special license. With a baby on the way, the sooner the better. Besides, he hated having to sneak around the house to spend nights with Cassie.

Lady Kiri Mackenzie was the matron of honor, and exotic dark-haired Kiri and gloriously red-haired Cassie made a pair dazzling enough to make any man swoon. Peter was Grey's best man, and there had been some hushed female remarks about how striking the pair of them looked side by side.

Since Grey was no longer available and had zero interest in any other woman, speculative female gazes were evaluating Peter, not that it would do them any good. After Peter was accepted into Mr. Burke's theater company, Lord and Lady Costain had resigned themselves to his choice. Now he was more interested in acting than marriage. Before the service, Peter urged Grey to be sure that he produced a male heir so his brother would never have to worry about inheriting.

Guests were lining up on the porch to offer personal best wishes, and Grey was delighted to see that two of his old classmates had made it in time for the ceremony. "Ashton! Randall! I'm so glad you're here."

Smiling widely, the Duke of Ashton shook Grey's hand with both of his. "Randall and I were delayed by a broken carriage wheel, but we were determined to make it even if we had to ride the post horses. I never thought I'd see this day!"

"Nor I." Randall, lean and blond and military, clapped a hand on Grey's shoulder. "Frankly, I'd given you up for lost, Wyndham."

"And good riddance, I'm sure." Grey grinned as he took Randall's hand. "I hear you've taken on a foster son who's one of Lady Agnes's students. How do you like fatherhood?"

Randall responded with a smile far happier than any he'd had as a boy. "I recommend it, especially if you can start with a twelve-year-old like Benjamin. That way you skip the messy stages."

Lady Agnes, General Rawlings, and Miss Emily had come from the Westerfield Academy to celebrate. Everyone in the Summerhill community was there, of course. They liked knowing that the next generation of Costains was secure.

The St. Iveses were present in full force,

including George, the youngest son, down from Oxford. They couldn't have been happier if Cassie really was their daughter and sister. Her uncle had walked her down the aisle, though there had been no nonsense about him "giving" her to Grey. She'd been her own woman for too many years.

Last in line was Kirkland, his handsome, saturnine face relaxed. "Remember those lists I always made in school to keep track of everything I needed to do?"

Grey laughed. "Who could forget? You were fearsomely organized even then."

Kirkland pulled a worn piece of paper from his breast pocket along with a pencil and held it up for Grey to see. The name "Wyndham" was written in the middle of a list where everything else had been crossed off. With a flourish, Kirkland drew a line through the name. "I now have one less thing to worry about!"

Grey laughed, then turned serious. "I'll never be able to thank you for everything you've done. You gave me freedom, and Cassie." Grey put an arm around his wife. "All I need to make my happiness complete is Régine."

Kirkland grinned. "I trust Cassie isn't upset by the implied comparison."

As he moved away, Cassie nestled comfortably against Grey's side. "In another fortnight or so, Lady Agnes will allow you to have her."

"Only because Lady Agnes is keeping a puppy to spoil."

Cassie glanced up. He could happily drown in those deep blue pools of patience and wisdom. She asked, "Is the crowd bothering you?"

He knew better than to lie to Cassie, since she could see through him. "A little," he admitted. "But this is home and these are friends, and during the wedding breakfast I can slip away for a few minutes when I need to. Will you slip away with me?"

She grinned. "Of course. People will notice and enjoy thinking scandalous thoughts."

The Costain carriage pulled up in front of the church to take Grey and Cassie to Summerhill for the wedding breakfast. The Costains and Cassie's aunt and uncle had already been taken in another carriage while other guests were walking along the lane that led to the great house. There would be an indoor feast for close friends and relatives, and an outdoor festival for the community. Inevitably the two groups would mingle.

Grey helped Cassie into the carriage, then followed. As soon as the door was closed, he pulled her into his arms for a smoldering kiss that would have been scandalous in the church.

By the time they came up for air, her flowered chaplet had fallen and left a trail of pale pink petals on her lovely bare shoulder. Cassie smiled at him with a tenderness that turned his heart inside out. "Tonight we sleep in our cottage by the sea, my golden lord. Even if it is really a farmhouse."

"It was worth ten years in prison to have found you, my one and only love," he said softly.

Cassie cupped his cheek. "I never believed fortune would bring me to such happiness." Her gravity dissolved into laughter. "Along the way I was warned by several people that you'd never, ever marry me. I always agreed with them wholeheartedly."

He joined her laughter. "That's a good reason to have two weddings." He kissed one of the delicate petals on her throat. "So there is no mistaking the fact that we are well and truly married, now and forever more." Abandoning seriousness, he added, "Any time you want me to marry you again, just ask!"

Author's Note:
The Truce of Amiens

Britain and France fought on and off for centuries. The war triggered by the French revolution ran almost continuously from 1793 to 1815, when Waterloo ended Napoleon's empire. The main break in hostilities was the truce following the Treaty of Amiens, which was in effect from March 1802 to May 1803.

War was expensive and the allied nations that had been fighting France wanted peace. Once the treaty was signed, highborn Britons flocked to Paris to party. However, Napoleon used the peace to consolidate his power and continued his belligerent and expansionist ways. As relations among France, Britain, and Russia deteriorated, many foreign visitors wisely returned home.

Britain recalled its ambassador to France and declared war on May 18, 1803. On May 22, Napoleon abruptly ordered the imprisonment of all British men between the ages of eighteen and sixty. His action was denounced as illegal by all the major powers, but Napoleon was never very interested in anything but power. Hundreds of men were interned and many did not return home until 1814, after Napoleon's abdication.

The provincial town of Verdun was the official place of residence for wellborn British internees, most of whom were joined by their womenfolk. British tradesmen who were also interned set up shop to cater to the well off, so British grocers and tailors sprang up. A fairly comfortable, if limited, community of expatriates was formed.

In all this upheaval, it's easy to believe that a particularly impertinent young English lord might have vanished into a private dungeon.

Center Point Large Print
600 Brooks Road / PO Box 1
Thorndike ME 04986-0001 USA

(207) 568-3717

US & Canada:
1 800 929-9108
www.centerpointlargeprint.com